The Last Daughter *of* Highdown Hall

ALSO BY CATHY HAYWARD

The Girl in the Midnight Maze

The Last Daughter *of* Highdown Hall

Cathy Hayward

LAKE UNION
PUBLISHING

This is a work of fiction. Names, characters, organizations, places, events, and incidents are either products of the author's imagination or are used fictitiously. Any resemblance to actual persons, living or dead, or actual events is purely coincidental.

Published by Lake Union Publishing, Seattle

www.apub.com

EU Product Safety Contact:
Amazon Media EU S.à r.l.
38, avenue John F. Kennedy, L-1855 Luxembourg
amazonpublishing-gpsr@amazon.com

ISBN-13: 9781662521751
eISBN: 9781662521744

Cover design by Emma Rogers
Cover image: © Jannis Tobias Werner © MaCross-Photography / Shutterstock

Printed in the United States of America

For Zara

Chapter 1

Zoe

Spring 2025

The skin on her hands and feet is tinged grey and purple now. Like a giant bruise creeping across her body. Zoe lays her mother's hand back on the sheet and looks up at the nurse.

'It won't be long now, Zoe,' says the nurse, her eyes soft. 'It's long past time to call them. They do have a right to know. To be here.'

Zoe nods and strokes her mother's hand, skin like tracing paper stretched across her knobbly veins, but still as soft as she remembers from holding as a child. Her finger catches on her mother's loose gold wedding band and she slips it back into place.

Do they have a right? she wonders. They've known Mum was seriously ill for months, years. But they've each had their justifications for not coming back home to Highdown Hall. To leaving Mum's care to her. She twists her three silver bands around her thumb.

Fiona she can almost excuse. Singapore is a world away and the last thing Zoe wanted was Fi flying back and forth to London every time Mum dipped. More pointless emissions. Best she stayed there until there was no choice but to return. Is that now? She swallows and looks up at her mother's face. Her eyes are shut, the silver scar on her temple barely visible now her skin is so pale, her slack mouth revealing her yellowing teeth. Zoe hasn't brushed them for over a week now. It upset Mum the last time she tried and the nurse says not to bother. You know you're ill when they tell you not to brush your teeth. Mum has enjoyed the occasional Zoom with Fi, although the time difference has been tricky recently with Mum's erratic sleeping. Fi all dressed up in smart suits and gold bling, picking up the laptop to show Mum the skyline of a city she'll never see.

Sara is busy with her three children. Zoe glances at the photo on the bedside table – a soft-focus studio shot of Sara holding the baby with the twins smiling down at her. There's the familiar twist in her stomach. Mum insisted it be moved there from the drawing room though there's not really enough space with all the medical paraphernalia. But the Surrey Hills are only forty miles away. There are trains. Sara did call last week to see how Mum was, and she asked how Zoe was doing. Which Fi never does. But still. Sara's got a husband to look after the kids. Zoe blows air up into her fringe.

It's Steph's silence Zoe can't understand. She only lives ten miles away. No children, no big job. And she's the eldest. Traditionally, it was the eldest child who took responsibility for everyone. Steph has never done that. She's always been the first to run away from any family issue, the first to give her excuses not to attend something. She was late for their father's funeral, for God's sake. But then Steph has always been different from them all. Distant. Reclusive. Happy to rescue anything with four legs, but no interest in her own family. So it's been left to her, Zoe, to nurse their mother. Zoe refills her mother's beaker from the jug, water sloshing on to her hands as she clicks the sippy lid back into place. She wipes them on her dungarees and looks back at her mother.

But they are her sisters and they should be here, she knows that. It's been hard getting any definite timings from the nurses. The new nurse who came yesterday said that patients can surprise you and recover, even at this stage. *Maybe that's why she hasn't called them*, Zoe thinks. There's still hope. Maybe. The doctor said a while ago that Mum probably didn't have long. But what does that actually mean? Illness and death seem so wrapped up in euphemism. They gave her a leaflet about what to expect at the end. But it was Helen, her hospice nurse friend, who gave her the best advice. If the patient is getting worse month by month, they've got months left, she said. If they're getting worse week by week, they've got weeks left. If they're getting worse day by—

Helen didn't have to finish. Mum has become less responsive every day this week.

The nurse is leaning over her mother, checking her pulse. She's very still and for a moment Zoe's own heart seems to stop. Is it? Has she? But then the nurse jots something down on the clipboard. Zoe lets out the breath she didn't realise she was holding.

When her mother sees her sisters, will she know that the end is near? Could it actually tip her over the edge? Zoe wouldn't want to scare her into going before her time.

The nurse lifts the duvet to check the syringe driver. 'I'll be back at around five p.m. but you know the number to call if you need us before then.'

Zoe nods. 'Thank you.'

She squeezes Zoe's shoulder, then looks back at Mum. 'Goodbye for now, Milly,' she says as she always does, then leaves the room. The syringe driver exhales.

Zoe stares at her mother's chest, waiting for the tiny movement of the cotton nightie. It seems an age until it comes. Will this be how it ends? No last words, no fanfare. Just a breath not taken. And then another not taken. And another. Stillness.

Zoe picks up her phone, pushes her fringe out of her eyes and starts scrolling through the numbers. Which of her sisters should she call first?

◆ ◆ ◆

Milly

1987

Steph never listens. 'I'm not saying that at all. I'm just suggesting that if you listen more and don't talk back, and do your homework, then you won't get into trouble.'

Steph gives a theatrical sigh and flicks her hair.

'*I've* done my homework,' a voice chirps from the back seat. I catch Fiona's eye in the rear-view mirror and paste on a smile.

'Well done, darling.'

'Yeah, but your homework is like two plus two. Or find the capital of France on the map,' says Steph.

My jaw tenses and I try to relax it.

'Teddy wants to know who France is,' says Sara, swinging her bear from side to side with one hand, the thumb of her other hand firmly in her mouth. Her hair is a scribble on top of her head. I must brush it before she goes into the school nursery.

Steph laughs.

'It's the country just underneath us. We can get the ferry there. They speak a different language to us,' I say, as cheerily as I can. 'Now take your thumb out of your mouth, darling.'

'Just underneath us,' Steph mimics. 'Don't you mean south?'

My jaw is tense again. 'South.' I smile in the mirror at Sara, who hasn't moved her thumb.

I indicate to turn off the main road. Not far now.

Next to me Steph puts her hands over her ears, and screws up her face. 'Stop doing that,' she says.

'Doing what?' There's a queue of traffic and no gap to get through on to the school road. Why don't people leave a space? They're supposed to.

'The indicator. It's so annoying. The tick tock, tick tock.'

'I've told you before, I need the indicator so I show the traffic behind me that I want to turn right. It wouldn't be safe not to use it.'

The traffic is beginning to move. Thank God.

Steph leans over, flicks the indicator off and shoves my hand from the steering wheel. In my panic, I stall the car.

'That's dangerous.' I glare at her and slam my foot on the brake, taking it out of gear. I turn on the ignition, put my foot on the clutch and engage first gear. I'm not sure what happens but I stall again. Someone behind me hoots. As I try again my feet are shaking so much that I instantly stall. There's now a cacophony of hooting.

The car behind me goes up on the grass verge to get past on the left. 'Women drivers,' he shouts out the window as he passes.

Steph gives him the V-sign. There are pricks of blood on her hand. Her eczema's flaring up again.

'Steph,' I say. 'Don't do that.' I admire her though, for taking a stand.

Two other cars follow, and Steph gestures at both of them. 'Stop picking at your skin, darling, you've made your hand bleed.'

'What's Steph doing?' says Fiona, craning forward.

'Put on your seat belt, Fi. And you, Sara.' *For God's sake, breathe, breathe. Don't stall again.* In the rear-view mirror, I can see there's a queue of about twenty cars. The vehicles the other side have cleared.

I manage to start the car and turn right into the senior school road, ignoring Steph's cheer. 'Now then. After school, I'm going to pick up you first, Steph, and then come back to the village for Fiona and Sara as it's ballet tonight.'

'It's okay, I'm going out with my friends after school. You can pick me up later. Or Alice can.' Steph's looking out of the window.

'No, I can't be running back and forth from the village to town. I'll pick you up straight after school and then collect Fiona and Sara and we'll all go to ballet together. You and I can chat while Fiona's in her class.'

Steph curls her lip. 'I don't think so. I'll wait for Alice.'

'Alice is leaving early today, she's got something on.'

I pull up outside her school and she's out of the car before I've even stopped the engine. 'I'll be right here at three. Please be waiting.'

She laughs, slams the door hard and throws her bag over her shoulder as she saunters away. I lean across, the seat belt digging into my chest, and roll down the window. 'Three p.m. here, Stephanie,' I shout. A group of girls near the car turn and giggle, but Steph completely ignores me. The horn makes a satisfyingly loud noise. 'Stephanie!' But she's too far away to hear now. Probably.

Okay, okay. I'll speak to one of the mums and get them to wait with Fiona and Sara. Then I can wait here for fifteen minutes for Steph to show up. And I'll have just enough time to get back to the village to pick up Fiona and Sara. Not ideal, but. If she doesn't show . . . My whole face is screwed up and I consciously relax it.

'Is Steph in trouble?' says Fiona, a smile on her face.

'Not at all. I'm sure she'll be here later.' I put the car into first and pull away. It will all be fine.

'She won't,' says Fiona. 'She never is.' I grit my teeth. Fiona knows her sister too well.

With Steph out of the car, I push in a Beatles cassette and the three of us sing along all the way back to the village. Outside the school, Fiona jumps out of the car, hugs me and joins a group of friends. Sara gives me a sloppy kiss as she says goodbye outside the nursery door. The feel of her warm pudgy hands across my back makes up for the earlier stress and I feel myself smiling. In the car, I turn the music up to full volume for the short drive back to Highdown. 'Can't Buy Me Love'. How very true. Everyone tells you that wonderful little girls one day become sullen teenagers who despise your very existence, but nothing actually prepares you for what that feels like. Was I like that with Mum? Probably, I can't remember.

◆ ◆ ◆

The library door is ajar. Paul must hear me come in as he shouts out, 'All okay?'

I push open the heavy door. It's gloomy inside, the room lit by a pool of green light spooling around the desk lamp. He moves aside a pile of paperwork and slides a paperweight on top.

I shake my head and drop on to his lap. 'I just feel like I can't do anything right.'

He strokes my hair. 'We'll get through it, Milly. She'll be fine.'

He's right, of course. I just didn't think it would start this early. Thirteen is so young to be properly stroppy. 'I was thinking, at least our three girls are all four or five years apart. Imagine if they'd been born closer together. We'd have two Stephs in the house at the same time.'

He makes a face and gives an exaggerated shudder. 'How are you feeling? Any better?' He glances at my stomach.

I shrug. What is there left to say? This time last week I had the beginnings of a baby in me. Ten weeks old. Now I'm empty. Again.

At least this time they've diagnosed the problem – an incompetent cervix – so they might be able to fix it. Incompetent cervix, incompetent mother. Steph certainly makes me feel that way.

Paul's hand is soft on mine as he strokes it. 'We'll get there,' he says. 'Zoe or Tommy will be born before you know it.'

I try to smile to make him feel better. I'm thirty-eight. He knows as well as I do that as every year passes it'll be much harder to get pregnant. We should start trying next cycle, whatever the doctors say. Zoe or Tommy. I know Paul wants a boy and who can blame him after three girls. But secretly I want another girl. Little girls are so wonderful. Zoe. Steph, Fiona, Sara and Zoe. The house would finally be full then.

'What are your plans for today?' he asks.

'I've got a few bits to do here then I'll take out the dog for a W-A-L-K before going back to school. Ballet tonight.'

Woody thumps his tail. He must be learning to spell in his spare time. I'd like to spend all day just sitting in here with Paul, reading and watching him work, but he glances back at his papers. It's hard to drag myself away. 'What are you doing?'

'Sorting out some repairs on Honeysuckle Cottage,' he says. 'The back wall is crumbling and needs rebuilding before there's an accident. I need to have a proper look at the roof on the oast house. Since your parents moved up to Scotland, it's all become a bit dilapidated in there. And then I want to walk over to the Wilsons' later – I need to talk to them about crop rotation. There's been a few issues. Come with me?'

He always knows exactly what I need. 'I will,' I say, 'thank you,' kissing him on the head as he bends back over his papers. However hard he works, there's always so much to do across the estate. In my grandfather's time, they'd have had a team of people doing Paul's job. Now it's just him and some odd-job men.

Woody gets up and stretches. 'Not yet, matey,' I say, scratching behind his ears.

He follows me upstairs and along the gallery, his claws clattering on the wooden floor. Mum's portrait glares down at me. Maybe I'll write to her, I haven't responded to her last letter from more than a month ago. It's still in the bedside table drawer. I take it out and begin to read, and the first few lines remind me why I have stalled on replying. *I did warn you against marrying Paul. If Stephanie's difficult, it's bad blood from his side. We've never had anything like that in our family. You must make the best of it. Perhaps some time away might help, bring the girls here in the holidays?*

The very idea of spending time with Mum and the girls in Scotland makes my jaw constrict again. Fiona and Sara would love it, Steph would go mental with all the rules. Mum would be judgemental and it'd be a disaster. Woody puts his paw on my knee, looking up expectantly. I slide the letter back into the drawer.

'C'mon, boy, let's go out. Enjoy the weather.' As we pass Steph's bedroom door, he starts growling and scratching at the wood. 'What is it?'

He barks twice, and pushes his nose against the door. I turn the handle, holding on to his collar. There's nothing obvious that he could have been barking about when I open the door, just the usual heap of chaos. Unmade bed. Desk covered with bits of paper. As I let Woody go though, he dashes to the far side of the bed and starts barking at a cardboard box covered by a towel. I drag him away and put him outside the door. Underneath the towel, hunched in the corner of the box, is a crow, its wing splinted with what looks like lolly sticks. I don't know what I was expecting, but it wasn't this. The crow stares up at me, unblinking. From the bottle of water and half-empty box of seeds underneath the bed, he's been here for a while. Why haven't I noticed? The poor thing must have been terrified with Woody barking at him. I cover the box back with the towel. I wish Steph had told me. I could have helped somehow. No wonder she insisted the cats sleep elsewhere at the moment. I knew it wasn't a sudden allergy but I didn't press it with her. I straighten the duvet, careful not to move too fast and disturb the crow.

That's very Steph though, to be nursing a crow back to life. She's always been different from the others, even as a young child. So impulsive, so willing to take risks and never behaving quite how you'd expect. It has often felt like she's wired differently from the rest of us. But give her an animal and she's amazing – all the empathy she finds so hard to express to other humans.

There was the incident a few years ago when she took a rabbit from a cage in the garden of one of the old biddies in the village, because she didn't feel it was well looked after. She just couldn't see that it was wrong. But maybe she was right.

Voices drift up from the front door. I finish plumping the pillows and go over to the window. There's Alice talking to the postman. How can she not have noticed the crow if she's here every day? The window is slightly ajar and as I open the catch to close it, I see a flash of red. I know what it is before I see it properly. A lighter. *Bloody hell.* I pocket it, and shut the window. Smoking at thirteen. *Bloody hell.* I'll wait until later to tell Paul.

'Morning, Milly,' says Alice as Woody and I come downstairs. 'How are you feeling?'

'I'm okay,' I say. 'Feeling stronger every day. Just got to keep going.' I don't know what I'd do without Alice, she's so thoughtful.

She nods. 'Do take care of yourself though.'

'I've just been in Steph's room. Did you know about the crow?'

'Crow?' She shakes her head. She's a poor liar. She and Steph have always been very close. It's rather lovely, especially as Steph has few friends.

'I'll speak to her about it tonight,' I say. 'I don't mind but she needs to tell us. Perhaps don't clean in there today. Woody's already upset the poor bird. Any more noise might finish it off.'

At the back of the top shelf of the pantry is my emergency packet of Silk Cut. Just the feeling of the white and purple packet in my hands makes me relax, though when I open it there seems to be fewer than I remember. Again. I thought it was Paul who was nicking the occasional one, but maybe it's Steph. I shake my head. I'll have to find a new place to hide them. On the back doorstep, I light one, pulling the smoke into my lungs. And relax.

Chapter 2

Zoe

Spring 2025

The crunch of tyres on the gravel outside Highdown Hall is followed by a car door slamming. Zoe, Steph and Sara look at each other.

'That'll be Fi,' says Sara, taking her arm from Zoe's shoulders. Since she arrived a few hours ago, Sara has taken charge – making constant cups of tea, as if that would wash away her grief. *Or maybe it was to assuage Sara's own guilt for not being here before now*, Zoe thinks. Then she pauses. *We've all lost our mum*, she reminds herself, *we just cope in different ways*. It just all feels so sudden, despite the months of waiting.

Opposite them, in the drawing room, Steph turns in her chair to stare out of the long windows that line the front of their childhood home. Behind her Zoe sees the lights of a sleek dark car moving away from the house. It curves around the old stone fountain, empty for the last decade, and continues down the driveway, zigzagging around the larger potholes. Steph turns her gaze back to the room and Zoe watches her eyes flick away from the stag heads above the fireplace, their grandfather's trophies – and glance over at the picture frames on the grand piano in the far corner of the room. Her legs are crossed and she's tapping her foot repeatedly. Steph's older than

Zoe remembers. Her hair is almost entirely grey now, lines bracketing her mouth, criss-crossing her forehead. She always thought her eldest sister had blue eyes like her own, but they're puddle-coloured, a luminous grey, as they dart around the room.

'Hello?' Fiona's voice calls.

'In here,' says Sara.

Steph seems to press herself further into the velvet armchair and recrosses her legs. Nobody moves when the drawing-room door opens.

'Where is she?' says Fiona, standing on the threshold in a smart navy dress, carrying a briefcase. She speaks in capital letters.

Zoe glances at Steph, who's picking the skin on her hand. She can't say the words again. Sara stands up and squeezes Fiona's. 'I'm sorry, Fi, she went this morning. The funeral home people have just collected her.'

'What?' Fiona staggers slightly and leans against the sideboard, dropping her briefcase. 'She's gone?'

'Yes, I'm sorry.' Sara guides Fiona to the armchair next to Steph.

Fiona sits down, covers her face with her hands and mumbles something. When she eventually looks up, her face is streaky, her eyes bright. 'I literally got the first flight out of Singapore. I left the office as soon as you called,' she says to Zoe. 'You should have phoned me before, so I had time to say goodbye.' Her voice catches on the last word.

'Fi, calm down.' Sara leans forward to rest her hand on her knee. 'I didn't get that chance either. Nor did Steph. She died before any of us could get here. It was very sudden.'

Fiona grips Sara's hand, and then they hug. *They fit well together somehow*, Zoe thinks. *They'd always got on as children.*

'I can't believe it,' Fiona says, her head tipped back. 'How was she?' She looks back to Zoe, and swallows. 'At the end?' Under the smart outfit and the make-up, she looks exhausted. She covers her mouth with a perfectly manicured hand, the red nail polish a blood stain on her face.

'There was nothing dramatic. No last words. She just stopped . . .' Zoe rubs her eyes. She knows she should have called them days ago. But it felt like defeat, admitting that their mother was dying. And there was something fitting about it, that after all those years alone with her mother, all those months caring for her, she should be the only one with her when she died. The guilt twists inside her as she sees Fiona's distraught face.

She looks around at the three of them filling a room that has been empty for years.

'But why didn't you call us before? I could have been here. I wanted to be here,' says Fiona.

'Fi,' says Sara, shaking her head.

But Zoe can't stop herself. She jerks her head and her heart starts to thud. 'You could have come at any time. She's been seriously ill for more than a year. No one was stopping you.' Anger soothes her guilt. She twists the rings around her thumb and sees Sara and Fi catch each other's eyes and look away.

'I thought the dying knew when the time was coming and held on until everyone had gathered around their bed to say goodbye,' says Fiona quietly. 'I thought I'd have time.' She falls into the chair and Sara sits back next to Zoe.

'It's not a movie, Fi,' says Zoe, hugging a cushion, feeling her anger fall away as quickly as it came. 'People die when they're ready. She hadn't seen you all in so long. Especially you.' She looks at Steph. 'Not even a short visit or a call. And you're the closest.' Steph looks into her lap and pushes herself further back into the armchair.

'Steady on,' says Sara. 'I tried to help. When you had that work thing a while ago, I came and sat with Mum for the weekend.'

'One weekend in two years,' Zoe mutters, but feels her heart constrict again. She knows she's being unfair and horrible but she needs to blame someone, something, now that their mother has gone.

'It's really hard with the children and everything . . .' Sara trails off.

A chime from the grandfather clock reverberates through the room, making the other three visibly jump. It is so part of the fabric of her day that Zoe barely notices it. She watches them count the eleven other chimes, each lost in their own memories. The clock – and its partner in the hall – were their father's passion. He had wound them every Saturday morning. She'd stood next to him when she was small, as he opened the glass door, and inserted the key near the number three. As she got older, he taught her how to push the key into the winding hole, his hand holding the clock face steady while she turned the crank, reminding her to check that the weights were rising. She's done it on her own since he's been gone.

Tears sting her eyes and she blinks them away. It's their mother she should be thinking of now, but seeing her go has taken her back to their father's death five years ago. That was the last time they were all together at the house. But Mum was here then to tell them what to do, to fuss over Fiona and particularly Sara who brought the newborn twins with her.

Fiona is glancing around the room. When the vibrations eventually fall away, she says, 'It's lovely to see Highdown again. A little bit older and tireder but still here . . .' She trails off.

'Like all of us,' says Sara with a small smile.

Zoe looks around the room too. She hasn't done more than glance around the door at it for the past few months. Suddenly she sees it through her sisters' eyes. It's not just the layers of dust on everything. The bald poinsettia encircled by leaves on the grand piano. The blackened silver photo frames. The rugs so threadbare, you can see the parquet floor underneath. The curtains punctuated by moth holes. Huge cobweb garlands decorate the oak beams. Two mottled damp patches are growing from the sides of the French windows, almost meeting in the middle. Through the windows, what remains of her father's giant topiary ducks stare down reproachfully at her from the stone gateway leading into the formal garden. Highdown Hall, she suddenly acknowledges with a twinge of guilt, has seen better days. She should have done more to keep it going, it was her responsibility with Mum so ill. Guilt needles at her again. She should have done so much more.

A gentle silence falls over them. Zoe wonders what they're thinking. Is it about all the times they've been in this room together, playing games as children, the fire lit, Mum and Dad here with them, making tea and crumpets, Terry and June stretched out on the huge hearth, the dog jostling for space and retreating when they scratched him on the nose? Or when Mum and Dad would host extravagant parties, and she and Sara would lie on the gallery looking down into the hall as glamorous people arrived? They'd go to sleep to the tang of cigar smoke and the sound of their mother playing the piano, laughter and chinking glasses.

Her eyes are full with tears. Missy slinks past the door and pauses to survey the room. This is usually her domain, with a choice of seats to curl up on. But she appears to welcome the newcomers, strutting in and wending in and out of their legs.

'Beautiful tabby,' says Steph, reaching down to stroke her. Missy stops and lifts her chin to be rubbed. 'Lovely colouring.'

'She's Terry and June's granddaughter,' says Zoe.

'Terry and June,' says Sara. 'I'd almost forgotten all about them. God I loved them when we were young. They must have been gone years.' Zoe smiles at her, surprised and pleased she remembers. 'They were part of the reason I got cats for my children.'

Silence falls over them again. They can't just keep sitting here. Zoe gets up and walks towards the door. 'Mum left instructions for her funeral and stuff. It's in an envelope in her room. We might as well start looking at it. Now we're together.'

'Surely that can wait until tomorrow, Zoe?' Sara says. 'It's late now, we should be going to bed. Especially poor Fi who's been flying all day.'

'I got a few hours' sleep,' says Fiona. 'I was in business.'

'Nice for some,' says Zoe, stopping herself from rolling her eyes. She's being unfair, she knows it. She tries to physically push down the rising resentment. *Be kind. Be kind.*

'It was the only seat they had at such short notice,' Fiona says, wiping her hand across the side table. 'Zoe's right though, there's a lot to organise now. And I'm glad I'm here to help.'

Although Zoe feels slightly irritated by them being here, the thought of the four of them sleeping under the same roof for the first time since they were children is strangely comforting. She doesn't want to sleep in this huge house alone. When they came after their father died, Sara and Steph just stayed for the day and returned for the funeral. Fiona must have stayed in the house but Zoe can't remember. 'You can all sleep in your old bedrooms,' she says. 'If you want? I mean, I haven't been in them for a long time.'

'I'm sure Alice has kept everything nice, ready for when we came back,' says Fiona.

Zoe stares at her. It's like she's from another planet. 'Alice hasn't worked here since Dad died,' she says. 'There was no money to pay her. There's no money for anything. But there's clean sheets in the airing cupboard on the top floor.'

'Oh.' Fiona's mouth is a perfect circle.

'I did wonder,' says Sara. 'Everything seems a little . . .' She doesn't finish.

Zoe feels another surge of indignation. But what is it about her sisters being here that's turned her into such a cow? It's like she's reverted to her prickly teenage self.

'But I totally understand you've been focused on Mum,' says Sara.

'I had to move back into the house six months ago. It had got to the stage where Mum couldn't be left alone.' Zoe has missed the independence of the old oast house, half a mile from the main house on the other side of the estate. Moving to the hall marked the end of her relationship with Ben too – he hated coming into the main house as if they were teenagers, and then she couldn't leave Mum overnight so she couldn't even stay at his place. 'I had to take time off work. And then because I didn't know when I could come back, I had to resign.' Zoe exhales. 'Obviously I wanted to, for Mum's sake, but it's been hard.' She feels the tears rise up again and moves towards the door to focus on something else. 'Anyway, let's just get the will over with. Mum wanted to have the funeral quickly. No faffing around, she said the other day.' Her voice catches on the words. Sara starts to rise but Zoe is already out of the room.

As the door closes behind her, Zoe hears someone mention her name, but it shuts before she can hear what exactly is said. In the hall mirror, her eyes are heavy with tiredness, the reflection from the crystal chandelier making her skin appear translucent. She touches the gilt frame, blowing off a cobweb. Life seems to have stood still for months.

She avoids the bottom two steps where the wood is dark and spongy underneath the tatty runner. On the first-floor gallery, the portraits of long-forgotten DeProse ancestors stare down at her. She blows dust off the bottom of the frames as she walks past, conscious her sisters will soon be up here. Next to her mother's bedroom door is the painting of her grandmother Evelyn DeProse, wearing an emerald-green cocktail dress and a stern expression. The artist brilliantly caught Granny Evelyn's character in those few strokes around her mouth. Zoe runs her finger along the frame but she knows there's no dust. This is the one portrait she's religiously cleaned. Her mother hated the idea that her own mother would have to look through grime to survey the house she loved.

Her mother's bedroom has already changed. Someone has folded up the camp bed she used for the past few weeks, and stacked the bedding on top. The duvet has been pulled back from her four-poster bed, as if her mother has just got up to make a pot of tea and will at any moment reappear and slide under the covers. Zoe puts her hand on the dip in the middle of the bed, where the sheets are creased. Is she imagining the slight memory of warmth? This morning, Mum was lying here, alive. She stayed in the drawing room after the funeral people brought her down. Zoe doesn't want to say 'her body'. Not yet. Sara sorted it all out. Steph sat fidgeting next to her, a tangle of awkward limbs.

In the cupboard of the bedside table is the large brown envelope her mother had talked about. *Not to be opened until after my death* is written across the front in her mother's hand, clearly done several months ago when she was still able to hold a pen. The seal is sellotaped shut.

As Zoe opens the door back into the drawing room, a cork pops. Fiona stands pouring red wine into four lead crystal glasses on the table. They must have been in the sideboard, unused for years.

'Would you like some, Zoe? I thought we'd toast Mum.' Fiona holds the bottle poised over the fourth glass.

'Where did you get that from?' Zoe asks. In the old days, the cellars were full of wine, but they haven't been used for ages.

'I picked a couple of bottles up in duty free. I thought Mum might fancy a glass.' Fiona sighs. 'Silly of me . . .'

'Understandable,' murmurs Sara.

Zoe nods at Fiona, who fills up a glass. She hasn't had anything to drink for months.

'Not for me, I don't really drink,' says Steph. Fiona ignores her and hands her a full glass. Steph takes it, slopping some of the dark-red liquid on to her hands. She wipes them on her jeans.

'To Mum,' Fiona says, and they all lean close enough to clink glasses. Somehow it feels wrong to be drinking wine, as if it's some sort of celebration.

Zoe sits down next to Sara, puts the wine glass on the floor and peels back the strip of tape from the envelope, drawing out a sheaf of papers. 'There's quite a few pages,' she says, leafing through them. A couple of months ago, her mother mentioned there would be something after her death that she wouldn't like or understand. Zoe tried to press her but her mother had been having a bad day and waved the questions away, and there hadn't been another opportunity to bring it up. As she flicks through the pages, Zoe wonders if she was referring to the funeral or an odd clause in the will, but the funeral arrangements all seem to be as she expected.

'When did they take her body?' asks Fiona. The word hangs in the air, suspended between the old beams.

'Not long before you arrived.' Zoe hears Sara's swallow. 'It's so warm this spring, the funeral people didn't want—'

Fiona takes a sip of her wine, and then looks back at Zoe.

'She wants a service at the church here in the village. No surprises there. It all looks a very traditional service. She's listed all the music. "*O mio babbino caro*" for the entrance of the coffin.' Zoe bites her lip as she reads. 'She was always playing that. Then "*Abide with Me*" and later "*Lord of all Hopefulness*". She's listed the readings and prayers too. She wants us to do one reading each.' Zoe glances up at her sisters.

Zoe hands around the envelopes on which their mother wrote their names in her distinct sloping hand. She opens her own envelope and there's a few lines of text with her name at the top. She puts two fingers on her name and brings them to her lips. Her mother wrote these. Probably the last time she wrote Zoe's name.

> *In the midst of our grief, we pray for unity among those who gather to remember our mother. May this shared experience bring us closer together, reminding us of the bonds that transcend the challenges we face. Help us find strength in one another as we navigate this emotional journey. Thank you for the unity we find in times of sorrow. Lord Hear Us.*

She blinks away her tears. She checks the envelope. There's nothing else. No personal letter. She doesn't know what she was hoping for, maybe just a few words about how much she was loved, appreciated. Something more than just a funeral reading.

There's silence as they all read their text, their heads bent over the papers. Sara takes a gulp of wine. Nobody offers to share and Zoe wonders what the other readings say. Maybe they're all about unity. Their mother's last attempt to bring them all together. She should make that effort, for her mum's sake if nothing else. Steph folds up hers and stuffs it back into the envelope, her hands shaking.

'Have you got a long reading, Steph? It looks like you've got a couple of bits of paper?' Zoe tries to push away the twinge of jealousy. This is bringing out the worst in her, she thinks.

Steph glances up at her, her eyes blinking rapidly. She shakes her head and waves the envelope at her. 'No, just a reading for the funeral,' she says. 'It's about unity. What's yours about?'

Zoe could have sworn there was another sheet of paper. 'Mine's about unity too.' She lets out a long breath and looks back to the other documents. 'Mum's included numbers of the people to call and invite to the wake. Mainly locals, but a few from elsewhere.

She wants to hold the wake here. After the service, she wants to be cremated and then interred in the family plot in the cemetery.'

They all nod. Their mother had made no secret of her fear of being buried alive, always cutting out newspaper articles about coffins being dug up with scratches on the inside. There was one still stuck to the fridge which she had put there when she was able to walk down the stairs. Zoe must take it down before someone throws it away. She focuses back on the pile of papers and starts to open the one labelled 'My Will'.

'Here's her will,' she says, sliding her thumb underneath the flap.

'I imagine it will be fairly straightforward,' says Fiona, still looking at her reading. 'A split of Mum's assets, with perhaps some specific gifts and charitable legacies.'

'I suppose by assets you mean Highdown?' says Zoe, staring at the faint line of grey on Fiona's blonde hairline. A chink in her sister's perfect armour. She must have been due a hair dye before she left Singapore.

Fiona looks up. 'It's just a term, Zoe,' she says. 'We all know Highdown is your home, and that you did a fantastic job looking after Mum in her last years.'

'And Dad,' says Zoe.

'And Dad,' repeats Fiona, looking at Sara.

'I suspect there will be some provision that Highdown has to stay in the family, be kept for the next generation,' says Fiona.

But who are the next generation? thinks Zoe. *Only Sara has children.*

'I bet she's left something to the women's refuge in Lewes,' says Sara. 'She was always on about the work they did.'

Zoe can't remember Mum ever talking about a women's refuge. She takes a sip of wine, feeling the warmth slide down inside her. Fiona opening the wine was a good call. She starts to read the legal paragraphs silently.

'I don't understand,' says Zoe quietly, finding it hard to swallow. She flicks back a page.

'What's the matter?' asks Steph, leaning forward, still gripping her envelope.

'I don't understand,' Zoe repeats, her voice catching. She thinks back to the conversation with her mother about something that she wouldn't like or understand. And here it is.

'What is it?' says Fiona.

'Mum's will—' Zoe looks up, her eyes wide. 'I'm not in it. Highdown goes to the three of you. But not to me.' She drops her wine glass and the heavy crystal shatters across the floor.

◆ ◆ ◆

Milly

1987

'Jesus.' Steph stands, her hands over ears. 'You go on about our table manners, but Sara drinks better than you.' At the end of the table, Sara looks up and gives her sister a toothy grin.

'Steph, sit down. There's no need to be so rude,' I say, taking another sip of tea as quietly as I can. She flinches, but sits down. Thank God. There's a faint twinge in my stomach and I tense. *Please, no.*

'Now please can you lay the table for breakfast,' I tell her, getting up to return to the Aga to stir the porridge, knocking the cats' basket. Terry cracks open one eye, staring reproachfully at me for the interruption. His sister June doesn't stir.

'I thought you wanted me to sit down.'

'Just do it, darling,' I say in what I hope is a calm voice, without turning around.

She opens the drawer so violently the cutlery smashes together and Terry flees out the back door. I grit my teeth. It's not yet nine, and I already feel on edge. *Calm down*, I tell myself. I wish I could have a quick ciggie, but it's too great a risk. Sara slides down from her seat and puts out the place mats, takes the cutlery from the drawer and lays the spoons and knives on top. Steph sits in her chair staring into the middle distance.

If I reprimand her, it will only cause more tension, and today is supposed to be a good day. My hands are in fists at my sides and I try to release them. Breathe. There's another twinge and I bite my lip. I'm a day late and I really thought— I keep stirring the porridge.

Small arms grip me round the waist. I turn and it's Fiona. 'Hello, darling. Have you been reading all this time?'

'I've finished that one now. Can I get the next in the series?'

'Of course. We'll go to the bookshop in town on the way back today.'

'Where are we going?' asks Fiona, sliding into her chair.

'It's a surprise, a nice family day out,' says Paul, coming into the kitchen with an empty coffee mug. He pulls me to him. Even after all these years, I love the feel of his body next to mine. The solidity, the safety. 'Mum and I have decided we're all going to the fair in town.'

'The fair? Why d'you want to go there? It's so babyish.'

We specifically chose it because Steph always likes it so much.

'Oh, don't be silly, munchkin, you love the fair.' Paul ruffles Steph's hair and she flinches.

'I'm not going,' says Steph scowling. 'I'm meeting up with a friend.'

'Steph, it'll be fun,' I say, in what I hope is a relaxed voice. 'A family outing, as Dad says.'

‘I’m not going,’ Steph says again. ‘I have plans.’

‘You are going and that’s the end of it.’ I wish Paul wasn’t so combative with her.

There’s a massive smash behind me. My heart races and every part of me seems to tingle. I jerk around and the new honey jar is in splinters on the floor, the honey oozing out over the shards of glass.

‘Sorry, accident,’ says Steph, taking a sip of tea.

Sara has her hands over her ears, Fiona is beginning to cry.

‘Keep Woody out of here until I clean up,’ I say to no one in particular, and get the dustpan and brush out. Paul picks up the larger shards and mouths ‘sorry’ as he catches my eye.

◆ ◆ ◆

‘The last time I remember seeing her was when we were all at that stall watching Fiona trying to hook the ducks out of the pond,’ I tell the policeman. My heart is racing. This can’t be happening. She was just there. ‘Sara was angry she wasn’t allowed to hold a rod. D’you remember? I looked around and Steph wasn’t there.’

Paul is white. ‘I just don’t remember. She just disappeared.’

The policeman is writing it all down in his notebook.

‘And you say five foot five; long, messy blonde hair; black jeans; black jumper. Was she carrying anything – a bag, say? Or anything else distinguishing?’

I can’t even picture her face. What if we never see her again?

‘I just can’t remember,’ says Paul.

The policeman mutters something into his radio. There’s a crackle back.

‘Follow me,’ he says.

I wait with Fiona and Sara in the back of the police car, listening to the radio traffic. Paul is out there looking. I see him darting between rides, seemingly randomly. My legs are fidgety. Why am I stuck in here? I want to be out there, looking for her. My little girl. Paul can't see anything even when it's straight in front of him.

'Please, please can I look for her too?' begs Fiona for the umpteenth time. I grip her arm, though I know there are child locks on the police car. She's already tried to get out.

'No, I can't lose you too.'

Sara is asleep in my lap, the occasional hiccup a memory of her earlier tears.

The radio crackles more urgently this time and the policeman talks into it. My heart thuds.

'Is this—'

He shakes his head. 'Just some animal libbers,' he says. 'Stealing goldfish.'

'Goldfish?'

He shrugs.

Later Paul comes back to the car. His breath is ragged, his eyes darting around. 'I just don't know where she could have gone,' he says.

'It might be best if you go home,' says the policeman. 'She may well have gone home or come home later.'

I shake my head. 'There's no way I'm leaving her here. It's not safe.' Why did I force her to come? She would have been safer with her friends. It's all my fault.

Paul cups my face in his hands. 'Take the girls home, darling, I'll stay here and keep looking. Then one of us will be wherever she is.'

But what if she's not here or there? Something tells me that she's not here anymore. She was here, but she's gone. What if she's been taken? I try to push away the images of her being tied up in the back of a van, or worse. *No, no, don't think about it.*

'Is there really nothing you can do? Put up roadblocks? Search cars? Vans? She may have been abducted.'

The policeman shakes his head. 'I know this is really awful for you both, but the reality is that she's probably just wandered off with friends. Teenagers do that. The chances are she's safe somewhere and she's lost track of time and will come home later. Try not to worry.'

The chances are. But she's my child. I don't want to take chances. I want them searching every car boot leaving the fair, stopping all vehicles trying to get out of town. They have her, I know they have her.

'I'll walk you to the car,' Paul says.

'I can't drive, not like this,' I say, my whole body shaking.

'That hurts, Mum,' says Fiona, pulling at her arm. I loosen my grip slightly, Sara still asleep on my shoulder.

'We'll drive you,' says the policeman. 'And one of us will stay with you until Stephanie returns.'

'Thank you,' I say. Paul kisses me on the forehead and stands watching us as we pull away. Next time I see him, Steph will be with us. Next time I see him, Steph will be with us. Next time I see him, Steph will be with us. If I keep saying it, it will be true.

Fiona is silent, staring into space.

We draw up outside the house and the policewoman comes inside to check Steph's bedroom. Thank God the crow healed a while ago.

I put the TV on in the drawing room for some background noise, and we sit there staring at it. The policewoman's radio crackles and we all jump but it's nothing. She turns it down.

Hours pass. The girls eat spaghetti hoops on toast but my stomach clenches at the smell. I'll never eat again if she can just come home. *Please God.* Sara seems totally unaffected, but I can tell from Fiona's darting eyes, the way she jumps at any sound, that she's waiting for Steph. Eventually I put Sara to bed, which feels like admitting defeat – a day is ending. Fiona and I stay downstairs staring at the TV. The policewoman is wandering around the hall.

Much later, car headlights swing up the driveway. I jump up, but it's just Paul on his own. 'The fair's shut now. There was no point waiting around.'

The policewoman looks sympathetic. 'She'll come home, they always do,' she repeats.

Fiona is curled up asleep on the settee. I put the kettle on. We sit together holding hands like we're on a first date. Or meeting parents.

It's after midnight when a figure starts forming through the darkness. 'Steph? Steph? Thank God, thank God.' I'm out of the house, running down the drive, half hugging, half shaking her. 'Oh my God, we've been so worried. Are you okay?'

She shrugs. 'I just . . . I just . . .'

'Where *were* you? Are you okay? We thought you'd been abducted. You just disappeared.'

I put my arm around her and guide her back to the house. Fiona's pale face looks out of the drawing-room window.

'We've been worried sick. You've been gone hours,' says Paul.

'Ten hours!' I say, the relief seeping into my bones.

'Are you alright, love?' The policewoman comes forward. 'They always come home in the end.' She smiles at me.

'I'm fine.' Steph pushes away from me, runs past the policewoman and into the house.

The police car edges down the drive, and Paul and I lead Fiona up to bed. The poor lamb is dead on her feet. I knock on Steph's door and go in. She's pretending to be asleep, her whole body tense, her beautiful hair spread across the pillow, her long lashes stroking her cheek.

'Are you okay?' I ask gently, but there's still no reply. 'We were so worried.' I stare at her taut body and then walk out and close the door as quietly as I can. I'll speak to her tomorrow. The main thing is that she's safe.

In our bathroom, I brush my teeth and then realise I've bled through my trousers. Another month and no baby.

Chapter 3

Zoe

Spring 2025

She wants to climb into her mother's bed and curl up. She's done that quite a bit over the past year. Not just when Mum has been really poorly, but earlier when she didn't feel like going out into the world. They'd spend Sundays with the papers spread across the duvet, putting the world to rights, good coffee on the bedside table. More recently, Zoe had lain next to her when she was in pain and the tablets didn't seem to work, just to hold her and talk to her, read her stories as if she were a small child who'd had a nightmare. Happy memories.

Now she kneels by the side of the four-poster, her hands to her face, tears dripping on to the worn sheets. After everything she's done for her parents, how could she not be included in the will? She was born in Highdown Hall – in this very room – learned to walk in the hall, her fingers clinging on to the wood panelling, learned to read sitting next to her father in the library, and has lived here or in the oast house all her life, caring for her parents as they gradually deteriorated and then eventually died. Since she had to let Alice go, she's cleaned what she could manage – her and her mum's bedrooms, the hall and the kitchen, mending and repairing along the way. But now it's owned by her sisters? They all grew up here – the house is pre-Tudor but has been in the family since the 1700s, different generations modernising along the way – but they've been here only occasionally since they left home almost as soon as they could. Steph never came back from boarding school, Fiona went to Singapore and Sara to university and then to her husband's house. This is Zoe's home. She thought she'd die in this house. It's part of her.

Zoe looks around the room she's come to know so intimately over the past year. The mantelpiece crammed with family photos above the fireplace which she lit every day this winter as her mother struggled to keep warm, dragging up logs and coal they could barely afford from the coalhouse. The huge armoire in the corner, where Mum's silk dresses and cashmere cardigans are losing the battle with the moths, despite the bunches of lavender Zoe cut from the garden and strung up. The dressing table, which Mum sat in front of every day looking into the ornate mirror, now cloudy with age, as she massaged thick cream into her face. Her powder pot, with its faded gold trim, still sits in the centre. When was the last time she was well enough to put powder on her nose? To lift up her lipstick brush and outline her lips?

Yesterday afternoon, Mum raised her arm from the covers and drew two fingers to her mouth, loudly breathing in and out, before laying her hand back on the blanket. Over the next few hours, she repeated the gesture occasionally, her face relaxing into a smile each time. It took Zoe a while to realise that she was pretending to smoke – or thought she was smoking. Who knows what she was thinking? She hardly spoke for the last week. Zoe doesn't remember her mum ever smoking, but clearly she did once. Are there other things from Mum's past that she doesn't know about?

Suddenly it feels like the woman she nursed for the past year, and lived with for the past thirty-five, was a stranger. How could she not leave Highdown Hall to Zoe? Or at least part of it? Zoe could have taken it on, looked after it. She thought she was the closest to her mother – the much-wanted youngest child.

She thinks back to the conversation a few months ago, perhaps their last proper conversation, when her mother hinted that difficult things were to come. Zoe thought it was about her deteriorating health, the process of dying, the funeral itself, the difficulty of arranging everything with her three sisters who are strangers in all but name. But perhaps all along it was about the will? The fact that Zoe wasn't going to receive a share of their childhood home. It is inexplicable. She always thought she was the favourite. And she believed that because she'd lived here so long, she'd be given Highdown, she'd be the one to take it on for the next generation. Zoe had even started having some thoughts about how she could do that – letting out the barns and the oast house to fund repairs on the main house and then, once it was back to its former glory, renting it out for weddings and parties. She'd read about loads of similar families who'd done that with their country houses.

She thought that her sisters would get the art or the jewellery or the books or whatever else of value. The things her mother refused to sell to fund the most basic of the much-needed repairs because they were family heirlooms. She bites her lip.

There's a gentle knock on the door and Sara comes in. Zoe sits back on her heels and wipes her wet cheeks.

'Are you okay?' Sara says, crouching down next to her. 'Silly question, I know. Of course you're not okay.' She rests her arm on Zoe's shoulder and it feels good to be in human contact, to feel someone. 'What a shock.'

Zoe nods, her head bowed.

'Fiona's read through the rest of the will and you are in it. You have what they've called a lifetime interest in Highdown. Basically, you have the right to remain in the house until you die, or choose to move out. Nothing will change.'

Zoe looks at Sara through her tears. 'Really? I can stay?'

Sara smiles at her. 'Yes, this is your home. You can live here for as long as you want, or the oast house, whatever. That doesn't change. And Mum's left you most of her jewellery – with only the proviso that we can have one thing each as a memento and that they be passed down to the next generation.' She's stroking Zoe's back.

Zoe rests her head on Sara's shoulder. 'It's such a shock. First Mum going and now this.'

'It's horrible for you,' Sara says. Zoe wonders if this is what she does with her children. It feels comforting. She takes a deep breath and lets it out slowly.

'It's horrible for all of us,' Zoe says.

'But particularly you, because you spent so much time with Mum.'

Zoe draws back and looks at Sara. Her face is soft, wobbly. 'Thank you for coming up here, to check on me.'

'I'm your big sister, Zoe, that's what I'm here for. And I'm also a mum.' Sara tries to smile but Zoe can see the tears behind her eyes.

Zoe sits on her heels. 'I'm relieved I can stay. This is my home. I was born here, I've never lived anywhere else. I've barely left the house for the past six months while I was looking after Mum. But it feels odd that now it doesn't even belong to me.' She gets up and moves to the mantelpiece, looking at the photo of Mum and Dad, their arms around Steph and Fiona, a toddler Sara in a pram against a seaside vista.

'The twins now look so like Fiona in that picture,' says Sara, standing beside her. 'We all look so sweet.'

The twins. She really should remember their names. What are they? She turns back to the photo. If Sara was two or three, then Zoe was not even a thought at that point. She rarely considered the life the five of them had before Zoe came along. But of course they had years before she arrived on the scene. Had those times meant more to Mum than the ones she shared with her?

Years ago, when she was about eight, Zoe overheard a conversation between Mum and another woman at a parish fete. The woman was commiserating over what she called Mum's happy accident. 'I bet you wish you'd been more careful,' she said. 'You'd be out the woods by now. As it is, you've still got years of mothering to go.' She saw her mother glance at her and smile slightly, and realised the woman was referring to her. A happy accident. She thought it was because she'd arrived early – her mother had always said she wasn't due for ages and the labour had come on suddenly overnight with no chance to get to hospital.

Now she sees it in a different light. Happy accident. Or not-so-happy accident. Was she ever wanted at all? Had her mother been done with having babies and got pregnant accidentally? Was she just the millstone around her mother's neck who happened to have made herself useful as a nursemaid to an old lady in her last few years? Was she just not loved like the others?

◆ ◆ ◆

Milly

1988

'I think we should call the police now,' I say, as the grandfather clock finishes its midnight chiming. 'The buses have stopped running, there's no way she's going to be able to get home.' It's pitch-black outside, those few hours of summer night. At least it's warm.

'We can't call them every time she doesn't come home. We're wasting their time,' says Paul.

'But the bowling alley closed three hours ago. She wasn't there when you drove by earlier so she must have already left to come home. Something's happened on the way home.'

'Was she even at the bowling alley?'

'What do you mean?' My skin goes cold. All evening I've been picturing her bowling. It felt like a wholesome, safe thing to do. And for once she's with friends. I've always worried that she doesn't have many friends.

'I think that was a lie to get out of the house,' he says with a sigh. 'She's never gone bowling before.'

My legs feel weak and I sink into a chair. 'I hadn't thought of that.'

'We should have punished her when she came home late last week,' Paul says. I know he's still annoyed with me about that. He thinks that if we punish her, then she won't do it again. Mum thinks the same. She's always writing to me saying we need to come down hard on her and then things will be easier.

I stand up. 'I know you think punishment is the way to go, but I don't think it'll make a difference. She doesn't care what the punishment is. She'll just take it and then do whatever it is again.' There's something odd about Steph when you tell her off. She'll stand there and look at you. Even slightly smile sometimes. Which can be infuriating. 'Where are you going?'

'I have to work tomorrow, I'm going to bed.'

'Bed? But Steph isn't home. She's fourteen, for God's sake. We need to wait.'

'Milly, she'll be fine,' he says from the doorway. 'She always is. Come to bed with me. You can't stay up like this. It's not good for you. Remember what the doctor said. Relax and you'll get pregnant. There's nothing physically stopping us now you've had that op.'

I shake my head and stand looking out of the window into the darkness. Where is she? I know something's happened. I can feel it. She's in danger.

He sighs and walks out of the room. I'll just sit down and wait.

◆ ◆ ◆

It must be the front door opening that wakes me. It's full daylight as I rush into the hall and there she is. 'Oh, Steph.' I grab her and pull her to me. 'I've been so worried.' *But I managed to fall asleep*, a small part of my brain reminds me.

'Oh, Mum, it was awful,' she cries into my shoulder. I hug her tightly, my heart thudding. I will kill whoever has hurt her. I will find them and kill them. I'll get Paul's shotgun and—

'We managed to rescue about three hundred of them but we had to leave the others behind. The mother and babies were left.'

Her body is shuddering against me.

My mind is spinning. 'What?' I ask, pulling away from her so I can look at her face.

'Rats and rabbits. Mainly rats. We couldn't take the mother and baby rats because of the stress of transportation. And there wasn't space in the vans.' She's sobbing, almost hyperventilating. 'You could smell the shit and fear from them as soon as we got in the room.'

It's like she's a complete stranger. I can't even work out what she's saying, what she means. 'You're making no sense, Steph. What are you on about?'

'Even the ones we rescued are in an awful state. The cages are so, so small, Mum. It would break your heart. How can anyone do things like that?'

My mind is on overdrive. Rats and rabbits. She was rescuing rats and rabbits? Maybe Paul's right. I was too sympathetic when she rescued that rabbit years ago, I should have shown her it was wrong and told her off and maybe she wouldn't be doing this now. Maybe this is all my fault.

I lead her into the kitchen and she sits down at the table as I put the kettle on.

Terry jumps up on to her lap, and settles down straight away. She strokes him under his chin.

I sink into a chair. 'Right, start from the beginning. What were you doing?' But she's not listening, she's in her own world.

'Some have open wounds on their skin, some burns from where they're testing stuff on them. Make-up, cosmetics. Can you imagine? All that suffering for some anti-wrinkle cream?'

My mind whirrs. The kettle clicks off and I automatically stand and go through the rigmarole of making tea. I slide the mug in front of Steph and sit back down.

She sniffs the mug. 'Actually, can I have coffee?'

'Coffee before bed? It'll keep you awake. Have the tea, it's got sugar in it. It'll help you relax.'

She shakes her head. 'Coffee helps me focus enough to sleep. It stops all the thoughts.'

Thoughts? What thoughts? Is she suicidal? She seems quite positive in a manic sort of way, not depressed. I put the tea in front of my chair and make her a coffee instead. 'Where was all of this? Who were you with?'

'There's a laboratory outside of Uckfield, tucked away in the Downs. You'd never know it was there.'

I go cold. 'Uckfield is miles away. Did you not go bowling?'

Steph looks confused. 'Bowling?'

'You said you were going bowling. In town.'

She laughs. 'Oh no, that was just to get out of the house.' So Paul was right. 'We've been staking out this place for months. Watching the security guard's routine, opening and closing windows to see how good the security is, working out the best places to get through the fence unseen, where to stand as a lookout.'

My mind seems to be working in slow motion. I can't understand what she's saying, what it all means. I hand her the sweet coffee. She cradles it in her hands. Her eczema's bad at the moment, the skin split and a mix of blood and clear liquid oozing out. I wish she'd use the steroid cream the doctor prescribed. Another worry.

'We'd worked out that the guard walked the perimeter of the building on the hour, every hour. But he wears headphones with music so loud we could hear it from the other side of the fence.' She starts smiling for the first time that morning. 'I thought it was Guns N' Roses he listened to. But P— Well, the others think it's U2. Anyway, he then sits in a box room for the rest of the time so we could easily get in and rescue the animals.'

'Who were you with?' The 'P' has not been lost on me.

'Oh, just the usual gang, but there was more of us this time. We needed all the people we could find to get the animals safely out.'

'The gang?' Gang doesn't sound good.

'It's just an expression, Mum. The ALF.'

'ALF?' The gang. This is some weird nightmare. Who is P?

'Animal Liberation Front,' she says.

Animal libbers. Oh my God. Of course. It all slips into place now. She must have been with them at the fair last year, though she refused to say. The policeman mentioned animal libbers rescuing goldfish. 'But they're terrorists,' I say. I've read about them in the newspaper. 'What they're doing is against the law – you could be arrested, sent to prison.'

'Oh, Mum, you worry too much. What we're doing is so important. We're taking a stand – no one else cares enough. If the public knew what was going on in those places they'd be horrified.'

Is she right? I really don't know. 'Where did you take them?' I ask, taking a sip of tea. Try to stay calm. Breathe. She's talking. Don't scare her off by freaking out. She never talks to me. Even though what she's saying is scary, I love that she's talking to me.

'There's a farm about ten miles away, near Pulborough. A lady called Mary. We loaded them off there into a barn. She said she'll start to rehabilitate and rehome them.'

'Where did you go after that?'

'Well, we dropped everyone off. And then—' She pauses for a fraction of a second. 'They came back here and dropped me off.'

They. If they is P, if they is a boy then they're old enough to drive. So seventeen. At least. And he didn't come up the drive, did he? Like a normal friend would. He dropped her at the end and scurried off, like one of the rats. Animal libbers.

'So they drive?'

'Yes.' She takes a sip of coffee. I can feel her start to calm down. She's coming off the high, the adrenalin of it all. I can't imagine what it would be like to break into somewhere like that, to do what she's done. She must be exhausted. 'They have to drive, to rescue the animals, otherwise—'

'I can't believe you're involved with animal libbers,' I say, not able to stop myself. 'It's so dangerous. It's illegal.'

She shrugs. 'It's worth it, Mum. We have right on our side.' Her eyes are starting to droop. I need to get some food into her and then her into bed.

'Let me get you some toast. Then I'll dress your poor hand, your eczema's bad again. And then bed. You need to sleep.'

'Thanks, Mum. And sorry I was so late. I thought it would be over much quicker. That you wouldn't notice I'd gone.'

I kiss the top of her head and get the bread knife out of the rack to slice the loaf. As I cut into the crust my hand won't stop shaking.

Animal libbers.

Chapter 4

Zoe

Spring 2025

The house is the fullest it's been in years, thinks Zoe, staring up at her bedroom ceiling. The hairline crack seems to have grown wider since she last slept in here, or is it her imagination? Something else to add to the list.

She wonders how her sisters are getting on in their childhood bedrooms. Nobody has been in them for years, since Alice left probably. She can't remember if they even covered things with sheets or if everything is covered in layers of dust. She caught the look on Fiona's face as they went up to the top floor to the old nursery and saw where the roof had caved in the year before. They have a new roof now, at least, but there was no money left over to repair the plaster and repaint. Maybe she should have dusted their rooms. Got some bedding out. But she didn't want to leave her mother's side over those last few weeks. Just in case.

The usual nurse came back yesterday evening. She always kept up a running commentary of what she was doing. 'I'm going to check your blood pressure, Milly, is that okay? How are you feeling, Milly, this evening? Any pain?' She checked the syringe driver, and scribbled something down on the notes. Then lifted up the duvet. 'Just looking at your legs, Milly. What lovely legs you have,' she jollied. The tide of mottled purple had risen from Mum's toes to her ankles and was now moving towards her knees. Mum hadn't moved her legs for a long time.

The nurse urged her again to call her sisters. She nodded and promised she'd do it that evening. But once the nurse had gone, and the only sound was her mum's rasping breathing – perfectly normal the nurse had said – she realised it was too late in Singapore. Fiona would be asleep. She didn't want to call Sara and Steph without having called Fiona first. Fiona would take charge, she knew. *It would wait until Monday morning*, she thought, as she lay down on the camp bed next to her mum.

Now she feels guilty that by the time she called them first thing Monday it was almost too late. She'd done what the nurse had said. Eventually. Sat by their mother's bedside, watching the loose bit of dried skin on her lip flutter against her breath, and finally called them. Fiona first and then Sara. Short conversations, the sudden intakes of breath, the catches in the voices, enough for her to know that they knew how serious it was. That they would come straight away. She even got an immediate reply from her text to Steph. Why hadn't she done it earlier? Perhaps there was a nasty part of her that wanted to keep her mother's death to herself after all the years of nursing her. She sighs. But it was also about not wanting to admit that it was the end.

If only she hadn't gone to make that toast when she did. Five minutes she was away at most. Three, probably. She wasn't even that hungry. It was eating from boredom, something she swore she'd never do, but sitting with someone while they were dying was a weird mix of boredom and stress. Until they were gone, and then you'd do anything to have even a minute of those weeks and months back. Zoe swallows and closes her eyes.

She gets up and tiptoes over to the door, opening it inch by inch, and creeping on to the landing. Highdown Hall is settling down for the night, slowly contracting around her, the creaks soothing in their familiarity.

Suddenly the door at the end of the landing opens and Fiona stands there, wearing an old pink dressing gown. 'Ah, Zoe, I'm glad you're still up. I forgot to ask, can I have the Wi-Fi password?'

Zoe shakes her head. 'We don't have Wi-Fi.'

'But I need to get online. And there's no signal in the bedroom.'

'There's a bit of signal in the library. I can sit on the window seat there, prop my laptop on the window ledge, tether off my phone signal. Sara phoned her children from there earlier. There's sometimes a bit of signal in the hall and kitchen too.' Fiona's body is drooping but her eyes are flitting from one thing to another. She didn't want to mention the signal in Mum's bedroom. Fiona would turn it into an office.

'That's ridiculous,' Fiona says. 'How can you live without Wi-Fi?'

Zoe shrugs. She stopped the Wi-Fi contract last year. Another thing they couldn't afford.

'I also don't have any clothes,' Fiona mutters. 'I only have what I was wearing and this dressing gown, which was on the back of the door. Did this used to be mine?'

'I have some you can borrow,' Zoe says. Fiona follows her back to her room, even though Zoe wishes she wouldn't, but she knows it would seem churlish to stop her coming in.

'Gosh, it's changed in here,' she says, looking around. 'It used to be all pink.'

Zoe laughs, the sound strange to her ears. 'That was twenty-odd years ago,' she says, handing her some loose trousers and an old t-shirt. 'This should do for now. I can give you more in the morning.'

'This is awful for you,' says Fiona, reaching forward. She touches Zoe's cheek, and the feeling of her hand makes Zoe jump. 'I'm sorry we weren't there to help.'

Zoe feels the tears start to swell up inside her again. 'I wish you had been,' she whispers. She knows that Fiona would have done a better job than her, the house wouldn't be in such a state if Fiona had been managing it, she would have found a way. Zoe swallows to push the tears down and turns away. She must stop crying. 'There's no hot water in the bathroom on this floor. There's some in the shower off Mum's dressing room. But you'll need to go round to the old nursery bathroom upstairs for a proper bath.'

'Right.' Fiona pauses. 'There's a huge damp patch on the ceiling in my room. It's okay, isn't it? It's not going to fall on my head in the night?'

Zoe laughs. 'It's fine. It's all dried out now. That was a leak from the nursery bathroom, caused weirdly by the roof caving in up there. We had to replace the whole thing last year. It hadn't been done in more than a century and was leaking all over the place. But there was no money left for replastering or repainting. And it's not something I could do myself.'

'That must have cost a fortune,' says Fiona, glancing around.

Zoe shrugs. 'There was no money, obviously.'

Fiona tips her head to the side looking at her.

'I sold the Chaumet necklace,' Zoe says by way of an explanation.

Fiona started. 'The pink one? But that was your twenty-first birthday present from Mum and Dad, wasn't it?'

Zoe nodded.

'Surely there were less precious things you could have sold first?'

It feels disloyal to tell her that Mum refused to sell anything, that she said all heirlooms had to be handed down. But she'd also refused to let out the outbuildings or even the oast house, not wanting strangers on the estate, apart from the cottages that had always been let. 'I didn't mind. It wasn't really my thing. Highdown's more important.'

'In the morning, let's go through what needs to be done. I'll put together a budget.' Fiona looks like she wants to say more, but just wishes her goodnight and climbs up the back stairs to the bathroom.

Zoe lies on her bed and listens to Fiona's footsteps, the cranking of the taps. She waits for her to come back and go into her room. When the door clicks shut, Zoe opens her door again and creeps on to the gallery. She glances at the other doors but Steph's and Sara's are shut and she knows the other main bedroom is locked, the furniture ghostly in sheets.

Her mother's bedroom feels more familiar than her own. On the bedside table, the half-filled plastic beaker is the only sign that illness inhabited this room. The nurse removed the medical paraphernalia not long after Mum died. A pair of reading glasses are neatly folded up on top of the book her mother was halfway through when she stopped being able to read. Imagine your eyesight going when you're halfway through a book. Maybe she should have offered to read it to her. It's too late now.

She feels better now that the body has gone. She can remember her mother properly, unencumbered by the body riddled with illness. She feels ashamed for hiding away when the funeral people came; she should have seen her mother off on her final journey out of the house she lived in for more than fifty years – that her grandparents had gifted her parents as a wedding present.

Zoe kisses the pillow, which is still impregnated with her mother's Chanel scent, and then retreats from the room, closing the door behind her, and turns the key. She doesn't want any of her sisters coming in here and messing up the memories. They're too precious.

Back in her room, she lies down on the bed. After weeks on the camp bed, she'd forgotten how comfortable a proper bed is. She stares back at the ceiling, tracing the crack. It doesn't feel like she's going to be able to sleep. Her thoughts career chaotically around her brain, colliding with each other like bumper cars. She wonders how her sisters are feeling. Her eyes start to droop. In that strange dream-state between waking and sleeping she sees her mother, young again, pushing Fiona in the pram, and the oddness of it jolts her awake. *Mum*. Is she okay? Has she called out? Is that what has woken her? Zoe turns over, sees the outline of her chest of drawers and realises she's in her own room. *Mum's gone.* Her heart constricts and the weight of it descends again.

There's a fluttery feeling in her chest. She takes several deep breaths but it doesn't improve so she sits up. The moon shines in through a gap in the curtains. She slips out of bed to close them and sees a fox strut across the drive and on to the lawn, disappearing into the woods. The trees look skeletal, haunting the skyline. An owl hoots. Something flits past her window, making Zoe shiver. She pulls the curtains together tightly.

If only she'd waited to have breakfast when the nurse arrived this morning, as she usually did. She'd known the minute she walked back into the room. She didn't need to feel for a pulse or check for breathing. Her mother had gone. Zoe didn't believe in a god, but she recognised that her mother's soul or life force or whatever it was had left her. She was no longer Mum but a body, a shell. She stood by the body for a few minutes, watching the flickering and flinching as it shut down. She touched her mother's hand but suddenly felt repulsed by it. She was touching a dead body, not her mother anymore. This wasn't Mum.

Of course she could never admit to the others that she hadn't been there. That after all those months of being by her mother's side, she'd missed being with her as she passed. She hadn't even told the nurse, who turned up for her usual visit fifteen minutes later. Just muttered something about it being peaceful.

She blames herself of course. All for a slice of toast and marmalade. But couldn't Mum have waited just a few minutes for her to come back? Fiona was right – some people waited for relatives to arrive from other parts of the world until they died, surrounded by everyone they loved. It felt like her mother had done the opposite. Waited until she left the room for a moment to make breakfast and then died. As if she had done it on purpose.

◆ ◆ ◆

Milly

1988

'I've managed to get hold of some soya milk from that health-food shop in town,' I say to Paul as we settle in front of the TV.

'Soya milk? What the hell's that?' He pulls a face.

'It's like milk but not from animals. I'm not sure how they make it. It was very expensive but I thought it would be good to show Steph we're making the effort.'

'You're too good to her.' He smiles at me as he picks up the TV remote. 'The vegetarian nonsense was bad enough. I don't get the vegan thing at all.'

'It's pretty harmless, Paul,' I say. 'She'll get over it.'

'I get that she loves animals – who doesn't – but it's the way she goes about it. All those letters to the minister. Did you read any of them? They were so visceral. Disturbing.'

'I did.' I helped her write some of them, though I wouldn't dare tell Paul that. He worked with the minister John Gummer occasionally. 'She's very articulate. She's clearly hugely bright and passionate about animals. It's all part of her wanting to be a vet.' I love how focused Steph is about it. The rest of her life – her bedroom, her school work – is complete chaos, but around animals she becomes completely focused. And it's the one time she actually wants to talk to me. I can't wait to show her the milk tomorrow. I'll put it on the table for breakfast. Perhaps make porridge out of it.

'That whole incident with Eddie's dog,' says Paul, 'cutting its rope. That poor old man is bereft without that dog.'

'To be fair, that dog should not have been tied up like that all day.'

'She used to love coming out on the estate with me, on the shoots, and now she doesn't even do that.'

'Paul, be realistic. She never loved the shoots. She hated them. She enjoyed the beating briefly but when she discovered why they were beating, she freaked out. Don't you remember her calling the new syndicate manager an animal abuser?' He was a bit odd, and I thought Steph might have a point about him.

'She called your father an animal abuser the last time he was here.' He glances up at the stag heads and then flicks on the TV. There's a police drama just starting. We sit there quietly for a while. I'm barely following the plot, but it's nice to be curled up with Paul. We spend too much time these days talking about Steph. We used to talk about so many other things.

I must update Steph and Fiona's school photos now that I've got Sara's first one, I think, glancing at the frames on the piano. Steph's is at least four years out of date. But she wasn't in school this year when they took them and managed to look peculiar in last year's one.

The programme suddenly goes quiet and it's then I hear the stair creaking. I turn, ready to welcome Fiona or Sara on to the sofa, thinking they're unable to sleep and need a cuddle. But it's Steph, dressed all in black like a panther, creeping down the stairs. Presumably she's trying to get out unseen. My whole body tenses. I feel like I'm on hyper-alert.

'Paul—' He turns and we both stand in unison. At dinner she agreed not to go out this week.

Paul moves first. 'Stephanie. We talked about you not going out tonight. That you needed to stay in, focus on your homework.' I can hear the irritation in his voice.

She's wearing some kind of black hat. There's a roll of fabric above her eyebrows. Oh God, it's a balaclava. Where is she going? Of course, it will be the animal libbers again. *P.*

'Steph.' He walks into the hall, his hands clenched. She takes another step down towards us, glancing at the clock. It's almost half past eight. She should be reading, being calm, finishing homework. Just like we said.

'I can't be late,' she says, shrugging, moving down another step. She's wearing her black school plimsolls. 'I'm always late and they tell me off.'

Late? Late? For what? And who tells her off? P?

As she turns a fraction, I realise she's holding something behind her back. It glints in the half-light of the hall. What is it? Is it a can of paint? It's two cans of paint. But why?

She takes another step down, biting the corner of her nail, or where her nail should be. Her cuticles are already raw. She sucks the side of the thumb. She must be bleeding.

Paul doesn't move. 'Come on, Steph, it's no time for you to be going out. You can't keep doing things like this. It's not good for you.' He's trying to stay calm but I'm worried he'll blow.

Only four more steps and then she'll be in the hall. The door is unlocked, as it always is. Maybe we should lock it in future. Paul needs to do something. Stop her. She can't leave. I can't do another sleepless night. I'm so, so tired. I just want to know she's here, safe.

She takes another step and I can see the paint cans properly. It's the red marking fluid Paul and the men use for the sheep. We've only recently started the marking so there must be most of the can there and an unopened can too. What's she going to do with it?

'Steph, please.' I'm walking towards her on autopilot. 'What are you doing? Where do you think you're going?' Paul's hand is on my arm, pulling me back, but I pull away. It's better me dealing with her calmly than him getting angry. She takes another step down. There's something written in felt tip on her arm.

She pauses, looking at me. I take a step towards her and hold out my arms. I'm not sure if I'm trying to hug her or stop her from leaving. I feel ridiculous, like some kind of lollipop lady. 'Put that paint down and go upstairs,' I say. Be firm, Mum and Paul say. I'm trying to be firm and calm. But there's a funny look in her eyes.

The clock starts up its half-hour chiming routine. She glances at it for a second and then leaps down the last few steps, lunging at me. Oh God. The balaclava falls down over part of her face. She looks like a pirate.

I must have closed my eyes in the moment because all I feel is a huge explosion against the side of my head. Someone screams and I feel myself falling backwards. I wait for the impact on the floor but it never comes.

'Milly, Milly.' Paul's voice drifts in. Everything's a bit patchy. Starry. I finally manage to open my eyes. There's the underneath of the hall table. It needs a clean. Something's throbbing. Wet. Sticky. My head. My right eye opens but I can't see anything from my left. 'I'm having a stroke,' I mumble.

Paul cups the back of my head. 'You're not having a stroke, darling.' His breath is jerky. 'Your face—'

I drag myself up, the room slowly spinning. I think I'm going to be sick. There's something wet dripping down the side of my face. Steph. I try to move my head and look around the hall. 'What happened?'

It sounds like he's going to cry. 'Steph caught you with the paint can—'

'Must have been an accident,' I mumble, pressing my hand to my temple. She didn't mean it.

'Yes, an accident.' His face contorts and looks ugly for a second. He stands. 'I'll get you something for that cut or it'll scar.'

The front door is wide open, a chilly breeze snaking around the hall. It was an accident. I shouldn't have got in her way.

Someone is crying. Is it me? But then Paul is on his feet going upstairs. Fiona is standing at the top, swaying slightly, staring at us, her eyes like saucers. She's holding Sara in her arms, shielding her from the sight of me.

Paul picks them both up. The hall spins again and I lie down. I really must clean the underside of the hall table. How did it get so dirty?

Chapter 5

Zoe

Spring 2025

'What's everyone's plans? I'm going to stay here until the interment.' Fiona lets out a slow breath. 'I can't exactly go back to Singapore.'

Sara nods, taking a slurp of tea. 'I'll have to see. It would be a long time for me to be away from my children. I've never even left them for a night before—'

'But we have a lot to organise, to help out here. We should all try to do it together,' says Fiona, cutting across her. Sara narrows her eyes and stares at her. 'Steph?' Fiona asks.

Steph sighs. 'I can't really leave the shelter for too long. I'll speak to Jay, see if he's able to stay for a bit. I can always pop back and forth if needed. It's not far.'

'It'll be good to have you all here,' says Zoe, surprising herself. 'It's been quite difficult doing this on my own for the past few months.' She stirs the porridge in the bowl but still can't bring herself to eat any.

'You should have called us earlier,' says Sara gently, eating the last of a slice of toast. 'It was a big responsibility just for you.'

She's right, of course, thinks Zoe. Even a few hours' sleep has given her a little more perspective on that. She can't now think why she didn't.

'Let's look through Mum's jewellery this morning,' says Sara, glancing sideways at Zoe.

'That would be a nice thing to do,' agrees Fiona, searching through the pantry. 'Then we can pop down to the village later to talk to the vicar about the service. Are there any eggs?'

Zoe shakes her head. 'I'm vegan.'

Fiona's mouth is an O, which despite everything makes Zoe want to laugh. Steph catches Zoe's eye and then looks away, slightly smiling. 'Well, we can stock up at the village shop on the way to see the vicar. I've also dropped an email to the solicitor whose name was on the will, asking for a meeting.' She looks down at her list. 'Is there anything else we need to do today?'

Zoe stares at her, impressed at her efficiency at such an awful time.

'You and your lists, Fi,' says Sara, a slight edge to her voice. 'Come on, let's go up to Mum's room. She kept it all in the safe in her bedroom, didn't she? I remember her showing me years ago.'

She and Sara walk up the stairs side by side. Zoe's not really sure what she should be doing. After months of her days being regimented by pills and nurses' visits, there's a vague sense now that the days will stretch ahead with nothing for her to do. At least Fiona is here to take charge, to organise things. She's not sure how she'd go about sorting out a funeral.

'I know you must be very disappointed by the will and the house situation,' says Sara as they reach the gallery. *Disappointed?* She must be making a face because Sara takes a deep breath and pastes on a smile. 'I'm sure when we meet Mum's solicitor, he'll have some answers. But Mum had some lovely pieces of jewellery. And they'll all be yours now. That's some consolation at least.'

She knows Sara means well. But jewellery? A consolation? Zoe twirls her helix piercing with her left hand. She never saw Mum wear any jewellery that she'd want to even try on in a million years. It was all huge ruby and sapphire brooches, diamond chokers and strings of pearl necklaces. She doesn't want to wear them, but she wouldn't want to sell them either. The idea of getting rid of anything that Mum once touched is too painful. And she knows Mum wouldn't have wanted that either.

Zoe takes the key out of her pocket and unlocks her mother's bedroom door. 'Maybe I can swap jewellery for bits of the house,' she says, gnawing at the side of her fingernail. 'A diamond brooch for the airing cupboard.' She laughs and Sara smiles at her, confusion in her eyes. She meant it as a joke, trying to make light of an awful situation, but it came out all wrong.

Zoe can't help but glance at the bed again as they walk in. Still empty. It feels so odd. This time yesterday, she'd gone but her body lay there. This time two days ago . . .

On the dressing table is a small mother-of-pearl box. Jewellery played an enormous role in her mother's life. Granny Evelyn had handed down her own collection on her death, and Mum had added to it over the years. She was the sort of woman who thought nothing of wearing a Cartier necklace on the school run.

In the top of the box is a key. The safe. Zoe opens the armoire and moves aside the leather overnight bag to reveal the safe behind. Security was never her mother's strong point. Inside are stacks of tiny boxes Tetrised together.

'Let's put them on the bed, like Mum used to do,' says Sara. 'Then we can take a proper look at everything.'

Zoe shakes her head. 'That's where Mum . . .' She swears she sees the faint indent of her mother's body in the sheets. A sort of Turin Shroud. But that turned out to be a fake, didn't it?

Sara touches her on the shoulder. 'Of course.' She stands at the side of the bed, staring at the emptiness. 'Isn't it strange? She raised us for all those years and now she's gone.' She sounds odd and Zoe moves to stand next to her. 'I'm sad to have missed her going, but I'm really glad that you were with her as she went. That she wasn't alone.'

Zoe swallows and turns away. 'We'll lay them across the carpet,' she says, starting to take things out of the safe. The flat, square necklace boxes nestle against the square ring boxes and the deep brooch ones. Zoe flips open the lid of one of the largest, a deep red with a gold border faded at the edges. Five rows of diamonds in a gold choker necklace glint back at her. She shows it to Sara who raises her eyebrows. 'It looks like something you'd see in *Dynasty*. Pure 1980s.'

Sara kneels down next to her and opens another box which holds huge yellow diamond drop earrings. 'That's like something Pat Butcher would wear on *Eastenders,'* Zoe says and then immediately feels guilty for criticising something of Mum's.

Another holds a gold brooch in the shape of a poodle, another a red enamel ladybird. Zoe gasps. 'I even remember Granny wearing this – I'd loved playing with it when I was small.' Zoe looks at the box – Cartier. She puts it aside.

They open all the boxes, unfolding brittle tissue paper that sometimes disintegrates in their hands to reveal strings of pearls or diamonds. The three-strand pearl necklace with the diamond clasp Zoe knows her mother's grandmother had given her on her wedding day. The wedding photo on the piano downstairs shows her touching them, perhaps conscious of the weight, as she gazes up at Dad.

'Oh look, the emerald bird brooch. I loved that as a child,' says Sara. 'It's so Mum.' She strokes it and then brings it to her mouth to kiss. 'This will be my one thing,' she says. 'And I can pass it on to the girls when I go.' Then, suddenly glancing up at Zoe, 'If that's okay with you?'

Zoe nods. 'Of course. There's loads of stuff here, you can have as much as you like. What shall I do with it all? Who will want to wear this now?' she says. 'It's so old-fashioned. The world this was created for has disappeared. Thankfully.' She opens another box. 'And Mum would have wanted it to stay in the family. Perhaps your children will want it one day.' She surprises herself by saying it. She can't remember how old they are now and immediately feels sad. She should have tried to be more involved in their lives – they are her nieces, after all.

'You might have children,' says Sara.

Zoe takes a deep breath but says nothing.

Sara looks at all the boxes, glinting in the morning light. 'I reckon there's thousands and thousands of pounds of jewellery here, Zoe. When you're ready, you should have it valued and then decide what you want to keep and what you want to sell.'

Sell. Mum had been funny about the jewellery. *She wanted to make sure it was handed down to her daughters, perhaps*, Zoe thinks. Not realising that times change, fashions change and they wouldn't want it in quite the same way. Meanwhile the house slowly decayed around them with no money to maintain it. Her small salary, Mum's pension and the cottages' rent had just about paid the bills and the estate workers and the day-to-day maintenance.

Zoe lies back on the rug, staring up at the ceiling, following the outline of the watermarks. She's been so institutionalised in this room, barely leaving, that it feels a relief to be back here somehow. It felt strange sleeping in her own bed last night, lingering over breakfast earlier and not rushing back to be here. Watching and waiting.

Death is funny like that. You spend all those months sitting with someone as they lie dying, wrestling with conflicting feelings and emotions. And then suddenly it's over.

Zoe feels bereft. Not just from her mum going. But from losing the routine of sitting with her every day, the nurses coming and going, the radio going through its hourly routine of news, music, chat, adverts. The finale of Schubert's 'Piano Sonata in A Major' was playing when her mum died. Or rather when Zoe came back into her room with her toast and marmalade and discovered Mum had died. Zoe waited until it had finished and the radio announcer said what it was. It felt important to know what Mum had been listening to as she took her last breaths. If she had been able to hear anything at all.

'We should show the others some of these pieces,' says Sara, holding a sapphire pendant up to the light. 'I think that's everything now, quite the collection.' Sara reaches into the safe. 'Oh no, there's something at the back.'

Zoe sits up as Sara brings out a narrow box which she hands to her. But when Zoe opens it, she realises that it doesn't contain jewellery. There's just a tiny brown envelope, the sort that people would have received their weekly wages in. When she opens it she finds a large iron key. Nothing else. Zoe frowns and looks at the envelope. It's marked *Kai*. How odd. Kai. She's never heard of a Kai. Is that even a name?

Sara cranes her neck to look and Zoe hands her the box and envelope. She holds the key up to the light. 'I don't recognise it, do you?'

Sara shakes her head. Zoe holds it to the door of the armoire, but the key is far too big. Likewise the dressing-table drawer. In her pocket is the key to her mother's bedroom and that's far smaller than this one.

'Maybe it's one of the doors downstairs,' says Sara. 'It looks really old so it may be from when the house was built.'

Zoe slips the key into her pocket. She takes the ladybird out of its box and pins it to her dungarees. It's actually very pretty. Nobody would know that it was worth anything – she doesn't look horribly pretentious in it.

◆ ◆ ◆

'I love the ladybird, Zoe,' says Fiona later, when they're back in the kitchen having a cup of tea. The day seems punctuated by tea; she hasn't drunk so much in her life.

'There's all sorts of funny things up there,' says Zoe. 'I've put them out in case you want anything. Sara's chosen a bird brooch.'

'Look,' says Sara, thrusting the drooping lapel of her blouse forward. 'Isn't it pretty?'

'I remember Mum wearing it,' says Steph. 'It was one of her favourites, wasn't it?'

'While you were upstairs, the solicitor called and he's coming round tomorrow to talk us through the will,' says Fiona, looking at a notepad.

'Thanks for doing that, Fi,' says Zoe, smiling at her older sister.

Fiona smiles back. 'We need to get this sorted,' she says. 'And I've been in touch with the crematorium. They're going to liaise with the church. They'll give the ashes to them a few days after the funeral for the interment. They'll add her name to Dad's stone. We need to decide on the wording. Something like *Beloved Wife, Mother, Grandmother and Friend*? Then her dates of birth and death?'

'Yes, we could do,' says Sara. 'Steph? Zoe?'

'Perhaps we should look at all the options,' says Zoe. 'There's no rush, surely. She's only just died.'

'Well, I do want to get it all sorted out,' says Fiona, tapping her pen on the side of the laptop.

'Let's have a look over supper,' says Steph, glancing at Zoe.

'Good idea,' says Fiona. 'Now I need to call the caterers. I was going to use the same firm who did Dad's wake, unless anyone has any objections?'

No one says anything. 'Great,' says Fiona. 'We need to think about clothes too. I presume nobody has black dresses here?'

'Isn't that a bit old-fashioned now?' says Steph, looking at Zoe again.

Zoe likes them looking at her to answer questions about their mother. 'I think Mum was quite old-fashioned really. She'd want us all in black – and the rest of the funeral is very traditional.'

'Perhaps we should go into town to buy some. I'll add it to the to-do list. I need to go into town anyway, to buy some clothes.' Fiona looks down at the creased tie-dye t-shirt Zoe gave her that morning.

'How are we going to pay for this?' asks Zoe. 'I have a tiny bit of savings that we could use but it's not going to cover that much.'

'That's okay, I understand,' says Fiona. 'I'm happy to pay myself and then we can sort it out afterwards. We can speak to the solicitor about it tomorrow.'

'Okay, thanks, Fi.' There's such a relief in Fiona taking charge.

'We found a very weird thing in the safe along with all the jewellery,' Sara says, looking at Zoe. 'There was an envelope, with a key in it. Show them, Zoe.'

'A key?' says Fiona.

'Yes, a large iron key. Very old-looking. The writing on the envelope was definitely Mum's. She'd written a name on it. Or at least I think it was a name.'

Zoe takes the key out of her pocket and lays it on the table. 'Look.'

'What was the name?' says Fiona.

Zoe screws up her face. 'I left the envelope upstairs. What was it?' She looks at Sara. 'Kai, that was it. K-A-I.'

'Kai.' Steph gasps.

Zoe turns to look at her.

'I've never heard of a Kai,' says Fiona, frowning. 'Mystery keys in envelopes is like some sort of Agatha Christie novel.'

'I doubt we're going to find a body in the library,' says Sara laughing, and then suddenly stops and looks down.

'Steph?' Zoe says. 'Does Kai ring a bell?'

Steph is pale. 'No. No, it doesn't,' she says. She slurps the last of her tea and stands up, turning her back on them to wash up her mug at the sink. 'Not at all.'

◆ ◆ ◆

Milly

1988

Overnight, the bruise has changed from a shocking red to a purplish black, starting at my temple and working its way around to my right eye. I press on the centre just to the side of my eye. There's something enjoyable about the stab of pain. I look haggard. There's no other word for it. My whole face seems to sag back at me in the bathroom mirror. Too tired to hold itself up. There are deep grooves bracketing my mouth, matching the tiny lines splaying out from my eyes.

Paul comes up next to me, spitting out toothpaste into the basin. 'I feel like I'm visibly ageing,' I say. 'I look much older even than yesterday. I'm not sure the bruise is doing much for me.'

He rinses out his mouth, looking at our joint reflection. 'You look as beautiful as you always do.' He turns to face me, cradling the left side of my face and presses his lips on my mouth. I feel myself relax under his touch.

He draws back and angles my face to look at the bruise, his lips pursed. 'She didn't mean to hit you,' he says, his eyebrows drawn together.

'Of course not,' I say, swallowing. 'It was an accident.'

'Yes, an accident,' he says. 'If I thought she'd done it deliberately, I'd . . .' He shakes his head. 'It's lucky that she caught you with the used paint can and not the full one or it would have been so much worse.' He pushes my hair away from the side of my face. 'But the bruise will go. In a couple of weeks you won't even remember it was there.'

I look back at my reflection, my right eye somehow shrivelled by the weight of the bruise. How will I ever forget this? Paul stares at our reflections. After a while he says, 'I don't think she would have hit you if you hadn't got in her way.'

'No,' I say.

'You put yourself in harm's way yesterday. You tried to physically stop her. You're shorter than her now, more slight. You can't confront her like that. You're only going to get hurt. I know I said we need to be more firm, but let me do that. She won't hurt me, even if it was an accident.' That word, accident.

'Yes,' I say. It all feels wrong. What if Paul felt that Steph did it deliberately? What would he do? 'Perhaps we could lock the front door to stop her going anywhere? I'm so worried about the risks that she's taking. Going out late at night, sometimes staying out overnight, with people we don't know, doing God only knows what. I've read about animal libbers in the newspaper. They're criminals. We should be bolting the doors and windows to stop her.'

And P. I need to find out who this P is.

Paul takes a deep breath. 'You know if we did that she'd find a way out. I know full well that she's been climbing down the drainpipe from her bedroom. I think the only reason she didn't do that last night was because she had the paint cans with her.'

I feel suddenly cold. 'She's been climbing down the drainpipe?'

He nods.

'How do you know?'

Paul shrugs, and reaches for his comb, dragging it through his hair. 'It's pulled away slightly from the bracket and there have been footprints in the flower bed beneath it.'

'Oh.' I don't know what to say. Why didn't I know? 'Why didn't you say anything?'

'I didn't want to worry you. But I'd prefer we allow her out the front door if she's going to go rather than her feeling she has to climb out in secret. It'd be safer.'

An image of Steph falling out of the bedroom window into the flower bed, lying with a broken leg, or worse, flashes across my mind. I shudder. 'Yes, you're right.'

'I just need to be more on alert. Stop her before she gets near the door.' He kisses me, smooths down my hair and walks back into the dressing room.

I look back at my face. The light has dropped out of my eyes. They seem flat. Over the past few months, I've felt the tension rising with Stephanie; she's seemed to be taking bigger and bigger risks. But I never dreamed she would hurt me, even by accident. She is such a complicated person, so difficult to understand at times.

At least she wasn't out too late last night. She got back at ten thirty, which still felt too late for a fourteen-year-old to me, but compared to recent weeks, it was positively early. It's funny how your expectations can change so dramatically. I'm still no closer to finding out who P is. She's becoming more and more closed. I know she's always with the animal rights lot, but I never know what she's doing specifically, what she's thinking. That's the frightening thing about having children. They start off inside you, part of you. Then after they're born, it's a gradual separation. Day by day, they move further from you. Until one day, they may still be living in the same house as you, you love them and you're still responsible for them, but they've become virtually a stranger.

I stare at the bruise. The foundation smooths on easily even though I haven't used it for years. I blend it in around my jaw, moving up to my eyes, muscle memory taking over. The purple gradually disappears under layers of skin-coloured liquid. I'm putting on a mask. A good-mother mask. I don't want Fiona and Sara seeing this. And especially not the school mums. I add eyeliner and mascara, and by the time I stand back and admire my reflection, you'd never know there was a bruise there. The person in the mirror smiles back at me. Uncertainly at first. I try harder and the smile is almost genuine. In my bedroom mirror I clip on the pearl necklace and add the Cartier ladybird for extra armour.

The clock marks seven. I need to wake up the girls. At least Steph's school is on a Baker Day so I don't have to face her yet.

◆ ◆ ◆

I'm hit by the sound of loud music as soon as I walk through the front door after dropping Fiona and Sara at school. That never bodes well. But I can't just let yesterday be forgotten. I need to talk to Steph calmly about it. And I want to see if I can find out who P is. If she's got a boyfriend, then we need to have a chat and take a visit to the doctor in town. Mum was always so coy about those things, but I'm not going to be like that. I want my children to have all the information they need, not words wrapped up in euphemisms.

I knock on the door and open it to a wall of noise. 'How can you possibly concentrate with music on that loud?' I know I shouldn't start off in this way, but honestly, the music is deafening. It makes my pulse race.

'You're supposed to knock. You promised,' she says, not looking up.

Oh yes. I did knock, but I bite my lip. 'Sorry.'

'Anyway, it helps me concentrate,' Steph says, focusing on whatever she's doing at her desk.

'I don't know how it can help you "concentrate".' I realise I sound like my own mother. I even did those stupid inverted commas in the air that used to annoy me so much.

'Well, it does.'

I sigh. Steph looks at me like she wants to kill me. I take a step back without meaning to. She sits on her hands. This is not going as planned. I take a deep breath and remember the good-mother mask.

'What are you doing?' I say, forcing a jolly note into my voice. I edge closer to her desk and lean over her shoulder. It's some kind of poster.

'I'm making a poster for the lab protest,' she says.

'*Close Down Manning Farms*,' I read. 'What's Manning Farms?'

'It's a laboratory a few miles away which is importing primates to sell to other places for animal testing.'

Animal libbers. How involved is she?

'Oh.' I'm not sure what to say but I want to keep the conversation going. 'Michael Jackson has a monkey,' I say. 'It's called Bubbles. I read about it in the newspaper. I guess that's wrong too.'

She looks up at me, her eyes like slits. 'Of course it's wrong. People shouldn't have monkeys as pets.' Her voice drips with sarcasm. 'They belong in the wild.'

This really isn't going to plan. I watch her for a minute as she colours in the curve of the S. My heart's rhythm feels like it's changed to match the beat of the music.

'You know, Steph, you can always talk to me about anything. Anything at all. I'm your mum, I'm here to help you. Whatever you do.' *Please talk to me about what you're doing with these people, with P.*

She grunts and doesn't look up. She starts drawing something clinging to the letter S. What is it? The felt tip screeches across the paper, making me wince.

'We need to talk about what happened yesterday evening. I think it's important that we do.' I've said it, thank God.

She swivels round to face me properly and looks taken aback. 'Why are you wearing so much make-up?'

'Why do you think?' I say, staring her straight in the eye. It feels oddly confrontational. I want to start again.

She shrugs. 'I dunno. You feel you look old? That's why most older women wear make-up.'

Stay calm, breathe. Stay calm, breathe. Get back to the topic in hand. 'You hurt me last night.'

She shrugs again and looks back to the poster, starting to colour in the other monkey.

'I think you should apologise.' I pull air into my lungs, but it's jerky, difficult to fill them up.

'Apologise for what? What have I done now?' She glances up.

I stare at her. Does she really not remember? It was yesterday evening, for God's sake. 'You hurt me, Steph. I know it was an accident but . . .' I touch the bruise and wince. 'What were you doing with that sheep-marking fluid anyway?' With everything that happened, I hadn't even thought to ask that question.

'We were targeting a vivisector's house. Not that far from here actually.'

'A vivisector?' Whenever I have a conversation with Steph, it always goes off on such a tangent.

'Someone who experiments on live animals.' Her voice has a rising inflection.

'I know what a vivisector is,' I say. 'I checked my face cream. It didn't have the bunny logo so I guessed it was tested on animals. I threw it away.' I thought it might help get her on side.

She nods and I sit down on the corner of the bed. This is going better. I must try to stay calm, whatever she says or does. 'So when you say "target", what do you mean?'

'We throw paint at their house and their car. Red paint, to be like the animals' blood. Sometimes we'll write things on the house with the paint.'

Oh my God. She could be arrested, charged, get a record that would affect the rest of her life. 'Steph, you can't do things like that. You could get in serious trouble with the police.' Thank goodness Paul doesn't know. And Mum.

She snorts. 'Last night was good because they were actually inside. The man was screaming at us as we covered his sports car, but he was too chicken to come out. He knows what he's done is wrong.' She's animated, her colour high, slightly smiling. She must have been terrified. But then something she said hits me with a jolt. Sports car? 'Whose house was it?' I ask, a heavy feeling in my stomach. Do I want to know?

'Andrew Wilson's place. Near Patching.'

Oh God. 'But he's dad's friend. He's not a vivisector. He works in a science laboratory trying to find cures for cancer.'

'He's testing stuff on animals, Mum.'

'But to cure cancer. Surely that makes it okay.' I lean forward and hold her arm. 'He's one of Dad's closest friends, Steph. He's a good, hard-working man. You can't be doing stuff like that to our friends. If you're caught, you'll be locked up, sent to prison.'

She curls her lip at me and tries to shrug off my hand.

'He's our friend. You used to go over there all the time, and their kids have come here. Fiona's really close with his younger daughter.' How can I tell Paul? That poor family. It must have been so frightening for them, especially if their children were home.

She shrugs. 'And?'

I can feel the heat rising in me. 'And? You hurt me last night. I'm wearing all this make-up to cover the bruises.'

She looks at her hands. 'I didn't mean to. You got in my way. I was just trying to get out the front door.'

Is what she did okay then? Because she didn't mean to do it? Maybe it's true. I just need to get over it.

'What did you expect to happen? You jumped in front of me. If you don't want to get hurt, stay out of my way. I'm old enough to go out when I want, and with who I want.' She's looking up now, staring at me. She tries again to shrug off my arm. I stroke her hand. *Stay calm, stay calm.* I need to keep close to her.

She reaches down with her other hand and twists the skin on my wrist hard, like we used to do as kids in the playground. It burns and I snatch my hand away. There's a small smile on her face, her eyes are a deep grey.

I jump up, my heart pounding and rush out of the door and down the stairs. What just happened then?

The library door is open. I walk in, flustered and confused, and sit on the side of Paul's desk. He smiles up at me. 'All okay?'

'I need to tell you something. It's not good.'

His eyes tighten. 'Stephanie?' He looks at my face. 'You're okay?' A vein in his forehead starts to pulse.

I nod. He's worried that she's hurt me. I put my wrist, red from the Chinese burn, behind me.

'What now?'

'She told me what she was doing with that paint.'

'Oh?' There's the beginning of a frown in his eyes.

'Andrew's place. They threw paint all over their house and car. Steph said Andrew and his family were inside at the time. Imagine how terrifying . . .'

I don't need to say any more. His face is in his hands. 'Oh my God. But why?'

'Steph says he tests things on live animals.'

'He's a scientist. He's trying to find the cure for cancer.' He massages his temples.

'That's what I said to her.'

'I wonder if he saw her, recognised her. This is awful. I'm going to have a bloody word with her. We need to sort this out once and for all.'

I wish I hadn't said anything. I should have kept it to myself. The last thing Steph or I need is him going in shouting.

The phone on his desk rings and he stares at it, and then at me. It carries on ringing until eventually he picks it up. 'Hambrough 233.' His face relaxes immediately. 'Oh Peter, thanks for calling back. I need to talk to you about that land over by the Cornfords'. Have you got a few minutes?'

I turn away; he's back in his world again. Hopefully he'll forget about Steph. 'Woody, come on. Walkies,' I say quietly.

The dog thumps his tail, still muddy from his earlier walk to school, and gets up, stretching. We slide out of the room, and head towards the wood.

Chapter 6

Zoe

Spring 2025

Zoe first tries the key in the drawing-room door, then the heavy-panelled door of the library and then the kitchen. But it's far too big for any of them. 'Let's try the cellar door,' says Sara. Through the scullery, behind a moth-eaten velvet curtain, is the way down to the cellar. But the key nowhere near fits in the keyhole.

Sara examines it more closely. 'Maybe there's something down in the cellar that it might fit. A huge trunk, or something. Another door, perhaps? If it doesn't, we could try outside.'

'I haven't been down there for years,' says Zoe. 'God knows what state it's in.' The door complains as they release it, a stillness of stale air greeting them. Zoe fumbles for the light switch, which she knows is somewhere on the right wall, and golden light slides into the corners of the stairs.

They pick their way down the stone steps, avoiding the animal droppings. 'This is disgusting,' says Sara, wrinkling her nose. 'And so close to the kitchen.'

'Mum doesn't store anything here because it's damp.' Mentioning our mother casually makes Zoe's throat tighten. *It should be 'Mum didn't', past tense, now.*

The further down they go, the more earthy the smell becomes. Zoe pinches her nose and breathes through her mouth but can taste the smell on her tongue. The tiled floor at the bottom is barely visible under layers of dirt and more droppings. The cellar is largely empty. At one end, a huge wine rack stretches from one side of the cellar to the other, bolted into the wall. A row of unlabelled bottles is covered in a thick layer of dust. 'I wonder if they're anything special?' says Sara, gingerly picking up one.

'I reckon that's Dad's old elderflower wine. It was like rocket fuel when he made it. It'd probably kill you now,' says Zoe. 'I'd forgotten it was here.' Sara slides the bottle back into the rack.

There's a row of Welsh dressers along one wall – a reminder of when this was used as a kitchen when the original house was first built in the 1400s. At the other end there's an old chest, which Zoe doesn't remember noticing before. 'Try it in here,' says Sara. The keyhole looks quite big and sure enough the key fits in. But it won't turn.

'Let me try,' says Sara, resting all her weight on it. It isn't the right lock. The key refuses to budge but the catch breaks off anyway and falls to the ground with a clatter.

'Well done,' says Zoe.

Sara grimaces, and lifts the lid of the chest. There's very little inside, save for some old dusty cookery books and some Ladybird books. 'Oh, I'll keep these for the girls. They'll love them,' she says, blowing the dust off the top. 'I wonder if we should try searching for Kai online.'

'We could try,' says Zoe. 'But just three letters isn't much to go on.'

Back in the kitchen, Fiona is sitting at the table on her laptop. 'No luck?' she says.

Zoe shakes her head. Steph is nowhere to be seen.

Sara gets out her phone. 'Kai, Kai,' she murmurs as she types. 'Hmmm, mainly just a fashion company, a Korean singer and a restaurant in Mayfair. It can't be any of those.'

'Why don't we try the attic?' says Zoe. 'I know there's loads of stuff up there. Old family bits and bobs, and boxes of paperwork. I had to move some of it when I patched up the roof last time. There may be something the key fits.'

Steph comes into the kitchen and stands by the Aga. Missy rubs her body against her legs, miaowing. 'Do you want to help get some stuff down from the attic?' Zoe asks her.

'Okay,' she nods, bending to stroke the cat.

The four of them traipse upstairs, past their bedrooms and then up the back stairs. What had once been servants' rooms and the old nursery was used as a playroom and sewing room for their generation, and has since been left empty. At the end of the landing is another set of narrow stairs to the attic. These open out into a huge space which runs the length and breadth of the house. A weak light penetrates through a tiny window, covered with decades of grime. Several old rugs patchwork the floorboards. In the far corner is a tangle of old wooden furniture. Lined up against the low walls are several old leather trunks, tea crates and sagging cardboard boxes. A huge chaise longue in a garish purple sits in the centre of the room.

'Bloody hell, there's a lot up here,' says Fiona, falling on to the chaise longue. 'When did this become purple? Wasn't this in the library for years?'

'I reupholstered it when I was in sixth form and doing textiles. Mum was horrified. She must have put it up here when I moved into the oast house ten years ago. Seeing it now, I'm not surprised.'

They laugh and Zoe feels warm inside. It's good to talk about Mum with people who knew her, who loved her too.

Steph delves into a crate, unwrapping the newspaper from an old teapot. 'Look at this,' she says. 'Didn't we used to have tea out of this?'

'Maybe,' says Fiona. They dig through the crate taking out orange and brown cups, saucers and small plates. 'These are just horrific,' she says.

'I reckon you could get a lot for these on eBay. People love retro stuff,' says Steph.

Under the tea set are a number of increasingly odd ornaments. An art-deco-style dancing woman menu holder. A figurine of a girl stroking an otter. A huge china toad eating a bird. 'I'm not sure anyone would want this stuff, not even the charity shop,' says Fiona. At the bottom of the tea crate are piles of *Financial Times* from the late 1960s. Fiona takes one out, lies back on the chaise longue and starts reading.

Zoe kneels in front of the first trunk and gets out the key. But the keyhole is far too small. The others are all the same. She wanders to the far end of the attic space, but there's nothing else with a keyhole. 'I can't see anything here,' she says.

'We should try the barns or the cottages,' says Sara. 'Like I said, it looks like it could be an outdoor key.'

'Yeah, I'll do that later.' Zoe hasn't been down to the cottages for ages.

Sara is sitting cross-legged in front of one of the open trunks. 'What's in there?' says Zoe, coming over to her. Inside are piles of old paperwork.

'Mum seemed to keep everything. Look, it's the milkman's bill from 1979. Half a dozen eggs were only twenty pence, a pint of milk was fourteen pence. And the milkman delivered chicken.'

'I remember that,' says Steph quietly. 'Dad had to build a special box to put it all in because the fox nicked it otherwise.'

'Is it just receipts and stuff?' says Fiona, putting down the newspaper and looking up.

'No, there's all sorts,' says Sara, rifling through. 'Photos, letters, bills, everything.'

'We really should bring as much downstairs as we can. We need to sort through all the paperwork anyway and there may be something in there that will help with the will.'

With all the focus on the key, Zoe has almost forgotten about the will. That she's now living in a house that is no longer hers. 'And give us a clue to who or what this Kai is, and what the key is all about.'

Steph opens a cardboard box. 'Oh my God, this is all fur.' She picks out a white stole, her mouth gaping. 'I remember Mum wearing this.'

'Me too,' says Fiona. She reaches over and lifts out a black floor-length cape with a hood, a white trim around it. 'This is beautiful. What animal would it be?'

Steph looks at it. 'Mink, probably.'

'Would anyone mind if I had this?' says Fiona, looking around.

'You absolutely can't wear it, Fi,' Steph says.

'I agree,' Zoe says, standing behind Steph. 'It's socially unacceptable. You'd get abused. And rightly so.'

'Not in Singapore,' says Fiona with a little smile.

'Fi, don't be daft. I'll take them. We can use these in the shelter. They're great for animal beds,' Steph says.

'For an animal bed? Oh my God, that's criminal,' says Fiona.

'I agree,' says Sara. 'I get that you might not want to wear them, but Fiona and I can split them between us. We'd both get wear out of them. My girls could wear them in time. It'd be a shame not to get use out of them. I wonder why Mum had them up here and not in her wardrobe.'

Steph looks down at the box. 'I begged her to put them up here when I was a teenager. I showed her pictures of the mink farms and how they're gassed to death and then skinned. She said it had put her off wearing them and she packed them up years ago.'

Fiona and Sara share a look and Fiona puts the cape back into the box slowly. 'Maybe you should take them back to your animal shelter. Use them as bedding, as you said.' Missy jumps into the box and nestles down on the coat. They all laugh.

'I think Missy's decided what's to be done.' Steph carries the box, with Missy inside it, towards the attic door.

Zoe opens up another box. 'This is paperwork too.'

'Okay,' says Fiona. 'Why don't we all grab a box and take them downstairs to the kitchen? Then we can go through them together and decide what to keep and what to throw away.'

Throw away? 'I don't think we should throw anything away,' says Zoe. 'Mum would have kept it for a reason.'

'A milkman bill from 1979?' says Fiona.

'There's a receipt here for a pair of Clarks shoes, May 1980,' says Sara.

'They must have been mine then,' says Steph.

'We can look through it all and there will be stuff that just needs to be thrown out, like the milkman bills, and other stuff that we'll want to keep,' says Fiona, lifting up a box and walking towards the door. The others follow her, the attic settling back into silence. There are footprints in the dust now, ornaments have been unpacked and left all over the floor. Already it's all changing and they've been here less than twenty-four hours. Zoe bites her lip to stop herself from crying. She wants it all left the same. Untouched. Just as their mother had it. But at the same time, it feels comforting to have them here, talking about Mum. People who really knew her.

She takes the key out of her pocket and stares at it. She knows that it must be significant in some way. Otherwise why would Mum have kept it in an envelope at the back of her safe, surrounded by expensive jewellery? Kai. Who is Kai? What does it mean?

The door opens and Fiona reappears with the others. 'C'mon, Zoe.'

Zoe stands, shaking her foot to get the circulation back. She takes a deep breath and picks up the nearest box and walks towards the stairs.

◆ ◆ ◆

Half an hour later, the kitchen is covered with tea crates and cardboard boxes. Sara fills up the kettle to make tea and the other three take a box each to look through.

'Look there's some photos here,' says Fiona. 'Of us on that train. Gosh, we look young.'

'What train?' asks Zoe, craning her neck.

'Before you were born, we went to the South of France on the train for a holiday,' says Fiona.

'I remember that,' says Steph, who has stopped reading the letter she's holding. 'We went with Mum and then Dad joined us later.'

'Yes, poor Mum having to take the three of us on the train on her own,' says Fiona.

'I must have been, what three, four?' says Sara. 'But I remember it quite clearly. All that beautiful sand. I can't imagine doing that with my girls.'

It's so annoying how she references her children at every opportunity. Like she's done something incredible by procreating.

'Mum constantly trying to put sun lotion on us and make us wear hats.' Steph smiles. *She has one of those faces that seems to look miserable most of the time*, Zoe thinks. *But when she smiles it completely changes.* Of her sisters, she feels she knows Steph the least.

'I remember the food most. Eating steak frites for the first time. Trying horse,' says Fiona. 'You were already a vegetarian then, weren't you? I think you had omelette for every meal.'

Steph laughs. 'Yeah, the French aren't known for their veggie cuisine. And especially not in the eighties.'

They all lapse back into silence again, flicking through the various papers, creating piles across the table. *Everyone remembers*, Zoe thinks. *Maybe Mum knew that after her death we'd all come to the house together like this. Maybe that's what she wanted.* She can't work out whether she wants them to stay forever or leave as soon as they can. She twists her thumb rings round and round.

'You'll get a blister doing that,' says Steph, stilling her hand.

Zoe jumps in surprise and snatches her hand away.

'Sorry,' says Steph, blushing.

'It's fine. It's just a habit. I won't get a blister. What's wrong with your hands, anyway?'

Steph spreads out her fingers, which are covered in patches of red raw skin. 'Childhood eczema,' she says. 'It comes back now and again. Stress, I guess.'

'It seems sore,' Zoe says, looking away. Stress. So perhaps this is as awful a time for Steph as it is for her. Mum always said their relationship was strained and maybe when someone dies after you've had a difficult relationship with them, it's harder than if you were close.

'I have some really lovely calendula and lavender salve upstairs. You can try some if you like. It might help.'

Steph looks at her and smiles. 'Thanks, that would be great. I didn't bring anything with me and it's come up so quickly.' She hides her hands in the box. 'Underneath all the old receipts are a load of letters,' she says. She has a stack of them on the table and is digging through the box on the floor. 'These ones are from before even I was born.'

'Who are they from?' asks Fiona.

'There's a few letters from who I think must be Mum's grandmother,' says Steph, turning over tissue-thin paper. 'She's writing about Dad. Listen.

> *'Dearest Milly,*
>
> *Who you want to marry, dear, is your choice. You're going to have to live with that person for the rest of your life – through all sorts of difficulties that you can't even imagine now – so choose wisely. Choose someone who is a solid friend as much as anyone else, whose mind you admire as much as his face. If in your heart of hearts you know Paul is that person, then ignore what your mother and father say. But take your time. It may feel like there's a need to hurry, but there isn't. Don't be in a rush to start your life.*
>
> *Come to the oast house one afternoon. We can go for a walk in the woods together.*
>
> *Love Granny.'*

Steph looks up. 'I didn't know Mum's parents didn't approve of Dad.'

'Yeah, I remember Mum telling me when I was getting married to Charles,' says Fiona. 'That I was lucky she and Dad approved of my marriage because that hadn't been her experience with her parents or her grandparents. Grandpa Edward forced Mum to have some sort of pre-nup, apparently. They thought Dad was a gold-digger.'

'Oh,' says Zoe, her forehead concertinaed together. 'How weird. Dad was so far from being a gold-digger. And he loved Mum. You could tell, right to the end. I wonder why she didn't tell me?'

'I guess she only told me because I was getting married.'

'But still,' says Zoe. 'So Mum's grandmother, our great-grandmother, lived in the oast house?'

'Yes,' says Steph. 'I think generally what happened was that as soon as a couple married and had children, the older generation would move out into the oast house or one of the cottages, and the younger generation would take over the hall. The hall was handed down as some sort of wedding present.'

'Some wedding present,' says Zoe.

'This place is a massive responsibility,' says Fiona.

'Tell me about it,' Zoe says, then tries to soften her comment with a smile.

There's silence as the four women flick through old bits of paper.

'Listen to this,' says Steph suddenly. 'It's another letter from Mum's grandmother to her. *The agreement is nothing to worry about, dear. It's just a precaution to ensure the hall stays in the family. We've had it for hundreds of years. It was passed to Grandpa on his marriage to me and we had to sign something similar, and the same when it was passed down to your father. You will pass it down to your children in turn. Please don't blame your mother for that, her hands are tied.'*

'That's the pre-nup,' says Fiona, looking up from a sheaf of photos. 'But they needn't have worried about Dad. He loved Mum fiercely. They'd never have split up.'

Zoe looks at the letter Steph hands her. Even later in life the love between her parents was obvious. They still held hands. She found love notes he'd written to her, caught up with shopping lists. Will she ever meet someone and feel like that? She thought Ben was that person, but he turned out to be as flakey as the rest.

Steph mumbles something about going to the loo and Zoe takes over looking through the pile of letters. She opens one dated 1972. *'Your mother told me about the miscarriage, dear, I'm so sorry to hear that. What an incredibly upsetting thing for you and Paul. Do take good care of yourself. Now is the time to nourish your body, put your feet up a little and prepare for the next pregnancy. Because there will be a next pregnancy, even if it doesn't feel like that at the moment.'*

'I didn't know Mum had a miscarriage,' Zoe says.

Sara stops sorting out receipts. 'Yes, she had several,' she says. 'One before Steph was born, then two between Steph and Fiona, then again before I was born and several before she fell pregnant with you. It turned out later she had a problem with her cervix, but they didn't realise that at the time.'

'I didn't know that,' Zoe says, looking back at the letter. There seems to be so many things she doesn't know about Mum.

'I guess she only told me because I'd had trouble getting pregnant and we went through all of the IVF. She wanted to reassure me,' says Sara. Zoe looks at Sara but doesn't say anything. There's so much she doesn't know about her sisters too. Somehow she painted them as uncaring in her mind. But she realises now that's not true. They all have their own lives, their own challenges. They're good people. She'll ask Sara about the IVF later, when they're on their own.

'It really is like looking for a needle in a haystack,' says Fiona. 'Her thinking behind the will may not even be among this stuff.'

'In some ways, that doesn't matter,' says Steph, coming back into the kitchen. 'I don't mean that badly, Zoe,' she adds quickly. 'Just that it's interesting to look back at this. To remember it all.' She picks up another letter from the pile. 'To find out more about Mum and perhaps parts of her life that we didn't know about.'

Zoe smiles at her. 'You're right, it is. It's important to remember all of this. I never want us to forget her.'

'She's our mum, Zoe, none of us will forget her,' says Fiona.

Zoe stands up and stretches. 'I think I might go outside and try that key in the outhouses.' She needs to get away, to think. She realises it feels lovely being here, the four of them. But she's so used to being on her own with Mum that it feels a bit much suddenly.

Steph stops refolding a letter.

'Good plan,' says Sara.

Zoe goes to pick the key up from the hall table but it's not there.

'I swore I left it here,' she says, lifting up the bowl, then rifling through the dusty potpourri. 'I don't understand. It's just disappeared.' She stands with her hands on her hips looking around the hall.

'It was in your pocket,' calls Sara from the kitchen.

'Yeah, but I took it out when we carried the boxes down from the attic because it's so big it kept digging into me. I definitely left it here.'

'It must be there somewhere,' says Sara. 'You just need to keep looking.'

Mum used to say that. Maybe all mums do.

'The key was here,' says Zoe. 'On this table. It was definitely here and now it's disappeared.' Someone has taken it.

◆ ◆ ◆

Milly

1988

The police car swings into the drive and I'm on my feet, running towards the front door. Outside, I can see Steph's silhouette in the back. *Thank God. Thank God.* Whatever else has happened, she's safe, she's alive. Paul is suddenly beside me, gripping my hand.

It screeches to a halt. Steph is staring out of the window but doesn't look at us. Something makes me stay where I am, rather than rushing forward as I would usually. A WPC walks round the side of the car and approaches us.

'Mr and Mrs Wright?' It's not one of the usual officers.

We nod in unison, like dumb puppets. This feels serious.

'I'm afraid your daughter has been involved in criminal activity. Can we come inside?'

Steph's face is blank as she walks past me next to the WPC. We all gather in the drawing room, perched on the edge of the chairs and settees. I stack up the plates decorated with crumbs, evidence of another night of eating to get through the hours. They decline a cup of tea, which somehow makes it feel even worse. The police who have brought her home in the past always have a cup of tea. Steph is staring into space. She's paler than usual. Tired, maybe. I wonder if she slept at all last night. She looks okay apart from that. But she won't catch my eye.

'I'm sorry that it's taken so long to bring Stephanie home,' the WPC says, glancing at her. 'We didn't realise who she was initially as she gave a false name. It was only when one of my team recognised her that we put two and two together.'

'A false name?' Paul says. I can feel the tension in him.

'She told us she was Milly Head,' says the WPC, looking at her notebook.

'Milly is *my* name,' I say.

'And Head is Patrick's surname, who was arrested with her and the others. We thought they were related.'

P. Patrick Head.

'What's she done?' Paul asks. I'm glad he can talk. My voice is now stuck in my throat. If I say anything I know I'll start to cry. Steph seems oblivious to it all. As if we're just sitting around talking about what to have for supper. She smiles slightly, as she did when I was telling her off as a young child.

'She was part of a group who smashed the windows of a department store,' the WPC says, glancing at her notes. 'She was recognised by passers-by and there was glass in her shoes when we arrested her at the squat a short while later. It's a straightforward case of criminal damage.'

The squat.

'That's not evidence.' Steph curls her lip. It's the first time she's spoken and her voice is unrecognisable. Hard. Mocking. I stare at her.

'Is there a lot of damage?' asks Paul.

The WPC nods. 'Every single window was smashed. Thousands of pounds, I'd say. The department store will support a prosecution. They always do in these cases.'

'But why, Steph?' Paul turns to her. 'I don't understand why you'd do something like that.'

'They sell fur,' says Steph flatly.

She's already talked to me about fur, and I promised to stop wearing it. We packed it up and took it to the attic.

'You're a bit young to be getting yourself mixed up with that animal-rights lot,' the WPC says. 'You're from a good family. I don't want you to ruin your life. They're bad news. They'll be in prison before long.' She swivels to face us. 'One of the ringleaders is a guy called Patrick. He particularly is very bad news. I suggest you keep firm tabs on your daughter and make sure she doesn't spend any time with him.'

The way the WPC looks at me makes me think that she knows it's all my fault. That I'm too busy socialising, or drinking or whatever to care what happens to my daughter. I bet she doesn't have children of her own. Or she'd know that actually you have very little control over a child once they reach a certain age. That in reality they can do exactly what they want and there's very little you can do to stop them. And if you do try to stop them, they can hurt you without meaning to. And there's nothing you can do about that. I pull my blouse down where it has ridden up my arm, revealing the faint outline of fingertips from where she gripped me a few days ago.

I need to say something, to show I care, that I'm responsible. 'How old is Patrick Head?' I ask.

The WPC looks at her colleague and shrugs. 'Mid-twenties, I think.'

Mid-twenties. What twenty-something-year-old man wants to hang out with a fourteen-year-old? Oh God, it's like the things you read about. Men who like too-young girls. And it's happening here.

Steph catches my eye and looks away. She knows what I'm thinking.

◆ ◆ ◆

Later, when the police have gone, and Steph is back in her room, I bring her up a cup of tea. She's lying on her bed. 'Thanks,' she says, taking a sip even though it will be too hot.

'You must be exhausted,' I say.

She nods. 'I didn't sleep much in the cell.' The cell. I never thought a child of mine would say something like that.

'It must have been very frightening,' I manage.

'I didn't like how small it was,' she says. 'I kept walking round it. One, two, three, four. One, two. One, two, three, four. One, two. There was a shelf that was a sort of bed. It had a blanket. There was graffiti over the walls. Weird stuff.' Her eyes are flitting around her bedroom, remembering it. She doesn't carry on and I wonder what I can say.

'Do you think you're a bit young for him?' It comes out before I can stop it.

'Oh, it's not in that way, Mum. We're all just there for the animals. We're activists. He's my friend, that's all.' She laughs. 'There's loads of us. Kids my age too. Patrick just happened to be there yesterday.'

I can tell by the way she talks that it's a lie. By the light in her eyes, by the way she says his name. There is something between them.

'Finally it all made sense. My life makes sense. This is what I'm supposed to be doing. Fighting for the voiceless. I know what it's like to feel voiceless like those rabbits and rats.'

I don't know what to say to that. How can she think she's voiceless? The whole family, everything we do, seems to revolve around her. 'Steph, I'm really worried about you. Getting involved with all this animal-rights stuff, taking so many risks, getting involved with an older man—'

'I've already told you I'm not involved with him.' Her voice is hard again, her teeth gritted. Her eyes are like flint. 'And it's not nonsense.'

I take a step back. But I can't not address it. That WPC thinks I'm a terrible parent because I'm not stopping her doing this stuff. 'It's very clear to me that you are involved with this Patrick and he's influencing you and making you do all these bad things. I really don't want you seeing him.'

'And what are you going to do if I do?' Her eyebrows are raised, like she's mocking me. She puts down the tea and swings her legs over the side of the bed. The languorous way she moves reminds me of a panther.

I can't admit to her that there's nothing I can do. 'I just want to keep you safe.'

She takes a step towards me. 'I am safe,' she says.

'Steph, you spent the night in a police cell. That's not being safe.'

She's quiet for a moment and stares at me. She's almost half a foot taller than me now. 'Mum, this is really important to me. I know you always thought I would be a vet, and maybe I will be, but right now I need to fight for these animals. Awful things are happening that the public don't know about. If you saw the state of these animals, you'd never eat meat or wear cosmetics again.'

She sounds so measured, so normal. Maybe it's me who's the mad one. Maybe I'm over-exaggerating all this. Mum always said I over-exaggerated.

'Steph, please. These people are terrorists. They're as bad as the IRA. They hurt people. You're getting deeper and deeper into something you don't understand. You're so impulsive, you're not thinking straight.'

Suddenly she's standing right over me. My heart starts to beat faster.

'Like the IRA?' she says, staring down at me with that look in her eye. I need to get out of her room. 'Why do you talk about things you don't understand? I try to tell you but you just won't listen.'

'I am listening,' I whisper. She's standing between me and the door.

Her breath is coming too quickly. She's going to start hyperventilating soon. I wonder where I left the paper bag. Downstairs, maybe. I put my hand on her arm. 'Calm down, Steph, it'll be okay. Just breathe.'

Her eyes are a deep grey and she looks at me for a moment but I get the sense she doesn't really see me. Then she half pushes, half flips me on to the bed. I feel my body fly through the air – how can she be so strong? – and my head collides with the top of the headboard, the carved mahogany slicing into the back of my skull. I crumple half on the bed, half on the floor. Black flashes above me. I close my eyes but it's still there. I slide to the floor. At least I'm nearer the door now. Something wet is creeping through my hair. There's a hanky in my pocket and I hold it against the back of my skull.

I edge closer to the door but she stays by her desk. *Thank God.*

Paul shouts up from downstairs. 'Milly, phone for you.'

I pull myself to my feet and stagger the last few yards and open the door.

'Let's talk later,' I mumble.

'There's no need,' she says, now sitting calmly at her desk.

I close the door quietly behind me and use the gallery railing to help me. It's hard to see much through the black stars. I edge down the stairs, holding tightly on to the banister, and collapse on the telephone seat in the hall. The library door is ajar, Paul's head bent over papers. He doesn't look up.

'Hello,' I say into the receiver using my best telephone voice.

'Oh, Milly, it's Jan. I heard what had happened and I wanted to check on you.'

News travels fast. But then Jan is married to Peter whose brother is in the police. I clamp my hand against the back of my head. The bleeding's getting worse. 'It's all okay, Jan, but thank you for asking.'

'It must be such a shock Steph being involved in criminal activity,' she says. 'Especially at her age. She was such a lovely youngster.'

I press my lips together. 'She's still lovely,' I say.

'Of course, of course.' There's silence on the line, just the crackle that tells me she's still there. 'She needs your support, doesn't she, as she adjusts to being a young woman. It's a challenging time.'

It reminds me of the last meeting we had with Steph's headteacher when she smiled and said, 'All Stephanie needs is a stable, loving home.'

'Well, I wanted to let you know that I'm thinking of you and here if you need anything. I can easily pop over,' says Jan brightly.

I need you to go away and mind your own business, I think.

'Anything at all,' she repeats.

'Thanks, Jan, and thanks for calling.'

'Take care, Milly.'

I settle the phone down in the cradle and take the hanky from the back of my head. It's completely drenched with blood. I'm wearing a dark-brown dress, so blood that's dripped on to it is barely visible. Steph's arrest will be around the village – and probably town too – within hours. I go back upstairs to clean up my hair before Paul sees it.

Chapter 7

Zoe

Spring 2025

Zoe wakes with a start and is already on the gallery on her way to her mother's room when she remembers. She stops, a dizziness spreading from her head down to her fingertips. *Mum's not here.* She drops her head, and retraces her steps back to her bedroom and stands at the window, where the dawn is already stealing through the trees and across the lawn. She knows she won't get back to sleep now.

Two days without Mum. It seems impossible. All the thousands of days she has been with Mum are behind her. She does a quick calculation. Almost thirteen thousand days they spent together. And now the days stretch out ahead without her. Until eventually, when she's an old lady, she will have spent more time without Mum than with her. What a strange thought.

She sees a black figure emerge from the woods, and momentarily freezes. But it's only Fiona running. She must still be jet-lagged.

Zoe puts on her dressing gown and goes downstairs to put the kettle on, just as Fiona comes through the kitchen door.

'Morning,' Fiona says, standing on one leg and pulling the other behind her to stretch the muscle. 'Today's the day. Hopefully we'll get some answers.'

Of course, Mum's solicitor is coming. Zoe forgot.

◆ ◆ ◆

Later that morning, the four of them wait in the drawing room, their mother's copy of the will on the table. They sit in the same positions they were in that first evening. Steph on a sofa alone, Zoe and Sara opposite her, Fiona in their father's armchair. *Funny how we're all creatures of habit*, Zoe thinks. It is the same at mealtimes. They all sit where they did as children, but with two empty places at each end of the table.

The sun comes out from behind a cloud and there's a sudden flash of light from the grand piano. One of her sisters has polished the frames and the silver is glittering in the sun. Zoe gets up and looks at the photos. Mum and Dad on their wedding day, the lifelong love evident in the way her mother is looking into his eyes. Granny Evelyn with her tiny cinched-in waist flowing into a long, full skirt holding Mum in her christening gown, a besuited Grandpa Edward behind her. A faded yellowed photo which she knows to be of Mum's grandparents even though they died before she was born. A rather awkward one of Dad's parents on a wind-swept beach. And then school photos of each of her sisters. Mum chose her favourite ones through the years. Mainly from when they were old enough to pull a smile but not look sulky. Then separate ones of Sara's three girls.

The door knocker goes. 'At last,' says Fiona, getting up.

The solicitor's grey suit is too tight across his shoulders and too long in the arms. He looks like he's dressing up for a work-experience day. He takes the cup of tea Steph makes him and settles himself into their mother's wing-backed armchair. None of them have sat in it since she died and Sara winces as he lowers himself down. Zoe sits back on the sofa.

'I'm very glad to meet you all,' he says, looking at each of them in turn. 'I only met her twice but Mrs Wright spoke very fondly of the four of you. I'm very sorry for your loss.'

They all nod a fraction, waiting.

He takes out an old leather folder from his bag and removes a sheaf of papers. 'I understand from what you said on the phone that you've already seen the copy of the will your mother kept here.'

'Yes,' Fiona jumps in. 'We know what's in it, we're hoping you can shed some light on it. Why it was written that way, what we can do about challenging it.' She has a pile of the letters from the boxes with the will.

The solicitor must be about the same age as Zoe but has the manner of someone trying to behave as if he were much older. 'Well, I may not be much use to you.' He flicks through the papers until he gets to what must be the will and lays it on top. 'I didn't draft this will. I work at the local practice and your mother asked me to hold a copy of the will and to be the executor.' He takes a sip of tea. 'When the time came.'

'You didn't draft it?' Fiona repeats, her voice rising at the end of the sentence.

The solicitor shakes his head. 'It was drafted by a London solicitor. I believe they were your mother's mother's solicitor.' He looks down at the papers. 'Wilson Cartwright Esq. of the Temple. The full version here is dated nineteenth of May 1991.'

Fiona looks across at Zoe. 'Not long after you were born,' she mutters. 'So you had nothing to do with this will? You didn't help put it together?' she asks the solicitor.

He seems to clench his jaw. 'I am the will's executor. I am legally responsible for carrying out the instructions in your mother's will and handling her estate. Now, in this case, although the property and its contents – art, furniture, books, etc. – was left to the three oldest sisters, the rest of your mother's estate was left to the youngest daughter. When looked at from a financial perspective, the value of the jewellery is equal to a quarter share of the property.'

Zoe's teeth start to ache and she realises she's been grinding them. The jewellery seems so inconsequential when compared to the house she's lived in all her life.

'It's slightly unusual in that I'd expect a house like this to be left to the eldest child which is . . .' He looks down to consult his notes.

'Me,' says Steph. 'Stephanie.'

'Yes,' the solicitor says. 'To be handed down to the next generation. But in this case your mother split it equally with her three older children.' He takes another sip of tea.

Zoe looks sideways at Steph and wonders whether she feels aggrieved. Houses like this are usually left to the eldest child. Why did her mother not do that? Steph has a right to feel annoyed and upset. But she's sitting there, her foot tapping on the floor. Zoe bites her lip. She's been so caught up feeling sorry for herself, she hasn't thought about her oldest sister. She tries to catch her eye now, but Steph's gaze is darting around the room, not fixing on anything.

'You need to agree what you want to do with it. There's a stipulation that it cannot be sold. The only way it can be disposed of is to pass it down to the next generation. But you can rent it out, live in it yourself or whatever else. The will stipulates that Zoe, the youngest sister, has a right to remain on the estate until she dies.'

A right to remain in her own home. Highdown Hall was bought by their great-great-great-grandfather in the 1700s with the fortune he made from textiles. It is impossible to think about dividing it up in some way. They've already had to sell so much land over the past thirty years, just to keep going.

'We will need to get the property valued by three separate agents, just for the paperwork, whatever you decide to do with it. The other issue that you need to be aware of is inheritance tax. This is a sizeable estate and the death duties are going to be significant. It may be that you need to sell something to pay these. But we can discuss that further down the line.'

Fiona uncrosses her legs and leans forward. 'I understand that when my grandparents died, my parents gave a painting to the National Gallery in lieu of inheritance tax. That's one option we could look at, as our mother died with very little capital left.'

Zoe stares at Fiona. She had no idea that was what happened. Their mother never mentioned it. She's torn between admiration and annoyance, but ultimately grateful that Fiona is taking charge.

The solicitor shuffles papers together. 'I've never come across that,' he mumbles.

'Well, that was what happened.' Fiona clears her throat. 'Anyway, what we're interested in today is why the will was written like it was – if Mum decided not to leave the house to Steph, as would be traditional, why it was not split equally between us, including Zoe. And what we can do to challenge it.'

The solicitor is scribbling with a cheap biro. He jerks his head up at the word 'challenge'. 'You want to challenge your mother's will?'

Fiona nods. 'Yes, we want to find out why it was written like it was and how we can challenge it and split everything equally. Even though, and I'm sure we all agree, we want to keep the house as it is. It's part of our family.'

Zoe relaxes. *Thank God.*

The solicitor looks at each of them in turn, scratching his cheek. 'That's not my role. I'm here to ensure that your mother's wishes are followed through.'

Fiona sighs and raises her eyebrows at Zoe. 'The thing is, I don't think this was our mother's wishes. She was always fair, always treated us the same. She wouldn't have wanted Zoe not to receive a share of the house she'd lived in all her life.'

'You don't think the will reflects your mother's wishes? But that's exactly what a will does. Reflects the person's wishes.' He shakes his head slightly as if they are all particularly dim children. *Pompous. That's the word for him*, thinks Zoe, staring at his too-bright tie and shiny shoes. 'This will was written some time ago, that is true, but there's no reason to believe that it doesn't reflect what your mother wanted. I agree that for one child not to receive a share of the family home seems irregular in this day and age. But if you look back in history, it was usual for only the eldest child to inherit the house, to avoid the issue of splitting up homes.'

Irregular makes it sound like some sort of French verb she should be practising. She stares at his face, which is without expression.

'It may be that you decide that Sara should live here, as she is the only one with children currently as I understand it.'

Sara laughs nervously.

'Look, is there anything else we need to know from you at the moment?' Fiona glances at her watch.

'Well, I will need to do a thorough analysis of the estate, in order to calculate the tax due. The value listed in the will is only approximate. It may be that items have been sold or purchased since this was written.'

'Mum refused to sell anything that she considered an heirloom. I've sold a couple of paintings which were in storage and some of Dad's first editions,' says Zoe. 'To fund repairs on the house.' The idea of this man's too-pale hands raking through her mother's jewellery, touching her books in the library, makes her shiver.

The solicitor's biro scratches across the paper. 'Noted,' he said. 'Perhaps after your mother's funeral, I can arrange a time to come again to go through things.'

'Perhaps,' says Fiona, in a voice Zoe remembers from her childhood when she was asking for something and Fiona didn't want to give it to her.

Fiona stands and nods at Zoe to do the same. The others follow, and the solicitor is left scrabbling around to shove his papers back in his folder and the folder in the briefcase.

He turns at the drawing-room door, Fiona right behind him. 'I'm very sorry for your loss,' he says again. 'I appreciate it's a difficult time and I'll try to make this as painless as I can.'

'This way,' says Fiona, her arm pointing into the hall. Zoe sinks back down and hears the front door slam.

'What a waste of time,' says Fiona, striding back into the room. 'He's clearly out of his depth.'

Sara nods. 'Yeah, he didn't seem to get what you were trying to say. Pompous little man.'

'I can't imagine Mum dealing with a solicitor like that, somehow,' says Steph, who was mostly silent the entire time he was here. Zoe smiles at her.

'Yeah, exactly,' says Fiona. 'I doubt he was even alive in the 1990s when she lodged the will with the firm. It was probably an older partner. I'm going to drop my own solicitor a note.' She opens her laptop. 'He can help us challenge the will and ensure Highdown is split equally. Then we can all decide what to do.'

'Thanks, Fi,' says Zoe, looking around the drawing room. Split Highdown. She hates the expression but she's grateful that Fiona wants to sort it out.

'I can't understand what Mum was thinking,' says Sara. 'Highdown has always been your home. It's right that you should have it – or at least an equal share of it.'

'Let's see what my lawyer says.' Fiona is punching the keys. 'Either way, just because we own Highdown now – or rather we will when probate goes through – we're not going to throw you out, Zoe. In fact, we can't legally throw you out.'

Sara nods and grips Zoe's hand.

'Absolutely not,' says Steph. 'It's your home.'

'We'll get to the bottom of it,' Fiona says.

Zoe glances around the room. They never really felt like a family to her. The six-year gap between her and Sara was bad enough, but eleven years between her and Fiona meant by the time Zoe was a teenager, Fiona had already left home. Steph she barely knows at all. But somehow, them all being here together, they feel like her family for the first time. Maybe it is the love of their mother that has brought them all together. Their lives might be completely different. She thinks back to how she has dismissed them in her own mind – Fiona for flying round the world like there's no climate crisis. Sara a total victim of consumer capitalism, always needing to buy the latest thing – and she feels guilty. She's judged them without really knowing them. And despite resenting Steph for never being here, she seems to have more in common with Zoe than the others.

The doorbell rings and Fiona looks at where the solicitor was sitting. 'Please don't tell me it's that man again.'

Steph is on her feet, collecting up the empty mugs. She glances out of the window. 'It's not the solicitor,' she says, craning her neck. 'It's a woman, I can't quite make out who.'

'A neighbour from the village, I expect,' says Zoe. *Come to nose around.*

Sara walks into the hall to open the door and squeals. 'Alice. Oh my God.'

Alice, of course. She would have found out straight away. Zoe follows Fiona and Steph to the front door.

Alice stands on the threshold, a Tupperware container wrapped in tinfoil and a bunch of daffodils in her hands. Zoe's face and neck suddenly feel hot. She should have told her about Mum.

'I'm sorry to barge in,' Alice says. 'I heard the news and wanted to give you my condolences.' She hands the flowers to Sara and the Tupperware to Steph. 'It's a vegetarian chilli. I know Zoe's vegan and I guessed that you'd still be a veggie, Steph.'

Steph smiles. 'Thank you, Alice, that's really thoughtful of you.' She takes the pot, opens the lid and sniffs. 'Smells delicious.'

'Come in,' says Sara, opening the door wide. 'I haven't seen you properly in years.' She leans forward and gives Alice a hug, crushing the flowers between them.

Their father's funeral would have been the last time, thinks Zoe. But Sara didn't stick around for long then. Funny how they've all stayed on at Highdown as if their mother's death is truly the end of something.

Alice stands in the hall, looking around and rubbing her hands. Zoe follows her gaze. The table gleams with furniture polish, the bowl empty of years-old potpourri. What happened to that? Mum had potpourri in there for as long as Zoe could remember. The glass in the clock face and mirror is polished to a shine. It looks like Sara and Steph have even waxed the floor. Maybe all Highdown Hall needed was them all here bringing it back to life together.

'Come into the kitchen, let's have something to drink,' says Fiona, leading the way. 'It's so good to see you.'

Steph sets about putting on the kettle and getting out more mugs while the four of them settle around the kitchen table. Zoe can't catch Alice's eye. Ever since she had to tell her that they could no longer afford for her to come every day, or even the twice a week they'd reduced it to, she's tried to avoid Alice – even when she came to Highdown Hall to visit Mum in those last few months. It feels like it's her fault that after Alice worked for them all her life, they had to let her go in her sixties. Maybe she should have tried harder to persuade Mum to sell something. It's not like they haven't needed Alice's help, or her company.

'I'm so sorry to hear about your mum,' Alice says, as Steph is sitting down. 'She was quite a woman.'

'She was,' says Sara, pressing her lips together.

'She'd be glad to see you home, I'm sure. Especially you back from Singapore.'

'Sadly we didn't make it in time to say our goodbyes,' says Fiona. Zoe grinds her teeth. *This again.* 'But at least we're together now.'

'You're all so properly grown-up,' says Alice. 'Your mum was so proud of you.'

They sit in silence, basking in this praise.

'How are your three children?' Alice asks Sara. 'Your mum spoke often about them, always showed me pictures.'

'Oh, they're so wonderful,' says Sara, grinning. 'Hard work at times, but just wonderful. We feel really blessed to finally have children.' She looks down at her hands. 'This is the longest I've been away from them. I video-called them last night to read the twins a bedtime story but I'm not sure they really got it. I miss them.'

Zoe feels the familiar irritation. There's a brief silence. 'Will they come for the funeral?' asks Alice. 'Do you have a date yet? I guess it's early days.'

'We do,' Fiona says. 'We spoke to the vicar yesterday and he's suggested Monday morning at eleven fifteen in the church. Mum had planned all the details so there's not actually that much for us to do.'

'John will bring the girls for the day. We're going to have a small celebration back here afterwards, if you're free,' says Sara.

'Of course I'm free,' says Alice. 'Now tell me what I can bring. You four have enough to be getting on with at the moment, you don't need the hassle of baking.'

A warmth spreads through Zoe and she can feel that she's starting to cry.

'That's so kind of you,' Sara and Fiona say in unison, and then laugh.

'Some of your cheesy stars would be amazing,' says Sara.

'I was going to say it's okay because I've sorted out caterers, but now you've mentioned cheesy stars, then yes please,' laughs Fiona.

'And that apple cake you used to make,' says Steph quietly. 'Not for the funeral, but for afterwards.'

'Oh yes, the apple cake,' says Sara.

'We're just like kids again,' says Fiona. 'Squealing over what you've baked us after school.'

Alice looks at each of them in turn. 'I know you're grown women now but I will always think of you as the children I knew. All those years tidying up after you, the cheesy stars, the walks into the woods for a picnic.'

Sara sniffs. 'Gosh, that seems a long time ago.'

'What's in those boxes?' asks Alice, nodding towards the tea crates and cardboard boxes stacked in the corner of the kitchen. 'You clearing stuff out already?'

There's a long pause.

'Well, actually we're looking for answers,' says Fiona eventually, glancing at Zoe. 'Mum's will was—' She stops.

Alice looks between them.

Zoe glances out of the window. 'Mum's will didn't include me,' she says.

'What?' says Alice.

'It did include you, Zoe,' says Fiona, sighing. She turns to Alice. 'But Highdown and its contents is split equally between Steph, Sara and me. Zoe gets the jewellery but has the right to remain in the house for as long as she wants.'

'I see,' says Alice, and takes a long sip of tea, though it must be too hot. She puts the mug back on the table and looks up at the ceiling. 'That must be very difficult for all of you.'

'You could say that,' says Zoe. She knows she sounds like a petulant child, but she can't help it.

There's a long pause.

'As you're here, I – we – wondered if you could shed any light on it. You knew Mum for years and years. Can you think of a reason why she would set up her will like that? The local solicitor was hopeless,' says Fiona, leaning forward.

Alice gives a quick, high-pitched laugh. 'No, I can't think why your mum would do that. She loved you all very much, you were her world.'

A longer pause. 'She desperately wanted a fourth child, Zoe. She talked about you for years before you came along – even by name.' Alice shakes her head.

They sit in silence for a while, Alice deep in thought.

'How's your husband?' asks Sara.

'Good, good.'

'And your children?'

'Yes, they're very well. I'm a grandmother now.'

'Oh, congratulations,' says Sara. 'And you're still in the same place?'

Alice nods and takes another sip of tea. She rubs her hands together and then stands up. 'Well, I've just remembered I promised Mary I'd pop in and see her for lunch. I'd completely forgotten . . .' Her voice trails away.

The four sisters stand with her.

'Do count me in for the baking for your mum's wake. And anything else.' She glances around. 'I'm happy to come and help you clean for a few hours. No charge. You've got quite the task sorting this place out. It was tough for Zoe to manage it all alone when your mum was so poorly.'

'That's very kind of you,' Fiona says, walking with her into the hall. Sara follows her, but the front door is already closing behind Alice.

'That was odd,' Sara says, coming back into the kitchen. 'She seemed so happy to see us but then in such a hurry to leave.'

'Very odd,' says Fiona. 'Do you think she knows something?'

'What could she know?' asks Zoe, a shiver running down her back. First the key disappears and now this. Highdown Hall seems to be holding so many secrets.

◆ ◆ ◆

Milly

1988

Out of the corner of my eye I see Emma coming and turn to avoid her, fiddling with Fiona's school bag.

'Woo-hoo, Milly,' she shouts, waving her hand. As if I could possibly miss her in that turquoise tracksuit.

'Hi, Emma.' I smile and then turn back to Fiona's bag, pulling on the straps.

'Mum, what are you doing?' she says. 'That's way too tight.'

'Sorry,' I mutter, grateful for something else to do. 'Take it off. It'll be easier to do without it on your back.'

She slides the bag off her shoulders. 'It's okay, Mum, I can do it in school.' She slips her arms around my waist and hugs me. I don't want it to end, but then she's off, running across the school playground.

'Milly, I was thinking of going to the coffee shop after I've dropped off the twins. It would be lovely if you could join me. I haven't seen you for so long.' Emma's perfectly made-up face smiles back at me, even her ponytail swings jauntily.

'Thanks for the offer but I'm a bit busy this morning,' I say. 'I have to get back to help Paul.'

Behind me, Sara clambers out of the car. 'C'mon, Mummy,' she says, pulling at me.

'Sorry,' I say to Emma, following Sara towards her nursery classroom.

'That's okay,' she smiles. 'I've got to have a quick word with Mrs Hickey anyway.' Behind her, her twins wait, standing side by side like dolls. We walk together. How am I going to ditch her? The last thing I want is to go for a cup of tea. Everyone will know about Steph. There was even a picture in the paper that some reporter had snapped – Steph, rock in hand, in front of another shop. They hadn't named her, but everyone knew. And I know they loved talking about it. The DeProses cut down to size.

I give Sara a quick kiss and turn away, walking at double pace back to the car. But Emma jogs next to me, unhindered by her perfect pregnancy bump. 'Gosh, you're in a hurry today,' she says. 'Come on, come for a coffee. I miss your company. We haven't caught up since before the summer holidays.'

'I would really love to,' I say, my hand on my car door. 'But I have to get back. Paul needs me.'

Emma's face colours. 'It's Paul I want to talk to you about, actually,' she says.

Oh. 'What about Paul?'

Emma looks around her as if the other mums, busy with the routine of dropping off children, might eavesdrop. 'I think it might be better in the privacy of the coffee shop.'

I sigh. If I go to the village coffee shop with her, everyone else will be there. I really don't want to get caught up with them. I know they're supposed to be my friends, but right now, it's just easier on my own. She grips my arm over my cardigan, on a bruise, and I wince. She glances at my arm and withdraws her hand. 'Please, Milly. It'll just be the two of us. Ten minutes. And I haven't heard about your trip to France. Fiona told the twins about the train, it sounded like a real adventure.'

I drop my head. A real adventure was a polite way of putting it. 'Okay,' I say, and follow her like a dog across the road and into the steamy village coffee shop. There's a group of farm workers having full Englishes in the corner but no sign of anyone familiar. We slide on to a table on the other side.

'You're brave, taking three children on the train to France on your own.'

What does she want to say about Paul? I want her to get to the point so I can escape before anyone comes in who we know. 'Well, Paul had to stay here to deal with some issues on the estate, so I didn't have much choice really. But the girls were pretty good.' That was a lie and I wonder how much Emma knows about what Steph did on the train. It was awful for Fiona and she might have talked to her friends about it.

'How was the weather? It rained the fortnight we were in Norfolk, so I'm very jealous if you had sun.' She rubs her bump and I look away.

The waitress, the same one who's been here for decades, comes over and takes our order, taking her time to write it all down. I grit my teeth. *Hurry up.*

'It was glorious.' I lift the corners of my mouth into a smile. 'The girls loved it.' Or rather Fiona and Sara loved it. Steph largely stayed in her room, oscillating between hiding under her bedcovers and shouting – and worse – at me.

'Milly, I want to talk to you quickly before anyone we know gets here. In private.' She readjusts her ponytail, making it slightly skew-whiff, and then taps her fingers on the table.

The waitress comes over with two black coffees and two teacakes and lays them out in front of us.

When she's gone, Emma starts talking again but doesn't look at me. 'This is a really difficult thing to bring up, but I'm really worried about you, Milly. I'm your friend. And I'm not the only one to notice . . . but . . . well, you've had a few bruises over the past few months.' She puts her teaspoon in the coffee and starts stirring. She can't meet my eyes. 'I've seen bruises on your arms, and a few weeks ago you seemed to have a black eye . . .'

Oh God. I pull my cardy down over my wrist. *Please stop talking.*

'With everything you've got going on with poor Steph, is everything okay between you and Paul? You really need Paul to be supportive . . . and I'm really worried for you.'

I look up. Paul. I guess that makes sense. Because who would even guess that your teenage daughter is hurting you? That would be unthinkable.

I finally catch her eye and she gives me a small smile. 'I want you to know that I'm here for you, to help you in any way I can. We all are.'

We all are. So the school mums have all been talking about me, talking about me being a battered wife. I can't have them thinking it's Paul. Obviously I can't have them thinking it's Steph either. But poor Paul, he doesn't deserve this. He's trying his best too.

'It's really not what you think,' I say, low enough that no one else can hear. 'Paul's not hurting me.'

'I thought you might say that,' Emma says, leaning in. 'Women in your position are often in denial. I read a leaflet about it in the doctors' surgery when I was in for my antenatal check-up.' She fiddles around in her bag and slides a pale-green piece of paper across the table. The corner of it soaks up some spilled coffee, the stain drawing through the paper to blur the words.

Women. Are you at risk from violence? Do you need a safe place to go? If you are threatened by physical, emotional or sexual violence in the home, Women's Aid can give you advice and help.

I shake my head. This is awful.

'There's a women's refuge in Brighton. If things got really bad. They accept children too.' She takes a sip of coffee, her eyes darting from the cup to me to the builders having their breakfast and then back to the cup. She picks up the sugar shaker and lines it up with the napkin dispenser. 'But we don't think you should leave Highdown. It's your family home. You should kick him out.'

This is what happens when you tell people too much. I should never have mentioned the pre-nup. I pick up the leaflet and stuff it in my bag as I stand up. 'It's not what you think,' I mutter. 'Paul's not hurting me, I promise you.' I walk as quickly as I can to the door, without looking back. As soon as I'm on the street, I run to the car and start the engine, pulling away before Emma has the chance to get out of the coffee shop.

How awful that they think it's Paul. But it would be more awful if they knew it was Steph.

But things aren't great with Paul either. When I get home the library door is shut. In the old days, I would come in from the school run and sit with him for a bit, just chatting about nothing in particular. But over the past year, it's all become about Steph. What to do about Steph. What Steph has done. What she might do next. Where she is. And we disagree on how to deal with her. Paul keeps using that awful phrase 'come down on her like a ton of bricks' and wants her locked in her room, or sent to Scotland to stay with my parents. Which means I don't tell him what she's up to, or what she's been doing to me. They're the first secrets between us in all these years together and it's already changed things. I think back to last night when we were getting ready for bed.

◆ ◆ ◆

One, two, three, four. The purple bruises look like the finger painting we did when the girls were small. A bracelet around my upper arm, the thumb print the clasp underneath. The mark on my hip is yellow now, it'll be hardly visible tomorrow. I examine my face in the mirror. Tired, as always. But no bruises to cover.

'What are you doing in there?' I can see him in the bathroom mirror peering over the top of the newspaper as he lies waiting in bed. I shift to the side just in case he can see my reflection.

'Just getting ready for bed.'

'You usually do that in here,' he says. I can hear him fold up the newspaper and the bed creaking as he comes to join me in the bathroom.

I grab my nightdress off the rack and slide it over my shoulders so it covers my arms.

He kisses me on the back of my neck as he picks up his toothbrush. We stand side by side and look at each other in the mirror while we brush our teeth, as we always have. I have to look away sometimes. I worry about keeping secrets from him. But I worry more that if he knows the truth, it will set him off and he'll send Steph away. Or worse. And surely the best thing is her being with us, with people who love her? Even if it feels like she's breaking us apart.

◆ ◆ ◆

And now he has started shutting the library door when I come home from the school run. The few times I've knocked and gone in, Paul's either been on the phone or has barely looked at me. He says he can't cope with Steph and it's disturbing his work thinking about it. As if it's easy for me and I don't worry at all. And as if his work isn't actually running my family estate.

I think about knocking now and telling him what Emma said, but maybe I'll wait until later. I should tell him what people are thinking. But if I do, then I'll have to admit that I've been hiding bruises and the ones he has seen aren't accidents. Or are accidents. Because I know she doesn't mean it. She's just lashing out.

I can hear Alice playing her radio upstairs, so I go into the kitchen, put on the kettle and get the biscuit tin, opening a new packet of Rich Tea. There's something enormously comforting about biscuits dipped in tea. By the time Alice comes downstairs to start on the drawing room, I realise I've eaten the whole packet with two cups.

Just inside the cellar door are the emergency cigarettes. I grab one, take the matches from the Aga, and then decide to go back to get another cigarette before stepping outside, where the air is crisp and autumnal. I wave to John who's busy pruning. I wait until I'm out of sight of the house to light up. Though who's actually looking? Nobody cares. In the woods, I find the usual log and sit down and strike a match, drawing the smoke into my lungs. Deep breaths. The nicotine makes me pleasingly dizzy. Another month without a baby. I deserve a ciggie.

The woods are a tapestry of colours. Vibrant greens to warm shades of amber, gold, and crimson. When I've finished I grind out the cigarette into a carpet of fallen leaves and twigs and light up the other. The morning sun filters through in dappled patterns.

Paul and I used to come here when we were first married. We'd bring a blanket and wine and lie down and watch the light. A few times it went further and we made love, laughing that there was no one for miles around who could see us. It's hard to imagine those days now. We seem to be growing further and further apart. I wish I'd brought the whole packet of cigarettes.

Maybe Mum and Dad were right to insist on that agreement about Highdown. Maybe they were right about the marriage. I shake my head. *Don't be silly. Things will be fine. We will be fine. It's just a bit of a bad patch.* I stand up and dust myself down. Everything will be fine if only Steph could be happier. Or our version of happy.

Chapter 8

Zoe

Spring 2025

Unity, unity. Zoe reads the piece of paper with the prayer for the funeral on it for the umpteenth time. This time tomorrow, the service will be over and Mum will be on her way to be cremated. A few more days and Zoe'll be alone again.

'C'mon, stop reading that, you know it by heart,' says Fiona, looking up from her laptop.

'Well, stop working then,' Zoe retorts. 'You're always on your laptop.'

'I was just seeing if the solicitor had got back to me.' Fiona closes the lid and sighs. 'He hasn't.'

The sound of the vacuum cleaner drifts down from upstairs. Sara and Steph never stop cleaning. They're all trying to find something to do to fill the time. And get the house presentable for the wake.

'We need to get rid of these boxes so the caterers can use this space tomorrow.' Fiona nods towards two cardboard boxes. Missy is curled up on top of one. 'Why don't we get rid of the obvious stuff and then we can stack what's left in the library? I thought we could use the library for coats tomorrow, but nobody will notice if we have a few boxes in the corner.'

Zoe dips her head, and lifts up the box Missy isn't sleeping on. They start taking out more old receipts for long-forgotten clothes and some photos of Mum as a child. There's a part of Zoe that doesn't want to get rid of anything of Mum's but she knows she's being ridiculous.

'Here are some more letters from Mum's mum to her,' says Fiona, unfolding the fragile pieces of paper and scanning the spidery text.

'Let's have a look,' says Zoe, holding out her hand. Fiona gives the letter to her and goes back to the box. 'She's talking about how lovely it was seeing you and Steph.' Zoe lets out a stream of laughter. 'Apparently you pushed Steph into the pond in her ballet outfit. Granny seems to have found that hilarious.'

Fiona shrugs. 'I don't remember that. But look at this. Mum when she was at school. Look at the straw boater. How sweet does she look?'

Zoe smiles. It's strange reading through all these letters. Everyone is now dead, and it's just the four of them left to carry on the history, the traditions, Highdown Hall. Whatever happens to the house now is immaterial really. It's what happens in the next generation that matters. Fiona, Steph and Zoe don't have children, so it'll likely be Sara's children who eventually inherit the house. What a responsibility.

She flicks through another letter but it's talking about family members she's never heard of. When everything's over she'll go through these more carefully. Perhaps plot out a family tree to work out who's who. Mum had once said they could trace the family back to the late 1600s. That must be somewhere in the house.

She picks up another letter. This time Nanny sounds worried.

Stephanie did seem to be a little off at lunch. All that moaning about having to eat meat. Very strange. Just keep an eye on her, dear.

Be as supportive as you can. Girls start to behave a little differently as they become women and it's likely no more than that.

Poor Steph, she was clearly before her time. God knows what Granny would have made of Zoe being a vegan. 'Granny seems like a right tartar,' says Zoe.

'Oh, she was lovely to us,' says Fiona. 'But she didn't take any prisoners. She and Mum had a bit of a tricky relationship, I think. She never forgave her for marrying beneath her, as she described it.'

'I only recall meeting her a few times,' says Zoe. 'Here and then in Scotland.'

Fiona shakes her head. 'There was a bit of a falling-out between her and Mum and they rarely spoke to each other. It was all over Dad, I guess. Granny couldn't get it out of her head that Dad worked on the land rather than owning the land. They moved to Scotland when we were quite young. That's where Granny was from. We visited quite a lot when I was small, but after the falling-out, we only saw them occasionally.'

'Oh,' says Zoe, opening another letter. Her eyes immediately fall on to the words *Please don't do it.* 'Listen to this,' she says to Fiona. '*I've just come off the phone from you. I know you won't listen to me, but I want to say it again. Please don't do it. It's a terrible idea that will have far-reaching consequences for everyone involved, particularly Kylie. Poor little Kai. We can help support you all if you don't go ahead. There is a much better way. Please, please don't do it. Mother.*'

Fiona's mouth is wide open. 'Bloody hell.'

'Poor little Kai,' Zoe repeats. 'Poor little Kai.'

Fiona reads the letter over her shoulder. 'Kylie and Kai. Who *are* they? And how are they linked to that key you found?'

'We should show the others,' says Zoe, taking out more letters and wondering whether there's anything else in the box that can shine more light on it.

Sara comes in dragging the vacuum cleaner behind her. 'Christ, I'm exhausted.' She drops the hose on the floor and sinks into the chair, peeling off her rubber gloves and folding them in together. 'There's just so much to do. I can see how you struggled, Zoe, especially with Mum to look after.'

Zoe smiles at her. 'It was pretty impossible.'

'Mum must be the last person in the country to have bowls of potpourri – it's everywhere. I got rid of the stuff in the hall and the cloakroom yesterday but I've just found loads of it upstairs in all the rooms. I didn't realise that they still sold it. I hope you don't mind, but I threw most of it away. It was all so full of dust.'

Mum would have a fit, but Zoe tries to smile. 'Of course, it's revolting stuff.'

'What are you two looking at?'

'Those letters and photos, from the loft,' Zoe says. 'But read this.' She hands her the letter mentioning Kylie and Kai.

Sara pours herself a glass of water and drinks it in one. 'Wow! I wonder what the terrible idea was? And who are Kylie and Kai then? And what's the connection with that envelope with the key in it?'

Steph comes in with an armful of cleaning sprays and cloths. 'Well, that's the top floor done,' she says, dropping all the stuff in the sink. 'Funny being back in the playroom again. I remembered it being so much bigger. Some of our drawings are still on the walls.'

Sara hands her the letter. 'Look what the others have found. All very strange. It mentions Kai again but also someone called Kylie?'

Two splashes of colour stain Steph's pale cheeks as she reads. Her gaze flicks to Zoe and then back to the letter. 'How should I know?' she says, getting up again and throwing it on the pile of receipts. 'I might start in the library while it's still light. People are bound to go in there tomorrow.' She picks up the cleaning products and walks out.

Fiona rolls her eyes, but Zoe sees Sara's questioning look. Steph reacted oddly when they first found the envelope with Kai written on it and the key inside. And now she is equally odd about the mention of Kylie. Kylie and Kai. She definitely knows something.

'Let me help go through that box with you,' she says to Fiona. 'The answer must be in there somewhere.' Zoe moves it across the table slightly and they pull out loose black and white photos of stiff, formal people in black suits and dresses. But there's no further mention of Kylie or Kai.

◆ ◆ ◆

They share a bottle of wine with the remains of the veggie chilli for supper. Afterwards Fiona opens another bottle and they lie about in the sitting room, sipping wine and reading or looking at their phones. Fiona reinstalled the Wi-Fi yesterday. 'I can't believe you managed to live without Wi-Fi,' she said, as if it were on a level with shelter, food and clothing.

'Do you remember Martha Stewart?' Sara says to Fiona. 'She was in my year at school. Red hair, load of freckles.'

Fiona looks up. 'Yes, yes, I do. Her older brother was in my year, I think. Weird kid. Why?'

'Oh, she's just commented on my post. She's mentioned about the time Mum decorated the treehouses, put all the lights up and—'

'What post?' says Zoe, feeling her jaw tense.

'I put something up about Mum's funeral.'

'Why?'

Sara pauses for a moment. 'Well, I just wanted people to know. I have friends who knew her, like Martha—'

'When was the last time you saw Martha?' asks Zoe.

'Oh, I don't know, a few years ago, I guess.'

Zoe rolls her eyes. 'Let's see what you've said.' She puts out her hand and Sara gives her the phone. Sara's post is inevitably saccharine, accompanied by photos, some of which she recognises from the boxes in the attic. One of the photos is Mum with Sara's children, which makes Zoe's stomach twist again. Another is the six of them together – Mum, Dad and the four daughters. Sara has clearly spent time putting this together. But why? 'I can't believe you posted about Mum dying just to get some attention.'

'I didn't post about it to get attention,' says Sara, a flush starting to rise up her neck.

'And you included pictures of me without my permission. Without any of our permissions,' Zoe says, glancing at Steph and Fiona.

'I posted something about Mum too,' says Fiona, shrugging.

'You too? Bloody hell. Why?'

'It just seemed like the easiest way to let everyone know.'

'Why didn't you just send out a press release? Isn't that what you do? Carefully curate the truth?'

Fiona sighs. 'There's nothing wrong with posting on social media, Zoe.'

'There's everything wrong with it. What about you, Steph?'

Steph glances up and their eyes meet. 'I don't have social media,' she says. Zoe sees herself reflected in Steph's grey eyes.

'Thank God for that.'

'For God's sake, Zoe, lighten up. I'm going to have a bath.' Fiona stands up and walks out.

Sara presses her lips together. 'I think I'll have an early night, tomorrow's going to be a big day.' She collects her and Fiona's wine glasses and takes them into the kitchen.

Steph glances at Zoe. 'Are you okay?' she asks.

Zoe nods. 'I just really hate social media, it . . .' She can feel her chin wobbling and the tears come, even though she desperately tries to push them back. She doesn't hate social media really, she doesn't know why she's making such a fuss and being so horrible to everyone.

Steph opens her mouth as if to speak but then says nothing. She eventually shifts across the sofa and slips her arm around Zoe and hugs her. It feels awkward and Zoe wants to push her away. She takes a deep breath. In a few days they'll all be gone. Fiona's already said she'll book a flight for the day after the interment. In a few days, she'll be alone with Mum's memory again. She wants it more than anything. But there's also a growing sense of dread. What will it be like without her? She's never been in this house alone. She must try to make the best of this time with the four of them together, as awful as it is in many ways.

◆ ◆ ◆

Zoe doesn't see Fiona and Sara again that evening and she lies in bed regretting being so harsh. Of course there's nothing wrong with posting on social media. It's part of grief, letting people know, getting sympathy, people sharing stories about the dead person.

The village church bell marks the hour with three chimes. Tomorrow they will be inside saying their final goodbyes to Mum. Zoe needs to sleep or she's going to feel even more awful.

Maybe a cup of tea will help.

Steph's bedroom door is wide open, the side lamp illuminating a pile of tangled clothes on the floor, an upended book, its pages splayed, and a bath towel in a heap. It is just like how Zoe imagines a teenager's room would be. She smiles and walks down the stairs.

Steph looks up from the kitchen table, illuminated by the moon. She's aged so much since their father's funeral – her hair was blonde when Zoe last saw her, now it's a sullen grey, a permanent cloud over her head.

'Can't you sleep either?' asks Zoe.

Steph shakes her head. 'I keep thinking about tomorrow. D'you want a tea?'

'Yeah.'

'I'll put the kettle on.'

Zoe slides down on to a kitchen chair, her feet cold on the flagstone floor, watching Steph. Steph slides a mug of tea across to Zoe and sits down opposite her. 'Highdown's looking great,' she says. 'All ready for tomorrow.'

Zoe glances around. 'You and Sara have worked so hard. I know it was a dump. I could see the way the three of you looked at it. But I had no time to do anything, and there's no money.'

Steph taps her nail against the mug. 'It was the same when we were children. It was always a bit dilapidated, wasn't it? There was never enough money to fix it, once they sold off the land and didn't get that rent.'

Zoe nods but she wonders if it's true. She remembers the house always being perfect. Glossy. She was proud to bring friends back here.

The silence stretches along the length of the table, taut between them. The grandfather clock strikes the quarter hour.

'Are you still doing the Extinction Rebellion stuff?' asks Steph.

She didn't think Steph would remember. 'No, I'm not doing anything with them now. Or rather I am now and again, but on a minor level, helping with some of the legalities.' Zoe sucks her bottom lip. 'Mass participation movements like XR can only happen at certain times in history. Something about 2019 made it all happen but that energy seems to have died away.' She misses the excitement of XR, the feeling that you were really making an impact.

Steph is still looking at her, waiting for more. She seems genuinely interested.

'I took some of the lessons I'd learned with XR and in my old job I was helping organisations work towards net zero. Basically reducing their impact on the environment. I also went into local politics to work from the ground up. Talked to people individually about why the climate crisis matters to them and why we need to change the way we live. I was a Green Party councillor for our area, but also had to resign from that when Mum became properly ill. It's not a job you can do half-heartedly.'

'That's amazing,' says Steph. 'Mum must have been very proud of you.'

'She was and she wasn't.' Zoe pauses and thinks back to Mum finding out about the funeral cortège protest she organised to go through the village, the coffin representing the planet. She'd been devastated that someone might find out Zoe was behind it. 'But I think she preferred the politics to the activism. Less embarrassing.'

Steph laughs. 'I can imagine.'

'I used to deal with everything from parish councils, campaign groups, community initiatives and sort out people's problems.'

'That sounds like a busy job. Lots of responsibility.'

Zoe nods. 'It was. I spent the first six months with serious imposter syndrome. But I really liked the feeling I was helping people, often those in desperate situations. I hope I can go back to it.'

'I'm sorry I never made it to that XR protest. I lost the leaflet.'

'What protest?' says Zoe, her head on one side.

Steph swallows and looks away. 'Never mind.'

Another heavy silence falls over them.

'I'm sorry about the will,' Steph says eventually. 'I want you to have my share of the house. I don't need it. I have everything I need at the shelter.'

Zoe glances up. Is she serious? 'That's kind of you but it's not just about that. It's about feeling that maybe Mum didn't love me like she loved you all.'

'I think she loved you best of all,' says Steph, taking a sip of tea. 'You were the golden child, the one who could do no wrong. And you proved it by staying and looking after her. If she had a favourite, it was you.'

'Do you think?'

'Yes,' says Steph. She gets up and puts her mug in the sink and walks towards the door.

'Thank you,' Zoe says to Steph. 'For telling me that. It helps.'

Steph smiles slightly and walks back up the stairs.

Zoe stares at the space where Steph has just been.

If she had a favourite it was you.

◆ ◆ ◆

Milly

1989

The woman from the council – Child Protection, or whatever she calls herself – advised me to talk to Steph when we were both calm. Talking together in a quiet moment, she said, can help foster a good relationship which can support us through the more challenging times. I understand what she means but there are fewer and fewer calm times. And far too many challenging ones. And in the rare calm moment, you just want to have a lie-down and enjoy the peace, not start creating new problems. Even my bones ache with tiredness.

And I hate having people from outside interfering with our family. Mum would hate it if she knew. But after Steph's arrest, Child Protection turned up on the doorstep and I couldn't turn them away.

I switch on the kettle and get out two mugs. On the lawn, Alice is playing catch with Fiona and Sara, Woody racing back and forth between the three of them, desperate for a dropped ball. I wonder how much they're affected by what's happening. Sara very little, I reckon – she seems oblivious to most things. I think back to when I was five and I can remember almost nothing. Tiny fragments of school. An old doll I had. The books with the ant and bee which I read until the spines disintegrated. And Sara is close to Fiona, worshipping her, rather than her oldest sister. Steph must almost be an adult in Sara's eyes.

But Fiona is different. At ten, she sees everything. I can tell by the wariness in her eyes. I wonder how much Steph talks to her about what's going on? The two are often together, tucked up in bed chatting, sitting on the roof outside Steph's bedroom though I've told them a million times that it's dangerous. Fiona's regular bed-wetting over the past few months must be linked in some way. She never did it as a young girl and when we took her to the doctor he found no physical reason. I try to talk to her too but she just clams up.

I take a packet of biscuits out of the pantry. I'm failing. I'm failing all of them. I have one job. Be a mum, raise the girls, and I can't even do that. I munch through the first biscuit.

Now I'm forty the chances of having another child are diminishing by the day. Another thing the doctor said. Fertility falls off a cliff after forty. So there's not likely to be a boy for Paul after all. No Tommy. Even the most recent miscarriage was a girl, they said at the hospital. I called her Zoe even though she was too small to be called anything. And Paul and I will have to be closer for the prospect of another child. He even slept on the old sofa in the library last night, after we rowed about the idea of Steph going on the pill. He's so naive if he thinks she won't be having sex. In our bed alone, I hardly slept a wink.

There's a squeal as Sara misses the ball and Woody grabs it in his jaws, circling around them joyfully, proud to finally be part of the game. 'Woody!' Sara screams, chasing him. I pour boiling water into the pot, stir the teabags around and fill up the cups, eating another biscuit in the process.

Steph's door is closed, but I remember to knock on it. There's no reply but I doubt she can hear it over her music. There's something behind the door and I have to put all my weight against the door to open it. There's a thump on the other side.

'For Christ's sake, Mum,' says Steph. 'I didn't say you could come in.'

I edge through the gap, past a bedside table which has been pushed against the door. On the floor is a stone lion. It takes me a moment to recognise it. 'That's from the garden,' I say needlessly. 'I've told you not to just take other people's stuff.'

Steph looks up from her bed. 'It's not "other people's"'. She makes the inverted commas in the air that she so hates me doing to her. 'It's all of ours as it's in the garden. In a common area. I'm just borrowing it.'

'What on earth do you need it for?'

'You won't let me have a lock on my door so I wanted something heavy behind the door to stop you coming in.'

I take a deep breath. 'Would you like a cup of tea?' Holding out one of the mugs.

'No, thanks,' she says, turning away. I grit my teeth. Another great start. Maybe I should just cut my losses now – it's not going to go well, I can tell. Wait for a better moment. But there are no better moments. At least she's not shouting.

I sit down on the side of her bed, next to Terry and June who are curled up on her pillow, and put her tea on the bedside table. 'Biscuit?' I hold out the packet of Rich Tea.

She looks at them for a moment and nods, so I throw a couple across to her.

'Ergh, I don't want the ones you've touched,' she says, beckoning for the packet. I reach forward and pick up the ones I threw to her and start to eat them. She immediately covers her hands with her ears. 'For God's sake.'

I swallow the biscuit hurriedly. There's a pain in my oesophagus as the biscuit works its way down too fast, and I take a slug of tea. Steph screws up her face.

'What do you want?' she asks.

And here it is. 'I want to have a chat with you about Patrick,' I say as calmly as I can.

She stares at the duvet, her eyes narrowed, but says nothing.

'I want to make sure you're being careful.'

'Careful about what?' She talks through the biscuit, flecks of it on her lip. I consider saying something but think better of it.

'I wondered if it would be useful to go down to the family planning clinic in town.' Paul would hate me for saying this, but I really need to. Although she doesn't need my permission to go on the pill anymore.

She munches her way through another biscuit and I wonder if she's heard me. 'Steph?'

'Stop it, Mum.'

'Stop what?'

'Stop trying to be my friend.'

I take a sip of tea. Calm, calm. 'I'm not trying to be your friend, I'm your mum and I'm trying to keep you safe.'

She gets up from the bed and stands at the window, looking out.

Maybe I should just leave. 'When are you seeing him next?'

She doesn't turn round. 'It's none of your business.' Her voice is raised.

'It is my business. You're fifteen and—'

'And what?' She turns to face me but doesn't look at me.

'You're still a child and I need to look after you and make sure you're safe.'

She curls her lip and laughs. 'Make sure I'm safe. You haven't got a clue about anything.'

I stand up, draining the last of my tea and take the leaflet out of my back pocket. 'There's some information here about the pill. I thought you might find it interesting. You can have a read and then you can decide what to do.'

She doesn't react so I walk towards her, the leaflet in my outstretched arm. 'Here.'

'I don't want that. Just leave and make sure you close the door on your way out.'

Something inside me snaps. 'Why do you have to be so rude all the time? I'm just trying to help.' I'm so fed up of being stuck between the two of them.

She turns suddenly, her eyes dark. 'Because you're a shit mum. A shit human. You don't care about me, about us, about anything. All you care about is what people think.'

I do care what other people think, that's true. Is that wrong? But I care about my family more.

'That's not true, Steph,' I say, trying to reach for her. 'I care about you all. I just want everyone to be happy.' I feel the tears coming and try to squeeze them away.

'We'd be happy if you weren't here, if it was just me and Dad and the girls. Why don't you just fuck off somewhere far, far away?' She pushes her hands hard against my chest, enough that I stagger back. *I was just off balance*, I think. I right myself.

'Don't push me like that,' I say.

'I'm always asking you not to touch me and you take no notice, but if I touch you, that's a different thing.'

'I'm just trying to help.'

'You're a pathetic human being,' she spits. She pushes me again and I back away. I shouldn't have got so close. I trip over the bedside table, but get back my balance in time.

'Fuck off out of my room.' She's properly shouting now. She lunges for me.

There seems too little space with the bed, the bedside table and the stone lion. I trip again, and hold on to the door handle. She grabs my wrist hard and twists it.

'Let go, I'm trying to get out.' I try to say it quietly but it comes out as a shout.

There's a snapping and a surge of heat in my arm. I look down at my hand and there's something wrong about the way it's hanging. At a funny angle. I cradle it with the other hand, trying not to think about the pain. I've broken it. *She's* broken it.

Steph stands back and looks at my wrist. Her hands flop by her side then she steps away and sits on the side of the bed, her head in her hands.

'Well, the offer about the family planning clinic is there, if you want it.' I step back and open the door with my foot and sidle out.

'Mummy.'

The voice makes me look up. Fiona is standing on the gallery with a tennis racket. She must have come down from the playroom.

'Oh, hello, darling, what have you got there?' I try to speak normally through the pain.

'Why were you and Steph shouting?' She's sobbing. I cuddle her with my good hand, the pain excruciating.

'It's nothing, darling, we were just talking.'

'You were both shouting,' she says through the tears.

'Where have you got to, Fiona? We're waiting for you.' Alice's sing-song voice comes up the stairs from the hall.

Fiona looks at me and then runs down the stairs.

'There you are,' says Alice. 'What took you so long, poppet? Oh dear, why are you crying? Let's dry those tears up and go and play tennis.'

I slide down the wall outside Fiona's room, the stabbing feeling in my arm making me nauseous. Fiona is crying to Alice but the sound is drowned out by music suddenly thumping from Steph's room. I start to cry again. I really need to strap up my wrist.

She always said before that it was an accident when I got hurt. But she deliberately twisted my wrist. Or was I just slow leaving? Was it my fault? If I'd left earlier, when she first asked, I wouldn't have got hurt. When do you say this is no accident, and start taking a stand? And what does that look like? All the advice from that battered wife leaflet is to leave an abusive husband. But I'm a battered mother and there's no advice for that. You can't leave your own child.

Chapter 9

Zoe

Spring 2025

The coffin is larger than she expects. How odd to think that Mum is inside, all dressed up for her final journey, wearing her favourite pearls. She wouldn't be Mum without those pearls. Zoe stands outside Highdown Hall, wrapping her arms around herself though it's another warm day.

Fiona comes out of the house with a mug, still wearing slippers. 'Mrs Gunn's done a good job with the flowers,' she says. The *MUM* on the top of the coffin picked out in daisies does look beautiful.

Fiona has organised it all single-handedly, thinks Zoe. She feels like she's been in a daze since Mum died, unable to really focus on anything.

'Everything's set for the wake. The caterers will bring the food while we're at church.'

'Thanks for doing all of this.' Zoe waves at the coffin.

Fiona squeezes Zoe's arm. 'She was our mum,' she says gently. 'Of course I was going to do it.'

'I'm sorry again about last night. I was being silly.'

Fiona smiles. 'It's okay, Zoe, I get it.' She goes back inside, picks up her make-up bag from the hall table and stares into the mirror. She seems to stand for a long time looking at her reflection. Zoe wonders what she sees. Are we who we see in the mirror, or what the world sees? Are they the same thing? After a while, Fiona pushes her hair behind her ears and carefully draws on her smile with lipstick.

Zoe turns back to her mother. The funeral people said they'd remove the pearls before they cremate her. They'll receive those back with her wedding band and ashes early next week ready for the interment in the village graveyard alongside the other DeProse family. And then after that, her sisters will all go back to their separate homes. *What will happen to her?* Zoe wonders. Everything seems so uncertain since they found the will. She takes a deep breath and looks back at the coffin.

When they take off the wedding band before they cremate her, it'll be the first time it's been removed since Dad slipped it on in the same church more than fifty years ago. Zoe was always moved that Mum continued to wear it after her husband had died, as if their love transcended this world.

Zoe walks forward and touches the end of the coffin, lying on its base in the hearse. Two men in dark uniform stand at the front of the car, turned away from her.

The grandfather clock in the hall strikes eleven. 'It's almost time,' calls Fiona from inside.

Missy jumps up into the hearse and curls up next to Mum. There's something about this small gesture that makes her eyes tear up again. She knows. The cat knows. 'You can't come with us,' says Zoe, picking her up and stroking her head. Missy purrs and Zoe buries her face into her fur.

Fiona emerges from the house with Sara, both looking immaculate. Steph follows, her dress baggy in the wrong places, and they stand by the coffin, as if they are at a macabre coffee morning with their mother. Sara picks cat hair off Zoe's dress.

One of the men closes the car, encasing Mum in glass, and they start the engine. It's only a five-minute walk to the village church but it seems to take ages to even get to the bottom of the drive, walking uncomfortably slowly, the sun hot against their black dresses. This house must have meant so much to Mum that she wanted to start her final journey from here. Which makes Zoe not getting any of it all the worse. But she's not going to think about that now.

Through the gates, the hearse noses its way on to the main road into the village. Someone Zoe doesn't recognise stops and stands, head bowed, as the hearse passes them, and this small gesture makes the tears prick her eyes again. They walk past the village school, which they all attended until they were thirteen, and next to it is the church, the spire picked out against the blue sky. The hearse stops outside and the men open it up and gently slide out the coffin.

The sisters wait while a couple of latecomers sidle past and slip through the entrance. The pall-bearers lift the coffin on to their shoulders and then the four of them automatically fall into step behind it. Zoe and Sara, followed by Fiona and Steph, walking in a strange half-shuffle. The church is packed, the pews crammed with people. Mum lived in Hambrough all her life and had played a big role in the community. Fetes, committees, the WI, chair of governors of the school, helping out in the church. If there was something to be volunteered for, Mum had put her hand up.

They walk down the aisle behind Mum's coffin to Mahler's 'Adagietto' from *Symphony No. 5 in C-sharp Minor*, as Mum requested. All four dressed in matching black dresses, sombre bridesmaids. Her legs are heavy and it's an effort to put one foot in front of the other. She can't keep her eyes off the coffin, imagining Mum inside dressed in the floor-length dusky pink summer dress she and Sara chose. Mum's favourite. It seemed such a waste to burn that beautiful dress, but what was the alternative? It might be environmentally friendly being cremated with no clothes but it would be odd to think of Mum naked inside the coffin. She shakes her head. Why is she thinking such odd things?

There are so many familiar faces. The whole village is here and some of the townspeople too. Mum was the last to carry the DeProse name. Mum's friends, many now leaning on sticks or slumped in wheelchairs. A day out. At the back, there's a man leaning against the pillar. Ben? Is it Ben? She can't turn her head enough to see. There's Alice standing with her husband. Then near the front, Sara's husband John and her three children have come for the day. Will Sara go back with them and then just return for the interment? Will that be the end of the four of them together at Highdown? Her stomach tenses. Having hated having them here at the beginning, she now can't imagine the house without them. Her sisters.

At the top of the aisle, the pall-bearers stop. She turns to see if it is Ben by the pillar, but no one is there now. There's a moment when the coffin tips slightly and Zoe holds her breath. Suddenly she's back with Mum watching Queen Elizabeth's funeral. Mum said what a responsibility it had been for the young pall-bearers to hold the Queen's coffin throughout the day. Into Westminster Abbey, then off to Wellington Arch and then on to Windsor. The two of them spent the day glued to the TV, Mum in black, with what she considered a tasteful Union Jack flag hung from the gallery, because the old flagpole had rusted solid, a full afternoon tea, including finger sandwiches which Zoe loved, in the late Queen's honour.

The coffin slides on to the catafalque by the altar flanked by two lines of tall candles. The men melt away and Zoe finds herself alone in front of the coffin, unable to move until Sara grabs her hand and brings her back to the front pew where the rest of her sisters are sitting.

'"I am the resurrection and the life,"' saith the Lord; "he that believeth in me, though he were dead, yet shall he live: and whosoever liveth and believeth in me shall never die'," starts the vicar. She tries to listen to all the words he says – some of it about Mum but mainly the humdrum words of the standard Church of England funeral service. Her mind keeps reeling back though to Mum doing the flowers for the harvest festival arrangements.

We plough the fields, and scatter the good seed on the land.

It's a warm day – they all seem to be unseasonably warm these days – but she's unable to stop shivering. Sara puts an arm around her and draws her close, until one of her children behind grows jealous and clambers over the pew to nestle in her lap, Sara burying her face into her daughter's hair. Zoe watches her curl into her sister and feels strangely envious. Not because she hasn't got her own children, but never again will she be able to do that with her mother. She thinks that in an odd way she's an orphan now. Can you call yourself an orphan at thirty-five? Probably not.

Sara gently hands back her daughter to her husband, stands up and Zoe realises it's time for the intercessions. They stand in a line, in the same place as she had to say the same prayers when she was at the village school. But this time she's not staring at Mum smiling back at her in the congregation but at her coffin. Does she have her eyes open? Is she still watching them? Or is she somewhere else in the church checking they've done it all as she instructed?

The microphone crackles as Fiona passes it to her. 'In the midst of our grief, we pray for un-un-un-ity among those who gather to remember our mother,' she says. Mum will be cross she's stumbled. Unity, unity. She glances down the line of her sisters, all dressed identically to her. Like they never did as children. Why did they do this now? Before Mum died, she'd never felt a sense of unity with them. She hates to admit it even to herself, but she'd actively disliked them for abandoning her to look after their parents, and felt they didn't deserve to be part of their mum's death and funeral. But just a week later, she feels differently. They are her family, for better, for worse, for richer, for poorer. 'May this shared experience bring us closer together, reminding us of the bonds that transcend the challenges we face. Help us find strength in one another as we navigate this emotional journey. Thank you for the unity we find in times of sorrow. Lord hear us.'

'Lord graciously hear us,' the congregation murmurs, faces warm with sympathy. For her mistake or for the loss of their mother, or both. The coffin is silent. Zoe can't help touching it as she files back past. *Sorry, Mum.*

Later Fiona stands to give the eulogy. They offered it to Zoe as the one they believed was perhaps closest to their mother, but what could she say? She has too many memories of her, too much to say to fit in the standard five minutes. And she knew she wouldn't have been able to get through it. Her throat tightens just thinking about it.

'Camilla Constance DeProse was born in Highdown Hall in 1949, the eldest child of Evelyn and Edward DeProse.' Fiona's first line sounds like a history lesson. 'She lived at the hall, or on the estate, her entire life and went to what was then called Hambrough Village School from the age of four until she was thirteen when she went away to boarding school. A lover of the English countryside, she met my father Paul on a shoot on the estate when she was just eighteen. She was a gun and he was a beater and our family initially disapproved of the relationship. Mum argued and argued and eventually got her way – as she usually did.' A murmur of laughter ripples through the church. Fiona smiles.

'And they were eventually married here in this church in 1971. Time was to prove Mum's parents wrong, for Mum and Dad's was a true love affair lasting more than fifty years. Testament to her love is that she is still wearing her wedding band, more than five years after my father died.' Fiona swallows and glances towards the coffin. *So Fiona noticed that too,* thinks Zoe.

'Mum played a big role in the village community throughout her life,' she continues. Zoe turns and glances around at the congregation, their faces watching her sister. Alice is already dabbing her eyes. The lady at the post office who Mum had waged war with is smiling at Fiona's mention of Mum's campaigning. The headmistress laughs at Fiona's comment on Mum spending more time in the school than some of the pupils. Everyone here loved her in some way, or at least respected her. It gives Zoe a warm feeling that so many people have come to see their mother off. Would it feel different if there were just a handful of people to witness her funeral? She'd been to funerals here with Mum when there was just the deceased's immediate family and a villager or two. Being part of a big congregation makes her grief feel bigger, more important. But she supposes it feels exactly the same if you loved someone and were the only mourner.

'Mum had always said she wanted a big family,' continued Fiona. 'She only had one sister, Josephine, who sadly died as a young child, and she felt the three of them had rather rattled around in the hall. Stephanie came along in 1974 and, like clockwork, Mum and Dad had another child roughly every five years – me in 1979, Sara in 1984 and Zoe in 1990. We were all christened in this church too. Milly was a wonderful mother – always willing to listen, to help with homework, to create a craft project, to build a den in the woods.'

Zoe knows the thickness in her throat is a sign she's going to cry, like your mouth watering before you're going to be sick. The tears come and Zoe wipes her nose with the back of her hand. Someone pushes a tissue into her fist and she presses it to her face.

At the pulpit, Fiona pauses for too long and Zoe realises she's also struggling. Her steel-like sister swallows and looks down at her notes.

'Mum took to being a grandmother as enthusiastically as she had to motherhood. The arrival of my twin nieces Charlotte and Isabelle and then little Katy was an enormous joy for her.

'My parents had the sort of relationship that it was impossible to imagine one without the other. When her beloved Paul died in 2020, that was the start of my mother's own decline. She never quite recovered from the grief and it seemed to weigh her down each day.' So Fiona listened to what Zoe had said. Zoe wipes the tissue against her nose. Poor Mum never got over Dad's death.

'When she turned seventy-five last year, the age my father was when he died, it was as if she'd had enough. After the celebration with Zoe and Sara and her family, she started complaining of pain in her torso which was soon diagnosed as cancer. She took the news as you might expect, stoically, and looked on the positive side. She would soon reunite with Paul. While I didn't manage to get there for the end' – was it Zoe's imagination or did Fiona still say that through gritted teeth? – 'my sister Zoe was with her as she died peacefully in the house she loved so much, as she had been for the weeks and months before that.'

Across the aisle, tissues are being raised like white flags. Sara sniffs and wipes at her eyes. Only Steph sits silently, staring directly ahead at something Zoe can't see. It's funny how they all show their grief differently. Zoe thought Fiona's organising drive was evidence that she hadn't felt as close to their mum, hadn't missed her. But it was just her way of coping. Just as Steph said little, and kept it all inside, and Sara fussed around and mothered them all.

A dropped hymn book echoes through the church as Fiona slowly walks back from the pulpit, touches the coffin, mouthing something, and then takes her seat next to Zoe.

‘Well done,’ Zoe whispers. ‘That was beautiful.’

Fiona presses her lips together and takes Zoe’s offered hand. Her eyes are full, a tear teetering on the edge of her eyelid. Fiona wipes it away with a manicured finger.

The vicar Mum had bossed about for years, finally given the chance to take the lead, is finishing the service with a blessing. He nods to someone and the pall-bearers reappear, carefully picking up the coffin. Fiona stands, then Zoe and Sara. She feels Steph move behind her and they file out to walk behind their mother to some piano music Zoe doesn’t recognise. What was it Mum chose? She can’t remember now.

That’s it, it’s all over. The tears come again and she stumbles momentarily. Steph grips her arm, keeping her upright. Zoe smiles at her and then keeps her eyes on her mum as they walk out into the sunshine and the men slide the coffin back into the hearse. She watches it inch its way down the street. A postwoman walks alongside the hearse for a while, pushing her red trolley on the pavement, huge headphones clamped over her ears. Next door, children are screaming in the school playground. For everyone else this is a normal day. But for her, it’s the final day. They won’t see Mum again. Next time, she will be a pile of ashes in a box ready to be placed in the cold earth next to their father. The hearse picks up speed, heading away, and the four of them turn towards Highdown Hall. Behind them, the congregation follows.

◆ ◆ ◆

This is the only time she envies smokers – the ready-made excuse to go outside, to get away. If one more person asks her how she’s feeling, she’ll scream. And bloody Fiona for organising the caterers. If it wasn’t for them, she could escape into the kitchen and fiddle about with the food.

'Are you okay?' Zoe turns towards the voice, about to explode, and realises it's Alice.

She feels her shoulders drop as she shakes her head. Alice envelops her in a hug, just as she had when she was small and she'd fallen out with friends, or been told off at school. She relaxes into it.

'It's a tough day for you – for all of you,' Alice says, stroking her back.

'It is,' says Zoe, taking a sip of her wine. People are everywhere. Sprawled on the sofas, plates and glasses resting on laps or on tables without a coaster. Mum would have had a fit. Even in the hall, the table is cluttered with glasses, surrounded by people red from talking too loudly and drinking too much. From her vantage point in the corner of the drawing room, she can see they've spilled out into the garden, grinding discarded cigarette butts into the gravel. Even the shade has retreated to the far corners of the lawn. Flitting between them like swallows are catering staff in black and white offering top-ups and plates of canapés. She knows from the looks and the occasional question about Highdown Hall that word has got out about her not inheriting her own home. Zoe wonders which of her sisters said something. It couldn't be Steph, she hardly speaks. But Sara and Fiona are far too sociable, too willing to chat about everything and nothing. She's seen them both with different groups of villagers, smiling and chatting. She just can't bring herself to do it. To act like this is some sort of party, one of the many parties her parents used to have. But then, across the drawing room, she sees the solicitor in another ill-fitting suit, a shiny black tie around his neck. He catches her eye and looks away. So much for confidentiality. It was probably the most exciting will he'd ever come across.

'Lovely food,' says Mary Billingham, flakes of pastry decorating her bosom. 'I'm sorry to hear about Highdown Hall. Very difficult for you. What was your mother thinking?' She takes a gulp of her wine. 'It's far more usual for houses like this to be left to the eldest child to carry on the tradition. We were all wondering what Stephanie was going to do with it when the time came.'

'I'm not sure it's our business, Mary,' says Alice, smiling and tipping her head on one side.

Mary Billingham blushes a fraction and then rallies. 'I think the future of the house is everyone's business. Imagine if it gets turned into flats . . .'

Zoe doesn't hear anything else. She is thinking she'll just quietly go upstairs when she sees Joy Philips. Her hair is a startling white against her black dress, her face a map of wrinkles. She's talking to another woman who Zoe doesn't recognise. They both look up as she approaches them.

Mrs Philips rests a blue veiny hand on her arm. 'I'm very sorry for your loss, dear.'

Zoe nods. 'Thank you,' she says automatically. 'Can I ask you something?'

'Of course, dear.' There's a piece of something between her two front teeth and Zoe wonders for a moment whether to mention it.

'You have something in your teeth, Joy.' Alice has come up behind her.

Mrs Philips colours and puts her napkin over her mouth, while she fiddles around with her fingernail and then swills it down with a mouthful of wine.

'Sorry about that,' murmurs Alice. 'That was completely wrong of Mary to say. People are such gossips.'

Zoe swallows. She knows it's what they're all thinking. That their beautiful home will be turned into luxury apartments. *Magnificent apartments for sale in former manor house in heart of Sussex countryside.* She can see the brochure already. They absolutely cannot let that happen. She can feel the weight of the stares of the DeProse portraits looking down at her from the gallery.

Mrs Philips has recovered. 'You wanted to ask me something, dear,' she says.

Zoe nods. 'Years ago, you were talking to Mum – we were at a parish fete, I think – and you described me as a happy accident.'

Mrs Philips puts her hand over her mouth, her eyes wide. 'Did I?' she says faintly. Alice seems to stiffen beside her.

'Yes, you did,' says Zoe. 'I wondered what you meant by that.'

'Well, well,' she stammers. 'I don't remember saying that at all. It's not the sort of thing I would have said. But if I did, it was probably just that your parents were a bit older by the time you arrived. Perhaps you were . . .' She swallows and looks through the front door to the drive. 'Unexpected,' she says at last.

Unexpected. Happy accident. Had her parents not planned for a fourth child?

'That's nonsense, Joy,' says Alice. 'I know for a fact that Milly tried for Zoe for years before she came along. She was a much-wanted child.'

Zoe turns to go upstairs but Sara is standing in the way, little Katy asleep over her shoulder, talking to an old man. She catches Sara's eye and goes over. 'God, this is awful,' whispers Sara, smiling gratefully as a waitress refills her glass.

Steph comes to join them, deep circles beneath her eyes, clutching an empty wine glass. The waitress refills it.

'Your mother was such a character,' says Mrs Philips, clearly pleased to have the three sisters as an audience. 'The village won't be the same without her.'

'That's true,' says another lady dressed in purple, incongruous among all the black. 'I remember the fantastic lunches she'd put on for the shoot.'

'Not just the lunches, it was the home-made sloe gin.' Another woman, bending heavily on a stick, joins them.

'The sloe gin, oh yes!' says the purple woman.

When will they all go? wonders Zoe. Steph finishes her glass and accepts the refill from the waitress, who also fills up the glasses from the other women.

'Elevenses was never the same without Milly's sloe gin and prosecco.' A man joins them, his black tie askew.

'It's called a sloegasm,' giggled another woman who Zoe doesn't recognise.

'Mabel!' says Alice.

Mabel giggles again. 'That's what Milly herself called it.'

'She did,' chuckles another man, his teeth stained red from the wine.

'Your mother was a saint,' says the purple lady, addressing Steph, Sara and Zoe. 'She will be so missed.'

Steph grunts and takes a gulp of wine. Zoe paints on a smile and takes a sip of hers. 'We will miss her, that's for sure.'

'We all will,' says the woman with a stick. Zoe knows she should remember her name.

'She was always so kind to everyone. She seemed to have endless time. She played bridge with my mother and aunt every week for years. Once they were housebound she was almost their only visitor, apart from family and the nurses.'

That must be Mrs Cornford's daughter, thinks Zoe. She remembers her mother visiting them.

'No one plays bridge anymore,' grumbles the old man.

'Mum was still playing bridge a few months before she died,' says Zoe, taking a slug of wine.

Sara smiles. 'I remember her teaching me. I could never get the hang of it.'

'Your mother was an ace player,' slurs the man, holding out his glass for a refill. 'Hard to beat.'

A burst of laughter comes through from the drawing room into the hall. *There's just too much wine flowing*, thinks Zoe. They should have stopped topping up the glasses ages ago. Steph is leaning against the staircase. *How much has she had?*

'Let's all just agree that Milly was a saint,' says Mabel. 'I will really miss her. We should raise a toast.'

'Hardly a saint,' Steph mumbles.

Everyone's glasses freeze mid-air. They all stare at Steph, who looks down into her glass.

'What do you mean by that?' says Zoe, her jaw tense.

Steph takes another slurp of wine. 'Just that she's not as saint-like as everyone is making out.'

Sara licks her lips. 'I don't think this is really the time.' She hands Katy to John who has come up behind her, puts her glass down on the newel and reaches for Steph's arm. 'Let's go upstairs.'

Steph tips her head on one side. 'If now's not the time, then when is?' Her words are tripping over one another in her hurry to get them out. She takes another sip. 'Everyone's talking about Mum and how wonderful she was. I'm just saying that she wasn't always that wonderful. Just giving a balanced view.'

'Stephanie . . .' Alice stares at her, shaking her head. 'Not now.'

'It's never the right time though, is it?' Steph is properly slurring now. 'You're all making her into a saint and she wasn't.' She waves her hand around at the crowd of guests and catches the top of her wine glass against the banister. It falls to the floor, shattering, the pieces splintering across the hall, the wine like blood among the shards of glass.

The crowd gasps and retreats as two of the catering team rush forward to collect the pieces.

Steph stares at the stem of the shattered glass she's still clutching. 'Mum did some terrible, terrible things. Inhuman things.' Steph's face is twisted. She picks up Sara's half-full wine glass from the newel and gulps it down.

'Stop it,' shouts Zoe, the fizzing in her stomach moving into her throat. 'Just stop it. Can't you just be pleasant, be normal?' Alice's hand is on her arm.

'Normal,' shouts Steph, her breath rancid with alcohol and staleness. 'What the fuck is normal? This family's not normal, that's for sure.'

Out of the corner of her eye, Zoe sees people melting away, going slowly into the library to gather coats, their eyes wide. Fiona marches through the front door, a lit cigarette still in her hand. 'What's going on? What's all the shouting?'

'I'm just giving everyone some home truths,' says Steph. 'Everyone seems to think that Mum was a saint. Well, sometimes she could be a right bitch.'

The adrenalin surges through Zoe and her hand stings as it makes contact with Steph's cheek. The crack echoes around the hall and up on to the gallery. It feels good to defend Mum, to do something to make Steph stop. Zoe can't remember ever slapping anyone before, so she doesn't even think about taking evasive action. Then Steph's hand catches her straight on her right eye, the pain full and bright. Zoe staggers back and falls against the hall table, the abandoned wine glasses and canapé plates spiralling to the floor and skittering across the parquet in millions of pieces. Her head bounces off the parquet, and she feels dizzy.

'Oh my God.' Steph's face is in her hands and she sinks to the hall stair. 'Not again.'

Alice stands between them, flapping her hands.

Sara rushes over to Zoe and helps her up, picking the bigger pieces of glass out of her hair.

'Why did you slap her?' Sara asks Zoe. 'It's Mum's funeral, for God's sake.'

'You heard what she said about Mum,' says Zoe. 'On the day we're supposed to be celebrating her life.'

Steph mumbles something unintelligible from the staircase. Fiona is sitting next to her, her head in her hands.

Sara disappears into the kitchen. More catering staff appear with dustpans and brushes and cloths and try to clean up. One of Sara's daughters is crying. Zoe can hear the murmur of voices from the drawing room and from outside but everyone seems to be leaving. That's one good thing. She struggles to her feet, her hand bloodied from the broken glass. She pulls a splinter out of her palm, the pain fresh and a relief.

Fiona slips an arm around Steph's shoulders. 'I know your relationship with Mum was difficult.'

'She was awful to me.' Tears are sliding down Steph's cheeks, the imprint of Zoe's hand still visible.

Fiona looks up to the ceiling. 'You were awful to her too.'

Steph glances at her and clenches her hands.

'I was there,' Fiona says, staring Steph straight in the eye.

'I know,' Steph mutters. 'I don't know what happened really.'

Sara comes back from the kitchen with two glasses of ice. She wraps several pieces in napkins and passes one to Steph, who holds it against her cheek, and the other to Zoe who presses it against her eye, wincing at the cold and the pressure against the bruise she can feel forming.

Brushing glass shards off her dress, Zoe stands over Steph sitting on the bottom stair. 'How dare you say all that at her funeral,' she hisses. 'And in front of everyone Mum knew. She would be ashamed of you. She *was* ashamed of you, actually – that's why she sent you away.'

A surge of pleasure mixed with guilt fizzes through her as she sees the shock on Steph's face, and the open mouths of Fiona and Sara. Zoe runs up the stairs, across the gallery and into her old childhood bedroom, slamming the door behind her.

◆ ◆ ◆

Milly

1989

'We need to do something about Patrick. Things were fine before he got involved with Steph. If he wasn't around, it would go back to being fine.' Paul's red in the face, breathing heavily. I wonder if he's been drinking but I can't smell anything on his breath.

'What could we do?' I ask.

'Shoot him?' He laughs but it comes out wrong.

'Don't joke like that.' I get up from his desk and walk over to the library window.

'I'm not.'

There's a silence. There are lots of silences between us these days. And secrets.

'There's not much we can do, except try to talk to her. You know we can't keep her in.' But still. We have to do something, he's right.

Paul rubs his face. 'A twenty-four-year-old man is taking our fifteen-year-old daughter away from us, and you say there's nothing we can do?'

'The police are on it, you heard them. They're trying to build a case against him, and the others.' The whisky in the decanter has gone right down. Maybe he has been drinking.

'But that's for the protests, and nothing to do with our daughter. By the time they've caught up with him, Steph will be firmly in his clutches. If she isn't already.'

'I don't know what you're suggesting,' I say. 'That we go and talk to him? We don't know where he lives.'

'There are ways of finding him. Town's not that big. People will know.'

I breathe out. 'Just don't do anything that will upset Steph. If she finds out, she'll be really angry.' And I will bear the brunt of her anger.

'I'm not suggesting I kill him, although that's tempting.' He tries a laugh again. 'Just frighten him. Perhaps hurt him slightly. Not put him in a wheelchair or a grave.'

'Paul, stop.' I turn to face him. 'This is too much. Steph is almost sixteen. She's almost an adult, she can make her own decisions.'

'What if he wants to start sleeping with her? Would you be happy with that? A man sleeping with our daughter?'

I swallow. Jan mentioned that her sister had seen Steph in the family planning clinic. I think she only said it to shock me, but I was glad. At least she's being sensible. I just hope she remembers to take the pill every day. She's so chaotic and I worry she'll forget. But I don't want to remind her because then she'll know I know.

'Well?' Paul is looking at me. 'Do you want that man having sex with our daughter?' He has had a drink. There's no way he'd talked like that usually.

'She's almost an adult, Paul.'

'But she's not an adult. There's something about how she behaves – she doesn't act like a normal person.' I realise as he says this that it's true. I hadn't really formulated the thought properly before but there is something different about her. 'She's incredibly impulsive, you know that. She never thinks about the consequences of what she's doing. It's not normal.' He sighs and looks down at his desk.

'She's just a typical teenage girl,' I say, trying to dismiss it. 'They're all a bit difficult at this age. Other people I speak to say the same thing.' The room suddenly feels very stuffy and I try to open the sash window.

'Leave that to me, silly,' he says, coming up behind me and opening it easily. 'You can't do that with your arm in plaster. And knowing how clumsy you've become recently, you'll make the whole thing collapse on your head or something.' He laughs and looks a lot like the old Paul. I smile back and he kisses me briefly on the lips.

He slides back behind his desk and I stay by the window. I look down at my plaster cast. I feel broken by trying to hold it all together, mentally and physically. I can't talk to Paul about anything. Maybe I could talk to someone else. I think of Emma in the coffee shop all those months ago. I've avoided her since, and everyone else. Could I talk to her? Maybe I should try at least. She was once my closest friend.

◆ ◆ ◆

Emma hands me a bunch of flowers as she comes through the front door. 'It's so good to see you, Milly, it's been ages. I was really glad to get your note.'

In the kitchen, I busy myself with the kettle and arranging the flowers in a vase.

We sit down on chairs facing each other in the drawing room, the tray of tea on the side. 'I haven't been at Highdown for a long time,' she says. 'A couple of years, at least. I remember all the parties you used to have.'

It seems like such a long time ago that we've had people round. In the before time. But she's right, we used to host big parties here. Highdown would be full of noise and laughter, bowls of punch on the hall table, people spilling out into the garden, cigarette butts ground into the gravel and the lawn. Kids running between legs. In my mind it's like some kind of Gatsby-esque golden time. I can't ever imagine that again. Being relaxed enough to have people round, not worrying about what could happen.

'I miss those times,' I say, nodding. 'It was fun.' Everything was fun. Before.

'Maybe you should host a summer party,' she says, cradling her enormous bump. 'It would be lovely. I'd help.'

I shake my head. 'Things are a bit tricky at the moment.'

She glances at my plaster cast again. I saw her clock it the minute she walked in, the slight opening of her mouth, the widening of her eyes. 'Your arm?'

I lick my lips. 'It's not what you think,' I say. 'I fell down the stairs, missed my footing on the runner where it's frayed. I keep meaning to get it fixed.'

A quick smile, she accepts the lie, knows it's a lie. We both know it's a lie.

'It's been quite difficult ,' I begin. 'Steph's going through a tricky time.'

'Yes,' she says, her eyes soft. 'I'm so sorry about that, it must be very hard.'

I wonder how much she knows. How much everyone knows.

'It feels like it's more than the usual teenage angst,' I say.

She tips her head to the side but doesn't say anything.

'It feels like she's gone completely off the rails in the last couple of years,' I start. 'She's so far off the rails, she's in another county.' I laugh in the way that I know Paul hates. But I have to laugh or I'll just be permanently crying.

'What's been happening, Milly?' Emma leans forward and touches my knee.

I lick my lips. 'Well, I guess it started with just the normal stroppiness. You know, rudeness and so on.'

She nods.

'But it's sort of escalated. She fell in with the wrong crowd. Actually, I don't know whether they are the wrong crowd. They're animal-rights activists. I've looked into it, and learned a lot from Steph, and I broadly support what they are arguing for. You know, that we shouldn't test products on animals, that we should treat all animals with respect.' I see her glance at the stag heads on the wall. 'I agree with all of that,' I repeat. 'But it's the way they go about it. Violence and so on.'

'It's good to have a cause, Milly. At least she's passionate about something. Most girls don't think beyond whatever's in *Just Seventeen*.'

'It's not just that, though.' I take a deep breath to steady myself. 'In some ways, I think she became involved in the group for the sheer excitement of it all. No, that's wrong. She's always been very passionate about animals. Do you remember when she took Mrs Petworth's pet rabbit out of its cage, and released it into the woods, because she thought she'd been mistreating it?'

Emma takes a sip of tea. 'Oh yes, Brenda was furious. But to be fair to Stephanie, she wasn't looking after that rabbit properly.'

'Yes, she's always been into animals, but it feels like she's used that as a sort of excuse to become more extreme.'

'Extreme.' Emma's eyes are wide now, and I see her glance at my wrist. She's guessed what's coming, maybe.

'It started with small things. Just shouting at me, swearing sometimes. But it's built up over the past few months, years.' I stop and look out of the window. Terry is walking along the wall of the formal garden, delicately putting one paw in front of the other.

'She started pushing me when we were arguing. And then I tried to stop her leaving one day and she caught me with a paint can on the side of my head.'

'A paint can?' Emma whispers.

'And it's just gone from there.' I hold up my wrist.

'Oh, Milly.' Emma slides on to the settee next to me and puts her arm around me. 'I'm so sorry, I thought—' She shakes her head a fraction. 'I didn't realise it was Steph.'

I give her a sad smile. 'It's unthinkable, isn't it? That your own child would hurt you.'

She nods, and I can see that she's trying to work it out in her mind.

'Please don't tell anyone about this. I can't have this getting around, it's just too awful.'

Emma shakes her head. 'Of course not, Milly. I'm one of your best friends, I won't tell a soul.'

I swallow. 'It feels like it's getting worse. The incidents are bigger and it's happening more often. I feel like I can't cope.' Saying the words out loud makes it feel more real. I can't cope. My mouth has articulated what my brain has been afraid to admit.

'What are you going to do? Can Paul help? What's Stephanie like with him?'

I sigh. 'I can't talk to him. I worry that if I say anything to him about what she's doing he'll send her away or something. Or worse.' I think of the look on his face after the paint can incident. 'So I've lied, told him the injuries are accidents.'

'So Steph only hurts you when you're on your own?'

I nod. She's rude and difficult in front of Paul, but only violent when it's just the two of us. Or am I imagining that? 'I'm frightened of her. And frightened about what the future holds for her.'

We sit there in silence for a while, letting the words settle around us.

'The strange thing is, just as I think I can't face anymore, that I'm going to call up the police and ask them to take her away or walk away myself, she comes up, the anger completely gone, and gives me a hug and says, "I love you, Mum".'

I bury my head in Emma's shoulder and sob.

'I feel so ashamed. Of what she's doing but also that I've failed as a mum.'

'Oh, Milly.' She strokes my back. 'I had no idea. I thought Paul . . .'

'It would be easier if it was Paul in a way,' I say through the tears. 'I could walk away or make him leave. There are places to go. Like you told me about. But you can't leave your own child, even when they're hurting you.' I lean back. 'It's not even something you can talk about openly.'

'Where's Steph now?'

I shrug. 'I don't know. I last saw her the day before yesterday. She wasn't there when I went to pick her up from school. I worry so much. What's she doing? Is she safe? But then when she's here I worry for me.'

'And how are the other girls?'

'I worry for Fiona too.' The school said the other day that Fiona's not playing with her friends and not listening in lessons. With everything that's going on I haven't paid her enough attention.

'You think Steph would hurt her?'

I shake my head. 'No. Never.' I somehow know that instinctively. 'It's just me.'

'This is impossible Milly. What are you going to do?'

Chapter 10

Zoe

Spring 2025

Whichever side faces up, Zoe's pillow always feels hot and clammy. The hours tick by, punctuated by the village church. Two, three, four. She shouldn't have said it. What was she thinking? She was just so shocked that Steph hit her back. It was like something out of a soap opera. Zoe presses her fingertip into her eye socket, enjoying the spongy tenderness of the bruise.

Highdown Hall is silent now. From her bedroom window, she watched the last of the guests hurry away yesterday evening. She heard Fiona's voice calmly ordering the house back to normal. The catering van eventually left, then the drone of the vacuum seemed to go on forever. It would be Sara doing that, unless she'd gone home with John and their daughters. Or maybe Steph. Steph. She sighs, touching her eye again.

Why did Steph say such terrible things about Mum? She knew they had a strained relationship at times, but to call her a bitch at her own funeral. It was awful. Zoe takes a deep breath. But Zoe shouldn't have slapped her, and then said Mum was ashamed of her. That isn't true either. They both behaved really badly.

Mum struggled with Steph, Zoe knows that. She hadn't really understood Steph. Years ago, when Zoe was at sixth form, Mum thanked Zoe for being such a good teenager, an easy teenager. Zoe laughed at the time and asked Mum what she'd expected. All-night parties, nights in the cells and teenage pregnancies? Mum had paled and forced a laugh and called her a silly thing. Obviously Steph's teenage years hadn't been so straightforward.

Zoe lay on her bed last night waiting for one of them to come to see her. Not Steph, obviously. But she thought maybe Sara or Fiona. After several hours, she realised they were leaving her alone. Maybe they blamed her? As she stands at the window staring out towards the dark woods, Zoe realises they would be right to. Steph was drunk, emotional. She should have taken her away upstairs, not publicly confronted her and slapped her. And then she said those awful things.

She feels her eye again and yawns. She's so tired, but just can't sleep. She's desperate for the loo. She didn't dare to show her face last night in case Steph was on the gallery. Zoe creeps out of her room, avoiding the creaky boards, and goes into the bathroom. She slides the lock, and looks at herself in the mirror, the moonlight highlighting the darkness of her right eye. It's already bruising.

Downstairs, everything's immaculate. You would never know that several hundred people crowded into these rooms yesterday, eating, drinking, smoking, fighting.

Two plates are stacked on the draining board. They must have had supper after everyone left. In the fridge are clingfilmed leftovers from the wake. Zoe's tummy rumbles and she takes out a platter, selecting the mini falafel and humous wraps. Sitting at the kitchen table, she works her way through them, washing them down with tap water. As she puts the platter back, the light from the fridge catches on a folded piece of paper on the table. It's been torn from her father's writing pad in the library.

She unfolds it. Unfamiliar handwriting scrawls across the thick paper.

Dear all,

I'm so sorry about yesterday. I didn't mean all those things I said about Mum. I don't know why I said them – I found the whole day horribly stressful and drank too much to try to cope with all the people and noise. It was overwhelming. I'm sorry I hit you, Zoe. You were right to say those things and I think they're true. Mum was ashamed of me. I was always the difficult one, the one who messed things up and that's why she sent me away. And I've messed things up again.

I think it's better if I don't stay for the interment. It will just be awkward for you all and give other people more chance to gossip. I don't want to cause more damage than I already have.

The last few days have been some of the happiest I've ever had in this house. I never thought I'd say it but being here with you has been unexpectedly wonderful. You are all great people.

I'm not sure we'll ever be together like this again. With Mum gone, it feels like the end of an era. Fiona, when you speak to the solicitor, please arrange for my share of Highdown to go to Zoe. That feels right and proper. I'll sign anything that's needed.

Love always,

Steph

Oh God, thinks Zoe, covering her mouth with her hand. *Poor Steph.* She surely can't have left already. Zoe rushes out the back door but there's a gap between Sara's four-by-four and the estate's old Land Rover where Steph's van was. She must have waited until she'd sobered up enough to drive.

Zoe glances at the Land Rover. The nearside tyre is completely flat, she's been meaning to do something about it for ages. There's no way she can follow Steph. And she wouldn't have a clue how to drive Sara's posh car. The kitchen clock says five thirty. It's too early to wake the others. *What a mess.*

Zoe goes back upstairs slowly, pausing at where she slapped Steph and Steph then punched her. Their mother would have been so ashamed of them behaving like kids, fighting in the hall. And in front of everyone. The early morning light seeps through the gap in her curtains and she pulls them tight, sliding between the bed covers and turning the pillow over.

She knows sleep won't come. She'll just lie here until it's seven and then she'll wake Fiona and Sara. Fiona will know what to do. She always does.

It's all her fault, she thinks.

It's bright daylight by the time she wakes, groggy with interrupted sleep. Zoe sits up with a start. She stares at the alarm clock. Ten o'clock. Ten! How could she have fallen asleep for so long?

She must speak to Fiona, talk about what to do next. But when she goes downstairs, having hurriedly pulled on an old pair of dungarees, there's no one around. She goes back up and checks their bedrooms, but the beds have been made, the curtains drawn. Downstairs, she sees two empty mugs on the drainer. At the back door, she realises Sara's car has gone. They must have gone to find Steph. *Thank God.* There's a note on the kitchen table but it's only Steph's original note. She sinks into the kitchen chair. Why didn't they wake her, or at least leave a note? She goes into the hall, waits for the signal on her phone to kick in, but there's no message.

She paces the hall waiting for something to happen but it's all quiet. The grandfather clock goes through its quarter-hour routine. It's the first time she's been in her house on her own for months and months. Above her the DeProse ancestors watch her, just as they watched her and Steph fighting yesterday. She can sense their disapproval. *Sorry, Mum.* She thought she'd talk to Mum all the time after she died, have proper conversations, but she hasn't felt her presence at all. She sighs. Maybe she'll come when everyone has gone home.

She goes out on to the drive but there's no one there, no sign of anyone. It's like she's the last person in the world. She sits on the bench and something digs into her thigh. The keys to the oast house. She could move back in there now that Mum's gone. But there was something rather wonderful about the four of them in the house together. Until she messed it up. Looking at the small ornate key makes her think of the other key. The mystery key, which still hasn't turned up. *Kai. Kylie and Kai.* Who are they? And who took the key? It must be one of her sisters, it couldn't have been anyone else.

She needs to be doing something. She walks around the back of the house past the walled garden and looks at the locks on the three old barns, but she knows the Kai key would never fit them. Then she walks across the lawn to the summer house, but the lock there is far too small. By the herb garden is the garden shed and the greenhouse but it doesn't look like it would fit either of those. She knows it won't fit the oast house. She listens out for cars but there's just birdsong. If she sees a potential lock, she can't even try the key out.

She walks up to the cottages, slightly out of breath by the time she reaches them. Mrs Crawford is planting herbs in pots in her front garden.

'Hello, Zoe,' she says, standing up and brushing her apron. 'That was a very beautiful service yesterday. Very traditional, just like your mum would have wanted.'

Zoe nods. 'Thank you.' If Mrs Crawford witnessed the fight, she doesn't say anything. Zoe looks at the front door of the cottage but even from this distance she can see that the key would be far too large for the slim lock. All the cottage doors are the same, so the key can't be for any of them.

Mrs Crawford puts her hands in her skirt pockets. 'There's no rush on this, but I wondered if you'd got my email. The shower hasn't been working for a while. The electricity arced in the bathroom again and set fire to the shower switch. We haven't been able to use it since. Could you get the same man back again? I don't mind contacting him. I know you're busy . . .'

She has a vague memory of an email. 'I'm so sorry,' Zoe says, examining her hands. 'It's been such a difficult time.'

'I understand. Are you happy for me to contact the electrician again?'

'Of course,' Zoe muttered.

'I'm sorry to bother you with it all, at a time like this,' Mrs Crawford says. 'It's just that it's been a couple of months now . . .'

Zoe pulls her face into a smile. 'Don't be silly, of course you should.' She looks around for something else to say. 'Your garden looks beautiful.' It's true. The little cottage garden is already a kaleidoscope of colours and it is only April. Rosebuds have formed along the wall, and shoots of delphiniums, hollyhocks and foxgloves are competing to be the tallest. The lavender along the path is bursting into life. Climbing roses and clematis are curling around the old wooden door. It's worrying how early everything comes out these days.

'Thank you, dear. Your mother and I loved our gardens.'

Zoe smiles and turns away. She planned to walk around the cottages but now she remembers another unanswered email about a broken back door. And didn't the new tenants at Jasmine Cottage mention something about an overflowing drain the other day when she bumped into them in the village? She can't face anyone else and turns back in the direction of the house.

Eventually she finds herself by the pond again and sits on the stone lip, trailing her hands through the thick green algae. It's surprisingly warm. Maybe the algae keeps it warm, she's not sure how it works. She'll look it up one day.

When she was a child, they had fish in here. But that seemed too cruel. *It was too small a pond for fish*, she thinks. Now tadpoles come here naturally and then turn into frogs. Missy seems to instinctively know when they are due and sits on the side of the pond, her paw poised to grab them as they take their first tentative hops. Nature is cruel.

She wonders if they're back yet, if they managed to persuade Steph to come home. Home. Is this Steph's home? Is home the place you grow up in, or where you choose to live as an adult? They must be home by now, it's only ten miles to Steph's place. But when she rushes on to the drive, already breathless, Sara's car still isn't there. Her heart thuds. Steph must be refusing to come back. And that will be her fault.

There's a figure on the drive and she starts. But it's only Alice. She hugs Zoe. 'I've just come to see if you're all okay,' she says.

Zoe shakes her head and then starts to cry. Alice draws her into another hug, patting her on the back like a child. 'C'mon, let's go inside.'

'I messed up,' says Zoe, falling into a chair at the kitchen table as Alice makes tea. 'I can't think why I slapped Steph, it was an awful thing to do. And now she's left and she won't come back. I know she won't.'

Alice puts two mugs on the table and reads Steph's note. She rubs her face and suddenly looks very tired.

'It's my fault, isn't it?' says Zoe, holding the mug.

Alice shakes her head. 'It's not your fault,' she says. 'You should all have sat down and talked a long time ago,' she says. 'You, your sisters and your parents. There's been far too much sweeping things under the carpet. And it's come to this . . .' She waves her hand at Steph's note. 'And yesterday.'

'Mum would have been so angry, wouldn't she? That we behaved like that.'

Alice nods slowly. 'Yes. But your mother is not blameless in this. And nor is your father.' Zoe looks up at her, her head tipped to one side. *What does she mean?*

She's about to ask her when there's a scrunch of tyres on the gravel and the sound of a car engine. Zoe jumps to her feet and rushes into the hall. There are three silhouettes in Sara's car. *Thank God.*

'She's here,' Zoe calls over her shoulder to Alice and runs back into the kitchen, suddenly worried that the three of them will see her watching.

'Good,' says Alice. 'Now perhaps the four of you can start to talk.'

◆ ◆ ◆

Milly

1989

I crack open Steph's door. It's the usual riot. Clothes strewn all over the four-poster bed, paper covering the desk and much of the floor. On the dressing table is some black eye pencil I haven't noticed before, fresh pencil shavings crushed next to it. I pick up Fiona's Barbie pencil sharpener and put it in my pocket. She'll never see that again otherwise. Steph's terrible at taking other people's things and forgetting to return them.

The tie-dye material Steph's rigged up for curtains for the four-poster is actually an improvement on the heavy brocade curtains that used to hang there. They made the room so dark. I wonder where she put them, they're probably valuable. I should really pack them up properly and put them in the attic. Now it's a clash of purple and pink, blue and black. Somehow it suits Steph. The pile of laundry Alice put on the bed yesterday has tipped over. It looks like Steph slept on some of it. I start picking up t-shirts – brushing off cat hair – folding them and sliding them into drawers. Inside the drawers themselves, everything is a tangle of fabric. I pick out my striped blue and white t-shirt – I wondered where that had gone – and throw it by the door. At the back of the top drawer is the unopened tube of eczema cream. Steph refuses to use it, even though her skin is terrible, because the company tests other products on animals. And meanwhile her hands are red raw and getting worse. The lavender salve I bought from the health food shop does nothing. I want to cry with frustration, but there's no point. I put the cream on top of the chest of drawers in case she changes her mind. Maybe I can sneak it into the lavender salve when she lets me dress and bandage her hands.

It feels soothing to reorganise everything. Pants, bras and socks at the top, t-shirts and jumpers in the next drawer and jeans and leggings underneath. There are dirty knickers under the bed, some stained with period blood. I throw them into the empty washing basket. There's the purple t-shirt she was looking for last week and said she'd looked everywhere for. I'll wash it and get it ready for when she's back. She's always losing things, I've never known anyone like it. The other two girls are so different.

She liked it the last time I sorted her room out for her. Said that it was such a relief for it to be tidy – she gets overwhelmed with the mess and doesn't know where to start. I can understand that. Maybe this will help her and bring us closer together.

The paper on the floor is covered in doodles. It looks like the start of more protest posters. But as I get closer I realise it's Steph writing her name over and over again. But instead of Stephanie Wright, she's written Stephanie Head. Patrick's name. Stephanie Head. Stephanie Head. Stephanie Head. It's suddenly hard to breathe. The others are protest posters and I carefully stack them together on her desk and put the felt tips back in the chipped mug. I don't want to look at the doodles. Stephanie Head. At least she's passionate about something. Some teenage girls are only interested in the latest make-up and perfumes, at least Steph has a cause. That's what Emma said. I should be grateful.

She frustrates me at every turn but I can also feel so proud of her, of how different she is from other girls her age. Carving out her own path and not following others. Stephanie Head. It's just a childish thing. We've all done it. I did it with Paul's name when we first met. Writing Milly Wright for the first time was exciting, made me feel so grown-up. So much more normal than Camilla DeProse. That's what it's about, that's all. But Patrick is nine years older than her. A man. And we've still never met him. He's an ethereal figure floating round the edges of our lives.

Both bedside tables are covered in half-filled mugs of tea, one with a mouldy top, which I gather up and put outside the door together with two plates of crusts and a half-eaten apple, brown with age. The coffee rings look ingrained into the wood but maybe Alice will be able to do something about them. The drawer of the dressing table is half open, and the glint of something metallic draws my attention. Before I even think about it, I've opened the drawer and am staring at three condoms in shiny red wrappers.

My arm feels heavy as I reach out to touch them. They weren't here before, when I last looked. I'm shocked at the visible confirmation that she's having sex. I'm about to close the drawer when I spot a tiny plastic bag at the back of the drawer. I open the drawer completely and take out a small bag of browny-green crumbly stuff. Hash. My fingers get stuck trying to open it, but the woody, earthy smell is familiar. Paul and I shared the occasional joint when we were first together. Steph is only fifteen. *Bloody hell.* I reseal the bag and put it in my pocket. I can't leave it here, it's illegal for starters. I rub my face and stand up, closing the drawer.

On the gallery, Mum stares down at me disapprovingly. Alice is in the kitchen crashing around with dishes, Paul sounds like he's on the phone. Not that I'd tell him about the condoms – that will just be between Steph and I – but he should know about the hash. I take the plates and cups downstairs and leave them on the hall table. I can't face talking to Alice so I go up the back staircase to tidy the playroom. It's hardly changed since I was a girl, though Mum called it a nursery then. The doll's cot that Josie and I played with still sits in the middle of the rug, a tangle of dolls under an old tea towel. I haven't thought of her for a long time. Would things be easier now if she'd lived? She would be someone to share things with, moan about our parents to? The wall is covered with Sara's drawings, with a favourite few of Fiona and Steph's on the cupboards. I touch Steph's drawing of Highdown drawn ten years ago. Three pencil figures standing outside, one with an exaggerated pregnant belly. They were happy days.

Next door, the sewing machine gathers dust, the pile of offcuts still waiting for me to make the patchwork quilt I talked about when Fiona was born. The smaller rooms are barely touched these days, it seems such a waste. We really should do something with them. I wander downstairs back on to the gallery just as the front door slams. *Steph.*

She looks washed out as she drags herself up the stairs, her bag falling off her shoulder. 'You're early,' I say. 'What happened? Are you okay?'

'I didn't feel great so they let me go home.'

'You should have called. I would have picked you up.'

She shrugs and pushes past me.

'How did you get home?' I ask, but she's already inside her bedroom, the door shutting.

She could have taken the bus, I suppose. But she hates the bus.

Her bedroom door opens again, and she stands in the doorway. 'What's happened to my room?' she says, her voice quiet, face blank. I smile and walk towards her. Maybe this can be the start of repairing things.

She flinches as I put my hand on her arm but doesn't move it away. 'I tidied it up for you. I remember you saying that it was overwhelming when it was so messy, so I did it for you.' I walk past her into the bedroom and open the chest of drawers. 'Look, I've reorganised all your clothes so it'll be easier for you to find everything. Bras and pants are in the top drawer, socks next to them.' I smile over my shoulder at her but she just stands there looking around the room.

'I liked it as it was,' she says. 'I liked it as it was. You had no right.' Her voice gets louder.

My heart starts thudding and I close the drawer. 'But you liked it when I did it last time. You said it helped.' I try a smile, but her eyes have darkened to a deep grey, almost black. I step back.

'I liked it like it was,' she screams. She pushes the pile of paper off the desk and it confettis to the rug. She pulls the quilt off the bed and stamps on it. Then she advances towards me, and pulls a drawer from the chest of drawers, throwing all the carefully folded t-shirts on the floor. She throws the empty drawer across the room and there's a sound of splintering wood.

I swallow and try to edge past her. 'I'm sorry, I didn't mean to upset you. I thought it would help.'

'You thought it would help to touch all my stuff?' she shouts, her spit flicking on to my face. Her mouth is contorted. Suddenly her hands are around my throat and she pushes me up against the wall. 'I hate you. You're ruining my life. I'd be much better off without you.'

I'm choking and try to pull at her hands. But she's stronger and taller than me, and my wrist still isn't properly healed. Black stars dance in front of my eyes. I can't breathe. I try to remember what Mum said when I learned to swim. That you can be for a while without air so long as you don't panic. But her hands are tight around my throat, it feels like something's going to snap. Can your throat snap? I grip her hands, not wanting to hurt her but desperate now to breathe.

She lets go as suddenly as she grabbed me and slams the heel of her hand into my throat. The impact pushes me backwards towards the door and I fall out on to the gallery, staggering, retching.

Back in my bedroom I kneel in front of my bed, burying my head in the duvet. She could have killed me. A few more seconds and I would have been in a crumpled heap, dead on her floor. I can't swallow and my throat feels like it's on fire. In the bathroom mirror my neck is bright red. I trace the scratch on one side, probably made by me trying to get her hands away. She tried to strangle me. I sit fully clothed on the loo, my head in my hands, tears pricking my eyes.

'Milly?' Paul is on the gallery coming towards the bedroom. I push the bathroom door shut and slide the lock across.

'I'll be down in a minute.' I don't recognise my voice – it's hoarse, raspy, as if I've smoked ten packets of cigarettes.

'You okay?' He's right outside the bathroom door. 'I heard shouting.'

'Yes, fine,' I say with as much enthusiasm as I can.

He's fiddling about with something in the bedroom and then I hear him on the gallery again. He's talking to someone. Steph, maybe?

I get up and go back into the bedroom. If I tell him what just happened, he'll go mad. In the top drawer of the chest of drawers is a collection of Mum's old silk scarves. I wrap one around my neck, finishing with a knot. It covers the worst of it.

I can't hear what they're saying. Steph's door is open and they're standing inside. I glance in on the way past – the t-shirts are still on the floor.

'You need to tidy this room up, pumpkin,' Paul says, using the childhood name Steph hates. But she doesn't react.

I glance in Fiona's room and everything is lined up meticulously. 'That scarf's pretty,' Paul says, catching me up, and putting his arm around my waist. We walk down the stairs together. 'You should have seen Steph's room, what a mess.'

I force my face into a smile.

In the hall he turns to face me. 'You okay?' he asks, his hands either side of my face. It reminds me of Steph holding my neck earlier and I shudder but try to turn it into a nod.

'You look like you've been crying.'

I shake my head and try to smile again. I don't trust myself to speak.

'Okay then,' he says, but I can see the concern in his eyes. 'I've got a bit more paperwork to get through then I thought I'd go over to the Cornfords' to talk about the new boundaries. Fancy coming with me? It's a beautiful day.'

He's right. Outside the sky is a brilliant blue. I nod. He kisses me on the forehead, like my father used to do, and disappears into the library. I can hear Steph crashing around upstairs so I walk out of the front door and head towards the woods.

Chapter 11

Zoe

Spring 2025

'I'm starving. We haven't eaten since those canapés yesterday.' Sara's voice comes through the front door.

'I told you to stop at that petrol station. We could have grabbed something.' Fiona.

Zoe sits at the kitchen table, her knuckles white against the mug. Alice touches her on the shoulder and then slips out the back door. Zoe wants her to stay, to help.

'There's a lot of leftovers from yesterday. We can start . . .' Steph's voice trails off as she sees Zoe at the table.

Zoe rises from her chair. 'Hi,' she says.

Steph swallows and looks down. 'I'm so sorry,' she says. 'For hitting you. Your poor face.' She comes towards Zoe as if to touch her eye and then stops a metre away.

'I'm so glad you came back.' Zoe steps into the distance between them and then suddenly they're hugging. Steph grips her tightly and Zoe winces as her eye catches the button on Steph's shirt. She draws away. 'I should never have said those things. I didn't mean them, and they're not true.'

'I think they are true,' says Steph, nodding. 'But thank you for saying that.'

Fiona and Sara stand in the doorway of the kitchen watching.

'I'm sorry to both of you too,' adds Zoe. 'For messing it all up yesterday.'

Sara squeezes her arm and starts taking more leftovers out of the fridge and putting plates and cutlery in the middle of the table.

Fiona nods and fills up small tumblers from the tap. 'I should never have ordered so much booze and so little food. Everyone was plastered, including you two,' she says, looking between Zoe and Steph. 'But the main thing is that we're all here together. Perhaps we can use the time between now and the interment to talk things over and get a few things out in the open.'

The four of them sit down and start picking through the leftovers.

'I know I've already said it, but I'm sorry I said those things, Steph. They're really not true. Mum wasn't ashamed of you at all.' Zoe picks up the pieces of falafel that have fallen out of the wrap. As she says it, she wonders again if it's true. Mum always talked about Steph differently.

Steph puts her sandwich down. 'We've never really talked about those years,' she says, glancing up at Fiona. 'I'm not sure how much you remember, Sara, but I know you do, Fi.'

'Yes,' says Fiona, taking a sip of water. 'I remember.'

'Remember what?' says Sara, spearing a cocktail sausage.

'It was difficult for a while,' says Steph, not looking at anyone.

'You and Mum had a pretty strained relationship,' says Fiona eventually. 'The others don't remember because they were too young. But I do.'

'Yeah,' says Steph, looking down at her hands. 'That's why, when you said what you said yesterday, Zoe, I flipped. It just brought it all back.'

Zoe swallows. The air feels thick.

'I remember you and Mum shouting at each other once,' says Sara, suddenly sounding very young.

Fiona looks like she's going to say something but doesn't.

'Yes,' says Steph, getting up from the table and standing at the kitchen window. 'It felt like the minute I became a teenager I couldn't do anything right in her eyes.'

'I'm not sure that's fair,' says Fiona, pushing her hair from her face. 'You were awful to her.' Fiona stares at Steph's back.

'Please don't,' says Steph without looking at Fiona.

'Why not? It's true. You were—' She takes a deep breath. 'You were violent towards Mum. I was there. I saw it. You broke her arm that time.'

'Mum said things were bad, but I didn't realise they were that bad,' says Zoe, her eyes wide. 'You broke her arm. How?'

'It's like I've blocked it all out,' says Steph.

'Nobody ever talked about it at the time, or afterwards, but you were scary,' says Fiona again. 'I don't want to be negative but we never talked about it and I think we should now.'

'I didn't mean to be. It wasn't like that,' says Steph, not looking up.

'I can't imagine any of my kids being violent towards me,' says Sara.

'I really struggled as a teenager,' Steph says, looking directly at Sara, before sitting down and tracing the grain of the wood on the table with her fingers. 'I can't explain it now. I can't even really remember it that well. Just this incredible restlessness and anxiety. Mum didn't get me and I couldn't understand her. I hate to think of the times I hurt her but—' She swallows and then carries on. 'Looking back, I know that a lot of the things I did – like staying out all night – must have been awful for her. But I just didn't think at the time. It's not like I was out partying, drinking and taking drugs. I was trying to make a difference, protesting, or going on raids or whatever.' Her voice trails off.

'You not coming home was worse, I think. The worry.' Fiona taps her fingers on the canapé platter. 'The first time it happened, Mum was beside herself. She kept coming into my room and asking if I knew where you were, or who you were with.'

'I'm sorry, Fi,' says Steph quietly, her eyes downcast. 'I didn't think of you being in that position.'

'I can't imagine what it must have been like for Mum if you stayed out all night,' says Sara. 'I'd be terrified if one of my children did that.'

Fiona sighs. 'Mum and Dad were so worried all the time. The police came, some of the neighbours came with torches and volunteered to search for you. It was horribly, horribly scary and stressful. I couldn't sleep when you were away. I was frightened of what you might have been doing, frightened of what Mum might do because she seemed like she was going crazy. She never slept either.'

'I remember it,' says Sara suddenly. 'On the drive, all the flashing lights. It must have woken me up.'

Steph's face is blank. A splash of colour stains her cheeks and she looks back into the hall. 'It wasn't something I believed I could control. It just happened. I'd get so angry that my body just took over. I couldn't help it. It sounds silly but it was like it wasn't me. I could feel it inside me yesterday, that flare of anger that I haven't had in years and years.' She catches Zoe's eye.

'Is that why you went away to boarding school then?' asks Sara.

Steph looks away. 'Probably. That first year at boarding school was awful. But being away helped a bit. And then afterwards, when I got the job at the rescue centre, I felt I found my place. Those animals, especially the injured dogs, needed someone to love them unconditionally. And they loved me back. In a way I never felt Mum did.'

'Oh, Steph.' Sara reaches forward and touches Steph's hand. 'Have you thought that you might be neurodiverse?' she says gently. 'Something like autism or ADHD? I've been looking into it because of one of the twins.'

Steph crosses her arms across her chest. 'Why do you say that?'

'Just that what you're describing sounds like it might be ADHD, and what I've seen of you this past week feels like you're wired differently. Not in a bad way, just different. I see it in Izzie.'

'I thought that too,' says Zoe, nodding.

'It might explain a lot,' says Fiona.

Steph glances between her three sisters. 'I've always felt different from other people. I never really understand why people do the things they do and then realise I've misinterpreted things and get really angry. So I tend to avoid other people.'

'It might be worth talking to a doctor about it, seeing if you can get a diagnosis?' Sara says.

'Maybe, though I'm not sure a diagnosis will change anything,' says Steph.

'Maybe not,' says Sara. 'But it might help you to understand yourself better. And forgive yourself.'

Steph wipes her eyes with the back of her hand. Zoe is close to tears.

'I really regret that Mum and I weren't close. That we never talked about things,' says Steph. 'And now it's too late. All this time we lived ten miles apart and we never spoke. I should have made the effort. Being here has made me realise that. She was my mum.'

There's a long silence, then Sara blows her nose.

'Being back here has made me think about it all again too,' says Fiona, biting her lip. 'I haven't thought about it for years and years. I think perhaps me going to Singapore was me running away from it all. I'd never realised that until now.'

'I don't remember it being like that at all. I had a happy childhood,' says Zoe.

'It was different with you. I think Mum felt she had a second chance,' says Fiona.

Steph opens her mouth to speak but then says nothing.

The four of them sit in silence for a while, picking at the food on the platters. 'We should spend the afternoon doing some more clearing out,' Sara says.

'Good idea,' says Fiona. 'Come on.' The chair squeaks as she pushes it along the floor.

◆ ◆ ◆

'Let's share our favourite memories of Mum,' says Sara. 'That would be a nice thing to do while we sort out her clothes. Something she would have wanted.'

Zoe looks at her. She knows she's trying to make everything right again, to take them all back to the morning of the funeral, before the unsayable was said. Somehow it feels that more should have been said. That they have only skated over the top of everything. Maybe they'll have a chance to talk more, before the interment. Maybe over a bottle of wine one evening. But just the one bottle this time.

Mum seems to have had a lot of clothes, although she only wore a few outfits over the past year or so. Her world shrunk after she became unwell.

'Good idea,' says Fiona, holding up a twenties-style flapper dress. 'This is exquisite. We should keep things like this. It's almost a family heirloom.'

It feels like the four of them have been here forever, although it's only been ten days. How easily they've slipped again into the routine of being sisters, a slight jostling for position, but with no parents left to tell them off.

Sara looks out of the bedroom window. 'It's just so hard to remember that far back.'

'It doesn't have to be from your childhood. Anything,' says Fiona, hanging up the dress on the back of the door, near the 'to keep' pile. Zoe leans forward from her mother's chest of drawers where she's sorting through her socks and tights, watching Sara.

'Well, I guess I remember when I had Charlotte and Izzie. She came to the house when I was in labour. In fact, she'd come once before but it was a false alarm. But this time it felt different and I called her straight away and she was brilliant. She helped me get to hospital and stayed all the way through. We must have been up about sixty hours by the time they were born. John kept taking himself off to sleep, but she was constantly there. Holding my hand, making me drink and eat, encouraging me. And when the twins were checked over and came back, her face.' Sara sniffs again and her eyes fill. 'She was so proud to be a granny.'

Zoe glances at the photo of Sara and the three girls on her mum's bedside table. Her mum had been looking at that a few days before she died. Zoe's stomach twists.

'And then Katy arrived. She wasn't with me for her, but she looked after the twins with Sheri, John's mum. Seeing her with my girls is – was my favourite thing.' Sara's properly crying now, and takes a crumpled tissue out of her bag and blows her nose.

'Mum often talked about your kids,' says Zoe. It shouldn't hurt to say that, but it does. Sara gave their mum something that Zoe probably never will. She thought she might with Ben, but that didn't happen.

Steph holds up a grey Fair Isle jumper. 'I remember Mum wearing this. I loved it, it was so cuddly.' *She looks almost wistful*, thinks Zoe.

'Your turn,' says Sara, looking towards Fiona.

Fiona bites her lip. 'Well, I haven't seen much of Mum these last few years, not since we left the UK. But I did like Zooming her.' She looks to Zoe, for confirmation. Zoe smiles. Mum enjoyed those Zoom calls, she realises that now. Fiona looks back to the dress, hanging from the door.

'It's actually a really small thing. Just a moment. It was a long time ago.' She takes a deep breath. 'I was in my room playing that Bluebells song "Young at Heart".' She looks at her sisters. '*Yooooouuuung at heart*,' she starts to sing quietly.

'I remember that,' says Steph.

Fiona glances at her and looks away. 'Well, I was playing it, probably quite loud. I was on the bed dancing, using my hairbrush as a microphone. Don't laugh,' she says to Zoe.

'Sorry, it just doesn't fit with how you are now.'

Fiona shakes her head. 'Anyway, she came in, and I thought she was going to tell me off. But she picked up my deodorant can and started dancing with me and singing at the top of her voice. *Youuuuung at heart*.' Her voice breaks on the last note. 'We danced and sang and when the song ended, she just put the can down as if nothing had happened and told me lunch was ready.'

'That's a lovely memory,' says Sara, squeezing her hand. Fiona grins at her. 'I suppose she was quite young really. She was what, only twenty-five when she had you, Steph, so she spent her twenties and thirties having babies, and just when we'd started to grow up and get easier she had Zoe in her forties. It wasn't until she was in her fifties she could actually start to do things just for her.'

Zoe thinks back to the conversation she overheard at the parish fete. Her being a happy accident. 'I have so many favourite memories of Mum,' she says quickly. She flicks through them in her mind but every time she focuses on one, it doesn't seem to be enough. It's not perfect, there's always a flaw. And the memory of that woman saying she was a happy accident . . .

'I suppose sitting with someone at the end of their life is a privilege. Not a happy memory, but it was good to be there with her right at the end.' Zoe pushes away the thought of the plate of toast and marmalade.

'It is a privilege. And it was so good you could be with her, that she didn't die alone,' says Sara, taking Zoe's hand. 'But think of something happier.'

Then suddenly it's there. School sports day. 'I was about eight and we were doing a three-legged mother-and-daughter race. We came last because we kept falling over. We were so far behind that they stopped the race before we'd even got to the halfway point. Mum just couldn't stop laughing. It was . . .' She can't swallow the lump in her throat and falls silent.

'It's those small things, isn't it? Those snapshots of memories that are wonderful, but hurt the most,' says Fiona, sighing. 'But it's good to share them, to remember those times.'

'Yes, it's good to talk about her. Somehow it helps,' says Zoe.

Sara reaches across and holds her hand. 'Isn't it funny,' she says. 'Although we're all sisters, we all have such different memories of our childhood, such different experiences.'

'I guess it was bound to be like that because we're all spread out in ages,' says Zoe. 'If we'd been born every two years, it would have been very different. But I literally have no memories of Steph when I was a child and hardly any of Fi either.'

'Your turn, Steph,' says Sara.

Steph stares at her hands.

'Steph? You must have more memories than any of us – you had five years with her before any of us were born.'

'But she was the one who left the youngest,' says Zoe. 'What were you, sixteen, seventeen when you went to boarding school?'

There's a long pause and for a moment Zoe doesn't think Steph has anything to say.

'When I was five, there was a fancy-dress competition in the church hall,' says Steph. They all look at her. 'Mum and I went together as robins. She made the costumes herself – matching. Hers was especially funny because she was pregnant with you, Fi, and her belly was huge, covered in the robin's red tummy. I'm not sure if Dad went as anything, I think it was just Mum and me.' Her face is soft, a small smile on her lips. 'Anyway, we won. And Mum was so proud. She hugged me and jumped up and down. I can't remember if we got a prize, but when I woke in the morning she wasn't there. She'd gone to hospital to have you. Maybe it was the excitement. That's my favourite memory.'

The four women are silent. Zoe has never thought about Steph having memories of their mum before any of the others were born. Zoe was there at the end of their mum's life. But Steph had been there before anyone else. She wants to talk to Mum about it, tell her what it's like, the four of them being back in the house together. But the one person she wants to talk to is no longer around.

◆ ◆ ◆

Milly

1989

'Ambulance, please.' I can hear Paul's breathing in the hall. 'My wife's cut her neck. It looks bad. Please send someone. Quickly.' There's a pause. 'Highdown Hall. In Hambrough. Please hurry, please.' Another pause. I close my eyes. The chill is working its way down from my neck to my hands, my arm into my body.

'Pressure. Yes, I understand. She's got a tea towel on it now. Yes, heavy bleeding. Thank you, thank you. Please hurry.'

He comes back into the kitchen from the hall and sits down next to me. 'They're sending someone straight away. What the hell happened?' he says, peeling up the corner of the tea towel, which I've been pressing against my neck to stop the bleeding. He properly looks me in the eye for what feels like the first time in ages. 'Are you okay?'

I try to nod but there's a stabbing pain in my neck and I feel a fresh gush of blood.

'Don't move. Just put pressure on it, they said.'

'Accident,' I try to say.

'Accident,' he repeats but without any certainty.

'Fiona, Sara . . .' I try to say, but I'm starting to feel dizzy.

'They're fine, they're in the library.' He's looking in the drawer, pulling out a stack of tea towels. He gently takes the one from my neck and replaces it. It's completely soaked with blood. My blood or Steph's blood? Or is it the same blood? She is my blood.

'Milly, you've got to stay awake, you can't drift off. That's what they said on the phone. The ambulance won't be long.'

'Stay awake,' I mumble. I'm always awake. It's impossible to sleep these days. I'm so tired, but it's so hard to sleep. And then I do and wake up like someone's jumped out at me. But I'm just so tired now. So cold, so tired. Has someone left the back door open? Steph. When she left. 'Close the back door, it's cold.'

'It is closed, Milly.' Paul is here. Why isn't he in the library? I can't feel anything. My head's so heavy, I have to lie down.

'Stay awake, Milly, don't close your eyes.'

I need to close my eyes. Everything is so heavy, so cold, so heavy. Just a little sleep. A moment. Mum always used to say that if there's a chance to sit down then take it. And if there's a chance to lie down, then do that. I'd like to lie down. There's something wet on the floor, it's seeping into my socks. 'Alice,' I say. 'The floor's wet.'

Paul is applying pressure against my neck. Is he strangling me? Then the room is full of noise and light. I close my eyes and retreat inside.

◆ ◆ ◆

'She's been very lucky, Mr Wright. The knife missed her carotid artery by millimetres. Otherwise we would be having a very different conversation.' The nurse smiles down at me and scribbles something on the clipboard, which she puts back at the end of the bed.

'How are you feeling, Mrs Wright?'

I try to nod but there's something on the side of my neck. 'I'm okay,' I whisper.

'There are some policemen here who want to have a chat with you.' The nurse looks down at her hands. 'I'm sorry but it's standard procedure with incidents like this, especially given your other injuries and history of incidents.'

Incidents like this. Oh my God.

'History of incidents?' says Paul, looking from me to the nurse and back again. I close my eyes.

The nurse plumps the pillows and helps me to sit up. I touch the side of my neck and there's a huge dressing. How am I going to explain this away on the school run? Maybe I can ask Alice to take the girls to school until it's better. Or Paul. In my other arm, there's a needle attached to a huge bag of blood. Everything feels woozy and confusing.

Two policemen come and sit either side of me. Paul holds my hand. 'I'm sorry, sir, but we need to speak to Mrs Wright alone.'

'But she's only just come round. I can't leave her.' There's a note of panic in his voice.

'I'll stay with her, Mr Wright,' says the same nurse, not meeting his eye.

He's ushered out and the curtains are drawn back round the bed in a flurry of blue.

'Now, Mrs Wright, can you tell me how this injury came about, and the various bruising the nurse mentioned?'

I think back to earlier this afternoon.

◆ ◆ ◆

'Would someone mind grabbing me the Oxo cubes from the pantry?' I say without turning round, stirring the onion, garlic and tomatoes bubbling in the pan.

'I will,' says Fiona, getting up from the table, disappearing into the scullery and then handing me over the tin box. I'm throwing away the foil when Steph starts to speak.

'You're not using Oxo, are you?'

'I always do, it adds a bit more flavour,' I say. 'Veggie lasagne needs a bit of extra oomph.' I've been getting better at cooking more vegetarian options over the past few months. Lasagne, chilli con carne, pies. Paul's not a fan but Steph is happy, and Fiona and Sara don't seem to mind. The fertility doctor even said it could be healthier, although I do miss the red meat.

'You do realise that beef Oxo has beef in it.' Steph stands up and moves over to the other counter.

I hadn't thought of that. My shoulders drop. 'Does it? Well, only a trace probably.' I try to smile.

'It's got meat in it, Mum. You're putting meat into vegetarian lasagne. Have you done that before?'

I shake my head and say nothing. I can hear the pan bubbling behind me.

'You have, haven't you? You've been making me eat meat for months.'

I'm so stupid. How could I have not realised? 'I'm sorry, darling, I just didn't think.'

'You just didn't think.' I can hear the anger and contempt in Steph's voice.

I try to stay calm and be jolly. I turn back to the pan. My hand shakes as I try to spoon out the brown Oxo powder.

Out of the corner of my eye, I see her slide a knife out of the knife block. It's the small paring knife I use for chopping vegetables. I've only just washed and dried it up from preparing the lasagne. She tests the blade on her thumb and flinches. A thin line of crimson bursts on to her skin.

It makes me lose my fear of her. She's my child again and she's bleeding. I drop the spoon back into the pan. 'What are you doing, Steph? You've cut yourself, you silly thing.'

I'm within a few feet of her when she holds the knife up to her own throat, the tip of the blade disappearing into the soft white skin of her neck.

My whole body tingles. Steph's eyes are dark grey, almost black, opaque, impossible to read. A drop of blood drips off her wrist, from her thumb or her neck, I can't tell. I take another step closer to her, so I can reach out and touch her, but my hands stay by my sides. I don't want to provoke her in any way. At the kitchen table, Fiona and Sara sit motionless, staring at her. I need to get them out of here, out of harm's way. They shouldn't be seeing any of this.

Steph's eyes widen, the darkness from her eyes spreading across her face. 'Don't come any closer.'

'Steph, darling, don't be daft. You're going to hurt yourself. Please.' I realise I'm begging but what else can I do? 'Please don't do this.'

Steph says nothing, just looks at me. More blood drips off her hand on to the floor. There's a sob from the table, Fiona or Sara, I can't tell. I glance at them and then there's a searing pain in my neck and a scream from Steph. Or is it from me? For a moment I think I've got a crick in it, when you move too quickly and then get a sudden shoot of pain. But then there's a stream of warmth down my neck and I realise she's stabbed me. *Shit.* Steph's face has gone white. 'Mum—' she says, her mouth hanging open. There's a clatter as she drops the knife on the floor.

'Steph.' I take my hand away from my neck and it's bright red. I stuff the tea towel up against it.

'Fi, darling, take Sara and go and get Dad. Quickly. He's in the library. Stay there. Don't come back with him.'

Fiona runs past us, pulling Sara behind her. Both are pale, their eyes wide. Steph stands still staring at me.

'Pony,' says Sara, starting to cry. 'I dropped my pony.'

'Forget your pony,' says Fiona, now dragging her from the room. 'Dad!' she starts screaming when she's in the hall. 'Daaaad!'

I hear the library door open. I sink on to the kitchen chair, my whole body starting to shake with cold. Steph is still looking at me, her mouth open, and then she turns and runs out of the kitchen door as Paul walks in.

◆ ◆ ◆

'So your husband wasn't present when this happened?'

I try to shake my head.

'How do you feel about your husband? Are you afraid of him?'

I try to shake my head again. 'Of course not,' I say. 'Paul would never hurt me.'

'You're saying that you and your daughter had a bit of a tussle while you were chopping vegetables and she caught you with the knife in the process.'

I try to nod but it's difficult with the dressing. I wonder where she's gone. How she's feeling. She looked as shocked as me at what happened. I wish she'd stayed. It would have been easier for us all if she'd stayed.

'And what about the other bruising? The nurse mentioned that there was bruising around your neck consistent with being strangled, various bruises on your arms and legs, and you broke your wrist a few months ago.'

'I'm very clumsy sometimes,' I whisper. I close my eyes, praying they'll go away.

There's some whispered conversation and they bring Paul back into the room. His eyes flit between me and the police officers. I can see he's guessed what they've been asking. He grips my hand again. It's warm.

'We wouldn't get involved in cases like this. Rough play and so on. Children will be children, eh?' the younger policeman pipes up, looking pleased to have the opportunity to say something.

I close my eyes and rest my head back on the pillows. Children will be children.

'I'm not sure you understand,' Paul says, his voice rising. 'I don't think this was an accident.' His eyes have become dark, like Steph's do when she's angry.

No, Paul.

'Sir?'

'I don't think this was an accident at all. I think my daughter stabbed my wife in the neck. The nurse said she was lucky not to have severed an artery. She could have died—' He audibly swallows.

'But your daughter is a child, sir,' the older policeman says. 'It must have been an accident. What child would do this to their mother?'

'She's almost half a foot taller than my wife. She's an adult in every other way and—' He stops. 'I don't know what she's capable of.'

The policeman blinks again. 'This is your fifteen-year-old daughter you're talking about? Stephanie Wright?'

I close my eyes again. It's ridiculous. It sounds ridiculous and it is. She's a child. I'm frightened of my own child.

'There have been other incidents now I come to think about it.' Paul's eyes are darting around the room. He stares at me and then looks at the police officers. 'My wife broke her wrist a while ago. She fell down the stairs. Then she's had bruises . . .' He tails off.

'We've spoken to Mrs Wright about that.' The older policeman looks at Paul coldly and I can see what he is thinking. They get up, not looking at either of us.

Once they leave the room, Paul takes both my hands in his. 'I'm right, aren't I? Steph's been hurting you.'

I try to shake my head again. 'Don't be daft,' I mumble. 'Of course she hasn't. I'm just very clumsy.' He cannot know what Steph does.

'Milly, don't lie to me.'

'Where is she?' I ask. 'Has she come back?'

He shakes his head. 'Alice came to look after Fiona and Sara. But Steph wasn't there by the time we left in the ambulance.'

My girl. Out there again on her own. Or not on her own, which is perhaps worse. How can I feel such love for her but also fear her so much?

Chapter 12

Zoe

Spring 2025

They finish packing up the clothes and carry them down to Sara's car. 'I'll take them into town tomorrow,' she says, slamming the boot. *Mum's entire wardrobe reduced to black bin bags*, thinks Zoe. All those clothes she collected over the years, wrapped with mothballs and tissue paper; the cotton sachets she refilled every year with lavender cut from the garden so that when you opened her armoire, the scent filled your nostrils. Now all there is left is a few showy dresses and a small pile of clothes each. Zoe wonders if Steph will wear the Fair Isle jumper. She seemed keen to have it.

The whole house is a mess again. The boxes of paperwork and letters overflowing in the kitchen.

'I think I'll go for a walk,' Zoe says to Sara, who's just come off a video-call with her twins. There are a couple of dilapidated buildings on the other side of the woods. She wants to check the size of the keyholes, just to see if the key might fit. When she finds it. Out of habit, she checks the old potpourri bowl, now full of pine cones, and looks under the hall table, but it's not there.

'You still can't find that key?' says Sara, coming out of the kitchen.

Zoe shakes her head. 'It's driving me crazy. It was here. In the old potpourri.'

'It definitely wasn't there when I cleared that all out before the funeral,' says Sara, glancing underneath the table. 'I'd have seen it.'

'You sure you couldn't have thrown it away by mistake?'

Sara shakes her head. 'It was a huge key, Zoe. Not something you could miss.'

The thought of the key and the names makes Zoe feel strange, but she can't work out whether it's to do with the key itself or with it going missing.

She takes a deep breath and sets off past the formal garden towards the woods. The early spring has held, the sun still high in the sky, buds tricked into opening. *If there's a frost, they'll die*, Zoe thinks. Mum used to worry about an early spring followed by sudden frosts. She'd cover the buds in muslin to protect them. Now if the cold comes back, the buds will wither and die, no one to protect them. She skirts the overgrown kitchen garden, promising she'll tackle it another day. There's just so much to do.

Out of sight of the house, she stops by the algae-green pond and lies on the warm grass, the sun red behind her closed eyes. It feels decadent to just lie down and do nothing. Years ago, she'd come here with her books when she was supposed to be revising for exams, spread them all out on the grass and then plug in her Walkman and go to sleep. That same sense of well-being seeps into her now, but she guiltily pushes it away. Mum has only been gone just over a week.

After a while she gets up and continues into the woods. The hairs prick up on her arms and she wishes she'd brought a jumper. That's the trouble with an early spring, you get lulled into a false sense of security. She walks for a while, the sweet delicate scent of bluebells almost hallucinogenic in its intensity.

She hears Steph before she sees her – a strange keening, echoing through the trees. Zoe stops to listen and then sees her stumbling in the distance. Zoe steps behind an old oak and waits for several minutes. Steph almost walks past her.

'Are you okay?' asks Zoe, making Steph jump. Her face is blotchy, her mouth trembling.

'I'm fine,' says Steph, blinking at her. 'Just wanted to get away from things. It's been an intense few days.'

'It has. I'm sorry again. For slapping you. And the things I said.'

Steph smiles. 'I'm sorry for hitting you back.'

'We sound like a couple of kids making up after a playground fight.' Zoe laughs.

'I don't usually drink at all,' says Steph, biting her lip. 'It just has a really bad effect on me, makes me too impulsive.'

'I haven't really drunk much since Mum's been ill, there hasn't been the opportunity. And there was a lot of booze at the wake.'

'Too much!'

In many ways, Steph looks exactly like their mother. Bobbed grey hair, the same springy gait. Or rather Mum before she got ill and the weight slipped away. It all started after Dad died. Even though she'd obviously been the one who was in charge in the relationship, she seemed to shrivel after he went. Zoe saw her whole on the outside, but like an apple left too long in the fruit bowl which wrinkles slowly and then dries up. She was tired all the time. Zoe had put it down to the general exhaustion of Dad being ill and dying. But the grief pulled at her, pinning her to her bed and then, when Zoe insisted she get up, to the armchair. Even the smallest thing was beyond her. Her eating became erratic.

Then the grief manifested into physical forms. She started to feel constantly nauseated, and was often sick, which meant she stopped eating much at all. She complained of pain going to the loo, until eventually she was diagnosed with bowel cancer. Before

Zoe realised what was happening, she'd become her mother's carer, helping her to dress, bathe and eat. And then even that was taken away once the diagnosis became terminal and the nurses stepped in.

'I know how private Mum was. She'd have hated me doing that, creating gossip for the whole village again.' Again. Steph seems full of sadness, thinking about her childhood. Perhaps being back here for these weeks can help her start to heal and move forward. She said in the note that this was her happiest time at Highdown.

They walk back to the house together, not saying anything. Zoe likes that about Steph – she's good at being quiet, whereas the other two always feel the need to colour in the silence with noise. Even though they're in a wide-open space, Steph veers into her. She can't seem to walk in a straight line. She waves her arms in front of her in that weird apologetic way she has. It's a bit odd and perhaps a bit funny too. Sometimes Mum painted Steph as a thoughtless, wilfully difficult person. But she's been quite different these past few days. Quiet and thoughtful. It's Fiona who can be annoying – a bit too chatty and bossy. In comparison Steph is quiet, thoughtful, and respectful of how Zoe feels. Or at least she seems to be. Maybe she's changed since Mum knew her properly.

Suddenly Steph stops walking and turns to Zoe. 'I like your mermaid tattoo. It's really cool.'

Zoe rolls up the arm on her t-shirt so Steph can see it better. 'Thanks. I call her Sylvie.'

Steph seems to stare at Zoe's arm for a long time. She traces the mermaid's tail, which curves around her forearm, and Zoe shivers with the strangely intimate gesture.

'You've got some tattoos too, right? I saw the one on your wrist.'

Steph turns her wrist over and looks at the four entwined hearts. 'It's just a stick and poke I did as a teenager. I didn't think it would last this long.'

'What do the hearts mean?'

Steph's eyes flicker and she shakes her head. 'Just a teenage thing.'

She closes down so quickly, thinks Zoe. One minute she's friendly and open, and the next clamped tight shut.

◆ ◆ ◆

'Good timing. Supper will be fifteen minutes,' says Sara as they walk through the kitchen door.

Whatever's in the oven makes Zoe's stomach rumble. How lovely that someone else is doing the cooking. 'I'll just pop upstairs, wash my hands and then I'll help.'

Zoe sees something glinting on the hall table as soon as she comes down the stairs. The missing key. She looks again at the bowl. *It definitely wasn't there before*, she thinks, or she or Sara would have seen it. They emptied it out, she looked underneath the table. It couldn't have been there. She picks up the key and puts it carefully in her pocket. No one else has been in the house today. One of her sisters must have put it there.

Her three sisters look up from the table as she walks into the kitchen. Which one of them had the key? Maybe they're all in on it, some sort of conspiracy about selling the house under her nose. She slips into her chair, the key digging into her thigh. One thing's for sure, she's not going to mention the key again and she's not going to let it out of her pocket.

◆ ◆ ◆

'What are your children like?' Zoe asks Sara, as they all sit around the table for supper. She realises she knows so little about Sara's family and hardly spoke to them at the funeral. She should have made more of an effort, they are her nieces after all.

Sara looks up from her bowl and her face brightens. 'Well, Katy is two now and the twins are five. Charlotte and Izzie. Here. I'll show you some photos.' She brings out her phone and starts scrolling. 'This is the five of us last summer in Spain. And this is the twins' first day at school. Look how sweet they are in their uniforms.'

'They are. Which one is which?' Zoe says, a flush creeping across her cheeks. Strange to think that these girls are her flesh and blood and she barely knows them. As soon as life gets back to normal, she'll arrange to get the train over there. 'It was sweet seeing them with you at the funeral. You seem such a natural mum. Did you always want kids?'

'Always,' says Sara. 'You remember we struggled to get pregnant for a long time and the twins are IVF babies. I was told I probably wouldn't be able to have children, so we didn't use any contraception and then I fell pregnant with Katy a couple of years later. Quite the surprise.'

'I bet,' says Zoe. 'I can't imagine having a child.'

'You might still have children,' Sara says. 'You're only, what, thirty-five. Plenty of time.'

Zoe shakes her head. 'I don't want children, really. And I'd need a partner first.' She thinks back to Ben and swallows. 'I thought one day that I might foster. There are so many kids in awful circumstances. And I could do that on my own.'

'That would be an incredible thing to do,' says Steph.

Steph gets it.

'Did you never want kids, Fi?' asks Sara.

Fiona widens her eyes and does a mock shudder. 'God, no.' She turns to Sara. 'No offence to you, Sara, I'm sure being a mother is great. But it wasn't for me. And I couldn't be a mum and have the career that I have.' There is a sadness about Fiona that Zoe hasn't noticed before.

'You don't work, do you, Sara? I mean, outside the home. I'm not being offensive, I'm sure the kids are a lot of work.'

'You're not offending me, Zoe.' Sara smiles at her. 'I think because we'd tried for so long, I wanted to enjoy every second of it and was lucky that we could afford to live on just John's salary. So I gave up the job in the City when I went off on maternity leave with the twins.' She takes a deep breath. 'It's hard though, being a full-time mum. You're so busy all the time, but when you look back, you wonder what you've been doing all day. John's great but I'm sure he thinks I just sit around chatting. It's been good being here in some ways, because I've been away from the family and I feel we achieve a little something more every day. When Katy goes to school, I'd like to go back to work, earn my own money. And do something with my brain.'

'What do you think you'd do?'

'It would be hard going back to what I used to do. I don't think they'd accept me part-time and I couldn't go back full-time – the hours in the City are crazy and I'd never see the girls. So I might do something locally. Given how lucky John and I have been with money, I could do something to give back.' Sara's eyes glisten.

Zoe reaches forward and clasps her hand. 'That sounds great, I'm sure there are loads of things you could do in your local community. Flexible hours to fit around the girls.' Suddenly her irritation about Sara and her daughters melts away. Now that she's seen them at the funeral, she understands. They're part of her sister, literally flesh and blood.

Steph leans forward. 'You're a bit far from me, but you're always welcome to help out at my shelter.'

'Thanks, Steph, but it probably is a bit far away. And I love animals but I'm not as passionate about them as you. I was thinking maybe something with children. Training as a teaching assistant, or even just starting out as a volunteer in schools.'

'That's important work,' says Zoe. 'What about you, Steph?'

Steph turns to face her. 'What about me?'

'Are you happy at the rescue centre?'

Steph nods. 'Yeah. I've worked there forever and then took it over when the previous people retired and I love it there. What we do makes a real difference to the animals. But also to the people who want to adopt a pet.'

'Mum said you'd wanted to be a vet when you were a kid.'

Steph sighs. 'Yes, when I was young I was desperate to be a vet. But I had some tricky times as a teenager, as you know.' She swallows and looks away for a second. 'By the time I'd got back on track, it was too late to go down that route. And I'm not sure it would ever have been for me anyway. But I've learned so much about animals from this work. Obviously I'm no vet but I can treat them for most things. And I'm happy. And that's the main thing. It feels like you're happy too?'

'I am,' says Zoe. 'I loved working with XR and still miss the buzz. But helping to improve people's lives every day with my consultancy work was a massive thing for me. I never thought I'd go into politics, but I loved it. And the net zero agenda is really important for me. I can't wait to get back to it.'

'So three of us are sorted and happy. What about you, Fiona? Do you like Singapore?'

Fiona tips her head on one side. 'I do. I like the efficiency of it. The cleanliness. The fact that you can get any sort of food at any time. It's a real East meets West place. I love our lives there . . .' She trails off and looks away. 'You should all come out and visit,' she says quietly.

Zoe nods but doubts she'll ever go.

'And you, Zoe, now that Mum has gone, what are your other plans?' asks Sara.

Zoe sighs. She's started to realise over the past few days that she's always felt a little inferior to her sisters. That they all left Highdown Hall and have lives, careers or families and she just stayed. She thought she was making a difference but has it been enough?

'I feel that my career ended really, before it started. Mum's illness came at the worst time. I'd just become a councillor on the town council, the consultancy was going well. And I had to stop everything. And then there was Ben . . .'

'Ben?' says Sara, her head on one side. 'Who's Ben?'

'He was my boyfriend. More than my boyfriend, really. I thought we were going to be together forever. But when I had to move back into Highdown, it became really difficult to keep seeing each other. Mum was quite demanding . . .' It feels disloyal to say that, but it is true.

'You split up?' says Sara.

Zoe nods. 'Well, rather we argued and we both said some horrible things.' She laughs. 'I'm good at that. And I haven't heard from him since.'

'Not even when Mum died?' says Sara, gaping at her.

'Yes, he dropped me a note then,' says Zoe. 'But I was in such a state I didn't reply. I thought I saw him at the funeral, but I'm not sure.'

'Maybe it's not completely over then,' says Sara. 'Maybe once we've all gone, you could pick up that thread of your life again.'

Zoe smiles slightly. Maybe Sara is right.

For the first time today it feels they've all actually talked. Not about the will, or what needs doing in the house, but about their lives and what they want from them and a little about Steph's relationship with Mum. Maybe they are becoming a little less like strangers and more like family.

◆ ◆ ◆

Milly

1989

There are moments of peace like this that make me wonder if I'm imagining everything else. The girls' three blonde heads bent over the kitchen table, all focused on their different tasks. Steph drawing angles with her protractor, revising for her maths GCSE. Fiona putting the finishing touches to her Tudors and Stuarts project. And Sara practising her writing, which is already neater than the other two and she's only five.

'Mum, come and look at my b,' Sara calls, beckoning me over. I give the sauce a quick stir and then inspect her notebook. The b is perfect, touching all edges of the square with the top going through into the square above.

'That's very good, darling. Very neat.'

I glance at Fiona's history book. She's drawn some kind of figure at the top and then there are lines of text underneath. 'Would you like another piece of paper?' I ask.

She looks up, her eyebrows drawn together. 'No,' she says. Then she tips her head to one side. 'Why do you think Queen Elizabeth never married?'

Queen Elizabeth is married, to Prince Philip. But then I realise she means Elizabeth I. I try to think. I can't remember studying anything from the Tudors apart from Henry VIII and his six wives.

'She wanted to promote the cult of virginity.' There's something about the way Steph says it that makes it sound rude. I stare at her for a moment and she raises her eyebrows at me, before going back to her protractor.

'What's virginity?' asks Sara.

Oh God, I really don't want to go into this. The sauce is starting to stick, so I give it another stir and turn down the heat, before reaching into the Aga for the pasta dish.

'Someone who hasn't had sex,' says Steph, without looking up.

Sara and Fiona start giggling and I turn away to avoid Steph's look. I tip the packet of green tagliatelle into the pasta sauce before pouring it all into the dish.

'Why would anyone want to have sex with a boy anyway?' says Fiona. 'Queen Elizabeth had the right idea.'

'You'll find out one day,' says Steph in a knowing voice that makes me look up without meaning to. She's staring straight at me. I think back to the condoms in her drawer. I hope she's being careful if she is having sex. But of course she's having sex. That's where she goes the nights she doesn't come home. To that man. To Patrick. I'm grating the cheese so hard I grate a piece of my finger, leaving a smear of blood on the grater. It stings, but there's also pleasure in it.

'Ewww! I'm not having any of that, it's got your finger in it,' says Fiona.

I wash the blood away under the tap and then wrap my finger in a plaster. 'It's nothing,' I say.

'It's not vegetarian now,' says Fiona. 'And Steph will only eat vegetarian food.'

I sigh and slide the dish into the Aga to cook. Hopefully they'll have forgotten by supper time.

If we can just get Steph through these exams, then it'll be the summer and then just two more years of sixth form and our job is done. That feels like a long time right now. *Just take it day by day*, Emma said. I wanted her to tell me that it was all going to be fine next week, but in some ways that advice was good. Don't think beyond this day and then the next and the next. A bit like being an alcoholic. Just survive one day without alcohol or a major incident, then another day, then another.

Fiona snaps her book shut and pushes her chair back from the table. 'I'm done,' she says.

Sara copies her, closing her book with a flourish and following her out of the kitchen. Steph doesn't move.

My heart starts beating faster. I check the food in the Aga and then walk as quickly as I can to the kitchen door.

'Mum?'

Adrenalin streams through me. 'Yes?' I say as casually as I can, one hand on the doorknob.

'Can you help me work out these semi-circle angles? I can't seem to get it to add up properly.'

My hand is pulling on the doorknob, but part of me is back in the room, wanting to go to her, to sit with her and help in any way I can. Although I failed O-level maths so I don't think I'd be much help. But I've realised that the only way to protect me – and therefore protect her – is never to be alone with her. That the real violence only happens when we're alone. So if we're not alone, I'll be safe. And she'll be safe from Paul. There's been no real incidents since she stabbed me and Paul has started to relax a little, realise that he may have been wrong.

'I'm sorry, darling, I'm rubbish at maths, you know that.'

Her face seems to sag and I feel a stab of guilt. I should help her. She's reaching out to me, I should help her. Even if I can't really help, it'll be a gesture, something. I turn back into the room.

'Yeah, I forgot you're stupid.'

It's just words but I feel my eyes prick with tears. I seem to be constantly on the edge of crying at the moment. I'm on the back doorstep and then into the garden before I realise it. Woody has followed and dances around joyfully welcoming this unexpected walk. 'C'mon, lad,' I say, scratching his ears as I push the tears back inside.

Is this really the only way? Am I to avoid being in the same room as my daughter on my own forever? It's awful, awful. I love her with everything I have. But I hate her and am frightened of her at the same time. How can I be frightened of my own child?

Chapter 13

Zoe

Spring 2025

After the public nature of the funeral, the interment is a quiet affair. Zoe invites Alice, and Mum's old friend Mary from the village comes along, pushed in her wheelchair by her daughter.

'Though we are dust and ashes, God has prepared for those who love him a heavenly dwelling place,' the vicar starts. 'At her funeral we commended Camilla Constance Wright into the hands of almighty God. As we prepare to commit the remains of Camilla to the earth, we entrust ourselves and all who love God to His loving care.'

A light rain starts to fall. The vicar is still talking but Zoe can't keep her eyes off the small wooden box that he places in the ground. 'We now commit her mortal remains to the ground: earth to earth, ashes to ashes, dust to dust: in sure and certain hope of the resurrection to eternal life.'

Somehow this placing in the ground feels far more final than the pomp and ceremony of the funeral service. But also far more removed. It's just ashes. It might be Mum, but it's not her in the same way as the coffin was. Zoe wonders if she'll visit the grave, as Mum visited her parents' graves every week. She always thought it was a strange thing to do – an ostentatious thing to do, perhaps. A 'look at me tending my parents' grave' when she could have remembered her parents at any time – just by looking at their pictures in the gallery. Depending on what happens with the house, they should move the portrait of their mum from the library to the gallery, shuffle the paintings around. That is when she will remember her, every time she passes by her portrait. Not standing at this old family plot.

Zoe watches Steph, her face closed off, far away.

'Through our Lord Jesus Christ, who will transform our frail bodies that they may be conformed to His glorious body, who died, was buried, and rose again for us. To Him be glory forever.'

It feels over before it's begun and they say goodbye to Mary and her daughter and walk back to Highdown Hall, Alice with them.

◆ ◆ ◆

In the library, they sink down into the leather armchairs. 'I haven't been to church since I left the village. Twenty-something years ago. And that's now three times in two weeks,' says Fiona.

'Me neither,' says Sara, and Steph also shakes her head.

'The last time I went was with Mum, for one of her friend's funerals,' says Zoe.

'It was a lovely send-off for your mum,' says Alice. 'She would have been proud.'

'Thank you,' says Sara. 'The funeral was beautiful but this was really tough.'

'I think all funerals and interments are tough, aren't they?' says Fiona.

'There's a difference, though, isn't there? When a person like Mum dies at the end of a long life and when someone dies young. A child, say.' Steph is looking out of the window and speaking so quietly that Zoe struggles to hear her.

Sara nods. 'I can't even imagine losing a child. I've found it hard enough being apart from the children for this fortnight. Video-calling them every night just isn't enough.'

Steph glances at her and then looks away.

'I've missed Charles too,' says Fiona. 'The time-zone difference has been hard.'

It feels like everyone is looking ahead to getting back to their lives. But what's Zoe's life now? Mum's gone and somehow she needs to pick up the threads she dropped when Mum became ill. Move back into the oast house, contact her old clients, maybe drop Ben a text.

'It was another beautiful service,' says Alice again. 'Just like your mum would have wanted. Like she planned.'

'I'd definitely want to write down exactly what I wanted for my funeral, like Mum did,' says Zoe. 'I don't want whoever's left behind to choose it for me and mess it up. Play a song you always hated as you were going into the crematorium. That'd be bad karma.'

Fiona turns her hands up. 'But you wouldn't be around to know,' she says.

'Do you think?' says Zoe.

'Burials aren't just for the people being buried or cremated. It's for those left behind,' says Steph. 'To help them to start to get over the death of the person.'

'And to celebrate their life,' says Zoe.

Steph smiles slightly. 'They're for everyone, aren't they? So what music would you go for, Zoe?'

'Well, I have been thinking about it, actually. Just because Mum talked about it in the last few weeks. I thought "*Somewhere Over the Rainbow*" as they brought my coffin in. Then Sam Smith "*Lay Me Down*" and maybe something from Adele – "*Someone Like You*".'

'Oh, I'd go for a mix of classical and modern, I think,' says Fiona. 'Berlioz's "Shepherds' Farewell" and then Frank Sinatra singing "*My Way*".'

'You always did like your own way,' says Sara, laughing.

Fiona makes a face at her.

'I'd go classical,' says Sara. 'Elgar's "*Nimrod*", and "Ave Maria" then that piece that Dad had at the end of his funeral – what's it called, Fi?'

Fiona shakes her head.

'"*The Lark Ascending*",' says Steph quietly.

'That's right,' says Sara, smiling at her. '"*The Lark Ascending*". Beautiful.'

'What about you, Steph?' asks Fiona.

But Steph just stares out of the library window. 'I don't know who would organise my funeral. There isn't anyone really.'

What a sad thing to say. There's a long silence. 'I'm sure we could all sort it out, if you died first,' says Zoe.

Steph gives her a quick smile.

Eventually Alice turns to Fiona. 'When are you going back to Singapore?'

'Tomorrow morning,' she says.

Alice starts. 'So soon?'

'Well, I've been here two weeks now. I need to get back to work, to Charles.'

'I'm heading home tomorrow too,' says Sara. 'I'm so looking forward to seeing the children again but I've got used to us all being together. It'll be sad when we all go back to our lives. Like the end of something.'

Zoe watches Steph fidgeting, her face unreadable. 'I'll head off then too,' says Steph. 'We've just had a new influx of animals so I really need to get back to sort them out.'

'It seems a shame that you're all leaving. You haven't had much time to talk,' says Alice, looking between them.

'I feel like we've done nothing else but talk,' says Fiona, laughing. 'I'm not sure when we'll meet again, Alice.' She leans across and takes Alice's hands.

'It's been rather wonderful seeing you all again, the wonderful women you've become,' says Alice, her eyes full. 'I loved being part of your childhoods, it was such a joy. But even more wonderful now to see you grown. And you with your own children, Sara. It's a shame that you all have to part again. And so soon. Without perhaps properly . . .'

'Well, we still have to sort Highdown out, don't we?' says Fiona.

Zoe sees Sara raise her eyebrows at her.

Fiona turns to Zoe. 'You need to take as long as you need here,' she says. 'When you're ready to have a conversation about the future, let's all get together on Zoom and chat. As soon as I get back to Sing I'll speak to the solicitor in person and see what can be done.'

'Like Fi says, as long as you need,' says Steph, talking too fast. 'And I was serious about you having my share.'

Zoe glances between them and imagines the conversations that must have taken place without her.

This time tomorrow then she will be on her own, Zoe thinks. After two weeks of the house being full, it will be silent again. Quieter than it's been since when their parents moved in on their wedding day.

It feels good and bad. It feels like the end of something. But she's not sure if she's ready for it to be the beginning of something else.

◆ ◆ ◆

Milly

1989

'She'll be back, Milly, she always is.' Paul cracks open an eye and then turns over, burying his head under the duvet.

I grit my teeth and walk into Steph's room. I'll never get used to waking up and finding that she's gone in the night.

Her bed is made – the duvet tucked under the pillow like only Alice does – so she must have left before she even thought about getting into bed. Terry and June are asleep on her pillow as usual, as if *they* expect her back at any moment.

I've tried to talk to her about it, to ask her to tell me when she's leaving. That I won't try to stop her, but I need to know. For my own sanity as well as her safety. But she says she never knows, that it's always a last-minute thing. A phone call asking her to join them, though I never hear the phone.

On her pinboard above her desk is a picture of the two of them – Steph and Patrick – their arms around each other, staring straight at the camera. One of those photo-booth shots. She looks wild and free and happy in that picture. I never see her like that here. He looks, well, he looks like a man. Not a boy who should be dating my daughter. I look away from the photo.

I know that he's come to the house, though we've never met him. I've heard the owl hoot that isn't an owl hoot when I've been lying in bed at night. Then the telltale creak of the landing floorboard.

She'll be back. I repeat Paul's words and go downstairs to make coffee for us both. I stroke my belly, imagining the tiny life growing in there at last. Eight weeks. In six weeks' time, I'll be safe.

There's no sign of her in the village as I walk Fiona and Sara to school, but then I'm not sure what I was expecting. I'm not sure where she goes when she disappears. The police never found her when she was younger, never really bothered looking, so they're definitely not going to make the effort now. After dropping the girls off, I walk back to get the car and drive into town to Steph's school to see if she's there. I know the office staff well – I've been in and out for the last three years with one thing or another. Mrs Baker glances up from her paperwork.

'Good morning, Mrs Wright.'

'Morning, Mrs Baker. I just wondered if you'd seen Stephanie this morning? If she'd come to school?'

She picks up her glasses from the string hanging around her neck and pinches them on to her nose. 'She hasn't registered this morning, no. But let me check if she's managed to get past without registering.' Mrs Baker bustles off down the corridor. The eyes of thirty teachers stare at me from the display, judging me. They know me as well as I know them. Stephanie Wright's mother.

There's Mrs Longman who teaches science, who was quite a fan of Steph's as she showed such promise. Until Steph smashed up some expensive equipment when Mrs Longman brought in a rabbit to be dissected. Mrs Smith has been amazing supporting Steph over the past few years. *And me*, I think, remembering the times I've cried in her office when it all got too much. I'll be sad when Steph leaves here in a few months' time. It'll be the end of an era. The new sixth form on the other side of town seems so grown-up in comparison. I hope they're as supportive as this school has been. By that time Fiona will be here, hopefully making less of a name for herself than Steph has.

'No sign of her, I'm afraid,' Mrs Baker says, smoothing down her perm.

'Thanks anyway,' I say. 'It was a long shot.'

I drive home via the butcher's in the village to pick up some pork chops for supper. I'll do an omelette for Steph. If she's home. Highdown is silent as I open the front door. The library door is closed and I go straight to the kitchen for another coffee. The clock strikes ten. It's my day to play cards with the Cornfords, so I'd better get Woody walked and back before noon when I have to leave.

The Downs' green velvet hills don't soothe me as they usually do, though it's such a clear day that I can see as far as Chanctonbury Ring. There's something niggling at the back of my mind that I can't quite put my finger on. Yes, Steph is missing and yes, it's seriously close to her GCSEs. But that's not unusual in itself. She often stays out all night. Three years ago if you'd told me I wouldn't be a nervous wreck because my daughter had disappeared, I wouldn't have believed you. There's nothing like repetition to normalise trauma. I suppose that's why doctors and police officers and the like can cope with such stressful jobs.

The sense of unease stretches through the game of bridge with the Cornfords. I lose deal after deal, making silly mistakes. Old Mrs Cornford, who used to be as sharp as a tack until cataracts made the cards milky, asks me what's wrong but I just shake my head. I've talked so much about Steph to the three of them over the years but for some reason I don't want to admit that she's gone again. It might make it all the more real.

Fiona is unusually chatty on the walk home, talking about the teacher's reaction to her saying that Elizabeth I made a cult of virginity. I smile at her, imagining the teacher's face. She and Sara sit down for a snack and I cradle a cup of tea while I watch them munch through toast and Marmite. 'Neither of you know where Steph might be, do you?'

Sara shakes her head but Fiona talks through toast. 'Have you looked on the roof? She often hangs out there when it's sunny.'

'The roof outside her bedroom?'

'No, along from that,' says Fiona as if it's the most natural thing in the world. 'Here, I'll show you.'

Back in Steph's room, she opens the window and uses the desk chair to clamber out. 'Be careful,' I say, visions of her rolling down the roof and then dropping to the ground making my stomach plummet.

'It's fine, Mum. You just have to crawl along this bit and then you get to a ledge where you can see everything.' She disappears from view but then calls back. 'She's not here.'

I turn to Sara who's busy looking through Steph's desk. 'Don't move and definitely don't follow me.' I pull myself out of the window and go in the same direction as Fiona, careful not to look down, and place my feet firmly against the tiles. I round the corner to the side of the house and there's Fiona sitting on a wide ledge, surveying the woods and the garden. She moves along as I squeeze next to her, my stomach somersaulting.

'So Steph regularly comes out here?' I say, looking around.

'Yes, we both do,' says Fiona, looking very pleased with herself.

'You both do?'

'Only me occasionally,' she says quickly.

'But what do you do, just hide?'

Fiona glances to the left where an orange Sainsbury's bag is visible under the tiles. 'Nothing really, just talk.'

I reach forward and pull out the bag.

'Don't tell her I told you, she'll kill me,' she says.

Inside the bag are some papers, rolling tobacco, and a pack of condoms. There's nothing in here I haven't seen before. I stuff it back under the tile. 'Come on, miss, down you go. You go first. And for God's sake be careful.'

I glance again around Steph's room, but everything seems exactly as chaotic as it usually is. Downstairs we go through the routine of homework and supper.

'No sign of Steph?' says Paul, as he sits down.

I shake my head. 'Not yet.'

'She'll be back,' he says again.

'She will Mum,' Fiona says, touching my hand. 'She just needs more space than she gets here.'

What a strange and very grown-up expression for her to use. I look at Fiona, her blonde hair dipped over her plate. Half child, half adult. I hadn't realised how much Steph confided in her and wonder if she knows more than she should. How much impact has Steph's behaviour had on Fiona? I should spend more time with her.

After the girls' bedtime, Paul and I spend a rare evening together, even if it's just in front of the television. As always when Steph is missing, I'm on constant alert, listening for footsteps or, worse still, a car. How many times has she been brought home in a police car for one reason or another?

While Paul gets ready for bed, I check Steph's room again and turn on the bedside light. Just in case she comes home during the night, which has happened before. I think it's going to take me ages to fall asleep. I remember nothing after getting into bed, though at some point during the night I wake, my heart pounding. *That* was what was different about Steph's room.

I slide out of bed, careful not to move the mattress and disrupt Paul. I avoid the creaky bits of the landing and hurry into Steph's room. The wardrobe door is shut. That's what's different. It's always gaping open, clothes spilling out. I'm always nagging her about it.

I open it with difficulty and gasp. It's almost empty. All the clothes have gone, just a few old jumpers and a bag I meant to take to the charity shop at the bottom. My heart is like a stone. I swallow.

The main light floods the room and I go methodically through the room and then the bathroom. All her usual toiletries have gone – toothbrush, soap, kohl eye pencil. She left two boxes of tampons but maybe she already had more. Almost all the clothes she wears on a daily basis have gone. Her felt tips and even her school books. Her school books? So she's planning to go to school.

Paul groans as I turn on the main bedroom light. 'She's run away,' I shout. 'She's gone for good this time.'

'What do you mean?' He's sitting up, blinking against the light.

'All her stuff has gone.'

He's out of bed and in Steph's room and I show him the wardrobe. He rubs his face, which looks grey in this light. 'Oh God,' he says. 'Well, I'll call the police first thing in the morning, report her missing.'

'First thing in the morning.' I can't help but raise my voice. 'We need to look for her now.'

'Milly, she's already been gone over twenty-four hours, another couple of hours won't make any difference.'

We go back to bed but I lie there tense, still waiting to hear Steph creep back into her bedroom even though I know it's not going to happen. Paul is snoring within minutes. Maybe he's actually relieved she's not in the house. That she might have gone for good. The grandfather clock strikes three in its night-time tone and I creep out of bed again. Downstairs, I pull a light coat on over my nightgown and head out to the car. I must do something.

I don't know what I'm hoping to find, but the village is just as deserted as I would have expected at this time of night. I've often driven around in the early hours of the morning looking for Steph. A fox stares at my headlights and then swaggers across the road. I head out of the village towards town.

On the high street, a couple of boys, leaning against each other to keep upright, stagger past me. A homeless man is slumped in a doorway. I pass a boarded-up building and wonder if that's the squat that Patrick lives in. But I can just about make out threatening security notices pasted on the door. It doesn't look like anyone could be living inside. But there must be countless places like this, not maybe in this town but elsewhere.

Lights shine from the occasional terraced house and I wonder why people are awake. Shift-workers, perhaps. Party-goers. Is Steph in one of those houses? I consider knocking on the doors but then realise how crazy that would seem and that I'd probably end up being arrested.

I stop outside her school. I'll go back there tomorrow morning and explain the situation. The minute she turns up, I'll be waiting for her and take her home. Three years ago when she started, we were so excited for her, so full of hope. She was already excelling, and the school would give her a chance to do what she really wanted to do – study to be a vet. Perhaps that dream is still there, just. But everything else is in tatters. I wish we could go back three years, do things differently. I wish I'd been able to get through to her, to help her, then she might not have run away. I start the engine again and drive slowly back to Highdown, scanning the streets as I go.

Chapter 14

Zoe

Spring 2025

'I don't know how you have so much baggage. When you arrived from Singapore you barely had anything,' says Zoe, helping Fiona down the stairs with a huge suitcase.

'Well, I have been here two weeks now,' says Fiona, panting. 'I could hardly wear your clothes all that time. Especially for Mum's funeral.' The word lingers in the air between them. 'And I wanted to buy some things to remind me of here, of home.' Zoe realises it is the first time Fiona has referred to Highdown as home in years.

Fiona wheels the suitcase to the front door, just as the knocker clatters against the door. 'Oh, the taxi's early. I better say my goodbyes now,' she says. Missy wanders up to the suitcase, brushing her face against it.

'Sara! Steph! Fi's leaving,' Zoe calls up the stairs. But as Fiona opens the front door, it's Alice waiting on the doorstep, her chest heaving.

'Oh, you're still here. Thank goodness,' she says, resting her hands on her knees as she struggles to catch her breath.

'Alice, what are you doing here?' says Fiona.

'I need to talk to you,' Alice gasps. 'To all of you.'

Fiona takes a step back. 'To say what? I thought we said our goodbyes yesterday.'

'Come on in, Alice, what's up?' says Zoe.

'I need to talk to you all,' Alice repeats, glancing between Zoe and Fiona.

Sara bounces down the stairs. 'Are you off, Fi? Oh, hi, Alice.'

Alice nods to her and then looks up the stairs as Steph walks down, her bare feet silent on the marble steps.

'Alice wants to talk to us,' says Zoe. Steph stops on the bottom stair and looks directly at Alice.

Zoe glances between them. 'What?' she says. 'What's going on?'

'I've been worrying about it ever since you told me about your mum's will. I hoped you'd all have talked, but . . . you didn't. When you all mentioned you were leaving today . . .' Alice shakes her head. 'I've hardly slept for thinking about it.'

'Thinking about what?' says Zoe.

'You must tell them, Steph,' says Alice. 'It's surely what your mum wanted. You can't leave it like this.' Her voice is soft and low. 'After everything that was said the other day.'

Steph's eyes widen. She shakes her head and looks at her feet.

Alice goes towards her, the others parting to let her through, and takes her elbow. 'It's time, Steph,' she says, guiding her into the kitchen. 'It's time to tell the truth. I've waited to see if you'd do it in your own time, but—'

'What's going on?' says Zoe, her voice trembling. She follows the others into the kitchen, catching the anxious faces of Fiona and Sara looking at each other.

The four sisters sit around the table as Alice makes a pot of tea, and brings out mugs and the milk bottle. Steph's eyes are fixed on her hands in her lap; Fiona watches her. Nobody speaks until Alice sits down next to Steph and touches her arm. 'Do you want to start?'

Steph doesn't move.

The doorbell rings and a voice calls, 'Taxi.' Fiona glances towards the kitchen door.

'You need to tell them now,' says Alice. 'It'll be too late otherwise. They deserve to know.'

Steph looks up finally, flushes of pink in her usually pale cheeks. She swallows. 'I know why you didn't get your share of Highdown,' she says, her eyes flickering over Zoe. She taps her fingers against the side of her mug.

Fiona glances at her frowning. 'How do you know? Have you spoken to a solicitor?' There's a note of panic in her voice.

Steph's nails are tapping repeatedly on the mug. 'No, I haven't. But I think it's all about the pre-nuptial agreement between Mum and Dad,' she starts.

'Yes, yes, we know about the agreement,' says Fiona impatiently.

Alice rests a hand on Fiona's arm. 'Let her speak, Fi,' she says.

Fiona swallows and stares at Steph.

'I think there was something in that agreement that meant that the house couldn't be handed down to anyone who wasn't—'

The doorbell rings again.

Steph looks up at Alice, who nods at her.

'Who wasn't one of Mum's own children.'

Zoe closes her eyes. A negative of the bright kitchen imprints on her eyelids. Not one of Mum's own children. What does that mean? If you're not your mum's child, then that makes you nobody at all. Of course she's Mum's child. But even as she says it to herself, somewhere deep inside her it suddenly feels untrue.

Zoe opens her eyes and looks at Steph, whose face is pinched. She looks much older than when she arrived a fortnight ago.

'Steph?' says Sara, her head tipped to one side. 'What do you mean? Of course Zoe is Mum's child, so she should get a share of the house.'

Zoe closes her eyes again, and even with them closed can feel the others looking at her. Sara is still talking but Zoe can't hear what she's saying. 'Zoe?' Sara's voice. A soft hand on her arm. 'Are you okay?' Her stomach turns.

'What I mean is—' starts Steph.

Zoe flicks her eyes open and stares at Steph. Her oldest sister is breathing loudly, almost hyperventilating. Steph. The thought flits across her brain bouncing off all the other thoughts. Steph?

Fiona turns to her, her eyebrows raised. 'What is it, Steph?' She sounds impatient. There's something about the way that Steph's eyes are darting between the three of them, the way she's twisting the bottom of her shirt in her hand, that says she has the answer.

They wait and Steph swallows. She glances at Alice, who inclines her head. 'You're not Mum's daughter. Biologically, anyway.'

Zoe stares at her, willing her to look at her properly. Fiona and Sara are shaking their heads.

'But that's simply not true,' says Fiona, banging her palm on the table, tea sloshing over the side of her mug.

'Fiona,' says Alice, holding up her hand.

Steph looks her in the eye. 'You're not Mum's daughter,' she repeats. She takes a breath. 'You're mine.'

Mine. The word silences the table. Zoe is holding her gaze and sees all the emotions flit across Steph's face. Joy, fear, pain and then a tiny filament of hope.

'Oh God,' says Zoe, covering her face with her hands and squeezing her eyes shut. A sickness rises to her throat.

The doorbell rings again.

◆ ◆ ◆

Steph

November 1990

The first light came on just after 6 a.m., throwing a golden sheen across the frosty lawn. *Thank God.* I tried to wiggle my numb feet and hands, careful not to wake Kylie who, despite the sub-zero temperature, was still asleep mummified in the shawl and blanket. Only her tiny nose was visible, pink with the chill. There wasn't one part of me that was even slightly warm. I edged closer to the house, certain that it would be Mum up so early, but wanting to make sure. I couldn't face Dad. Not yet. Near the kitchen door I saw her for the first time.

She was yawning, pushing her hair out of her eyes as she spooned coffee into two mugs. *Mum.* She looked different somehow, like her skin had been filled out. There were grey streaks in her hair instead of the usual blonde. Maybe it was just that I hadn't seen her for eight months. As I touched the door handle, she started and her face drained of colour. But her eyes widened when she saw it was me, and she covered her mouth with her hand. For a moment we both stood there, staring at each other. Then she rushed forward and pulled the door open.

'Oh, Steph! Thank God, thank God.' She smelt of Mum.

She clasped me hard and it was then she realised I was holding something. Someone. 'Oh,' she said, moving the blanket aside gently to see Kylie's face. 'Oh my God, it's a baby.' She covered her mouth with her hand again, her eyes wide. 'Oh my God. Is . . . is it yours?' She looked down at Kylie, stroking the top of her head.

I nodded, my throat full.

'Oh Steph, is this why you ran away? You didn't have to leave. Not because you were pregnant.'

I started to shiver then, and she guided me to the table and sat me down as if I were a child.

She sank on to a chair next to me and gripped the tops of my arms. 'Thank God, thank God you're home. I've been so, so worried. Are you okay?' Her words fell over one another. 'Is the baby okay? Is it a boy or a girl?'

I looked down at Kylie, a sleeping witness to this homecoming. 'We're o—' But I started to cry before I could finish, big sobs rising from deep inside of me. It was a long time since I'd cried in front of someone. Mum leaned even closer towards me and hugged me, rubbing my back, Kylie an awkward lump between us. 'Oh Steph,' she said again. 'It will be okay now. You're home. Everything will be okay.'

It suddenly all felt okay. This was home. Safe. And warm for the first time in weeks. Why hadn't I done this before? She gently eased Kylie from my arms and laid her carefully on the kitchen sofa, wedging her in with cushions. 'You look exhausted,' she said. 'Let's get you sorted out and then we can focus on the baby.'

'It's been really hard,' I said, still shaking with sobs. 'With her, outside.'

Mum closed her eyes. 'I'm so sorry about whatever we did to make you feel you could never come back.' Her voice was hoarse. 'Whatever happened between us, this was always your home.' She held my hands. 'I love you, Steph. I will always love you, whatever.'

'I love you too, Mum,' I said, sagging against her body. It felt such a relief to be held, to be looked after.

On the sofa, Kylie mewled. 'What's her name?' said Mum, getting up.

'Kylie,' I said.

She smiled. 'Like the pop singer?' She unwrapped the outer and inner blankets and then slid her hand under Kylie's head and lifted her up. 'Hello, baby girl,' she said, bouncing her against her body and staring at her face. She looked at ease with her in a way I never felt. 'She's beautiful. She looks so like you did as a baby, that same little frown between her eyes, like she's thinking important things.'

It was hard to think I'd been a baby and Mum had been like me. Had she ever felt as scared as I did?

'You clever thing, having such a beautiful baby.'

I smiled. It didn't feel very clever, but she was beautiful and I loved her so, so much. I'd do anything for her.

'What are your plans?' she asked, her body swaying from side to side. Kylie was quiet.

I shook my head. I hadn't thought beyond this moment. Just getting home.

'And Patrick? She is Patrick's?'

I nodded and started to cry again. 'He—'

Mum slid down next to me and rubbed my back, holding Kylie in the crook of her other arm.

'I ran away from him. I couldn't do it anymore. It was so cold. Always so cold.' My whole body shuddered, as if in memory of that place, though I was beginning to feel warmer. The kitchen was as bright and homely as I remembered it, the Aga keeping it cosy.

'It's okay, Steph, you're home now. I'll look after you.'

I leaned against her. 'Thank you, Mum.' I needed to say it. 'I'm sorry – for everything.'

She paused for a moment and looked at me, stroking the side of my face. 'We both made mistakes. I'm sorry too. I'm just glad you've given us a second chance.'

'I need to start again,' I said. 'Go back to the beginning.' I wasn't even sure what I meant, it was just words.

Mum tipped her head to one side and studied my face. 'I understand. We can discuss all of that later. For now, let me make you a tea. Would you like something to eat? Breakfast?'

'I'm starving,' I said. It was true. I couldn't remember the last time I'd had a proper, hot meal. All I'd eaten were snacks for days – weeks, probably.

With Kylie still in one arm, she tipped oats into a pan and added water. She seemed to carry her so easily. My eyes were heavy so I leaned my head on my arms on the table, listening to her bustle around. The ping of the toaster. The click of the kettle as it turned off. The bubbling of the porridge. I could picture exactly what she was doing, even with my eyes shut.

'Sit up slightly, darling. Start with the porridge.'

She slid a bowl in front of me, orange juice and a steaming mug of tea next to it. A tower of toast soon followed on the side. I knew I'd burned the roof of my mouth with the first spoonful but I didn't care. My stomach cramped after I finished the porridge, but I ignored it, smearing jam over the toast triangles and cramming them in, crusts and all. I licked every last bit of Mum's plum jam off my fingers before looking up.

'You were hungry,' she said, her eyes full. 'You need to eat properly when you've had a baby. It takes a lot out of you.' She stroked my hair and then got up, tidying the breakfast things while I hugged the mug. The dirt was etched so deep in my nails, I wondered if it would ever come out.

'I think the baby's got a full nappy. Do you . . . ?'

I shook my head, not looking up. I'd reused that disposable nappy too many times as it was. Scraped off what little poo there was and tried to dry out the urine. But nothing would dry outside in this cold.

'Don't worry, I'm sure I've got some of Sara's old ones somewhere. I kept all the baby stuff. Just in case I— Lucky, really.'

She leaned over me and stroked my hair again. 'Your poor hands,' she said, looking at my cracked and blistered fingers. The cloying sweetness of Kylie's nappy curled into my nostrils. I was glad I didn't have to deal with it for once. 'I'll have a look at them later, dress them for you. But right now I'll change the baby and then why don't you feed her and then go to bed for a few hours.

You look exhausted. I'll look after her. Then we can talk about what to do.'

I nodded and lay my head back on my hands on the table, the surface still warm from the bowl. There was nothing to worry about, nothing to think about. My eyes closed automatically. I could relax, I was safe here. I must have slept a little, because Mum woke me stroking my cheek, dragging me out of the warmth.

'I'm sorry to wake you, darling, but Kylie needs feeding. Then I'll let you rest properly.'

Kylie grasped my nipple straight away. Maybe being warmer helped her too.

'She had quite bad nappy rash,' Mum said. I swallowed. She'd developed that after a couple of weeks and it had been impossible to shift. 'But I had some barrier cream so I've put that on her. It should clear it up in no time.'

I heard the footsteps on the stairs and stared at Mum. 'I've told Dad, darling. Like me, he's just relieved you're home. Nothing else matters.'

I held my breath as Dad came into the room. 'Steph. Oh my God.' He hurried forward but then didn't seem to know what to do. His hand rested awkwardly on my shoulder. 'I'm so glad you're back. Mum and I have—' He took a breath. 'I'm just so glad.' He sat down on the chair next to me, still touching my arm, as if he couldn't believe I was real. I'd often thought of home and of Mum and Dad, and Fi and little Sara. But I'd never really considered how they felt about me. If anything I thought they hated me for everything that had happened, for how I'd treated Mum.

We sat there, me in the middle of them as if I were a small child, as Kylie fed for a long time, Mum stroking my hair to the same rhythm as Kylie's suckling.

Eventually the clock in the hallway jerked into life. I felt the seven bongs reverberate through my fingertips. It's funny how you can miss a sound.

'I need to get the girls up and ready for school,' Mum said, glancing over at Dad as she stood up and collected the dirty crockery, piling it in the sink. She slid two cereal packets on the table and laid out bowls and spoons.

The clatter disturbed Kylie and she slid off me, her face damp and warm from the milk. She'd never been so relaxed. I should have come home a long time ago. As soon as we went on the run. What had I been thinking?

'Right.' Mum was standing at the end of the table. 'Your room is waiting for you. I'll put a hot-water bottle under the sheets to take off the chill.' I stood up, suddenly not sure what I should do.

'Let me take the baby, so you can rest.' I handed Kylie over to her like a package. A pass the parcel.

Through the kitchen door I could see the huge bowl of potpourri on the hall table. I wondered if Mum had changed anything since I left. I wanted it to all be the same.

We walked up the stairs side by side. As we rounded the top, I heard Fi talking to Sara and suddenly wanted to see her more than anything. I started towards her room, but Mum gripped my shoulder. 'Not yet, darling. Rest first and then you can see them this evening.'

My room was exactly as I'd left it, though Mum had tidied it. The curtains had been neatly tied back from the four-poster bed, the princess canopy over the dressing table had been rearranged and someone had neatened the desk. I never lined things up like that. On the pillow Terry and June were curled together. I sat down next to them and buried my face in their warm fur, stroking their heads. Terry started to purr. It was as if he knew it was me without even opening his eyes. 'I'm back,' I whispered, taking off my clothes and sliding under the covers, carefully pulling out the second pillow from under the cats.

Had my bed always been this soft, this warm? It was like being cuddled by a cloud. It all smelt of lavender. Mum closed the curtains tightly, and the room became womb-like. Terry settled back down to sleep. Kylie was sleeping in Mum's arms – full and warm. At least I was doing that right. Finally.

There was crunching on the gravel outside.

'Mum—'

She sat down on the side of the bed, tucking the covers around me. 'Yes?'

'He's going to come after Kylie, I'm sure he will. He won't let her go. Patrick.' My voice trembled. I thought back to how distraught he'd been the evening before.

Her face twisted slightly as she rose to look out of the window. 'It's just Alice.' She turned to face me. 'You'll be safe here. Dad will keep a lookout while I walk the girls to school. And Alice will be around all day. I'll wake you at lunchtime,' she said. 'Dad will keep Kylie until I come back and then I'll look after her so you can get a proper sleep.' My belly growled and my feet and hands tingled with warmth. She slid the hot-water bottle next to me but I couldn't seem to open my eyes. I could relax now. I was safe and warm and full and Kylie was safe with Mum.

Chapter 15

Zoe

Spring 2025

'But I've got my birth certificate,' says Zoe. 'It's clearly got Mum and Dad's names on it.' It's like being drunk – she's confused and disorientated, as if nothing is how or where it usually is. She stares at Steph who shrugs.

'I don't know how they got that. I presume they must have known someone, bribed someone, maybe. I never registered your birth.' Her voice cracks.

Her stomach is boiling with nausea, ready to erupt. Zoe covers her mouth with her hand and swallows. 'It can't be fake,' she says, her voice wavering. 'I've used it for all sorts of things. No one's ever questioned it.' She can feel herself begin to panic, to hyperventilate, her chest tight. It's written in black and white on her birth certificate. Her parents' names are there. But here she's being told by this woman, her distant older sister, that what's there isn't true. She tries to draw in a breath. Alice touches her shoulder.

'Your parents were influential people,' says Alice. 'They might have found someone who was prepared to write a genuine birth certificate, especially as there wasn't an original.'

'I just don't see how all this can be right,' says Fiona, shaking her head and looking at Steph. 'I remember Mum being pregnant. I remember Zoe being born.'

'You remember what you were told to remember,' says Steph. She pushes away the mug of tea.

Fiona turns to Zoe. 'You arrived overnight. We came down in the morning and Mum was sitting in the armchair holding you in front of the fire. You were there, Sara, so were you, Steph.' She pauses and looks up to the ceiling, rubbing her eyes. 'Mum said she'd gone into labour after she put us to bed the night before, when Steph arrived. She said she hadn't wanted to tell us before because we'd get too excited. But I remember her being bigger, pregnant. She was definitely pregnant . . .' Fiona tails off. Zoe can hear her breathing.

'I don't remember any of that,' says Sara, looking between Steph and Zoe.

'Mum felt it would be better for you to be her child, that people wouldn't accept you being my child, that your life would be easier.' Steph glances at Zoe. 'That my life would be better too.'

The sickness explodes and Zoe rushes to the sink retching. Just liquid comes out. Alice follows her and pats her back as she did when she was a child. Sara joins them, a glass in her hand. 'Let me get you some water, you've had a terrible shock.' She fills up the glass and guides Zoe back to the chair. Her legs are weak.

'But I never saw you pregnant, Steph. You were never pregnant.' Fiona's voice is shrill, her eyes wide. She's still shaking her head.

'I wasn't there. I'd run away.' Steph swallows.

'You ran away?' says Zoe, taking a tiny sip of water to try to get rid of the sick taste in her mouth.

Steph nods. 'When I found out I was pregnant with . . .' Zoe looks at her, and swallows again. Her mouth is dry. Alice pushes the glass of water towards her but she shakes her head.

Steph stumbles over her words. 'I knew Mum and Dad wouldn't accept it, that they would go mad, that they'd try to make me give you up, so I ran away.'

The five women sit silently, each staring at the table. Zoe rests her head in her hands. It feels better to just shut everything out.

'Are you sure, Steph?' Fiona says at last. 'This is not just one of your wild fancies?'

'Of course she's sure,' says Alice sharply. 'Steph has kept this secret for thirty-five years. It's not something she'd make up.'

Fiona doesn't respond.

'You never forget having a baby. I know I never will.' Zoe looks up as Sara takes Steph's hand. 'But Zoe was brought up as Mum's baby. How did that happen?' Sara's eyes are full.

'Hold on,' says Zoe, the sickness receding, leaving her with so many questions. 'So I wasn't born at Highdown. Where was I born?'

Steph is looking at her lap, still twisting her shirt. 'Not that far away. We were living in an old bothy on the South Downs. We'd been living in an abandoned warehouse in town but the police were after us so we went into the countryside. We thought it was safer.'

'Christ,' says Sara. 'I can't imagine that. With a baby. It must have been so hard.'

'It was quite comfortable,' says Steph. 'Warm and dry all summer. At least until the autumn came. It was an early winter that year.' She tails off.

'The autumn?' says Zoe, staring at her. 'But I was born on the twenty-first of November.' She looks at Steph who is shaking her head. 'Wasn't I?'

'You were born in August, the seventh. I came back to Highdown in November and that's when Mum—'

The doorbell rings again, but for much longer this time. Fiona sighs and stands up. 'Let me just pay off the driver. Don't say anything until I'm back.' She disappears into the hall and they all sit quietly as murmured conversation drifts into the room. A minute later, Fiona slides back into her chair and looks at Steph. There are black marks around her eyes where she's rubbed her mascara. 'I think you need to start from the beginning.'

◆ ◆ ◆

Steph

1990

I woke several hours later, my breasts aching. A cold light filtered through the flowery curtains. Terry and June had both disappeared. I stretched out, my fingertips touching the bed post. It felt amazing to be in a bed again after months of sleeping on the floor. Everything was so soft, so warm.

I'd only been away eight months. Nearly two school terms. But it felt like a lifetime. It *was* a lifetime. I touched my tight breasts and wondered if Kylie needed feeding. But Mum would have brought her to me if she had. Maybe she was still asleep. It must be strange for Kylie being inside. Maybe she was relaxing too.

What would Patrick be doing? He would have realised immediately that I'd gone and he must know that I could only have come home. This was always my home. I tiptoed to the window and peered around the curtains. He'd come for me eventually. He wouldn't accept me leaving. He couldn't lose Kylie, not after what had happened.

On the bedside table was a book. *Matilda*. Fiona had been reading this when I'd left. Why was it in here? I'd read it years ago. I opened it and started reading. It was like being a little girl again, tucked up in bed, reading an adventure story. A few pages in, I heard footsteps on the gravel outside. I froze, not even moving my eyes. Whoever it was didn't go straight to the front door, but was walking around the perimeter of the house. The footsteps stopped almost underneath my bedroom window. Something was wrong.

I wondered if anyone would hear me if I shouted out. Alice would be downstairs somewhere, but she probably didn't even know I was there. Dad did, but he was locked up in his library with Kylie on the other side of the house. Maybe I was being paranoid and it wasn't Patrick at all. It could be anyone. John the gardener. The milkman. A delivery man.

I inched off the bed, careful to make no sound, and crept to the window. It was shut but the old metal windows had bloated, leaving gaps. I didn't dare move the curtain but I pressed my ear as close to the window as I could. Whoever it was, was still there. Maybe it was Terry. There was a flower bed beneath the window with Granny's roses. I had the scars from falling into them. He might be pruning them, readying the garden for winter.

'Steph,' a voice called quietly. 'Steph, please don't do this.'

My heart hammered in my chest. It had only been a few hours but already his voice sounded foreign.

'Steph, I know you're in there. No one closes the curtains in the middle of the morning.'

What a mistake. He was just a few metres below me. I could almost hear his breathing. I tripped over the rug running away from the window but righted myself and launched into bed, pulling the covers over my head.

'Steph,' he called a little louder. 'You can't take her away from me. Not after everything we've been through.'

I slowly lifted the covers, enough to peek out. There was a strange scraping which I suddenly realised was the drainpipe. He was on the drainpipe, climbing up, just as I'd used it to climb down. But he couldn't be. He was terrified of heights. He always got someone else to do any roof work when we were doing surveillance. But the scraping was getting closer.

The hairs on the back of my neck stood up and I shivered. Any minute now I would see his shadow at the window. I wanted to close the curtains on my four-poster. Surround myself with the fabric, curl up in the dark.

'Can I help you?' said a voice from outside the house, in a way that suggested no help would be forthcoming. Alice. Thank God. She would know what to do. She certainly wouldn't let him in. The scraping stopped and there was a thump, the sound I always made when I landed in the flower bed. He'd jumped down.

'I'm looking for Steph.' He sounded almost polite.

'We're all looking for Steph,' she said. 'Mr and Mrs Wright especially. But why are you climbing up a drainpipe?'

'She's in there, inside that room, with my baby.'

'What on earth are you on about?'

'Steph has my baby and she's here. Inside there.'

He sounded desperate and my heart twisted. Kylie was his baby too.

'Steph is here?'

He must have nodded because there was a long silence. 'I think I know who you are and I know you're not wanted here.'

That was what he said his mum had said to him when she'd thrown him out aged fifteen. *You're not wanted here.* Those exact words. I sucked in air. *Oh, Pat.* I'd wanted to make him better, but I couldn't do that sleeping rough with a newborn baby. It was impossible. Maybe he could live with us. Mum and Dad could love him like his mum never had, take him on as their own. But even as I imagined this happy-ever-after scenario I knew it couldn't happen. He was from a different world, he was too damaged to fit in here. The extremes of the life we'd lived was all he knew. And it was good, exciting, until—

'I just need to see her. Please let me in.' He was crying as he banged on the drawing-room window below. 'Steph, please. Let me in. She's mine too. Don't do this to me.' He banged on the window again, so hard that I thought it might break.

'You need to leave. Steph is not here. We don't know where she is.'

'She was with me, but she ran away last night. I'm sure she's here. Certain. Where else would she go?'

'Right, that's it. I'm calling the police.'

I heard Alice's footsteps crunch away across the gravel and imagined her walking back to the front door in that determined way of hers. I got out of bed and ran to the window, flinging open the curtains. He was still down there, looking up, his face white. His beautiful face. What had I been so frightened of?

'Steph.'

'Pat.' I opened the window. 'Stay there. I'm coming down.' I glanced at the drainpipe but I knew my body didn't have the strength so I tiptoed to my bedroom door. The gallery was empty, as was the hall below and I ran downstairs. The library door was shut and I could hear Dad and Alice. We didn't have long. I ran outside.

'Steph.' He flung his arms around me, gripping me tight. His hands chilled my back. 'Why did you leave?' His voice was full of pain.

'It was too awful,' I said. 'K—' I swallowed and buried my face in his freezing coat. 'I couldn't face it anymore. Kylie needed to be somewhere warm or—'

'I know. But we should have talked together, worked out a plan.'

'We were out of plans, Pat. This was our only option for Kylie.' I gestured towards the house.

'Is she inside?' I guessed she was in the library with Dad and Alice but I wasn't sure.

I nodded.

'You can't take her away from me. She's all I've got. The only thing that's ever wanted me. Properly wanted me.'

I'd wanted him. I still wanted him. Didn't he realise that? I thought he'd come for me and Kylie, but now I realised it was just Kylie he wanted. After everything I'd sacrificed for him. I took a step back from him. My home. My family. I'd left it all for him and he didn't care about me, it was only Kylie.

I heard Dad before I saw him. 'Patrick. I don't think we've met. I'm Steph's dad.' He was holding out his hand.

Patrick glanced at me and then back to Dad and there was a strange look between them and then he shook it. 'Hi,' he said, in that awkward way of his. 'I wanted to see Kylie.'

Dad looked at him and gave a half-smile. 'She's safe,' he said. 'She will always be safe with us. We will look after her, I promise you that.'

Patrick's eyes darted between Dad and the house and I wondered if he was going to dash in and try to snatch her.

'The police are on their way. You should leave before they get here,' Dad said gently.

'Just let me see her first.'

Dad looked at me and I nodded.

The three of us went into the house and Dad led the way into the library. There was a Moses basket on the sofa that I remembered Sara being in when she was a baby. Patrick glanced around at the books, at the mantelpiece over the log fire, and then back to me as if he couldn't quite believe this was my home. Then he saw the basket and knelt by it. He touched her cheek.

'She's so warm,' he said, looking up at me.

'Yes,' I said.

The chair creaked as Dad sat behind his desk watching us.

'It was too cold there, wasn't it?' He looked around the room again. 'This is a good place for her to grow up. Better than I could ever offer her.'

'Yes,' I said again.

The faint drone of sirens filtered through the window. I could tell by the way his shoulders hunched up that he'd heard them too.

'I wasn't a good enough dad, just like my own dad.'

'It was nobody's fault,' I said. I knew it was my fault. If only I'd not written that number down wrong.

The sirens were close now, at the bottom of the drive, I reckoned.

'Look after her for me. Love her for me.' His lips were on her forehead.

'You'll see her soon. You won't have to do long.'

'They need someone senior to make an example of. And I'm that person. We always knew that.'

I wiped the tears off my face and nodded. 'I'll tell her about you. And when you're out you can come and see her.'

'Oh, Steph, my little optimist.'

There was a squeal of brakes outside. Radio static filtered through the window. Dad got up and went into the hall.

'Goodbye, little girl. My beautiful little girl.' Patrick picked Kylie up from the basket and for one moment my stomach twisted. Would he try to make a run for it with her? But he hugged her tightly to his body and then laid her gently back down. I wanted to bottle that moment forever. She stayed asleep.

The library door opened and a plain-clothed policeman and three uniformed officers came in, Dad behind them. The plain-clothed one came up to Patrick with handcuffs.

'Patrick Head. I am arresting you on suspicion of causing an explosion with intent to endanger life or cause serious harm to property. You do not have to say anything unless you wish to do so but what you say may be given in evidence.'

Intent to endanger life? He wasn't trying to hurt anyone. It was the opposite of that. He was trying to save lives.

'Turn round. Put your hands behind your back.'

'Pat, no,' I said, but he just smiled sadly at me and did what the policeman asked.

Once he was cuffed, the two uniformed officers led him to the car, half dragging him though he wasn't resisting. I followed them, walking next to Dad. He looked up as they pushed his head in the car and I held up my hand. Then the door slammed and all I could see was a dark silhouette in the back of the car as it drove away.

The other police car remained on the drive. Dad and I walked slowly back into the house. In the hall the uniformed policeman stood looking at his shoes next to the plain-clothed one.

'Hello, Jerry,' said Dad. 'Can I get you anything. Coffee? Tea? Something stronger? It's been quite a morning for us.'

The plain-clothed policeman laughed. 'Can we have a chat privately? We will need to talk to your daughter about what she knows.'

'I understand. But perhaps not today, she's exhausted and needs a rest.'

'Of course.'

'Come into the library.' Dad turned to me. 'You go upstairs and rest, Steph.' I waited, shifting from foot to foot outside the library as Dad shut the door. The uniformed policeman watched me. I wanted to go in and pick up Kylie. Thinking about her made my breasts tingle and a droplet of milk appeared on both nipples, which quickly became a small stream. I ran up the stairs and took a tissue from the dressing table and pressed it on to them until they'd stopped. I needed to feed her soon or I was going to burst.

Chapter 16

Zoe

Spring 2025

After Steph finishes speaking, there's a long silence.

Zoe wants to talk to Mum about it, ask her if it's true. To hear her mother laugh at Steph's fanciful idea and draw her into a hug. Stroke her forehead and tell her what a fantasist Steph is. Of course Mum is her mother. How could she not be?

The tears are hot against her cheek. 'Why didn't Mum tell me?' she sobs. 'She would have known it would come out after she died. It seems so cruel that she left it to you.' She glances up at Steph, who catches her eye and then quickly looks down at the table.

So is this what Mum was on about? The thing that would come out after her death that Zoe wouldn't like? *Wouldn't like.* She thought it was not having a share of Highdown Hall. Not a seismic shift in who she is. What she is. She's no longer her parents' daughter. She can barely hold her head up, she feels so weak. Can it really be true?

'I wonder if she had blocked it out, denied it to herself,' says Sara, sliding another tissue across to Zoe.

'She had plenty of opportunity to tell me,' says Zoe, blowing her nose and then sniffing again. 'She just chickened out.'

'Maybe she didn't have the words,' says Alice gently. 'She held that secret for a long time.'

'You knew from the beginning, didn't you?' says Steph to Alice. 'From that morning, when he . . .'

Alice nods and glances sideways at Zoe. She takes a deep breath. 'Your mother *was* pregnant again when you ran away – I found the pregnancy test in the bathroom bin.'

All four women gasp in unison, their eyes on Alice.

'But she was hospitalised months later and had a stillbirth. Another girl.' Alice's voice breaks. 'I came and stayed here for a few days to look after Fiona and Sara.' She lifts up the teapot, glances at the mugs and tops up her and Steph's mugs.

'I remember that,' says Fiona. 'When Mum had her appendix out.'

Alice looks at her and shakes her head. 'And then a few months later, you returned home, Steph, and then the next day Milly told everyone she'd gone into labour overnight and here was a baby. It just wasn't possible.' Alice took a sip of tea and looked at Steph. 'The baby was small but it definitely wasn't a newborn. I've had three babies, I know what newborns look like. But your mum had put on weight over the past year or so, so perhaps other people believed her.'

She sighs. 'And you were in such a state, you poor lamb. I knew it was more than what you'd been through when you'd been away. Your parents then deliberately kept you away from Zoe.'

'Did Mum ever talk to you about it?' asks Steph.

Alice shakes her head.

'And you never said anything, to anyone else?' says Zoe.

Alice presses her lips together. 'It wasn't my story to tell. And I'd worked for your parents for a long time.'

'I remember you talking about Patrick, when you used to creep into my bed at night,' says Fiona. 'At the beginning you'd talked how much you admired what he was doing, how much he cared for the animals and how brave he was, risking arrest to free caged rabbits and monkeys and stuff like that.' Fiona stares out of the window. 'But I noticed how your face changed when you talked about him, how you were slightly breathless, excited. And then a few months later you told me you'd kissed.' Fiona laughs. 'I remember being so shocked. My sister, my big sister, had kissed a boy. So it was Patrick.'

'Patrick,' says Zoe, tasting the name in her mouth.

Nobody says anything for a long time.

'I think I'm going to cancel my flight,' says Fiona eventually. 'I can go another day.'

Sara nods. 'Yeah, me too. Let's all stay here tonight, then decide what to do later. It feels like we need to let this rest a bit.'

'I think I might go upstairs now.' Zoe stands and the four women look at her, a mixture of pity and worry clear on their faces.

Steph half stands but Zoe shakes her head at her. 'Not now,' she says, and turns to the door.

Back in her bedroom, she lies down on the bed. When she got up this morning, she thought she knew what was coming – saying goodbye to her three sisters, not certain when she'd see any of them again. She had not even the tiniest inkling that a few hours later it would be revealed that everything she knew about herself and who she was isn't true.

Her mother tried to warn her, she realises that now. After more than three decades of keeping it a secret, she wanted to tell her. Was it because she knew that Zoe would probably find out anyway? Or was the heaviness of the secret weighing on her all this time?

Mum had tried to bring it up a little over a month before she died. Maybe she knew that she was fading and that this would be one of the last times she'd be able to have a proper conversation. Have the energy and the brain power to structure a sentence and listen to the reply.

'It's difficult to understand other people's lives, isn't it?' she'd started, gripping Zoe's hand between her two hands. 'When I'm gone there will be things that will be said, that will happen, that you won't like.'

'What do you mean, Mum?' said Zoe, leaning forward over the bed and squeezing her mum's hand in return.

'I made decisions when I was younger, that I thought were for the best. For everyone. But looking back all these years later, maybe they weren't.' She tailed off and stared into space, her eyes glassy with cataracts.

'Oh, Mum, it's natural when you're coming towards the end of your life.' She swallowed. The nurse had said that she should be honest with her mother, but her tongue stumbled against the cruel words. 'To . . . to look back and think of the things you did well, and the things you could have done better. But you've had a good life. You've been a wonderful mum to us four.'

The hand gripped hers tighter. More strength than her mother had shown for many months. 'That's just it. I haven't always been. I made decisions that I thought were for the best, that I did for the best of reasons. But looking back now, I think I was wrong. And it's now too late to put right.'

'Don't be daft, Mum. We've all turned out all right. Well, all but Steph, maybe.'

Her mum winced and Zoe laughed. 'But that's not your fault. Steph's just a strange one, that's all.'

'Things may come out after I die that you don't like. That hurt you. And I'm terribly sorry for that. I've always loved you very much.' Her mum sighed and closed her eyes, the grip on Zoe's hand releasing. 'You were the best thing that happened to me and Dad.'

Now Zoe thought it had been unkind of her not to tell her then, when she had the chance. To leave it to Steph to be forced to reveal it now, when they were all grieving, seemed an added cruelty. Poor Steph. Her mother should have had the courage to tell her herself. Having been so close to her, having looked after her for months and months. Now it feels that Mum was just a complete stranger who she happened to know very well.

Her grief has been turned upside down. She's not grieving for her mother, but her grandmother. That suddenly seems less important, like her grief has been taken away from her. Reduced in value. Now she's also grieving for the relationship she hasn't had with Steph, her true mother, though that doesn't feel real either.

The worst is that Zoe can't now ask Mum questions about it. She can't find out why she took her on as her child, how she felt about it. Her mind flicks back to what Mrs Phillips said at the fete. Happy accident. But Zoe wasn't a happy accident that her parents had later in life. She was a granddaughter they took on from their eldest child. To replace their own much-wanted baby. The other Zoe.

Why did they keep it quiet though? Zoe thinks. It was 1990. Not 1950. Being an unmarried mother wasn't such a stigma then. They could have helped Steph out, and told Zoe who her real mother was when the time was right.

There's a quiet knock on the door. Zoe turns her head, her gaze catching on the mysterious key which she left on the mantelpiece. She could stay silent and they might think she's asleep. Or gone somewhere. The knock comes again.

Who does she want it to be? Bossy Fiona? Caring Sara? Or Steph. Her weird older sister. Distant. Reclusive. All but estranged from the family. And all along her mother.

'Zoe?' The voice is so familiar, and yet a stranger's.

◆ ◆ ◆

Steph

1990

My breasts had never felt so full. Kylie couldn't believe her luck. After three months of struggling to satisfy her, somehow there was more milk than even she could handle.

Mum sat on the side of the bed, stroking my hair. 'She's a good feeder, isn't she? Just like you were. You never turned down anything. Well, until you became a vegetarian, of course.' She laughed lightly but with less malice than she would have before. 'How are you feeling?'

I nodded. 'Better. I'm still so tired though. Like my bones feel tired. Like more sleep will never be enough.'

'Oh, darling, you've been through the most horrendous trauma. It's going to take you time to recover. But you're home, and we're here to support you through it. You don't have to worry about Patrick coming back. I spoke to the police and he's not going to be let out on bail. He'll be on remand until trial.'

I rubbed my eyes. Poor, poor Patrick. It wasn't his fault, it was mine. It was all mine. A chain of events that I'd started. If only I'd remembered the phone number properly. I took a deep breath, trying to force down the panic.

I leaned my head against her and she half-cuddled me as Kylie continued to feed.

'Can I see Fi and Sara?'

'Of course. I didn't say anything to them this morning as I was still in shock myself. But we can all have supper together. A proper family supper. We've all missed you, Steph. It hasn't been the same without you.'

A little fizz surged through me. I thought Mum would have hated me after everything I did.

'I'll do something special for you. How about a veggie cottage pie?'

My mouth watered at the thought. Food that wasn't from a packet. I never wanted to see another store-bought cheese sandwich again.

'Did you manage to eat well while you were away?' she said, her eyebrows drawing together.

I let out a long breath. 'Mum, it was awful.' Then I shook my head. That wasn't true. 'No, it was fine to begin with. After I left here, we moved to a new squat. An empty warehouse on the other side of town, near that sixth form I was going to go to. Where that carpet showroom used to be. So you couldn't find us.'

She winced.

'There was quite a few of us living there. Old carpet showrooms are comfortable places to stay. No shortage of decent floor coverings.' I laughed but didn't really mean it.

'Where did you have the baby?'

'In the squat.'

Mum screwed up her face. 'Oh my God, Steph, anything could have happened. You're lucky to be alive.'

During the labour I know I'd called out for Mum, I just couldn't help it. It was so much worse than I thought it would be. After the baby came, I'd drifted in and out of sleep. It felt nice. Like ecstasy. The pain had gone, just the odd cramp. People around me talked but I didn't really know what they were saying. Someone would tell me if there was something important.

◆ ◆ ◆

Baby, there was a baby. I knew that. Where was it? I pulled open an eye and saw Patrick sitting cross-legged next to me holding a baby. My baby. He had the baby.

'You okay, Steph? There's a lot of blood.' Merry's voice. I recognised it. I tried to nod but it was too much effort.

'Pat, drag your eyes away from that baby, there's a lot of blood.' Merry again.

'Shit, it's all over the mattress.' Patrick. 'We should have moved her on to one of those old carpets.'

'There just seems more than there should be. Don't you think?'

'How would I know?'

'Steph, I've got some pads here. I'm going to put them between your legs. Put some knickers on you to keep them in place.'

Merry was kind. She was always kind. I felt her move me, sliding the cotton knickers up my legs. That's what Mum would have done if she'd been here.

'Her legs are freezing. Pass me those blankets.'

'Don't get blood on them.' Patrick.

My heart was racing. Must be from having the baby.

Someone was panting.

'Her hands are cold too.'

Did we agree on Kylie for the baby? I wanted to call her Kylie. Was it a girl? I think it was a girl but maybe it was a boy. I wanted to ask but my mouth wouldn't move properly.

'Steph? What you trying to say? Shhhh, everyone, she's trying to say something.'

'Kylie,' I managed and then it started to go patchy and starry. The pain started to grow.

◆ ◆ ◆

'It was okay in the end,' I said quietly.

'Just the thought of you having a baby on your own, I should have been there for you.' Mum had her hands in front of her face.

'I wanted you there,' I said. Her face softened into a small smile.

'Did you? I would have been there, if I'd known where you were. I looked everywhere for you.'

We sat in silence, listening to Kylie suckling and gurgling.

'So how come you ended up outside?' she said eventually. 'Why did you leave the place you were staying?' She couldn't bring herself to say the word 'squat'.

I knew I shouldn't tell her, but I was just so tired, so tired of it all. I needed to tell someone. I needed to talk about it. 'We were targeting another lab. We'd made a home-made bomb. What we usually did was to plant it and then call in to warn people to vacate – cause maximum disruption – and then rescue the animals. But I messed up. I must have written the number down wrong. I basically called the wrong number with a bomb warning. So they didn't have notice to leave. No one was hurt, but—' My voice caught.

'Oh Steph, it wasn't your fault, of course it wasn't.' The words were right but I wondered if she meant them. Old Mum would always talk about me being a child, getting involved in grown-up things, that things weren't my fault, that I was incapable of making my own decisions. I took another breath through my gritted teeth. 'They blamed Patrick, of course, said it was his fault because he was the leader. We heard there was a warrant out for his arrest. So we had to leave. Kylie was a month old then. We stayed in different people's places for a while.' People were kind but nobody wanted a crying baby staying with them for long. And Kylie cried and cried all the time. 'But then eventually we ran out of options and we found an old, abandoned place on the Downs. It was fine until it started to get cold. And Pat couldn't work because he was afraid of being arrested. So we had no money.'

I couldn't go on. There were no words to describe the last month in that place.

'Oh, Steph, you've been through so much. You both have. What a start for poor Kylie.' She stroked Kylie's downy head. She'd finally had enough and had fallen asleep, her face pink and damp with milk. She really was the most beautiful thing I had ever seen.

Somehow now I could enjoy her. See her for what she was without the constant worry of whether I had enough milk, or where we were going to get water or food from.

'I'm just glad you're home now. You're safe and home with your family where you belong and we'll look after you and we can decide what to do next.'

I let my head roll back and took a deep breath, letting it out slowly. Now was the time to tell her. I had to tell her if I was going to make it right. I had to be honest with her. 'Mum.'

'Yes?' She had her head tilted to the side, a small smile on her face. Happy to have me back, to have all her children safe and sound. I knew what I said next would destroy all of that.

'There's something else I haven't told you. Something awful.'

Her smile started to fade.

◆ ◆ ◆

Mum walked beside me down the stairs. 'I've told the girls there's a surprise,' she said, her mouth curving into a smile which didn't reflect in her eyes. Halfway down she stopped and turned to face me. 'Look, Steph, I don't think we should mention the baby for now. Dad and I have talked about it . . .'

I wondered what she'd told Dad. I hadn't seen him since Patrick had been taken away. The words 'intent to endanger life' still rang in my ears. I curved my arms around my stomach.

'It'll be too much for them to take in at their age. Let's just focus on your homecoming. That's the exciting thing and it will be easy for them to understand. Then we can introduce the baby later.'

My shoulders dropped. I'd been so excited about showing them Kylie. They were both her aunts now, which seemed strange when they were so young. I'd always thought of an aunt being an elderly person. 'Okay,' I said. It wasn't like I had much choice. I never had much choice in this house.

'She's fast asleep now anyway. After such a busy few weeks I think she needs to catch up,' said Mum.

A busy few weeks. She had no idea.

I'd missed Fi and Sara almost as much as I'd missed Mum and Dad. It's funny how things that you think are really annoying at the time are the things you miss the most when you no longer have them.

Dad opened the oven as we came into the kitchen, steam billowing out in big clouds. He lifted the cottage pie on to the table. The smell made my mouth water. Fi and Sara had their backs to me, filling up their water glasses at the tap. They both seemed taller and Sara's hair had grown much longer. I slid into my usual seat.

Fi screamed as she turned, spilling the water on the floor. 'Steph!' Mum took the glass before it smashed, as Fi threw herself at me. I pulled her into me. She smelt exactly the same as she always did. Sara slid underneath my arm, and the three of us stayed like that for what felt like forever.

'Surprise!' Mum said.

Fi looked up. 'When you said earlier there was a surprise, I thought you meant we were having Angel Delight for pudding!' She laughed, her whole face grinning. 'I can't believe you're back.' She gripped my arm. 'I've really missed you.'

Sara was more shy, staring at me, her eyes wide. 'Hi, Steph,' she said.

'Hi,' I said.

'Right, everyone, let's sit down. We don't want it getting cold.'

It had been eight months since I'd last sat down with them all. Suddenly that time concertinaed. It was hard to believe what had happened. I squashed an urge to rush upstairs to see if Kylie was real. Of course she was real. I knew she was real. I took a bite of the cottage pie, my taste buds fizzing with the joy of real, home-cooked food.

'Neither of you seem very happy that Steph is home,' said Fi eventually.

Mum and Dad glanced at each other. 'I'm over the moon,' Mum said simply. 'It's just been a shock and a tiring day. A lot has happened. But I can't tell you how wonderful it is that the five of us are around the table again.'

The warmth spread from my stomach into my heart and head and out into my fingertips. It had been the right decision to come home. Even though Patrick had been arrested. Kylie and I were safe and would be looked after and that was all that mattered.

'Can we stay up late and watch TV with Steph?' Sara had hardly spoken all meal. We turned to her.

'I think Steph will probably want an early night, but, yes, you can stay up a little later,' said Dad. Both Fi and Sara squealed.

As silence descended there was the unmistakeable sound of Kylie beginning to cry. Fi and Sara didn't seem to notice. I rose from my seat but Mum's glance told me to sit down. 'I'm just going to check on something.' She walked out of the kitchen, closing the heavy door behind her.

Dad picked at his food, occasionally glancing up at me. Like I was some strange exhibit in a museum. Fi ate with one hand linked through mine. Sara, opposite her, stared at us both, and I got the feeling that she wasn't entirely happy I was home. Perhaps she'd enjoyed having Fi to herself.

Mum came back as we were washing and drying. She smiled at me and nodded. Kylie was fine. Thank God. It was strange not being with her. I'd been with her non-stop, never parted for more than a minute for the past few months. With no pram, I'd carried her all the time. My arms felt empty, useless now. I dried a saucepan, and hung it from the hook.

'Dad's got the new video of *Who Framed Roger Rabbit?*,' said Fi, jumping from one foot to the other. 'Can we watch it, Dad, to celebrate Steph coming home?'

'I think so,' said Dad. 'Go and brush your teeth all of you, and get your pyjamas on, then you can watch it under duvets on the settee.'

The other two scampered upstairs and Dad went into the drawing room to set up the video.

'You too, Steph,' said Mum, scraping her uneaten dinner into the bin.

Chapter 17

Zoe

Spring 2025

'Were you never tempted to tell me?'

Zoe stops abruptly outside the half-closed kitchen door, her heart thudding so loudly she wonders if she's missed Steph's reply.

'So many times,' Steph says eventually. 'I couldn't believe that you couldn't see it. It seemed so obvious to me . . .'

'I'm so sorry, Steph, I feel like I've massively let you down.' Fiona's voice drifts through the gap. 'All these years, I had no idea.'

'It's not your fault, Fi,' Steph says gently. 'It was just what happened. What was decided.'

'I remember you coming back, after you'd gone missing, really clearly. Just being there when we were about to have supper. I was so excited.' She laughs. 'But I don't really remember much after that.'

'I was only home for a couple of weeks before I went to boarding school.'

There's a long pause before Fiona speaks. 'That seems so barbaric, to send you away like that.'

'Yes,' says Steph.

'I can't quite believe it all,' says Fiona. 'Why would Mum do that? Take your baby and say she was her own? And then send you away.'

'I guess she thought it was best for me,' Steph says.

'I can't imagine what you've been through.' Fiona again. 'Watching Zoe grow up and not being able to have a proper relationship with her.'

Zoe bites her lip. *Poor Steph.* This is as bad for Steph – worse probably – as it is for her. Somehow becoming closer to her over the past two weeks has made this news easier. Before this, she always thought of Steph as being difficult, reclusive. Now she's begun to see why she was like that, and how similar she and Steph both are.

Steph says nothing for a while. 'It was awful,' she says eventually. 'I couldn't deal with it. I wanted to be close to her but when I was it was painful. So in the end I kept away.'

'Secrets are like splinters, aren't they, buried deep in your skin, which eventually work their way to the surface,' says Fiona.

'I thought this secret would be buried forever,' says Steph. 'Until Zoe read the will, and then I knew it would come out. It had to come out then.'

Fiona sighs. 'And yet, if it wasn't for Alice, I would be on a plane back to Singapore right now. And it might have come out later when we were all apart. Alice did the right thing, I think. She made sure it happened while we're all together. So we can support one another.'

Steph's voice is quiet. 'I'm glad that we're all here together.'

'It's a lot for Zoe to deal with,' says Fiona. 'And just after losing Mum. I know she's in her thirties, but Mum always babied her. She's never even lived on her own.'

Trust Fiona to comment on that, thinks Zoe. Has Fiona ever lived on her own? She married Charles almost as soon as she left Highdown Hall.

'I think there was a reason for that – she wanted to keep her close,' says Steph. 'After we'd all gone away, Zoe was the one who had to stay.'

Yes, because everyone else abandoned Mum and Dad, thinks Zoe. She could have travelled, had her own children, married Ben. But even as she thinks it, she knows it's not true. Until now, until all these revelations, she was happy with her life. She felt she was making a small difference to the world. One person at a time.

There's the clatter of mugs being put into the sink and Zoe readies herself to walk into the room.

'When you first started to tell us, I think I realised before you said it what you were going to say.' Fiona's voice is quiet and Zoe has to concentrate to hear her. 'It's like the conversation had been floating in my mind for years, something I overheard as a child but didn't understand at the time. But I get what they were talking about now.'

There's a moment of silence, then the scrape and flare of a match.

'I didn't know you smoked,' says Sara. Zoe hadn't realised she was there too. The three of them cosy inside the kitchen, she separate. She pushes away the sting of jealousy. She wants to be in there with them. But she can't make herself push open the door.

'Only very occasionally. Do you want one?'

Sara must have nodded, because there's the sound of another match strike and then a slight cough, which must be Sara. Mum would have a fit if she could see them smoking inside.

'I remember I'd been sitting in the scullery, playing with my farm animals,' starts Fiona. 'Mum and Dad were in the kitchen. They'd been silent and I hadn't realised they were there really until Mum said something like, "No one will ever guess. Why should they? They probably think it's about time we had another anyway.

That we would try again for a boy." Dad said that was true. But then he said something along the lines of, "Is it the right thing to do? For both of them?"

'Mum said there was no alternative, that two lives would be ruined. She said they needed to act now – I remember very clearly that she said "this will be the best for her", presumably meaning you, Steph, and that you were Dad's favourite and that you were so bright, and could go on to do anything. Then you couldn't do that in the situation you were in, and something about giving you a clean slate.

'At the time, I thought at first they were talking about me.' Fiona laughs. 'I thought I was Dad's favourite. But the rest of it didn't make sense. Then I think I knew it was you because Mum said she'd been so worried about you and now the worst had happened and they could protect you. They were worried about people finding out later. And I remember sitting there while they sat quietly and then I remember Mum saying she'd "make the arrangements".

'And then they went upstairs. I sat in the scullery knowing I'd heard something important but not understanding what it was about. I guess my brain just filed it away with all the other useless information. I went into the kitchen after they'd gone. Both chairs were pushed back. The olive stones in the ramekin in the centre of the table were sprinkled with ash. Two cigarette stubs in the bottom. Dad had left the rest of the cigarettes and the lighter on the side. I remember picking them up and keeping them for you, Steph. There was a part of me that perhaps always knew. That had interpreted their conversation correctly but had denied it to myself for years without ever consciously thinking about it. But it all makes sense now.'

‘That’s where it was all decided then, I suppose,’ says Steph. ‘My whole life changed – Zoe’s whole life changed – by that one conversation. In this room, around this table. It doesn’t feel real.’

There’s a long silence. Zoe is about to go in, when Fiona starts speaking again. ‘I remember so many happy times, though, before everything. D’you remember all the times we sat on your roof smoking?’

Steph laughs. ‘God, yeah. I thought about that afterwards, when I was at boarding school. How bad I’d been getting you to smoke.’

‘I was ten when I had my first cigarette with you.’

‘Bloody hell,’ says Sara.

‘I remember the first time I found you smoking,’ says Fiona, ‘do you?’

‘When you almost locked me out on the roof?’

‘Yeah, I’d gone into your room and it was freezing, so I went to shut your window and then you shouted at me and then told me to join you.’ Fiona laughs. ‘I remember being terrified climbing out of the window, and creeping along the ledge to the side of the turret. We could see for miles.’

‘The views up there are still amazing. I went out on the roof the first night we came back two weeks ago. The night Mum died. The stars are so clear. Orion, Ursa Major, Cassiopeia. There was an old packet of tobacco in a plastic bag, stuffed under one of the tiles. It must have been there for more than thirty years.’

The three women laugh.

‘When you went missing, I used to go out there, y’know,’ says Fiona. ‘Sit in the same place and think about you and where you were. You’d left some cigarettes and some vodka up there. I drank it over the first few weeks after you left.’

‘Is that where you went?’ says Sara. ‘I knew you had a hiding place that I didn’t know about.’

They lapse into silence again. Zoe takes a step towards the door.

'Look, I've been thinking. Maybe you and Zoe need some time alone, to talk things through. This has been massive news for me and Sara but it's far more significant for you both,' says Fiona.

There's no response from Steph and Zoe's heart contracts. Does she not want to talk to her?

But then Steph's voice cuts across her thoughts. 'I'd like that, but it has to come from Zoe. I knocked on her door earlier and I know she was in there but she didn't answer. I don't want her to think I'm trying to impose something on her, that I'm going to try to be her mother now. I know that Mum will always be her mum.'

'I don't think she'll think that. But you two need to start talking sooner rather than later. The longer you leave it, the more difficult it will be.'

'Maybe.'

'I was thinking that you should get out of here to talk. Give yourself some space. This place has too many memories for all of us. Maybe go into the village and go to the pub or the Indian or something.' Fiona again. 'Get away from Highdown.'

'Yes, you're right. Sometimes this house feels too much, like it's crowding in on us,' says Steph. 'I'll try again now.'

There's a scrape of a chair against the brick. Zoe steps back and runs into the drawing room, hiding behind the door as she hears Steph's purposeful stride come out of the kitchen, cross the hall and go up the stairs. Zoe lets herself out of the French doors and half runs down the path towards the woods. She doesn't feel ready to talk to Steph. Not yet.

◆ ◆ ◆

Steph

1990

'It's for the best,' said Mum, steepling her fingers together over her dress.

'It will give the baby the best possible chance in the world and you a clean slate,' said Dad. 'The chance to start again. Just like you wanted.'

I didn't understand what they were saying. I was still so exhausted, despite sleeping for some of the day. My bones still felt tired. I stared at them, but their faces were closed.

'Steph, did you hear me?' Dad's breath sounded heavy.

'I don't understand,' I said. 'Kylie's mine.'

Dad nodded. 'But you're a child yourself, Steph. A child going through some challenging times.' He looked at Mum. 'We've talked about it, we've talked to Granny Evelyn and Grandpa Edward this evening, and we think it's best.'

My thoughts skittered around the room. I tried to grab them, focus on the one thing I wanted to think about. But there was too much noise – the clock ticked, the fridge hummed into life next door, somewhere a lawnmower whirred. Mum lifted her mug to her lips and sucked the tea into her mouth. Granny and Grandpa knew now. Why did she tell them? It was like she was trying to take over. I wanted to be the one to tell them.

A tiny fist appeared for a second above the wicker basket they'd brought down from the loft. She'd woken. She released a small mewl. She was hungry. And needed milk now. Over the past few months, I'd got much better at understanding her messages. The mewl sounded harmless enough but if she didn't get milk within the next minute, it'd build into a crescendo of almost unbearable noise. Patrick hated it, said it got on his nerves, so I got used to being ready to feed her at any time. The thought of him made my stomach twist.

I stood up and walked towards her, desperate to feed her. My breasts were hot and taut and I felt shivery despite the heat of the room. But Mum was already there, her hand under Kylie's bottom, lifting her on to her chest. I watched her, my nipples prickling. Mum walked over to the sideboard where there was a small saucepan I hadn't noticed before. Holding Kylie in one arm, she lifted out a bottle and wiped it on a napkin before walking back and sitting down. Kylie was building into a climax. Terry and June got up from their spot by the fire and stalked out of the room in unison.

Mum slipped the teat of the bottle into her mouth. She stopped crying and went to suck on it but immediately pushed it out of her mouth.

'Mum, she doesn't need that bottle, let me feed her.' The front of my jumper was completely soaked. My breasts were weeping for Kylie.

'Steph, this is the best way.'

'But she doesn't like it.' Kylie's face was a bright red tomato. An angry tomato.

'She had some earlier and got used to it eventually.'

She had some earlier. 'What? You had no right!'

'I just wanted you to get some sleep. And then you were having supper.'

It was only a few hours, I thought. *She should have woken me*. And I'd wanted to go and get her during supper. 'She's my baby.'

The milk was dripping through my bra, through the folds of cotton into the wool. A droplet fell on to my belly underneath my jumper.

'Steph, you've been sleeping rough with her for months.' Dad's words were like a slap. 'Months outside in the winter with a small baby. That's not what's best for her. It's neglect. It's cruel.'

Mum looked at him and swallowed.

'I had no choice,' I said to him, not looking at his face. I pressed my hands into my chest, using the wet fabric to cool my breasts. 'Mum, I need to feed her.' I stepped forward and grabbed the corner of the shawl, pulling Kylie towards me. Mum was pulled off balance and fell against the settee but she managed not to drop Kylie.

'Steph!' Dad shouted. Kylie was screaming, flailing at the bottle. My chest was wet with the milk she was so desperate for.

Mum steadied herself and moved back to the sideboard. She shook the bottle again and dripped a tiny droplet of milk into Kylie's mouth. Her pink tongue pushed it away and she screwed her face up. But it must not have tasted as bad as she initially thought. She paused for a moment. Mum dripped in more milk and Kylie licked it. She stopped crying and started rooting again. Mum slipped the bottle into her mouth. Kylie looked confused and tried to push it out but then suddenly grabbed it and started to suck.

'There, there,' said Mum, as she sat down on the sofa. 'That's better, isn't it, baby?'

My milk had stopped leaking, but my t-shirt was sopping wet. I sat down opposite her and watched her feed my baby, Dad with his arm around her, looking down at Kylie. The perfect family portrait. I'd been that baby once.

Then it was like I was watching myself watching her feeding Kylie. Like I was on the ceiling looking at everyone. And then suddenly I was back inside me, my belly churning. *Why don't they call her by her name?*

'Dad, she's my baby.' I tried to keep my voice calm but I could hear the tremor. 'I know I need help with her. I need Mum to help me. But she's mine, Kylie's mine.' I realised I was shouting.

'Steph, for once just listen.' Dad spoke as if he wanted to punch something. 'Given everything that's happened, I don't think the baby would be safe with you.' He glanced at Mum. 'You're not in the right frame of mind to look after a baby.' He cleared his throat. 'You've always been the clever one, Steph. You could really make something of yourself. But not with a baby at your age.'

I shook my head. 'I don't want to make something of myself,' I said, mimicking him. 'I'm a mother. That's what I am now. I can go back to school when she's older.'

'Steph, darling, I know you want what's best for the baby, don't you.'

Mum said it like a statement, not a question, but I nodded anyway. My heart was thudding so hard in my chest, it was making me feel sick.

'Of course you do. Every mother wants what's best for their child. I want what's best for you.' Kylie sucked rhythmically now. Her eyes shut, her hands clenched by her sides. My belly dropped. She'd betrayed me.

'I know this is going to be a very difficult thing for you, but if we bring the baby up as our child, you can start again. You'll still see her all the time, live your life with her, but you'll be able to focus on your education – you've really missed out recently. But you're so bright, I know you can catch up.'

'I don't want to go back to school,' I shouted.

'What kind of future can you offer her? You struggled enough before you had her,' said Dad, not looking up. 'Where would you live? How would you earn enough money to feed her, clothe her? Patrick's likely going to prison for a long time. Babies can't survive on love alone.'

'I'd live here with you. You'd both help me to bring her up. And when Patrick comes out of prison, then he can live here too.'

Mum winced and turned to Dad.

'Steph, that's not realistic,' he said, shaking his head.

'Please, Dad, just give me a chance. Give Kylie and me a chance.' I'd never wanted anything more than I wanted this. 'Please, Dad. No one need know, if that's what you're worried about. I promise not to leave Highdown.'

Mum looked out of the window and sighed.

'You haven't done that well for the past few—' Dad stopped, and I knew what he was going to say.

There was a long pause, he couldn't seem to speak. But Mum could. 'What Dad means is that we're worried about the baby's safety. You've had such challenges these last few years, that maybe it would be better for everyone – the baby but also you – that we bring her up.' She rubbed the scar on her forehead.

Dad closed his eyes, his hand still around Mum's shoulder. 'It's for the best, Steph. It's the best for you and for the baby.'

I felt like a rabbit in one of Dad's traps, who, too late, realises that being tempted by the carrot was a fatal error. I should never have come home. Even Patrick at his worst was better than this. My stomach turned and I shuddered.

'I'll tell everyone,' I said. I could just run away again. Take Kylie and go. But I thought back to the woods, and how cold it had been. And what had happened there.

Mum pursed her lips. 'If you do that, you'll be harming this beautiful baby.' Her face softened as she looked down at Kylie. 'Harming your own child. And we know where that leads. Child neglect and worse. K—' She looked at me with hard eyes and I knew what she was saying.

'Think of the baby and her prospects. If she's brought up as your sister, then everyone will accept her. She'll have the best of everything here. A future. And so will you. And you'll still have a relationship with her – a strong relationship. The two of you can thrive.'

Kylie had fallen asleep on the bottle, as she so often did on my breast. Mum took the teat out of her mouth and carefully slid Kylie back into the Moses basket. She looked so natural doing it. Like she knew what she was doing. I'd never felt that. She adjusted the blanket around her and smiled. Dad looked down at Kylie and shared another smile with Mum.

Kylie started and flung her arms above her head. Her cheek was pink. It would be damp from the milk. I stared at her, willing her to wake, to do something. Maybe Mum was right. Maybe this was better for Kylie. And what choice did I have, really? Where could I go now? Patrick was gone and that was all my fault too. In the past few days, I'd lost everything. It felt like there was nothing left to lose. At least this way she would be safe. And I'd be with her.

I stared at Kylie again. *Wake up. Show me what to do. Show me what to do like you've done before.* But she stayed asleep.

Chapter 18

Zoe

Spring 2025

'Go ahead, Jeremy,' says Fiona. 'We're all listening. I'm here with my sisters. Sara, Zoe and Steph.'

Her mobile phone is balanced on the butter dish in the centre of the kitchen table. The four women surround it, each cradling a mug. Zoe catches herself thinking of them as her sisters but then stops. They're not her sisters at all.

'Right. I've looked into the will in detail over the past week. I've talked to the son of the solicitor who drew it up.' The official voice pauses. 'His father is retired now but the son was able to speak to him, and because of the slightly unusual terms of the will, the old man remembered it.'

Steph is tapping on her mug with her fingernail. 'Will you stop that?' says Fiona. 'I can't hear what Jeremy is saying.'

Steph looks away but stops tapping her finger.

'To explain the will, I need to go back to the beginning. As I understand it, your late mother Camilla Wright came from a wealthy country family. The DeProses. There appears to have been some reluctance within the family to her marriage to your father who came from a less-well-off family.' He clears his throat.

'Yes, Dad was a farm labourer, we know that,' says Fiona.

'Your mother was eventually given permission to marry but only on the understanding that there was a pre-nuptial agreement. The pre-nuptial agreement set out the terms of what would happen in the event both of any divorce but also on the death of your parents and who could inherit. Happily, the marriage was a success and there was no need for divorce. But the pre-nuptial agreement had strict terms about who could inherit your mother's heritable estate – essentially Highdown Hall and the surrounding land – what's left of it now. Her moveable estate – cash, jewellery, books, etc. – she was free to do with what she pleased. But the property – Highdown Hall – was a different matter. This had been gifted to your mother by her parents on her marriage to your father. They wanted to ensure the property didn't pass into your father's hands if there was a divorce. They didn't really want it to go to anyone outside the immediate family. This is really the crux of it.'

Fiona waves her hand impatiently. 'Yes, yes.'

'Under the terms of the pre-nuptial agreement, which we see reflected in your mother's will, the only beneficiaries for the family home and land were to be Camilla's children – her own biological children. She was precluded from leaving the land to any organisation or anyone except her children. It had to stay in the family. There were separate conditions if they didn't have children, but obviously that was not the case.'

They all stare intently at the phone, although Zoe knows they're only going to hear what they already know. There's silence on the phone.

'Jeremy, are you there?'

'Yes, sorry, did you miss that? The line is a bit crackly. I said that under the terms of the pre-nuptial agreement, which is reflected in the will, the only beneficiaries for the family home and land are her children. So Stephanie, Fiona and Sara – in equal shares.'

Zoe's stomach seems to fall, as if she's jumped from a great height. To hear her mother's children listed by this official disembodied voice and for her not be in that list brings the reality of her situation crashing home. She's not her mother's child. She will never get used to that, no matter how many times she hears it.

'Well, at least we all know for sure now,' says Fiona. 'We know the reasoning behind the will. That it wasn't Mum's fault, she had no choice.'

'I think we already knew that, Fi, but anyway . . .' Zoe takes a sip of tea.

'While the will cannot be challenged, in reality, now that the three of you own the property, you can do what you like with it. If you, as the three daughters, decide that you want to gift a share to your mother's granddaughter, then that is your legal right to do. There will be tax implications, of course.'

Three daughters. Mother's granddaughter. She always felt separate from her sisters, different somehow, but to repeatedly hear it in this official language is worse somehow.

'My recommendation would be to wait for a while, to let the dust settle, and then decide what you want to do,' the voice says. 'I'll be here to support you through whatever you decide. It won't be as complicated as you might imagine.'

Zoe looks around the kitchen that she's been in almost every day of her life. Every nook and cranny is familiar to her. When the will was first read out, not having her share of Highdown Hall seemed like the worst thing that could ever happen to her. Now it feels like the least of her worries. She gets up and stands at the window, looking into her mother's abandoned herb garden. The rosemary and oregano are leggy with age while the parsley and basil's new shoots are growing through last year's brown, withered stalks. A huge weed strikes through the middle, adding to the wildness. Behind her she hears Fiona saying goodbye to the solicitor. There's a scraping of chair legs and then silence. Thank God they've gone. She just wants to be on her own. She really must do something about the herb garden. Her mother would hate to see it neglected.

She turns and jumps slightly when she realises she's not alone at all. Steph sits immobile at the table, hands planted on the wood, staring at something in the distance. In her hands is a folded piece of paper.

'You made me jump,' Zoe says, unable to stop the note of accusation in her voice.

'Sorry,' says Steph. 'I just wanted to say that if there's anything you want to know, from that time . . .'

Steph is biting the skin at the side of her thumbnail, her grey eyes watching her.

'I want to speak to Mum, that's what I want. To ask her why she lied all those years, why she didn't have the courage to say anything at the end. I feel so—' Zoe swallows. 'So angry,' she bursts out in a shout.

Steph recoils but then speaks so quietly that Zoe barely hears her over the sound of her own heart. 'I feel angry too. It wasn't what I wanted. I need to show you something.'

Out of the corner of her eye, Zoe sees her pick up the letter. She doesn't want to look at it. She doesn't care what's in it.

'D'you remember when you handed out those envelopes with the will readings in them? The day Mum died?'

Zoe stares at her. That feels like a million years ago. The before time.

'You said you thought there had been two sheets of paper in my envelope, rather than just the funeral reading.'

Zoe keeps looking at her, saying nothing.

'You were right,' Steph says, unfolding the piece of paper. 'The other was a letter from Mum.'

She smooths it out on the table.

Zoe grits her teeth. Steph got a letter from Mum, but she, the forgotten daughter, her non-daughter, got nothing. No letter, no explanation. Nothing. Just a posthumous disowning. A de-daughtering.

Steph slides it across the table towards Zoe.

Zoe sits down and stares at it, but the words blur before her eyes.

There's a long silence. 'Do you want me to read it?' asks Steph eventually.

She should read it herself, thinks Zoe. But she feels so angry, so let down, she worries that she'll tear the paper into tiny pieces, destroy her mother's words. Her grandmother's words. She nods, and Steph takes the paper back and then has a sip of tea. It must be cold by now.

> *'Dear Stephanie,*
>
> *'If you're reading this, then we have not reconciled and that is something I deeply regret.*
>
> *'I want to apologise to you for many things, things that I never had the courage to discuss in person while I was alive.*
>
> *'Firstly, for not having the courage to tell Zoe about who her mother is, and for leaving you to do it after I've gone. In the past few years, I've tried desperately hard to get the terms of the will changed, but my parents were clever and there was no legal loophole we could use to get out of it. So I knew that Zoe's heritage would come out once I'd gone. I'm sorry that that has been left to you at such a difficult time. I shouldn't have laid that on your shoulders.*
>
> *'Your dad always argued that Zoe had the right to know and you had the right to be her mother. Having reflected on this for the last thirty-five years,*

I know he was right. I'm sorry I didn't come to that conclusion when there was time to rectify it.

'I want you to know that I took Zoe as my child with the best of intentions. I thought it was best for both you and for Zoe. With everything that happened in the months and years before you left and what happened while you were missing, I was terribly worried that bringing up a baby wasn't the right thing for you. I was worried that you weren't in a position to be Zoe's mum and that could be detrimental to her. I was concerned you'd run away again and take Zoe with you and anything could happen.'

Steph falters. She swallows audibly and carries on. Zoe stares out of the kitchen window. The sickness in her stomach has never quite gone away and she can feel it growing now.

'But as the years have gone by, I've realised I maybe did it for selfish reasons. Dad and I had desperately wanted another baby. I was pregnant when you left – I realise we were actually pregnant at the same time, which seems so odd. But I lost that baby a while after you left and was very ill. We were told that we couldn't have any more. Somehow when you turned up with a baby and saying you wanted a fresh start, I mistakenly saw Zoe as my second chance. But now I realise that, with our support, you would have been able to raise Zoe as your own. Our relationship was so difficult at the time and I couldn't see past that. With time, I've realised that much of that was my fault. I just panicked so much about what was happening and didn't know what was for the best.'

Steph's voice breaks. Zoe wants to reach out to comfort her but hesitates at the thought of touching her.

Steph takes another sip of the cold tea and picks up the letter again.

> *'I'm sorry for not being the mother I should have been to you. I tried but I know I was often wrong and we ended up at cross-purposes. I know now that if I'd behaved differently and tried to get more of a support network for you, you may not have run away but would have come to me when you found out you were pregnant and everything would have been very different.*
>
> *'I wonder if you will show this letter to Zoe. I hope so as it will mean that you will start to reconcile and can begin a new life together.*
>
> *'I have tried many times to write to Zoe, but there are no right words really. What I did to her was as wrong as what I did to you. I know I deliberately turned her against you by talking you down. I was scared that she'd recognise you for who you are and she'd leave me. After you, Fiona and Sara had left, I was terrified of losing Zoe too. Especially after Dad died. So it was easier to continue with the pretence, than face facts and tell her the truth.*
>
> *'I'm so very sorry to both of you. I hope more than anything that you can start to reconcile.*
>
> *'With love always,*
>
> *'Mum.'*

Steph's gaze raises from the letter to meet Zoe's. *Is there a chance of reconciliation?* her eyes seem to be asking. Zoe swallows and turns to look out of the window at the kitchen garden. This all feels too much, too soon. To hear from Mum from beyond the grave. She wishes more than anything that Mum had left her a letter too. There's the sound of the door closing and when she turns back to look, Steph has gone. The letter settles on the table.

◆ ◆ ◆

Steph

1990

'Did you realise Mum was having a baby?' asked Fiona. 'She said that we'd get too excited if she told us beforehand, but it's not that big news. I don't get why she didn't tell us that she was pregnant and then leave it until she had the baby.'

God, she's stupid, how can she not see? But I just shook my head. When I told her I wanted it to be on my terms.

'It's so weird,' Fiona said, pulling a face. 'She's so old for starters.'

I shrugged. 'Forty-one.'

'Ancient,' said Fiona. I turned away so she couldn't see my smile.

Fiona flopped down on to my bed. 'I'd noticed that she was fatter but I didn't think she was pregnant. Mrs Edmunds at school was huge for months before she had hers.'

I wanted her to know, I wanted her to keep asking questions. 'Do you think it's her baby?'

Fiona propped herself up on her elbows. 'What do you mean?'

It's my baby, I screamed at her in my head. *Can't you see?*

'Well, she could have got it from somewhere.'

'Even Mum's not that weird.' She pushed her fringe out of her eyes. 'I just didn't think they'd still be doing it.' She pulled a face again and stuck her tongue out. 'Not at their age.'

From upstairs in the nursery, Kylie started to cry. Even though my milk had started to dry up, the sound made my breasts tingle. I crossed my arms.

'She's always crying too,' said Fiona, sighing. 'And Mum has no time for anything today. It's all about the baby. Baby this, baby that. Thank God you're back.' She looked up at me. 'Sara was so boring to play with.'

I smiled at her. *I'll tell her one day. Mum can't stop me. I'll tell them all. Fiona, Sara and Kylie. Kylie has a right to know who her mum and dad really are.*

'Mum said that you were sleeping on the street. Is that true?' Her eyes were wide, like I was straight out of one of her adventure books.

I shook my head. 'We stayed in Patrick's squat for a bit and then moved to a little hut in the woods.'

Fiona tipped her head to one side. 'How romantic.'

I think back to the ice on the inside of the windows in the morning, how it felt to be always some degree of cold. The ache in my belly that never seemed to be filled. 'It wasn't romantic, not really. Mum is a bitch but being at home is better than where I was.'

Fiona grinned at the word bitch. 'I hate her,' she said without feeling.

'Me too.' *She's trapped me here, taken my baby and left me with nothing. I'm warm and full but nothing else.* 'She's a bitch,' I said again, grinding my teeth against the word.

I lay down next to Fiona and we stared at the ceiling. I wondered what Patrick was doing. Had they really charged him with endangering life? That seemed so ridiculous. He wasn't endangering anyone's life. What they did was murder. Killing innocent animals.

I wondered if I could find him, write to him. I wanted to tell him what was happening, what Mum was doing to me. Maybe he could escape and we could grab Kylie and run away again. He'd talked about going up north. The ALF was growing up there too and needed new people. We could start again. The three of us.

'D'you wanna game of Connect 4?' asked Fiona, turned on her side, her eyes shining.

I nodded. Anything, anything to distract myself from Kylie. Hearing her, seeing her. It was a hunger, a need. I wanted to grab her and run. Whatever the consequences were for both of us. If only Patrick was here.

Fiona disappeared out of the room and then reappeared a minute later with both the Connect 4 box and Sara.

'Sorry,' Fiona said, shrugging. 'She insisted.'

Sara jumped up and down on the bed. 'We can come in your room again,' she said.

'Stop it,' I said, but I didn't mind, not really. They were the only good things about being home. That and Kylie seeming happier.

'How about me and you against Steph?' Fiona said to Sara. 'She's too good at this game.'

'Why don't we see if the baby wants to come and play with us too? It could be me and her against you two,' I said.

Sara pulled a face. 'The baby's boring. She doesn't do anything. I thought it'd be fun having a baby sister but she just lies there.'

'She can roll over.' She'd done it for the first time the day before we left, looking as surprised as I was to be staring up at the roof and not the blanket.

Fiona screwed up her face. 'Not that useful a skill for Connect 4,' she said, pulling the blue frame out of the box, pushing it down into the duvet and dividing up the yellow and red counters between us.

Upstairs Kylie started crying again, and thinking of her made me miss Fiona and Sara getting four in a row.

'We win, we win,' shouted Sara, jumping on the bed and turning the Connect 4 frame upside down.

Fiona laughed and I picked up the grid to reset it.

'I'm glad you're back,' Fiona said quietly, as Sara whirled around the room shouting.

My face started to wobble and I swallowed back the tears. Despite it all, I was glad to be back too. It was better that Kylie was safe and well, than spending the winter in that hut. I leaned forward and hugged Fiona.

◆ ◆ ◆

I didn't think I heard her right the first time. It was only when she said it again that I caught it properly.

'What did you call her?' I asked, watching the steaming water fill Kylie's bottles. Mum paused for a moment and put the kettle down.

'Baby Zoe,' she said, as she reached towards Kylie in the bouncy chair. 'Didn't I, baby?' she said in that irritating sing-song voice. An image of me punching her flashed across my mind and I was on my feet. But she'd got Kylie in her arms then, bobbing her up and down.

'Her name's Kylie,' I said, a sickness boiling in my stomach.

'I know that's what you called her first,' said Mum, using the baby voice. 'But Dad and I have talked about it and we just don't think it's a good fit.'

'A good fit?' I echoed. What the hell did she mean?

'People are going to think it's really odd that we'd name our child after an Australian pop singer. Stephanie, Fiona, Sara and

Kylie just sounds strange. Wrong somehow. We thought Zoe would be a better option.'

The sickness spurted up into my throat and I gagged, swallowing it back down. 'You can't change her name,' I said. 'That's what we called her. That's her name!'

'I think it's for the best, Steph.' Mum rested her hand on my shoulder. 'It's best for you too. It'll give you some sort of mental separation from the baby you gave birth to.' Her voice was odd, strained somehow. But her face was the same as always. Rigid. She seemed a different person to the one who'd opened the back door to me yesterday.

I was on my feet again before I realised it. It was like watching a film as I caught the underside of the empty bouncy chair and flipped it across the room, smashing into the fireplace, the poker and tongs clattering on to the hearth. A brown streak fled out of the door. Terry. Kylie's screams added to the chaos, and my heart twisted at her voice, but there was a stillness in the centre of the noise. I stopped running when I reached my bedroom and I threw myself on the bed, the thumping of my heart filling my ears.

'Steph?' She'd sent for backup. Dad's head appeared around the door, disembodied. I couldn't look at him.

'Can we have a chat?' *We*.

I said nothing but they both came into my room anyway. Mum took the chair from my desk and turned it to face me. Dad perched awkwardly on the bed.

The skin on my palms had split where the eczema had taken over and clear fluid had leaked out, mixed with specks of blood. It hurt but there was also a pleasure in picking it, waiting for Dad to talk.

'This is clearly not working,' Dad began. Something light began to grow in my belly. *They've realised they've made a mistake. They're going to give her back.* I started to sit up and look at them for the first time. But Mum didn't look contrite. Her face was closed, more set than usual. Dad looked as uncomfortable, as if he was about to explain the facts of life to a pre-pubescent child. My eyes flicked between the two of them. The lightness morphed into a hard ball.

'It's not working for you – you're clearly very upset – and I'm worried it's going to have a bad effect on Zoe, and on Fiona and Sara.'

'Kylie,' I said, 'she's my baby. You have no right to change her name.' There were bubbles of clear liquid under the skin. I pressed them, trying to burst them. How could it be so itchy?

'When we agreed that we'd take her on as our child – your sister – you promised not to call her your baby,' Mum said.

'We never agreed that,' I said, my voice rising without even meaning to. 'You forced me into that.' I focused on picking my skin, squeezing the fluid spots. If I had a pin it would have been easier. I loved the feeling of the pin pricking the top of the bubble and it then all seeping out. So satisfying.

'We didn't force you, Steph,' said Dad. 'We all agreed it was for the best. Best for you, but also best for the baby.'

'The baby, the baby. My fucking baby.' I was shouting then, but it was like it was coming from someone else's mouth.

Mum got up and closed the door. Dad stared at his hands.

'In order for this to work for everyone, we think you need a bit of a break from one another.' Mum spoke slowly, enunciating each word carefully, as if I was a particularly dim child.

'There's also the issue of school. You weren't around to sit your GCSEs, and you really should have started your A-levels now.'

Dad hadn't looked up but I could see the tension in Mum's face. *She's worried about how I'm going to react.* She was building up to whatever it was slowly. Treating me like a child. She shifted in the chair a fraction and looked towards Dad but he didn't move.

They wanted me to go back to school, I realised. But I'd have to go down a year, to sit the exams. *There's no way I'm doing that.* It would be excruciatingly embarrassing. There was a girl once who had to repeat a year. Tina something. Everyone took the mickey.

Mum's lipstick hade bled into the thin vertical lines around her lips. 'We think you should go back to school to do your exams.' And there it was. 'You had a bright future before all of this.' She waved her arm at nothing in particular. 'And we want you to achieve that.'

'I'm not going down a year,' I said immediately. 'It would be too embarrassing. Everyone would know.'

Mum and Dad glanced at each other and Dad nodded.

'We completely agree with you,' said Mum. 'That would be awful for you.' She paused a second. 'So we thought you could go to a new school where nobody knew you.'

Their faces were turned towards me as if they were waiting for me to say or do something. 'What school?' I said finally.

'Mum's found a lovely school that would allow you to go back a year to sit your GCSEs and then you could go on to do A-levels next year. With your brain, if you worked hard then you'd easily get good grades.'

Mum had glanced at Dad when he said her name but now looked back at me. 'It's a lovely school, beautiful grounds, there's a swimming pool, tennis courts, they play lacrosse. Just like those books you used to read.'

They were looking at me as if I was a ticking bomb. 'And?'

'Well, what do you think?' said Dad, visibly swallowing.

'I obviously want to go back to school. I can't not have any qualifications. And I get that having school to focus on will help everything with Kylie.' I emphasised her name and looked at Mum. *She's not going to win that one. My baby, my name.*

'Good, I'm glad you agree,' said Mum, starting to get up. 'We think it's for the best. It'll be a clean break, make it easier to separate yourself from her. When you come home in the holidays, you'll be able to see her as a sister.'

When I come home in the holidays? I stared at her and she stood still, holding on to the back of the chair. Dad smoothed down his hair.

'What do you mean "when I come home in the holidays"?' I asked, looking between them.

Dad leaned back.

'It's a boarding school, Steph,' said Mum, her voice wavering.

I heard myself start to pant. 'I'm not going to a fucking boarding school.'

'It's for the best, Steph. Fresh start. It'll allow you to come home and see Zoe as your sister, not—'

For the best. For the fucking best. It's all she seemed to say.

The bedside lamp hit her full in the face and she fell on to her knees. Redness seeped through her hands as she clutched her cheeks and nose.

'Oh my God!' Dad stood staring at me. 'Steph,' he said determinedly. I picked up the water glass and he held up both his hands and started to walk backwards. I threw it and it smashed against the wall behind him. He lifted Mum up by the elbow, his arm around her, and turned to the door.

'I'm not going to a fucking boarding school,' I screamed again, throwing a book against the closing door. I sunk to my knees and buried my face in the duvet. I should never have come back.

Chapter 19

Zoe

Spring 2025

Sitting opposite Steph in the Indian restaurant in the village that evening, they seem to have so little to say. Or maybe there's too much to say and it's impossible to know where to start. Perhaps just being in one another's company is enough for now. They say that if you can sit in silence with someone then that's the sign of a good relationship. But this isn't a comfortable silence, it's heavy. Expectant.

The waiter slides two beers on to the table and Zoe immediately takes a sip, grateful for something to do with her hands.

'Why did Mum do what she did?' She wasn't planning to say anything. Wanted to wait to see what Steph did. But it comes out without her knowing.

Steph's head looks up from the menu. She taps her fingernails on the laminate. The buzz from the curry house recedes into the background.

Zoe can hear the whine in her own voice, as if she's the sixteen-year-old. 'It was 1990, for God's sake, not 1950. There were loads of single mums.'

Steph sighs deeply. 'Single mums were still vilified in 1990. Thatcher was in power when I had you—'

They catch each other's eye. Zoe wonders if she'll ever get used to hearing Steph saying she is her mum.

'Thatcher was always attacking young single girls who she said deliberately became pregnant to jump the housing queue and get benefits. It wasn't until later, under New Labour, that that changed. Maybe it would have been different if I'd been born later.' Steph sighs. 'Mum did it for me but also for you. I can see that now.'

Zoe stares at Steph, waiting for her to continue.

Steph lines up the cutlery against the place mat. There's some kind of mandala on it. 'She didn't want me scarred by having a baby so young. I hadn't sat any school exams and she was worried about what that would mean for my future and what bringing up a baby would do to me. For you, she didn't want you scarred by being the child of a single mum. Yes, it was the nineties, but she was a forties child, when having a baby outside of marriage was a scandal. And she didn't approve of Patrick.'

Patrick. In all the shock of discovering Steph was her biological mother, she barely thought about Dad not being her father. It feels so disloyal even thinking it. Dad was always a great father to her. Especially once the others had left home and it was just the three of them. It is impossible to imagine he's not her actual father. 'What was he like?' She hates herself for asking the question, it feels disloyal to Dad, but she needs to know.

'He was complicated. He'd been brought up in care after his mum threw him out – children's homes mainly – and he was very hard, traumatised. But he found the animal-rights movement and it brought out the best in him. It gave him purpose.' She pauses and looks far away. 'I think in the animals he saw himself – someone who had been abused by the system and needed rescuing. He was a brilliant activist at a time when it was incredibly hard. He's included in several books about animal activism in the eighties and nineties.'

'Is that how you met?' asks Zoe.

Steph nods. 'We met on an operation to free some goldfish from a fairground.' There's a memory of a smile on her face. 'When I was thirteen.'

'And from what you said, he knew about me, you were together?'

'Yes, he was with me when you were born. He loved you very much. He'd been desperate to be a father. A good father.'

'Explain to me properly – why wasn't he able to stay with you, be my dad?'

Steph picks up her beer and takes a sip. She settles it down, arranging it carefully back in the same wet ring on the table. 'Just after you were born, we were part of an operation against an animal-testing lab in Sussex. Not that far from Highdown. I messed up, I was supposed to call someone at the lab and warn them about the devices we'd planted. But I dialled the wrong number. So the site wasn't evacuated and the bomb went off when there were people still on site.'

Zoe gasps. *Patrick killed someone?*

'No one was hurt,' Steph continues. Zoe feels herself relax. 'But Pat was caught on camera and an arrest warrant was put out for him. Which is why we went on the run and were living in the woods with you.'

Steph takes a sip of her drink. 'When I came back here, he followed me to beg me to let him see you. I'd never not wanted him to see you, I just couldn't face living rough anymore.' She shivered. 'Dad called the police when he came to the house. They came to Highdown and caught him and he was sentenced for all sorts of things. Intent to endanger life, possessing explosives, criminal damage, arson, escaping custody. He'd had a few past convictions because of his animal-liberation work and they basically threw the book at him. They treated him like a terrorist.' Steph looks down and sighs. 'It wasn't his fault he couldn't be involved in your life.'

'But I never heard from him, he never made any effort to contact me, to tell me the truth,' says Zoe. She knows it's the shock and rejection speaking but can't help herself.

'He was inside for a long time. They wanted to make an example of him.'

'What does he look like?' asks Zoe. 'Have you got a photo?'

Steph takes out her phone and does a quick internet search. 'Here,' she says, holding out the phone to Zoe. 'This is him. Patrick Head.'

'Oh my God! I recognise him,' says Zoe, her mouth open. 'He's come to a couple of public meetings I've led.'

'What?' says Steph. 'So he's still about? Local to Highdown?'

Zoe rubs her forehead. 'Yes. I think so. I think he lives not that far away. In the farm by the chalk pits. I went out there once.'

Steph nods. 'I remember that place. So what's he doing?'

'He does stuff with XR and animal-welfare causes.'

'That sounds like Pat,' murmurs Steph. 'He'd never give up that cause.' She looks into the distance. 'So after he was released from prison, he came back to be close to you, to see you.'

'To be close to you too,' says Zoe.

'To be close to you,' says Steph. 'Ours was no great love affair, or at least not on his side. I was in love with him, I worshipped him. But I don't think he felt the same about me.' She swallows. 'Until it turned out I was pregnant and then he couldn't do enough for me. He loved being a father – it was all he ever wanted.'

Zoe looks at her. A mother who ran an animal-rescue centre, a father who was an animal-rights activist. Maybe it explains how she ended up being a climate activist. It was in her blood all along.

'And you've not been in touch with him since?'

Steph shakes her head. 'No, I haven't spoken to him since the day he came here and the police took him away. We didn't have phones or anything. And then I went away to boarding school anyway and life took a different path. I wrote to him many times, through different people, but he never responded. He obviously knows who you are. I'm sure he'd want to meet you properly, as his daughter, if you wanted to.'

Zoe presses her lips together. How odd that last week she thought she'd lost both her parents and now she finds out that they're both alive. She's not even sure how she feels about it.

The waiter appears with a plate of poppadoms and bowls of chutneys.

'Mum always said she called me Zoe because it was Greek for "life",' says Zoe. 'I guess that makes sense now, that you would call me that.'

Steph puts down the piece of poppadom she's broken off. 'I didn't call you Zoe,' she says. 'That was Mum's choice.'

Zoe stares at her.

'I mean, it's a beautiful name and I think it suits you much better.' Two spots of colour highlight Steph's cheeks.

'Than what? What did you call me?'

'It was a silly name, really. But then I was just a kid.'

Zoe sits with her hands folded in her lap, watching Steph.

'I called you Kylie,' she says finally, her tongue catching on the name.

'Kylie. Wow. After Kylie Minogue?' Kylie rings a bell in her head. Where has she heard that name recently?

Steph nods. 'I loved her at the time, listened to all her music and did the dance routines. Sorry it's a naff name, I just really liked her.'

'I like Kylie, it's a sweet name,' says Zoe eventually. 'But how weird to think that I had a different name.' Kylie doesn't really suit her, she thinks. She's not a Kylie. Zoe sounds more serious, a proper name. Maybe Mum had the right idea. Or maybe the name you're given influences the person you become. Would she have been a different person if she'd been Kylie all her life? Would she have been a different person if Steph had raised her?

'Thank you,' says Steph, picking up her beer glass. She slops some of the liquid on to the tablecloth and then dabs at it with her paper napkin.

Didn't Mum mention Kylie in one of her letters to her mother?

They eat the poppadoms in silence and the main course arrives. They chat about Fiona and Sara for a bit and watch an awkward first date at the next table.

Then she remembers. There was the letter from Granny to Mum about a Kylie and Kai. She's Kylie so who is Kai?

'Is that everything?' Zoe asks. 'No other secrets?'

Steph looks down and tears a piece from a chapati, stuffing it into her mouth.

Zoe watches her methodically chew. 'Steph?' It's the first time she's used her name since she found out. She wonders if she will ever call her Mum, or ever think of her as her mum. But there's something wrong. She's ignoring her. She looks flustered. 'Steph? Steph, what is it?'

'There *is* something else,' she says, a tiny piece of the bread flicking on to the table in front of Zoe, who stares at it, waiting, dread filling every pore. 'It's linked to the key you found.'

'The key?' That isn't what Zoe is expecting. She's carried the key with her since it went missing. She takes it out of her pocket and lays it on the table. 'This key?'

Steph stares at it if it might explode. 'Only Mum knows this, and Granny and Patrick. We never told anyone else. Even Dad.'

'And?'

Steph picks at her nail. 'You have a twin brother,' she whispers.

That's it, thinks Zoe. *Kylie. Kylie and Kai. They were the names mentioned in the letter. Kylie and Kai.*

◆ ◆ ◆

Steph

1990

'You're a good lad, aren't you?' said Patrick, stroking Kai's cheek. 'Not like your naughty sister.' He sat on the wooden bench in front of the empty fireplace. It had been raining for days and the small amount of wood we'd found was too damp to light.

My feet and back ached from walking back and forth but it was the only way to keep Kylie's screams to a murmur. The minute I stopped she seemed to think she was going to be fed.

It was the coldest night by far, the sky stretching like a planetarium over us, the hole in the roof acting like a telescope. Last night I'd done star jumps for minutes at a time to keep warm. But we'd run out of food again and my limbs felt too heavy to lift.

'Can't you just feed her?' he said, as Kylie got louder.

'I've tried. You know I've tried. There doesn't seem to be anything there.'

'What do you mean nothing there?' He watched me over his shoulder as I paced.

'I'm just so thirsty,' I said, trying to squeeze some saliva around my tongue to lick my cracked lips. 'If I had a cup of tea or something, I'd have milk for them.'

'We all want a fucking cup of tea,' he said, resting his cheek against Kai's. 'He's cold, Steph.'

'We're all cold,' I said, briefly wondering if there was any part of me that was warm. When I'd peed that morning, I'd wanted to hold my hands in the stream just to feel something warm. When you've been that cold, it's hard to remember ever feeling warm. In the depths of winter when you're wearing every item of clothing you own, it seems impossible to believe that in six months you could be sweltering in shorts and a t-shirt.

'No, I mean he's really cold.' He stood up.

'You need to put him inside your coat, it's the only way.' Kylie was nestled between my jumpers and my coat, my scarf wrapped around her hat.

'He fucking wriggles too much. I worry he's going to suffocate. Kylie might scream but at least she's still.'

I took off my glove and touched Kai's cheek. My hands were so cold, it was hard to feel whether there was any difference with him. We were all cold. But he looked different somehow. Slower, maybe.

'Look, you take her and I'll put Kai under my coat.' The change in my pace upset Kylie. She started to build up to her drill-like scream. 'Hold her,' I said to him. Patrick shook his head and started shaking Kai gently. 'She's better with you. C'mon, my lad. He'll be okay.'

I went back to pacing from one side of the bothy to the other, avoiding the mud, now frozen to a slippery crust. Kylie settled into a low grumble. I fantasised about toasting crumpets in front of the roaring log fire at Highdown. I'd turn round and Mum would pour me a mug of tea. I'd gulp it in one, burning the roof of my mouth, and get her to pour me another. I'd slather Sussex honey on the crumpets and it'd melt and drip through the holes in the bottom, melding with the butter into a deliciously sticky and warm mess. Or maybe it would be one of Mum's home-made jams. I'd eat the whole packet and Mum would smile and open another and hand them to me to slide on to the toasting fork. I'd sit so close to the fire I'd singe my slippers.

‘Steph, Steph, he’s not moving now.’ Patrick’s urgency sliced into my fantasy and I was back in the starlit bothy. ‘Look,’ he said.

He held out Kai to me and I sat on the bench so I could keep Kylie inside my coat and hold Kai in my arms. I kissed his forehead, my lips immediately cooling where they touched him. He was a heavy sort of cold. A still sort of cold.

I shook him slightly, expecting his eyes to open, his mouth to start puckering with the beginning of a cry. But he stayed silent. ‘Kai, Kai, darling. Wake up.’ I took off my glove and touched his cheek. I still couldn’t tell how cold he was.

‘Kai, Kai.’ I kissed him again and then shook him, harder this time.

‘Careful, you’ll hurt him,’ said Patrick, leaning over.

My heart was thumping, adrenaline making me warm. ‘Kai.’ I was shouting then and Kylie started to cry louder.

I unzipped my coat and took her out, handing her to Patrick. ‘Put her inside your coat.’ He shook his head.

‘Put her inside your fucking coat.’ I ground out the words and he silently undid his jacket.

I took off my own coat and my top jumper and immediately started to shake uncontrollably. The jumper fitted twice around Kai and I slipped my arms back in my coat and slid him between my breasts. Despite being so cold myself, he made me colder. Even the proximity to the milk he had wanted earlier so desperately didn’t make him stir. *Fuck.* I breathed warm air down on his face, my breath jumpy. *Come on, Kai. Don’t do this. God, don’t do this.*

Maybe we were being punished for what had happened at the lab. Maybe that was it. But it wasn’t Kai’s fault. He hadn’t even been born then. I imagined being in the village church, kneeling in front of the altar, begging. *Please, please, God. I’ll do anything. I’ll go home, tell Mum, tell everyone I’m sorry and I was wrong. Tell the police what happened. I’ll tell them where Patrick is. Do everything and anything. Study. Sit my exams. Never go out again. I'll even help Fi with her maths.*

We stayed like that for a long time, my hips swaying with muscle memory. Kylie kept up a steady stream of protests inside Patrick's coat. He said nothing but watched me and Kai.

'Check him,' he said eventually.

I stared at Patrick. I didn't want to check him. I didn't want to know. The not-knowing was better. He was just chilly and I was warming him through. Like any mum would.

I'd do the Duke of Edinburgh thing Mum had been on about. I'd visit old people. I'd help John in the garden. If only Kai would be alright.

'Fucking check him, Steph.'

'I can't, I can't bear it if—' I tried to say, licking my lips. My tongue was swollen in my mouth. I looked down at the top of his head, hiding underneath my scarf. I wanted Mum.

'Here, there's a little water in the bag finally.' Patrick reached up and took one of the plastic bags off his water system. I sipped it, licking my lips and then holding the little water in my mouth. I offered it back to him and he shook his head. I drank down the remaining water. It felt like nectar slipping down my throat. I licked the inside of the bag to get any remaining liquid and handed it back to Patrick for him to rig up again.

Kylie was lying on the bench screaming, and my nipples finally prickled. *Thank God.*

Patrick wrenched open my coat, the zip tearing. He grabbed Kai and opened up the swaddling. There was no reaction from him. I sat down on the bench and picked up Kylie, shoving her towards my breast. I could feel some milk oozing out and she started suckling immediately.

'Give him here,' I rasped at Patrick. He handed Kai to me, and I slid him under my jumper positioning his mouth on my wet nipple. There was no reaction from him but then he'd always been a poor feeder compared to Kylie. I readjusted her and then squeezed the milk into his mouth but it just dribbled off and slid down his cheek on to my jeans. I took him out from my jumper and looked at him properly.

His face was grey, his eyes closed. I touched his cheek. 'Kai,' I whispered.

Patrick dropped to his knees next to me. He was sobbing. 'He's gone.'

Anger flared inside me. 'If you'd just put him inside your coat like I said—' He smacked me across the face, and I jolted to the side, gripping both babies tightly. Kylie screamed as she lost contact with my nipple. Kai didn't react.

'Don't fucking blame me. It was you who fucked up at the lab and brought the police on to us. It's your fault we ended up in this shithole. If he dies, then it's your fault too.' A blast of cold hit me as he disappeared through the door, which then swung back on itself, letting in another gust of freezing air.

I couldn't bear it. I couldn't bear it. I dragged Kylie back to my breast but she couldn't seem to get what she wanted. I put Kai on the other side and sat there, Kylie thrashing and Kai perfectly still. So still.

I wanted Mum. I wanted Mum here. She would know. She would make it right. What had I done? Patrick was right, it was all my fault. Calling the wrong number to warn them about the bomb had set off a whole trail of events – the lab not being evacuated; Patrick being named as a suspect; having to go on the run with the twins; running out of safe places to stay and then finding this hut; the money going and having no food; Patrick's temper meant we had lost the few friends we had; winter; cold. Kai had always been the smaller twin. Would it have been different if I'd had him in hospital? They had those plastic jugs of water in hospital. Food brought to your bed every few hours. Warmth. Clean sheets. I could have had that if I hadn't called the wrong number.

My arms had gone numb and I readjusted them. Kylie grumbled and shifted slightly. Kai was still. People who didn't have twins would never get what it was like to have two babies. One and one didn't make two, whatever they'd said at school. The weight of both of them in my arms.

After what seemed like hours Patrick reappeared. 'I'm sorry,' he said straightaway. 'I just couldn't—'

He saw me with the babies crossed against my chest and a spark of joy illuminated his face. I shook my head. He came over then, and knelt in front of me. Kylie had fallen asleep on my breast, her mouth still wet. Patrick slipped his hand under Kai and lifted him off. His face was stained with milk, the creamy white only emphasising the grey of his cheeks. Patrick was crying again as he wrapped him back up in the blanket. He stood there cuddling him for a long time. I couldn't look at them. I missed his weight already.

Eventually he sat down in the corner of the room, Kai on his lap.

'He'll be cold like that,' I said. But he just shook his head and looked at him.

I wrapped Kylie back up and slid her underneath my jumper, my forehead touching hers.

◆ ◆ ◆

I must have slept for a while because I woke with my heart thudding, wondering where Kai was. How he was. I stared around the room, then saw Patrick was asleep, sitting on the cardboard in the corner, leaning over Kai, his hand on him. The remembering was almost as painful as the discovery. My eyes pricked but no tears would come.

Kylie woke up but didn't cry; her anger at the pathetic amount of milk earlier had seemingly been exhausted. She looked up at me, her dark blue eyes unblinking. *Would she remember these months with her twin?* I wondered. She'd grown with him, entwined with him for nine months within my womb and then spent another three living with him outside, their bodies still entwined at times. Their feet would touch when I fed them together. It looked like they were playing footsie. Would she always feel there was a part of her missing?

Tell me what to do, I telepathed to her. She stared back at me. I asked her again.

The crescent moon cast shadows through the patchy roof. For the first time I noticed a faint tinge of blue on Kylie's lips. Maybe it was just from her crying. My torch battery had died a long time ago so there was no light and I didn't want to wake Patrick by going outside. I eased off one glove and her face chilled my already cold fingers. *She's freezing,* I realised. *Maybe it's only because she was born the biggest that she's the strongest, that she's survived this long.* My heart contracted and I looked into the corner of the room where Kai appeared to sleep peacefully on Patrick's lap in the Babygro he'd never grow out of.

What shall I do? I asked her again. *Mum, I need you. What should I do, Kylie?* Stiffly she turned her head towards the door. I glanced at it. We'd stuffed plastic shopping bags in the gaps, but still the wind had got through, creeping under the blankets to snap at our toes, seeping into every pore, every bone.

I held her close against my body. I tensed every muscle into moving as slowly as it could, inching across the room. I leaned over Patrick, and pressed my lips against Kai's cold cheek. I would never forget that feeling, that moment.

Before I opened the door, I looked round. There was nothing to take. All the things I'd so excitedly brought from home eight months ago had been stolen or sold. What was left was just squalor. Piles of rubbish from the snacks I'd bought or stolen from different shops and the twins' used disposable nappies, though most of those had been reused many times.

I gripped the door handle and pulled it open slowly, my eyes fixed on his face. I couldn't see Kai from the way Patrick was leaning. My baby and I slipped through the door, and I pushed it to, then I was running, tripping, the moon and stars lighting the way home to Highdown.

Chapter 20

Zoe

Spring 2025

The four women stand together outside the ice house in the woods staring at the moss-covered door. Zoe takes the envelope marked *Kai* out of her pocket and removes the heavy key. 'I can't believe I didn't check the ice house,' she says. 'I tried it everywhere but had completely forgotten this place.' She hands it to Steph who looks at it for a long moment, weighing it in her hand.

'After I'd told Mum what had happened that day, we went back to the bothy,' she says, still looking at the key. 'It was a twenty-minute drive and then a five-minute walk – that's how close I'd been all those months.' She looks up at Fiona and Sara.

'I thought you were in town, you know. In a squat or something. I somehow felt you were close,' says Fiona. 'I couldn't understand why they couldn't find you.'

'Mum said she'd walked near the place with Woody looking for me months before.' She takes a deep breath. 'When we arrived, he was still there. Kai was still there. Tidied into the corner. Patrick had covered him with the baby blanket our friend Merry had crocheted.' Steph puts her hands over her face, the key between them. Fiona rests her hand on Steph's arm.

'He was still perfect. It had been less than twenty-four hours but he was still perfect. Mum picked him up and cradled him, kissed him on the forehead.' She swallows. 'She was crying as she held him. We both were. She'd brought a bedsheet and a wicker basket, the one we had for picnics. She said that if anyone asked, we could just say we were going for a picnic. In November.' She gives a strained laugh.

Steph puts her hand out on to the outer wall to support herself. 'We walked back to the car like that and then she put him on the back seat.' She sighs. 'I wish I'd asked to hold him again, but I didn't dare. I don't know why.'

'Where was I?' asks Zoe. 'Did you take me with you?'

Steph shakes her head. 'You stayed at Highdown with Dad. It was still bitterly cold and Mum was worried that you'd spent enough time outside. I suppose she also didn't want me being seen with you. But I didn't think about that at the time.'

Fiona strokes her arm.

'I can't imagine what this must have been like for you, Steph. Just beyond awful.' Sara is crying now, tears tracking down her cheeks.

Steph nods. 'I think Mum had already decided on the ice house when I told her about Kai. I suppose it was an obvious choice. It was already a burial place.'

'It was never locked then,' says Fiona, glancing at the door.

'I think she only locked it afterwards.' Steph looks at the key again. She looks up at the other three. 'She dug the hole. She had brought a spade and a fork and I suppose she thought I would help, but I just couldn't. And really it didn't need two people. It was such a tiny hole.' Steph puts her hand over her mouth and turns away from the door.

Zoe strokes Steph's shoulder and Steph jumps under her touch. 'I'm sorry,' she says as she turns to face Zoe. 'I know this is as much your grief as mine. It's just all so fresh. It feels like it happened yesterday. I've never talked about this to anyone.'

'No one?' asks Fiona. 'Did you and Mum not talk about it afterwards?'

'No.' She takes a deep breath. 'I tried to talk but Mum always said it was best not to mention it, to leave the past in the past.' A sob gushes out of her closed mouth. 'But it was impossible. He was buried here. You were in the house, but as my new baby sister. And then within the month I was at boarding school to resit my exams.' Steph shifts the ice-house key from palm to palm.

'Steph, that's just barbaric. I can't imagine what any of that was like.' Sara wipes her eyes with her sleeve.

'Mum said it was for my own good, as much as anything. That I'd be in trouble with the police otherwise. If we'd been living here, or anywhere indoors, Kai would have survived. It was because of us being outside that he died. It was my fault. He was never as strong as you.' She shivered.

'But you were just a child,' says Fiona. 'You couldn't be blamed for that. How would the police have known about Kai anyway?'

'She was worried about it, said someone would find out. She said by hiding Kai and then taking Zoe as her own, we'd all have a fresh start, a good life. No questions would be asked and I wouldn't get in trouble. I think it was genuinely for both of us. She wanted us both to have a good life and she felt this was the best way. I was angry with her at the time, and devastated too. But I can't hold too much against her. She was from a different generation.'

Zoe looks down at the key in Steph's hand. 'I have had a good life. But now I find out that it was all built on a lie.'

'It wasn't a lie, Zoe. Mum loved you as if you were her own. It was so painful to see.' Steph covers her mouth with her hand again. 'When I came home for the holidays, you and her were such a little unit. You adored her. It was as if she'd made all her mistakes with me, relied too much on Fi – and that's why you moved away and are so hyper-independent – improved with Sara – who's a great mother herself as a result – and then perfected her mothering skills with you. She wanted to be a great mother, and you gave her that chance.'

'I'd never thought about it like that, y'know. Until recently, I'd never thought about your lives with Mum and Dad before I arrived.' How self-absorbed she'd been, thinking she was the centre of the universe.

'I tried not to think about your lives after I left. It just hurt too much. But then I'd see you occasionally and think about what could have been. But it was too late then.'

'Now I understand why you left,' says Zoe, touching Steph's hand.

'After Mum buried him, she locked up the ice house. I suppose she didn't want anything unearthing him. Or anyone finding out.'

'So that's why when Terry and June died, and then Tog, they were buried in the orchard and not here,' says Fiona. 'I wondered why Mum stopped burying the pets in the ice house, but then I'd always found it a bit creepy here, so I was glad in a way.'

They both stare at the door.

'There are no pictures of you with me as a baby. Holding me. And I don't remember you ever playing with me as a child.' Zoe looks sideways at Steph.

Steph holds her face to the sky. 'If Mum ever saw us together, she would intervene. She didn't want me holding you, said it would confuse you and be too painful for me. But actually having nothing to do with you, and then being sent away, was far more painful. I came back here a lot,' says Steph. 'It felt like my only link to him – and to you. The only place that was a witness to the three of us. I would sit against the door wishing I could get in and lie on his grave.'

'So you took the key after Zoe and I found it in the safe in Mum's room?' asks Sara.

Steph nods. 'Yes, the next day. It was on the hall table. After all these years, I wanted to see Kai. I had the key for a few days, trying to build up the courage to come here. But when I eventually got here, I couldn't bring myself to go in.'

'That's when I saw you crying in the woods that time,' says Zoe.

'Yes,' says Steph. 'I realised then that I wasn't going to be able to do it, so I put the key back.'

Zoe shivers. 'Shall we go in?'

Steph slips the key into the lock but it won't turn. She rattles the key.

'I can't imagine Mum ever came here,' says Zoe. 'Here, let me try.' She bends down and fiddles with the lock. 'It's rusted over.'

Steph takes out a can of WD40 from her bag. 'I came prepared,' she says and sprays it liberally over the lock.

Zoe coughs and covers her mouth.

Steph slips the key in again and, after an initial resistance, it opens. 'I haven't been in here for thirty-five years,' she says, standing on the threshold.

'You go first,' says Zoe, the blood pulsing in her ears.

But Steph just stands in the doorway peering into the gloom. 'I was sixteen when I was last inside here. You were three months old.'

Zoe stares at her. It's difficult to breathe. They wait there for several moments and Zoe wonders if Steph will be able to go on. She glances at her, but Steph's face is immobile. She looks behind her at Fiona and Sara, who stand motionless. Zoe takes Steph's hand, which is cold despite the warmness of the day, and draws her inside. 'It will be okay,' she whispers. She needs to see whatever is here. Steph stumbles after her, her breath catching.

Beyond the initial pool of light thrown through the door, it is as dark as night. Zoe flicks on her phone torch. Steph flinches.

They all tiptoe down the stone stairs, wet with grime and covered in moss. The air is cool and dank. At each step the birdsong fades until it's deathly silent. 'They used to put straw and sawdust between the brick walls to keep it cool,' says Sara, her palm flat against the brick to stop herself falling. 'I've read about it.'

Zoe can feel the chill from the stone floor at the bottom through her trainers. The torch's pool of light shrivels. She clutches Steph's arm.

'It's okay,' says Steph, leading her forward through a doorway. Zoe swings the torch above her head where the brick walls arch together. There's a flicker of movement.

'Bats,' says Fiona.

They tiptoe onwards through another doorway. At the very back of that room, the stone floor ends and gives way to bare earth. There are wooden signs, the lettering unreadable, a dog bowl, the metal catch of a lead. Steph steps over them and then stops in front of an unmarked wooden cross.

She stands silently staring at it. 'This is him. Your twin. Kai,' she says eventually.

My twin, thinks Zoe. She kneels down and places her hand on the chilled earth. How strange to think that another person she grew with for nine months inside this woman she's always thought of as a sister, and then who she lived with for another three months, feeding and crying and sleeping together, now lies under this earth. Years ago, she read that twins who didn't grow up with their twin for whatever reason could feel the loss. 'I never felt your absence,' she whispers to herself, covering her face with her hands. She spent all this time thinking that she was the daughter who looked at life differently, who really thought about the world, but in the end she was just as blind as everyone else, she thinks. Zoe turns and Steph is standing behind her, motionless, her hand on her chest.

'Can we give him a proper burial? A grave with his name on it?' says Zoe. 'It's awful him being trapped here. So far away from all of us. So secret. Like a stain.'

'Do you both want that?' says Fiona. 'There would have to be a police investigation, they'd talk to Patrick. The coroner would need to get involved. It would all come out about your parentage.'

Steph shivers and the light from the torch dances off the bricks.

Zoe realises she hasn't thought about that. The very last thing she wants is people digging around, asking questions, potentially Steph being in trouble. 'You're right, we don't want that. And Mum wouldn't want that.'

'I don't think it's actually down to Mum,' says Fiona. 'She's gone now, the decision is down to both of you.'

'It's whatever you want,' says Steph to Zoe. 'He is your brother, your twin.'

'Your son,' says Zoe, taking her hand. Steph grips hers in response and they stand looking down at the cross in the unmarked earth.

'My son. Kai. Kylie and Kai.' She swallows.

'Perhaps we could mark his grave with something more than a wooden cross. Have something made but not make it public,' says Zoe. 'Just so the four of us know.'

Steph nods. 'And let's get keys made for all of us, so we can come here whenever we want.' She looks around. 'I'd like to be able to do that. On his birthday and the anniversary of his death.'

Zoe lets go of Steph's hand and instead they link arms. Steph takes a shaky breath and together they clamber out of the ice house, Fiona and Sara behind them.

'You know you're always welcome here,' Zoe says to Steph. Then she looks at the others. 'All of you. Highdown is your home.'

'You said the other day that you had some ideas about its future,' says Fiona, closing the ice-house door behind them and locking it.

Zoe nods. 'Yes. I talked to Mum about it but she wasn't keen. Mum treated Highdown like it was a family home, because that's all she'd ever known. But things have changed. We don't need a family home but we do want to keep Highdown.' She looks round at Fiona, Sara and Steph, all looking expectant, smiling at her. 'I thought we could take out a mortgage against the house, enough to get it all done up, the barns and outhouses too, and then we could host weddings and big events here. People could stay in the rooms – there are twelve bedrooms when you count the old servants' quarters – and we could do bed and breakfast. And then rent out the barns as self-catering. I could run it from the oast house. I was going to move back in as soon as you all went home.'

'It's a great idea,' says Fiona. 'I could do the marketing.'

'From Singapore?' says Zoe.

Fiona pauses. 'I've been thinking about that. I'm not sure I want to be there forever. I'd like to come back soon, back home, and this could be the perfect thing to work on. It would bring in enough of an income to maintain the place and help us. Let's look at some figures on the laptop when we get back.'

'Maybe this is something I could help with too, get my mind thinking about work things again,' says Sara. 'It would be fun to get the place back to how it was in Mum and Granny Evelyn's day.'

'I'd like to be part of it,' says Steph. 'I'm quite handy. I do all the building work at the shelter. And I'm only ten miles away.'

A warm feeling spreads out from Zoe's chest. 'It seems like it's something we can all work on together, getting Highdown back to its former glory.' Perhaps they can be a proper family now. Maybe Mum knew that this would happen, that the crisis of the will and the unearthing of the family secret would cause great hurt but in the end bring them closer together.

Zoe links arms with Steph again and together they turn and walk towards the house.

ACKNOWLEDGEMENTS

Relationships between mothers and daughters are endlessly complex. I had a very difficult relationship with my own mum and she was absent for my teenage years. So I was completely unprepared for the tumult that hit when my daughters, born twenty months apart, hit their teenage years, just as I was reaching perimenopause. Those years are partly the inspiration behind this book but there are many people who helped me along the way.

Jenny Eden, the branch manager at the RSPCA Sussex North and Brighton branch, who kindly talked me through the joys and challenges of running an animal-rescue centre and showed me round the animal shelter she runs just outside of Brighton – the inspiration for Steph's rescue centre.

Ania Card, a fellow Brighton-based author, who talked to me about being a woman with ADHD as inspiration for Steph's character.

My oldest friend Sara Varela for answering all my questions about life in Singapore where the character Fiona lives.

Dr Mark Slater, who was once an XR activist and went on to become a councillor for the Green Party. He spent a couple of hours talking about his experiences which were the inspiration for Zoe's work.

Jackie Hunt for advice on policing in the 1980s and 1990s.

My lovely GP friend Dr Hilary R Nash for the medical input.

Esme Banks Marr for sharing her experience of growing up as one of many sisters. As an only child, this was invaluable.

The wonderful authors and writing tutors Lucy Atkins and Richard Beard who read the early sections of this book on an Arvon writing retreat and provided valuable feedback.

The Advanced Writers Workshops led by author Laura Wilkinson who workshopped sections of this book and helped me come up with the ending: Tom Alexander, Andrew Allen-Tidy, Aisling Bradley, Catherine Dooley, Ann Galvin, Suzanne Hillen, Jacqueline Hunt, Jenny Jones and Matthew Wells.

The 5 a.m. Writing Club in Kemptown Bookshop, Brighton where I wrote so much of this book.

My agent Sam Brace at PFD for her excellent counsel, always.

My wonderful editors Maisie Lawrence and Mike Jones, who are such a joy to work with.

My cheerleaders: Rachel, Jo, Hilary, Davina, Doo, Helen and the November Mums and the FM Wonder Women.

Jude, Zara and Katy – for all the adventures along the way.

To Richard, my beta reader, for helping me to carve out time to write and always being willing to discuss the motivations for the crazy characters who only live in my head until they're on the page. And for all your love and support, always. Truly the wind beneath my wings.

BOOK CLUB QUESTIONS

If you're choosing to read *The Last Daughter of Highdown Hall* in your book group, then a massive THANK YOU. I obviously love the idea that people are reading my book, but far more exciting is that you're sitting around talking about it with cups of tea or glasses of wine. I do love a book group. Here are some pointers for your discussion which I hope are helpful. If you haven't yet read the book, then stop reading this post now. There are spoilers ahead!

How did *The Last Daughter of Highdown Hall* make you feel?

Camilla has a difficult relationship with her own mother, herself traumatised by the death of her other child. How much do you think this impacted on her own experience of mothering? Do you think trauma can be passed down from generation to generation? How do you think traumatised families can break the chain?

The uncovering of Zoe's heritage and Steph's teenage years is a key part of the story. Would the sisters have been happier if they hadn't uncovered their family secrets? How would they have been different?

Out of the four sisters, who did you have most, and least, sympathy with?

In her eulogy, Fiona describes her parents' relationship as a true love affair which lasted more than fifty years. But as readers, we see inside the relationship during a difficult period when Steph is a teenager. Given what we know, do you agree with Fiona's assessment?

Much more is understood about neurodiversity now than in the 1980s and 1990s. How different would Steph's teenage years have been if she'd been born now?

Child and Adolescent to Parent Violence and Abuse is little understood with 40 per cent of those experiencing it refusing to report it, according to London's Violence Reduction Unit. How did Steph's treatment of Camilla have ramifications elsewhere in the family? Could Camilla have dealt with Steph's violence more effectively?

Alice is a mysterious character, a silent witness to many of the family secrets. Do you think she should have intervened earlier to ensure the secret is revealed?

Highdown Hall is a key character in the story and the reason why many of the tensions arise between the other characters. How would the story have been different without that setting?

The four daughters each experience their mother differently but only Sara has her own children. How did the complicated family dynamic impact the four women's desire to have their own children?

Why do you think Camilla and Paul decided to take on Kylie as their own child? Were they right to do so? Do you think it would have worked better if Steph had brought up Kylie while living at the hall?

Do you think Zoe and Steph will go on to have a strong relationship?

If the book was to be made into a film, who do you think would play the key characters – Camilla, Steph, Fiona, Sara and Zoe?

If you loved uncovering the emotional family secrets in *The Last Daughter of Highdown Hall* and found it incredibly hard to put down, then you'll love *The Girl in the Midnight Maze* by Cathy Hayward.

All her mother left her was a clue to a family secret. But is it a mystery best left unsolved?

Emma's strongest connection to her mother was a painting Margaret created before Emma was born, of a little girl lost in a maze. So when Margaret dies, gifting the painting to a total stranger, Emma is consumed by grief – for her mother, the little girl, and the relationship they never had.

When she discovers something that throws doubt over everything she's ever been told about Margaret's past, Emma must decide whether to pull at the thread of secrets and lies. Will the truth help her through her grief – or reveal a loss that runs deeper than she ever imagined?

Available now or keep reading for an exclusive extract!

Chapter 1

Emma

January 2019

Emma's phone rang as she was peeling potatoes for mash. She glanced at the screen but didn't recognise the number so ignored it, cutting the peeled potato in half before adding it to the pan.

Her son James wandered into the kitchen, headphones clamped to his ears. He grabbed a carton of milk from the fridge and lifted it to his lips.

'James! Use a glass,' she said, nodding towards the cupboard.

He rolled his eyes but poured the milk into a glass and sat down at the kitchen table. 'How long till dinner?'

'Thirty minutes,' she said. 'How was college?'

James shrugged and looked at his phone. 'Same, same.'

'Best bit of the day?' coaxed Emma. She remembered asking the same question when she used to pick him and his sister Libby up from primary school. Best bit of the day? Worst bit of the day? What did you have for lunch? She learned that after receiving a standard response of 'fine', they would compete on who could describe the most outlandish things that had happened. Now they were both teenagers she was lucky if they answered at all.

James didn't look up. 'I scored a couple of baskets in practice and coach asked me to join the first team.'

'James, that's amazing.' Emma smiled and rested her hand on his shoulder. A faint blush crept up his neck. 'You must tell Dad when he gets in.'

James nodded and focused back on his phone.

'How many sausages do you want?' Emma asked, slipping them out of the packet on to the grill tray.

'Six?' he said hopefully.

Emma laughed and got a second packet out of the fridge. 'D'you want any help with revision later? I could go through those index cards with you, ask you some random questions?'

'Yeah, okay,' he said.

Really she should try to finish off the survey for the new development. She'd only got halfway through before she'd had to leave to pick up Libby and take her to street dance. That was always the challenge – trying to fit what was a full-time job into part-time hours. But Emma loved her afternoons off. Since James started school, she'd only worked from nine to three, meaning she could pick him and Libby up every day and spend the rest of the afternoon with them. Even now they both tended to do their own thing – James at basketball or out with friends, Libby hanging around in town – she still liked being at home when they arrived and they knew she was there if they wanted her. She could finish the survey after she'd helped out with the revision.

Libby came in and sat at the table. 'I saw you with that girl at lunch,' she said to James.

James narrowed his eyes and mouthed, 'Fuck off.'

'I saw that,' said Emma. 'It still counts as swearing even if you don't say it.'

James rolled his eyes again slightly and looked back at his sister mouthing something Emma couldn't interpret.

Her phone rang again and she glanced at the number. It was the same one as earlier and she still didn't recognise it. She was about to answer when Nick came through the door.

'Hi, gang,' he said. 'Nice to see everyone here rather than hiding in your rooms.'

'The draw of dinner rather than my company, I think,' laughed Emma as he pulled her into a hug. 'How was your day?'

'So, so.' He screwed up his face. 'Client meeting was a compete fiasco. I spent most of the rest of the day trying to sort out the mess.'

'Oh, darling, I'm sorry. Why don't you change? Then dinner will be ready.'

'Fab, I'm starving.'

'Libby, James, could you lay the table, please, while I serve up?'

There was a general grunt of disapproval but they both slowly got up and reached for plates and cutlery as Emma started putting pans of steaming mash, peas and beans on the table. Nick joined them and Emma dished up, making sure to put plenty on Libby's plate. She had been looking too thin recently.

They were halfway through dinner when Emma's phone rang again. She put her fork down. 'I know we say no phones at the table, but I just want to check it's not that number again. Someone keeps calling me.'

'One rule for us . . .' said Libby.

'Libby,' said Nick. 'Enough.'

It was the same number. Emma clicked 'Accept' and said 'Hello?' as she walked out of the kitchen, closing the door behind her.

'Hello, is that Emma Bowen?'

There was something official about the man's tone of voice that made her heart beat slightly faster. 'Speaking.'

'My name is Mr Eals. I'm calling about Margaret Chapman – your mother, I believe?'

'Yes?' Had she had a change of heart?

'I'm sorry to inform you that Margaret died earlier today. It was very peaceful.' The voice was soft.

Emma felt her throat constrict. She held the phone against her chest, unable to speak. Almost immediately tears spilled down her face. Mum was dead. She'd always thought they might reconcile. She'd rushed to her mother's bedside several times over the past twenty years of her illness, as she had gone in and then out of remission. She'd become so used to her recovering that she thought they'd always have time to make things up.

She swallowed with difficulty and raised the phone to her ear. 'Hello?' she said.

'Hello, Mrs Bowen.' The voice was quiet, understanding. Someone who was used to delivering bad news. 'I realise this will be something of a shock for you. May I suggest we talk tomorrow morning, once you've had time to digest the news. We can then talk about the official arrangements. Is there a good time for us to speak?'

'Any time,' Emma managed. 'Thank you, Mr Eals.' Emma ended the call. She opened the kitchen door again and looked at Nick and the children around the kitchen table. They were laughing. Three faces turned towards her.

'All okay?' said Nick.

'It's Mum,' said Emma, her voice broke. 'She died earlier today.'

'Oh, Em.' Nick was on his feet, holding her as her knees started to give way. He guided her back to the table. 'What a shock.'

Both James and Libby stopped eating. Libby got up and put her arms around her mother from behind. 'Sorry, Mum. We love you.'

'Thanks, Libs,' said Emma, wiping her eyes.

'I'm sorry too, Mum,' said James, frowning at her.

'I think I'm going to go upstairs for a while,' said Emma, getting to her feet. 'Leave you to finish off here.'

'I'll come with you,' said Nick.

'I just need a moment on my own,' said Emma.

'I understand,' he said, giving her another hug.

Lying on her bed, she let the tears come. But what was she crying for? She and Mum had never got on. She felt guilty that she hadn't been there at the end though – especially when she'd dashed up to be with her the other times they'd thought she was near the end. Had she died alone? No, Mr Eals had said it was peaceful so there must have been someone with her. *As her only child, it should have been me*, Emma thought, crying harder.

But their relationship had always been strained. Even as a young child. There was a feeling of slight relief that it was at an end, and it made Emma feel even more guilty.

Later, when Nick came up, she sobbed into his chest. 'I don't know why I'm crying so much. I didn't cry like this when Dad died and we were always so close.'

Nick stroked the back of her head. 'I think it's because you're mourning the relationship you never had.'

And that was it exactly, Emma thought.

Chapter 2

Betty

March 1937

Betty lay in the bath, her white legs flushing a blotchy pink in the scorching water. The passage light leaked around the edges of the bathroom door, merging into the glow from the streetlamp, fractured through the frosted glass window. The mirror perspired in the heat, dripping into the basin.

She took another gulp straight from the half-empty bottle balanced on the corner of the bath where the mould bred between the tiles. Her face twisted at the gin's bitter burn, but the bottle was cool against her cheek as she pulled a breath into her tight lungs.

Her mother's knitting needle balanced on the cloth used to wipe her sisters' faces. As she leaned forward to feel the pointed tip again with her finger, the water sloshed over the sides of the bath, on to the floor. The muffled sounds of her sisters finishing off their tea in the kitchen next door mingled with her mother's muted scolding.

There wasn't much time. *Not for me, not for it. He*. Betty was sure it was a he. *He would look just like him. But not grow up to be the coward his father was. He'd have a proper job where he'd have clean hands, a smart suit and a bowler hat. Live somewhere posh like Epsom, not in this tiny tenement.*

The hum of buses grinding up Battersea Park Road past St Saviour blurred with the shouts of the men clocking off, heading to the pub, and the yelling of the boys playing football by the dim streetlights.

She reached forward, over the tightness of her belly, and grasped the knitting needle, then let it float on the surface of the scalding water until it sunk beneath the water line, turning almost gaily downwards. The intense heat made her drowsy. It was difficult to move.

The pain won't be bad. Not as bad as standing there, looking the best I've ever looked, wearing that beautiful dress, waiting for him. Father pacing up and down. Then realising he wasn't ever going to come. That awful journey back home.

Angry steps sounded.

'You've taken all me bleedin' hot water. There ain't none left.' Her mother was at the door, shaking the handle.

'I won't be long, Ma.'

'Least you could do is be 'ere helping me with this lot, not dilly-dallying in there. Betty?'

'I'll be there in a minute.'

'What you doing in there anyway? Dolling yerself up? Got yerself another fancy man already, 'ave yer?'

'I won't be long, Mum.'

'Bloody hurry up. Cheek taking all that water. Nothing for yer pa when he gets home.'

The sound of steps moved away, and Betty imagined her mother, her thin, faded housecoat wrapped around her ample frame, stomping back into the tiny front room. There was a shout from next door, the sound of a child being slapped and then whimpering.

The knitting needle had settled, resting across the dark mound of her pubic hair. She stared at it. One small movement. Over. Quick.

She closed her eyes. She had no choice.

Chapter 3

Emma

January 2019

Emma yawned. It had been such a long drive to Morecambe to the solicitor's office. She wasn't used to driving that far and she felt guilty for leaving James in the middle of his mocks. And work. She'd never finished the condition survey. And it was due today. She sighed and looked around the small solicitor's office. The window ledge hadn't been dusted for years. A dried-out spider plant was caked with decades of grime. The reception area, which doubled as the secretary's office, was chilly. There was a heater under the desk of the woman who had only reluctantly glanced up from her pile of paperwork to welcome Emma. She didn't look much younger than the building.

Behind the secretary's desk, Emma saw a figure emerging from a narrow corridor. Mr Eals, her mother's solicitor, looked even more dilapidated than his office. His dark eyes were sunken into his face, barely visible below untamed eyebrows. The hand he held out to greet Emma was equally hairy. Already a short man, he was bent over, as if from the weight of people's troubles he had shouldered over the years.

He was smiling. 'Ah, Margaret's daughter, Mrs Bowen. I was hoping we would meet. It's a pleasure.'

'Good to meet you too, Mr Eals.' They shook hands and he ushered her back down the narrow corridor, years of spilled coffee staining the carpet tiles. The back door was open, the chilly draught riffling the stacks of paper lining the corridor and breezing into Mr Eals' small office at the back of the building. The windows here were high up on the wall, so there was no view of whatever lay behind the office. But even if there had been big windows, Emma suspected the old solicitor would have found a way of covering them. Every single surface in the room was buried under piles of manila files held together by elastic bands, labelled in the same spidery script. The top of a mahogany glass-fronted bookcase, which was full of impressive-looking legal tomes, was stacked to the window ledge, and even the chair opposite the old desk had several newer-looking folders on them. Mr Eals slid them on to a pile on his desk and indicated where Emma should sit. He eased himself past another tower of files and sat on a well-worn leather chair opposite her.

He was watching her, the tips of his fingers pressed together, his elbows resting on the cluttered desk. 'You do look like your mother. I suspect everyone says that.'

Emma smiled. 'Not many of my friends knew her.'

The contours around his eyes rippled as the old man returned her smile. 'Your mother was one of my longest-standing clients. I'm sad that this day has come. As a solicitor, you follow a client through their lives, intervening at the crucial points. Births, marriages, divorces, deaths of relatives, house purchases, and, then eventually, death. It's the natural order of my professional life.'

'So you had known Mum a long time?' Emma didn't recall her ever mentioning Mr Eals.

'Yes, since her twenties. She was one of my more interesting clients,' he said slowly. 'Now, have you got the death certificate we discussed on the phone yesterday? It is a relatively simple estate so, with a fair wind, we should secure probate in a couple of months.'

Emma drew the envelope out of her bag – she'd got the death certificate from the town hall that morning – and handed it over to the solicitor. He took out his glasses and put them on his nose before examining the death certificate closely. He nodded gravely. Then he raised his arms to the sides of the chair and used them to push himself upwards, until he seemed to judge that his knees would be able to support him. He moved slowly over to a pile of files in the corner nearest Emma and selected an enormous series of folders second from the top. It was held together by blue elastic bands, straining against almost a foot of paperwork. What on earth had her mother needed to discuss over the years?

Mr Eals dropped it with a thud on to the desk with the look of a man surveying a job well done. He rolled off one of the elastic bands and slid in the death certificate.

'Thank you for arranging to get this so quickly and for offering to sort out her possessions. As I said on the phone, the will makes a number of stipulations about certain items. I always think it's better for relatives to manage that. It saves unnecessary solicitor's fees and allows for what the Americans like to call "closure".'

'I think I'd have to go through years of therapy to get closure with my mother,' Emma said with a grimace.

She'd meant the comment light-heartedly, but Mr Eals paused and looked down at the file, stroking it.

'I'm not a religious man,' he said quietly, 'but I believe there's a phrase in the Bible about walking a mile in another man's shoes. Until we have done that, we will never understand what it's like to be the other person.'

Emma glanced down at her hands and realised she was twisting her wedding ring around her finger. She placed her hands on the desk and looked up at the old solicitor, who was watching her over his glasses. She nodded. Emma had no wish to walk in her mother's shoes. Their relationship had been difficult at best.

He eased a couple of sheets of paper out of the file. 'I have your mother's will here,' he said, passing it across the desk, 'so you can see what needs to be done.'

On the top sheet *Last Will and Testament* was printed in large bold letters across the top.

'*This Will is made by me Margaret Chapman of Flat b, 487 Marine Road East, Morecambe on this day Monday the 21st of January 2019,*' she read.

Emma looked up quickly. 'This will was made the day before she died,' she said, her eyes wide. 'Didn't she have a will before, or did she change it?'

Mr Eals hesitated. 'Your mother made some small changes to her will just before she died, but it was easier to make a new one than add them in as a codicil.'

Emma frowned and looked down at the document. Her heart started to thud. Why would Mum change her will just before she died?

The solicitor continued. 'Now, after the usual blurb about revocation, executors – that's me' – he looked up – 'and funeral directions, you'll see there's a section entitled "Specific Gifts".'

Emma traced her fingers down the page. There was a list of items that her mother wanted distributing to different people. Books, ornaments, jewellery, a coin collection. Nothing that Emma particularly remembered.

'All these items are in her property,' Mr Eals said, 'and I've arranged a courier to come to collect them later today to save you having to distribute them yourself. Some of them are going to other parts of the country, although a couple are local.'

Emma reached the end of the list and gasped. '*The Girl in the Midnight Maze*. She wants the painting to go to someone called Clare Richens. But—'

'Yes, your mother's friend Clare lives close by. I've included her address and phone number on this sheet,' he said calmly, slowly sliding another piece of paper across the desk. 'If you prefer, I can cancel the courier and you can deliver it yourself?'

'But *The Girl in the Midnight Maze* is ours. Our family's. It can't go to a stranger. I love that painting, it's beautiful,' Emma said, suddenly finding it difficult to swallow. She thought of the little girl dancing in the moonlight in the centre of the maze.

The secretary appeared at the door with a tray cluttered with a teapot, cups, and a milk jug. She laid it gently between them and set out the cups either side of the tray. Mr Eals reached forward and carefully poured milk and then tea into two cups, both covered in roses, and slid one across to Emma. She picked it up, her hands trembling, and took a sip.

With his fingertips once more pressed together in what she realised was his habitual pose, Mr Eals spoke quietly. 'I'm afraid that's what Margaret's will says. She wanted the painting to go to Miss Richens.'

Even though Emma hadn't seen the painting for years, for much of her childhood it had hung in the sitting room of their family home in Sussex, watching over her as she grew. When she was tall enough, she would reach up and follow the labyrinth with her fingertips, trying to find an escape route for the girl in the white dress locked within the shadowy prison of green hedges.

Her shoulders dropped and she looked back to the will. She hadn't thought there would be anything controversial in it. How naive. Mum had always loved any opportunity to be contentious.

'There is also the matter of her property itself. If you turn to page two, clause seven . . .' The solicitor paused and looked up at her.

Emma flicked over the page, scanned down and read out loud. 'To Elizabeth Margaret Bowen I leave my property Flat b, 487 Marine Road East, Morecambe.' She looked up at the old man. 'She's left her flat to Libby?'

Mr Eals smiled. 'Yes, to your daughter. Your younger child, I believe?'

Emma covered her mouth with her hand. 'But Mum hated Libby,' she said, rereading the text.

'Hate is a strong word,' he said calmly, slowly opening a drawer and extracting a set of keys. 'These are the keys to your mother's flat. I'm afraid it's been empty since she went into the nursing home a few months ago, but I've been keeping an eye on it.' He reached up and scratched his neck inside his starched collar. 'I think you'll find it all in order.'

Emma nodded, staring at the keys. Some had a carefully labelled tag, written in an unfamiliar hand: *communal door, front door, meter cupboard.* A small brass key was unlabelled.

'The residue of your mother's estate goes to a selection of charities, as you'll see on page four. If you can box it all up and label it, I will arrange for all of that in my role as executor. I can perhaps book another courier to save you taking it to the various charity shops she stipulated.'

Emma nodded blankly and then blurted out, 'What was it she changed the day before she died? The property going to Libby or the painting going to' – she looked down at the will – 'Clare?'

The old solicitor shook his head. 'I'm afraid I'm not at liberty to disclose the content of her previous will. I'm sure you understand.'

Emma nodded again, her foot tapping the floor.

'Now, this final document' – he slid a sheet of paper across the desk – 'details her funeral wishes. The music, readings and so on. Margaret had been in touch with a funeral home and made all the arrangements herself. You will just need to contact them and arrange a date.'

Emma scanned through a short list of music and the contact details for a humanist celebrant. *How very like Mum to want something different to the norm.*

'If you need anything else, do get in touch.' Mr Eals pulled himself up by the arms of the chair and stood. 'I will be in contact about the probate in due course.'

She also rose, clutching the keys. 'Thank you for your help,' she said automatically and followed him out of the room, her throat tight with repressed emotion.

ABOUT THE AUTHOR

Photo © 2025 Dani Brown

Cathy trained as a journalist and wrote about everything from accounting and supply chains to football finances and port strategy before moving into public relations. In 2022, after having spent a lifetime pottering around bookshops, she bought Kemptown Bookshop in Brighton, where she has created a community hub that supports local authors and aspiring writers. In 2023, she took on management of The Creative Writing Programme, the leading independent centre for creative writing teaching in the south-east of England – the course that set her on track to be a writer. When she's not writing (or reading), Cathy loves pottering in other people's bookshops. She lives in Brighton with her three children and two rescue cats.

Follow the Author on Amazon

If you enjoyed this book, follow Cathy Hayward on Amazon to be notified when the author releases a new book!

To do this, please follow these instructions:

Desktop:

1) Search for the author's name on Amazon or in the Amazon App.
2) Click on the author's name to arrive on their Amazon page.
3) Click the 'Follow' button.

Mobile and Tablet:

1) Search for the author's name on Amazon or in the Amazon App.
2) Click on one of the author's books.
3) Click on the author's name to arrive on their Amazon page.
4) Click the 'Follow' button.

Kindle eReader and Kindle App:

If you enjoyed this book on a Kindle eReader or in the Kindle App, you will find the author 'Follow' button after the last page.

Printed in Dunstable, United Kingdom

82475672R00181